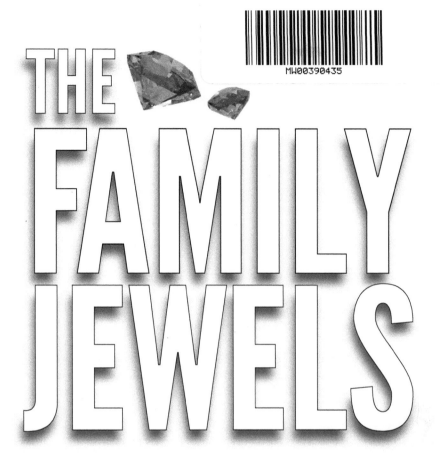

THE FAMILY JEWELS

Published by Mindstir Media, LLC
45 Lafayette Rd | Suite 181| North Hampton, NH 03862 | USA
1.800.767.0531 | www.mindstirmedia.com

Printed in the United States of America
ISBN-13: 978-1-7339571-5-1
Library of Congress Control Number is on file with the publisher.

MINDSTIR MEDIA

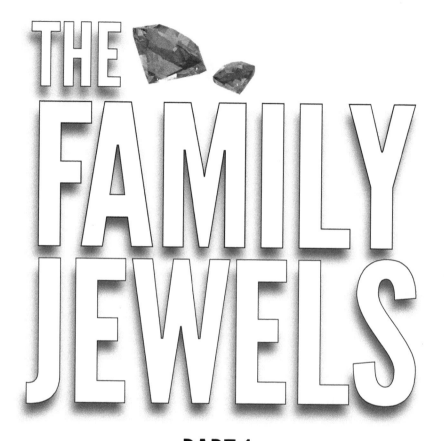

THE FAMILY JEWELS

PART 1
CROSSING THE LINE

ROB NORTHRUP

To Suzy – the love of my life, soul mate, and my inspiration.

Up on Cripple Creek she sends me

If I spring a leak she mends me

I don't have to speak she defends me

A drunkard's dream if I ever did see one

The Band, 1969, and Suzy since 1997

And to Christopher…

I'll remember the good times,

and by the grace of God, see you again.

PROLOGUE

'Deus Vult!' God Wills It! The chant had accompanied a papal call to arms to stop the advances of Saracens into Europe. Followers of the Prophet had pushed around the corner of the Mediterranean and colonized as far north as Romania, prompting Catholic leadership to muster their factions to first thwart the advances, then press through the Holy Land to free Jerusalem of the yoke of Islam.

Today, July 15th, in the 1099th year of the Lord Jesus Christ, Jerusalem had fallen. After the long siege, the battering rams finally breached the walls. When the stones gave way, the support beams used to shore the bulwarks of the Holy City fell into place, creating a bridge allowing the Crusaders easy access to the inhabitants. As the Christian army broke through, the chant of *'Deus Vult!'* rang on the wind.

Thus, began the slaughter of Saracens and Jews by the thousands, at the presumed will of God.

After three years, Roberto DeCorto was sick of it all. Wholesale carnage day after day.

DeCorto had done his share of pillaging along the arduous road to the Holy City and now had no taste for it. He longed simply to be back on his lands in the south of Spain. There his wife and two children waited. He hoped.

Now he stood in the heart of Jerusalem in light chain mail which he'd preferred over the heavy armor that had slowed many of his fellow Crusaders, ultimately being the cause of their demise in battle. Nor did he carry a huge broadsword as did many of his brethren. He preferred a lighter, faster blade. He'd also taken to the longbow; it too was light, quick, and could wield death or salvation (depending upon the hand holding it) from long or short range. The only piece of true armor he donned was a helmet that covered his head and nose with steel, offering protection for his neck with bands of thick leather fastened to the metal. Overall his carapace of war was slight, allowing him greater range of motion and the ability to capitalize on his speed in battle and quickness of his mind. The scars on his body told tales of many near misses by his enemies, yet his hollow brown eyes gave away the anguish that came with having slain so many on the road here.

Standing in the heart of what had been the object of their quest he felt relief. This fight was over; the city had fallen. Perhaps his days of killing had finally ended.

Roberto could only shake his head as he thought for the thousandth time—*Where in all this carnage was the God for whom he had taken up the fight?*

His fellow conquerors now went from house to house, forcing the inhabitants to divulge the hiding places for their treasures, great or small. Through torture, the Crusaders had learned the people of the region had taken to the habit of swallowing bezants of gold and other valuable items in the hope of retrieving those from their feces days after the battle and sacking had ended. His comrades inflicted unimaginable agony to find out where treasures were hidden, or which kin member had swallowed the riches. Upon revelation of the whereabouts of hidden ingots, bezants, and jewels, the Crusaders would confiscate the loot, then kill the males of the family, leaving their bodies to rot.

Those identified as having swallowed riches were rounded up and hauled to internment pens just outside the walls of the city. News spread through Jerusalem that one might be spared if he or she had eaten articles of treasure, and the pens would be a place to avoid the slaughter. People began volunteering they'd eaten riches to be taken to the safety enjoyed by those waiting for their excrement to pass when the riches would be salvaged. They hoped in the few days it would take to clear their bowels, their conquerors' bloodlust would dissipate, and they'd be set free, or perhaps be kept alive as slaves and servants.

The security of the pens was initially preferred to the streets of Jerusalem, which ran red with blood. That was the thought until the prisoners saw the huge fire pit prepared nearby. Then their fate became clear. They were to be burned, their ashes sifted to remove the treasures held in their bellies and bowels.

As in the cities sacked previously by the Crusaders, the people were put to the sword one by one, then their bodies thrown into the flames. The pyres lasted for days, and thousands perished this way. Untold riches were filtered from the ashes, most claimed by the clergy who supervised the operation of killing, burning, and sifting. Yet the leaders of the Catholic Church allowed the men who took part in the venture a generous portion of the take from the cinders. It was gruesome work, but many a Crusader filled a purse or chest with treasures sifted from the remains of the conquered people.

As DeCorto witnessed those being hauled to the pens, he knew well the fate awaiting them. Personally, he found the practice abhorrent. He'd amassed his own store of wealth on this venture by valiantly leading charges against the enemy and being the first to reach the cache of those they defeated. Most of the spoils secured were handed over to the papal contingent as required, yet he'd collected a solid share.

Any concept of doing the will of God had long ago been washed from his mind. The murder inflicted in their wake had purified him of the belief after only a few skirmishes with the enemy. The 'enemy' largely consisted of shopkeepers and merchants in the cities and farmers and herders in the open lands. On a few occasions, they had met organized Saracen forces, fierce warriors who flew at them, seemingly appearing from the sands of the desert on horseback, slashing quickly with their scimitars, then disappearing into the dust. Seldom did the Crusaders locate the camps of these marauders. And the steeds they rode were magnificent. Unlike the thick-bodied warhorses of Europe, they were sleek and fast, allowing the warriors on their backs to attack quickly, wield their swords, and turn and retreat before being surrounded.

He'd amassed gold and a few jewels in their victories, but in addition, DeCorto was collecting a different kind of treasure—the beautiful animals of the region. His prize possessions were four stallions and eight mares, stabled by slaves back at the camp, two boys he had spared after the conquest. They had each been with him for over two years now and had taken to him as their protector. He planned to take them to his Spanish lands where they would run his stables and breed the horses. The promise of a better life where it was rumored there existed more than rock, sand, and butchery excited the boys.

With the city now defeated and only massacre taking place, DeCorto turned to walk back to camp. He would make arrangements for his return home. Their quest was complete. He wanted no part of the sacking; the warrior's work was done.

As he made his way from the center of Jerusalem toward the now wide-open gates of the city, he passed a well where he found a bucket and a rope. He lowered the container into the well and filled it with water. Removing his helmet, he sat on a bench of brick and mortar. Picking the pail up, he dumped half the contents over his head, then scrubbed the gore of battle and the dust of the streets off himself. Placing his light armor on the bench with his sword and bow, he repeated the process numerous times until he felt relatively cleansed. Refreshed, he rose to continue on his way.

As he pulled his chain mail back over his head, he caught a glimpse of movement directly in front of him. Instinctively he rolled away and yanked the mail down quickly to open his field of vision.

To his dismay, he saw the sword he'd set down was now in the hand of a boy. Yet the blade was not pointed at him. The boy, or upon further evaluation, nearly a young man, looked excitedly around. Spinning first to see in all directions, he then focused on DeCorto. Roberto took a step sideways to get nearer to his bow. The lad did not attack but rather stepped away apparently ready to bolt. However, he did not run. Looking down, Roberto saw that the boy's feet were shackled with a chain. He must have been hiding behind the stone bench at the well.

"There he is!" The loud call came from nearby.

The boy stood frozen. A half-dozen men, all Crusaders, appeared from between two buildings and quickly surrounded him. Their heavy armor rattled as they trotted into position. With the sword leveled at his pursuers, the boy lunged at one of those who encircled him. The Crusader raised his broadsword in an arc and easily blocked the thrust with a clank of steel. The men laughed. The boy obviously possessed no knowledge of the sword.

DeCorto relaxed and crossed his arms to watch.

"He's found a toy. What a cute little blade!" laughed the man who'd parried the thrust. The others laughed along with him. With a smile of yellow teeth visible through the helmet, he said, "Drop the weapon, boy, and you'll be spared."

The boy spun quickly in a circle, blade out, forcing his assailants to step back. DeCorto's eyes widened at the speed the lad demonstrated. *What the boy lacks in skills perhaps he makes up in quickness.*

"Perhaps he does not understand you," Roberto said to the Crusader who had spoken. "Speak to him in Arabic."

"Neither I nor any of my men speak the cursed language of the Saracens," said the Crusader harshly.

"I will speak to him then. What do you want with him?"

The Crusader cleared his throat. "We want him for questioning. He may have knowledge in the disappearance of a priest."

Odd, thought DeCorto. *These men want this boy for questioning when they do not speak his language?* In Arabic, he said to the boy, "These men say they will spare you if you lay down your weapon."

"They are liars," the lad replied.

"Why do they pursue you?"

"They believe I have swallowed items of wealth. I am not of Jerusalem. I have come from the lands to the east where your armies have already conquered, and I have seen what happens to those suspected of containing riches in their bowels."

"Have you swallowed riches, lad?"

The boy's head snapped in DeCorto's direction, and they made eye contact for a brief instant. "No," he answered.

"Now you are the one who lies," he confronted the boy, still in Arabic. "So, you fear the internment pens and the fire that waits there?"

The boy's eyes met DeCorto's again. "These men have no plan to take me to the pens. They plan to disembowel me and keep what they find in my stomach and intestines for themselves."

"Where did you learn to speak Latin?"

"I do not speak Latin."

"Then how do you know of their plan?"

The boy's lips pursed as he was caught in another lie.

DeCorto laughed. "I may be able to help, but you must tell me the truth. If not, these men will kill you. Where did you learn to speak Latin?"

The leader of the Crusader band barked at DeCorto, "What do you two speak of? We wish to be on our way with this prisoner. Tell him to lay down his weapon!"

"I did not see you or any of your band at the charge of the wall. Nor did

I see any donning your colors manning the towers or rams," he replied. "You should show more respect for one who opened the walls so you could rob these people."

"We are guards of the church contingent. We do not fight with the commoners such as you. This is a matter of the church; you should not concern yourself with it," he returned. To his men, he gave the command, "Move in. Take the boy."

"Do not touch the boy." DeCorto's command was deep and strong. The soldiers froze.

After a moment, their leader regained his courage and stepped forward. "We wish no trouble here, yet you seem to seek it. We will take this boy, with or without your approval," he said as he bobbed his blade in Roberto's direction.

"You may take him when I am done speaking to him." DeCorto's voice was now somewhat softer, but methodical.

"We will take him now. Move in!" the Crusader barked as he turned to the boy.

He hit the dirt with a metallic clanking of his armor as Roberto tripped him backward, hooking his hands on the upper edge of the plating covering his back and yanking downward. The takedown was so fast the broadsword never swung. The weight of the massive blade took the Crusader's arm down to the ground, where DeCorto stepped on the wrist with his right foot, forcing the hand to open. The Crusader attempted to roll and grab a leg of his assailant, but in the ungainly armor, he struggled like a turtle on its back.

DeCorto's right foot left the pinned wrist and swiftly kicked the helmet, and with a dull 'thunk' of thick leather against metal, all motion stopped. The other five men stood silently, amazed at the swiftness with which an unarmed man had dispatched their leader.

"Your friend has decided to take a nap. I will continue my conversation with the boy while he slumbers."

The other men said nothing, and in unison, the tips of their swords lowered toward the ground.

In Arabic, DeCorto again addressed the boy. "Now tell me where you learned the language of the Pope."

"I wish to speak in private. Send these men away."

"These men do not understand us. Trust me." Looking at one of the men DeCorto said in Arabic, "Your birth is the result of your mother lying with a camel."

The man's expression did not change. Until the boy laughed. Pointing his blade at the youth, the Crusader stepped forward menacingly. The boy's smile quickly disappeared.

DeCorto continued in Arabic, "Your story. The truth."

Stepping back from the sword leveled at him, the boy began. "I was captured as your forces advanced. My family was put to the sword before my eyes. I too would have been slain, yet a priest took an interest in me. I was taken to his encampment as his servant, one of many boys. None over the age of fifteen years. I was eleven.

"My father was a trader who had traveled to lands far to the east and south. He amassed riches and possessions unheard of in these regions. Yet all was taken by the priests, and my family killed after the rape of my mother and sisters." The boy's look toward the Crusaders who encircled him turned to one of pure malice. For a moment DeCorto thought he might charge them with the stolen sword.

The boy continued. "I was taken into the tents of the priest. One by one he summoned the boys of his camp to his chambers for his pleasures."

"And you too?"

"I refused his advances for over a year. By working harder in the kitchen and learning the language, I made myself too valuable to kill. However, after a time, the priest decided his advances would no longer be refused," the boy said.

"That is the missing priest these men speak of?"

The lad swallowed before answering, "I am a man now, and no true man would allow the violations of this priest. I convinced him to take me from camp two days prior to a private place for our interlude. We went together. He will not return."

DeCorto nodded slowly. "You could have escaped, but you returned to reclaim the riches of your family, which you carry now within you.

"How did these men discover your act?"

"Another boy of the camp saw me swallowing articles from the priest's coffer. To swallow all at once could kill. I have seen it happen. So slowly, over days, I have eaten a large amount, with only a small bit of food."

DeCorto shook his head in amazement.

"I wished to reclaim what was mine by birthright. A jackal of a boy turned me in. That is why I wear these shackles. Now they want the treasures I carry within me as their own."

The second in command of the Crusaders, summoning lost bravery, interrupted the conversation. "We will take the boy now. You have talked enough."

Still in Arabic, DeCorto quickly addressed the boy. "What is your name?"

"Raji."

"Raji, throw me the sword you hold."

"No. I will be unarmed!"

At their new leader's urging the Crusader band again advanced on the boy, this time keeping an eye on DeCorto as they moved. "Kill him! We will carry his body with us!" ordered the man who'd taken charge.

As the men came within inches of Raji's outstretched blade, DeCorto said, "You are no match for these men. You must trust me. The treasures you carry I will claim as my own, but I will give you your life and your freedom. The sword! Toss it!"

"No! The jewels are of my family and shall remain mine!" Raji raised the blade for battle. A final act of defiance.

The Crusader in command took a mighty swing with his broadsword and knocked the weapon from Raji's raised hand. Falling backward as he absorbed the force of the blow, the boy hit the dirt with terrified, widened eyes. The Crusader's raised sword began its downward arc, and Raji closed his eyes, bracing for what he hoped would be only a brief second of pain before death. He was surprised when he felt no impact.

Opening his eyes, he was astonished to see the Crusader clutching at his throat where an arrow protruded, feather end on one side of his neck and point on the other. Blood gurgled from the man's mouth as he danced in pain clutching the shaft.

The shot was perfect, piercing the gap in the chain mail between the helmet and body armor. An inch higher or lower and the arrow might have bounced off the protective metal.

Raji silently thanked Allah for this deliverance. The Crusader fell to the ground, and the gurgling sounds faded as his life ended.

The four remaining men turned to see DeCorto standing tall, holding his longbow, bent with another arrow nocked.

"Charge him!" yelled one of the men.

The second arrow left the bow with a twang and found its mark in the throat of the man who'd ordered the charge. He too fell in his tracks, death only seconds away.

The three crusaders standing attacked DeCorto too quickly for the Spaniard to nock another arrow, and the bow he'd carried for over two years splintered as he used it to fend off the sweeping broadsword blade that nearly decapitated him. Roberto skillfully used the ends of the severed wooden bow to deflect the blows of the three as they advanced, yet with each dull thud of metal against lumber his protective staffs were shortened.

Knowing he could no longer hold his place, DeCorto decided to bolt. The heavily armored men would not catch him if he could break free of their encirclement. Saving this boy to claim his treasures had been an impulsive, and inherently wrong, decision.

Seeing an opening between the three, he feinted one way, then darted another direction as their ungainly swords swung wildly. He rolled free of the circle and rose to run.

The impact of a metal glove on the back of his head returned him to the ground on his knees. As he fought to keep the fog from overtaking him, he realized the leader whom he'd kicked to sleep a few moments ago had woken up and cut off his escape. A vicious kick to his ribs knocked the wind out of him, and he fell back to the dirt. Fighting to regain his breath, he rolled to see the leader of the men standing over him, sword high above his head.

"You will cause us no more trouble!" he yelled as he brought the sword down in a smashing blow.

With senses dulled from the wallop to his head and gasping for breath from the air kicked out of his lungs, Roberto summoned all the strength he could muster. He rolled to avoid the blade that sank into the dirt inches from his skull.

With one more rotation, he thought he might gain his feet and put some distance between him and his assailant. As he forced his body to move over once more, an obstacle stopped his motion.

He had rolled into the block bench at the well.

"Ha! You have run out of room to wiggle!" the voice boomed from above. This time the Crusader cocked the blade to the side to deliver his blow, which left Roberto no room to spin away. The arc of the sword would undoubtedly reach him.

But the Crusader's swing never started. Roberto saw the man's eyes widen in horror as a smaller blade came up under his armor and entered his body just below the armpit. Raji had launched himself and driven the stolen sword deep into the torso of the would-be executioner. The extension of the body necessary to swing the overweight weapon had exposed an area unprotected by the armor. His broadsword dropped, and he fell. This time he would not regain his feet.

Reenergized at his salvation, DeCorto rose from the ground and kicked Raji out of the way, yanking his sword from the trunk of the dying man.

Raji watched in amazement as DeCorto, brimming with new life and adrenaline, proceeded to spin, dance, and parry the attacks of the oncoming three Crusaders. He leapt deftly from the ground to the bench to the edge of the well, where one of the men made an overhand swing that missed him by inches. Fending off a blow from one of the others as he jumped down, Roberto hooked the ankle of the off-balance man with the instep of his own foot, and with his free hand hooked under the metal plating on his back, flipped the Crusader forward into the well. As he hit the water with a splash, the heavy armor took him down, and he drowned as the fight went on above his lifeless body.

Any thought of retreat had vanished from Roberto's mind as he battled on. He was too swift for the broadswords wielded by the armor-clad men, and in the heat of the afternoon soon their breathing became labored. Finally, one of the two remaining made the mistake of a forward charge. DeCorto had been patiently waiting for such a foolhardy move, and his blade caught the man at eye level as he sidestepped the onslaught. It was the first two-handed swing he'd used this day, and his aim was true. The helmet stopped the man's head from being severed in two, but the force of the blow crushed the protective metal backward three inches, ramming the Crusader's septum and eye sockets into the brain. As the man died instantly, Roberto twisted to face the final warrior.

Dropping his sword, the man began to run, his clanking armor slowing him to laughable gait. Roberto pursued and caught him after only a few steps, tripping him from behind. The Crusader sprawled on the ground, pleading for mercy.

"Please. I beg you! Let me live, and I will never tell of this encounter," he cried.

DeCorto drove the point of his blade into the man's throat, then twisted the handle of his sword, inflicting a mortal wound.

He looked around the area at the bodies of the five men, and at the well where the sixth had sunken to his death. To Raji, he said, "We must leave this place before more of our forces arrive. There will be questions I do not wish to answer."

Raji bent and picked up the heavy broadsword of one of the fallen men. Facing DeCorto, he said, "We will go separate ways."

"We made a deal. Your life and freedom for the riches within you."

"I made no deal. You assumed it only."

"The fact that you breathe now is evidence of your acceptance of our pact. Boy, you are shackled and hold a blade you cannot swing. Come with me peacefully."

"Sir, you are a great warrior. I have never seen such skill in battle. But I will not give up what was my father's, and my family's. You will have to take my life." Raji raised the weighty sword. "Engage me or walk away."

Roberto shook his head, then raised his weapon. He lunged toward Raji, who swung hard with the oversized piece of steel. The weight of the blade took him off balance as DeCorto easily stepped out of the way. With his body contorted and face exposed, the last thing Raji saw was a fist flying at his head. Then everything went black as the impact of Roberto's punch knocked him out.

As Raji dropped, DeCorto caught him and threw him onto his shoulder. He retrieved his helmet and put his sword into its leather scabbard, then continued the walk back to his camp, carrying the boy.

A week later DeCorto's entourage was encamped on the shores of the Mediterranean. Roberto had arranged passage on a ship bound for Western Europe. His dozen horses were loaded on board, and one of the stable slaves tended them. The other slave remained with him on shore and now delivered a bowl to DeCorto at the table where he sat.

"This is all?" he asked as he peered at the contents of the bowl.

"Yes. The boy has passed nothing in his excrement for two days. We will see no more."

"You have boiled these in water? And scrubbed them?"

"Yes. Four times as you requested. Just as with the others."

DeCorto opened a pouch he carried and poured the contents into the bowl. Large blue stones met others in the container. All were approximately an inch in diameter and an inch and a half in length. Twelve stones in all. "You did well," he said to the slave.

"It was not the most pleasant task you have given me, master," he answered flatly.

"I appreciate your effort. And how is Raji?"

"Angry. Especially that you fed him the potion that required his bowel to open. Then having us force water..." the slave hesitated then continued, "...to further clear his bowels has enraged him. It would be better if you had him killed, I think. He will not forget this."

DeCorto smiled as he dumped the jewels back into the pouch, careful to not touch the stones. Eventually, he would, but only after they were scrubbed and boiled a few more times.

"He will recover. The time has come to turn him loose," he stated, rising from the table and walking to the tent where Raji was shackled. Opening the flap, he found him sitting dejectedly on the makeshift cot provided.

"I will free you. You have fulfilled the pact," said Roberto.

Without looking up, Raji replied, "For the hundredth time, warrior, we had no pact. You have stolen what was my family's by birthright. Those stones you now possess are useless colored rocks in your hands. Like the rocks you carry in your head."

"It is war, boy. You should be thankful you have your life. You are an industrious young man, and you will prosper. Perhaps as a trader, as was your father," Roberto stated. He added thoughtfully, "Still, I am amazed you could have swallowed so many stones so large and survived."

"It was the will of Allah."

"Then Allah willed that I should possess the stones."

18

"No. That is the will of Iblis. Allah's preference will come to be before the end of all things."

DeCorto stated, "You will be released upon my boarding the ship. I will leave you with some bezants of gold to feed you until you start your ventures. I will also leave you with two of the stones; it is my way of showing gratitude for saving my life, which was nearly lost in the endeavor of saving yours."

Opening the pouch, he shook two stones out onto the edge of the cot. A purse was then dropped with a metallic clanking.

"Oh, thank you, master!" said Raji sarcastically. "Your benevolence is matched only by that of Allah himself!"

"You should be more gracious to your benefactor. Had I not intervened at the well you would now be gutted like a lamb at market."

"Sir, you and your people are *not* our benefactors. You come to our lands to take what is ours. You are a boorish people, dirty, and you smell. I have seen your men use the same hand they wipe themselves with to eat. You're a disgusting lot.

"Were it not for the divisions among us, we would overrun you and send you all home. Those few who were not corpses, that is. One day we will unite and drive you from our lands. Then we will come for you in your lands to make slaves of you all. That is a promise I make to you, by the will of Allah."

DeCorto said tiredly, "What happens here henceforth is of no concern to me. I will return to my family and my lands and raise horses.

"Our time together is ended. I wish you good fortune in the future."

Raji nodded in acceptance, saying, "Be gone then, thief. But know that this story will be told and retold through my family. The jewels will find their way back together and to their rightful owner over time. I will come, and if not me, my sons, or even theirs. Your lands may be a great distance, but the stones themselves will find the way. They have a great purpose."

"I'm sorry we cannot agree on rightful ownership of the jewels," said Roberto. "When the story is retold, those hearing must know that the very ears through which they receive the tale would not exist, save the intervention of DeCorto."

"The name will be remembered."

With a final nod between them, the tent flap closed behind the warrior.

CHAPTER 1

A THURSDAY AFTERNOON IN EARLY MARCH

Victor Cohen maneuvered the Suburban out of the hospital parking lot, smiling at the whoosh of the wipers sweeping the droplets off the windshield. With everything going on in his life, the mental cleansing of today's rain was a welcome respite.

Easing the big vehicle onto the freeway for the thirty-minute drive from Riverside south to his home in Canyon Lake, Dr. Cohen called home on the Bluetooth. His wife of thirty-nine years answered on the third ring. "Hi Annie," he said, "I just left the hospital. It's still raining here, so traffic will likely be backed up. It'll take a few extra minutes to make it home."

"No problem," Anne replied, "I guessed that. I'll put the chicken in the oven now, and we'll eat a few minutes after you get here."

"Okay. See you in a half hour or so." He almost said goodbye, but asked, "By the way, did you hear from Wojicki today?"

"Not today." She paused then added, "In fact, not at all this week. Is he out of town?"

"I don't think so. We're supposed to start trenching for footings on Phase II at Vineyard Meadows on Monday. He's probably been out at the job site. He's a stickler for details," Victor said.

"You're probably right. Drive safely. See you soon." Anne hung up.

Vineyard Meadows was the largest and latest in the line of housing subdivisions Victor and Anne Cohen had invested in over the past ten years. Vic was a partner with Tom Wojicki, a man who was once a patient and had convinced the orthopedic surgeon to invest in a small home subdivision a decade ago. The doctor had been easily convinced, but his wife Anne had an initial distrust for the man. However, after numerous dinner meetings and cost-analysis breakdowns, she warmed to Tom enough to give her husband her blessing to invest, as long as he had control of the finances. The partnership agreement was drafted with Victor Cohen and Tom Wojicki as equal partners. Vic was Chief Financial Officer, and San Jacinto Development had been born.

Over the life of the company, there had been tremendous successes along with a few minor failures. There were also the inevitable disagreements of partners.

In the initial subdivision, the structures sold at an average of ten percent over the estimated prices, garnering a profit far greater than expected. While the partners were more than happy with the outcome, Tom Wojicki was unhappy with how the proceeds were to be divided. He felt Vic and Anne Cohen should be happy to accept the amount originally estimated as their return, and he should receive the balance. After all, it was *his* expertise that allowed the company to reap such a large profit, and he had suffered with a meager income for months waiting for the proceeds from the sale.

Dr. Cohen had been amenable to a modification in the distribution of the proceeds. However, Anne was adamant the original agreement be followed. She reminded her husband that Tom had risked nothing in the endeavor, and they had paid his monthly draw from their personal accounts until the construction loan funded, above and beyond the terms of the agreement.

After a few tense meetings, they agreed the proceeds would be divided equally. Talk of disbanding the company and going their separate ways came up, but both Tom and Vic were too excited about the next project to dwell on any hard feelings.

They'd located two more parcels of land, and one even carried an approved subdivision map. Building could begin immediately.

San Jacinto Development had survived the minor disagreement and became a highly profitable sideline business for many years for Victor and Anne Cohen.

As he neared his exit for home, he decided to call the construction office to get a progress report. It was unlike Tom to not call for a week. He called up the office number from the memory of the phone. After three rings an electronic voice answered, *"The number you have called is not in service at this time. Please check the number and try your call again."*

Odd, he thought. He called again, receiving the same message.

It gnawed at Victor. The development company office was just ten minutes down the freeway; he decided to swing by. He phoned Anne to tell her he was taking a brief detour, but she didn't answer. She regularly took their dog for a walk just before dinner, and seldom took her cell phone. He decided to call again in a few minutes and didn't leave a message.

The Vineyard Meadows project was being built on a piece of gorgeous land east of Temecula in the wine-producing region. By the time the subdivision map was completed and approved, there was no market for the homes. The bloom had temporarily fallen off the rose in the Southern California housing market.

Due to lack of demand, the Cohens and Tom Wojicki decided to suspend development until the housing market made a comeback, but the decision had been made too late into the freefall of home prices. Their last subdivision lost over $1,300,000 at final sale. Tom had suggested they bail out and let the bank take the loss. He planned to liquidate his accounts and funnel the money into investments offshore. He'd declare bankruptcy after his funds were safely hidden away, and he urged Vic and Anne do the same.

The Cohens would have no part of the plan. Developing homes over the years had been lucrative, and the bank was not at fault for the market crash. The majority owner of the lending institution was a friend, and they simply couldn't deal him such a blow. A loss that size would not be pleasant, but it could be absorbed by the company. Although Tom was loath to do so, he begrudgingly contributed his share to pay off the construction loan. The company held onto the raw land, the site of their current project, Vineyard Meadows, and shut down to wait until the economic environment changed.

Tom went off to Nevada and continued building. Dr. Cohen saw patients and traveled with Anne, spending time at their home in the East Cape of Cabo San Lucas, something they had nearly given up during the years of development.

Yet sunshine and near-perfect climate would not be daunted. The allure of Southern California was too strong. Within two years home prices were on the rapid rise once again.

Dr. Cohen had called Tom and suggested they start working on the Vineyard Meadows project. Tom explained his own funds were invested. With all his working capital tied up, he had only his time, effort, and expertise to contribute to the project, basically under the same terms of the agreement they'd entered into many years ago. Profit would be split after Vic and Anne Cohen withdrew the funds they'd invest in the construction.

Vic Cohen jumped at the offer. Tom's project could wait. The amount of money to be made here was too great to pass up.

That was nearly a year ago, thought Dr. Cohen as the Suburban slid down the freeway exit.

The office of San Jacinto Development was located at the rear of a strip mall just off the freeway. The home sales took place from a beautifully decorated model home at the development site. The office here was for the construction details and didn't need to be fancy. Located within the office was their newly opened subsidiary company, Wine Country Escrow, a venture Tom Wojicki had assured the Cohens would further increase profits.

The closing officer at their escrow company was Cindi, a gorgeous blonde Tom had in tow when he returned. Vic and Anne guessed Cindi was twenty-seven years old at most, and while they didn't know for sure, they speculated Tom's age at just over forty-five. The woman, while young and pretty, seemed to know the escrow business. She was efficient and pleasant with clients. Tom made the commitment that if the escrow company lost money, he'd reimburse San Jacinto Development for her salary out of his share of the proceeds when the homes were sold.

As Victor pulled into a space in front of the office, he was relieved to see one of the employees moving a computer from one desk to another. The last vestige of daylight had faded during his drive, and no other people were about. The business phone being out of service had mildly unsettled him. A familiar face and the lights on were comforting sights. Especially *this* familiar face. Dr. Cohen knew Monk Phillips.

Monk was a huge man with longish sand-colored hair and an overly jovial disposition. He'd been an athlete at some point earlier in life, and the scar on his left knee led Dr. Cohen to believe he probably had played football somewhere before the injury, although Monk would never confirm nor deny the doctor's conjecture.

Maybe in the stack of monthly invoices we forgot to pay the phone bill, thought Dr. Cohen as he approached the office door and gave it a push. The portal didn't give way.

The lock was in place with the key inserted on the inside, he noticed. With a rap on the doorframe Monk looked up from the computer he was moving and waved as he recognized the doctor. As Monk walked across the small office, Victor Cohen froze in a moment of realization. Monk was not moving the computers and other office equipment within the building. The equipment was being loaded in crates, apparently for transport.

When Monk reached the door, he said through a mail slot in the glass, "Hey Doc, great to see you! Let me get the door open, and I'll explain what's going on."

With a smile on his face, he quickly reached down and turned the key.

Before Dr. Cohen could answer, Monk slammed his full weight into the steel doorframe, driving it outward. The frame caught the stunned doctor across the right side of his face, instantly shattering his cheekbone and opening a large wound under his eye. The jolt threw him off the concrete walk, and he went down hard on the wet pavement of the parking lot. As he struggled to get up and reached his knees, he clutched his mangled face with his right hand.

Disoriented with his vision blurred, Dr. Cohen knew he was in trouble. Escape became his foremost thought. He had one foot under him when he felt another impact under his right arm. Ribs snapped, and the air exited his lungs as Monk nailed him with a fully arched roundhouse kick to his ribcage. He was down again, left hand covering the cracked ribs and right hand over his broken cheekbone and lacerated face.

He tried to scream for help, but with no air inside his chest, only emitted a slight groan.

Then he heard her voice. He couldn't hear what she was saying, but the voice was familiar. With his left eye, he caught a glimpse of her legs. He couldn't lift his head high enough to see any more of her, but he certainly recognized the legs. Breathing as deeply as the spreading pain would allow, he moaned, "Cindi, run. Call the police." He coughed out a wad of saliva and blood and took another breath. "Monk's gone crazy. I caught him robbing the office. Run!"

The legs in front of him did not move.

Then came another blow, this one to his exposed abdomen. He retched in agony.

"Hey Doc, you're messin' up the parking lot," Monk said as he arched his leg for yet another kick. He delivered the blow, again to the abdomen. The helpless surgeon threw up once more.

"Stop kicking him, Monk. For God's sake! Tom's going to be pissed at you! Let's get out of here," Cindi yelled.

The last thing Dr. Cohen remembered was hearing the footsteps as they walked away, a distinct click-click-click-click of a woman's heels, and the dull thuds of a large man's work boots. He felt raindrops falling again, then the pain subsided as he drifted off into unconsciousness.

Two hours later his dinner sat cold in the refrigerator. Anne had eaten and was now reading on the couch. *An emergency must have come up at the hospital,* she told herself. It had happened before, but he usually called.

The phone rang, and she answered on the portable handset. It was the county sheriff's department.

"I'll be there as quickly as possible," she answered. As she hung up, she tried to fight the tears welling in her eyes.

CHAPTER 2
SATURDAY

"Today in the finals of the King of the Hill competition at Squaw Valley, we have the pleasure of seeing two of the finest mogul skiers in the world!" The announcer paused to let the crowd of three thousand-plus cheer for a few seconds. "On the red course, we have the overall points champion of the past three seasons. You all know 'The Jet.'"

The racer on the red course pointed his ski poles toward the sky and drew circles in the air. The crowd howled.

The announcer continued, "And on the blue course we have this season's points champion, headed next to the world championships, 'The Flyin' Hawaiian', Brian Chang." Again, a huge cacophony came from the crowd. The Flyin' Hawaiian was the new golden boy of freestyle skiing. Fans flocked to see him perform. The blue course competitor raised his poles above his head and clicked them together twice.

When the crowd quieted, the introduction went on. "In case you haven't been following the tour, this will be the third meeting between these two skiers this season. This will be the last chance this year for The Jet to avenge two prior losses. Folks, you're about to see the best there was versus the best there is right now on the Western States Freestyle Tour. Racers to the gates! Let's get ready to rock!"

"Smokin'" by the band Boston howled from the speakers lining the course at the top of Headwall, one of Squaw Valley's nastiest runs.

Brian Chang looked down his course outlined by the blue flags. He glanced at The Jet settling into the starting gate on the red course to his right. His friend and Racor's Edge teammate gave a thumbs-up and a quick nod. The idiotic smile that he'd seen a thousand times was broad across The Jet's face.

"Racers ready!" the starter barked.

The Flyin' Hawaiian tried to clear his mind to focus only on the starting horn, but all he could picture was the devilish grin of his competitor.

Beeeep! The starting horn rang out.

They were out, with Brian, focused on his competitor's smirk, a hundredth of a second behind.

Brian's knees worked like shock absorbers, bending with the impact of each bump, then quickly unweighting to allow the skis to turn as he rose to the top of another mogul. He was under control, looking for the first of two jumps built into the identical spot in each course. The Jet had a slight lead, but The Flyin' Hawaiian knew he could catch up.

They flew high, almost in unison as they spun inverted with their skis rotating overhead. On the landing, The Jet's lead had actually increased, and Brian saw him negotiating the bumps and skiing flawlessly.

He's too old to ski like that, thought Brian. He drove off his edges to gain speed and catch his opponent.

But the wily veteran skier was not to be caught today. By the time they'd reached the second jump, he had a five-yard lead. He flew high and rotated upside down once again, this time locking eyes with Brian at the point of being completely inverted. Their vision joined only for a split second, but the familiar daft grin was there on the red course. Brian focused on the sardonic smile and lost concentration, hitting the jump off balance, and crashing in a heap, losing his skis, and tumbling across the snow.

The crowd went wild, but the five judges at the base of the hill immediately raised the flags signaling a victory for the red side, even while the racer still had one-third of the course to cover.

When The Jet saw the flags raised below signaling his victory, he abruptly threw his skis sharply on edge and stopped above the finish line to look up the hill and see what happened.

Brian Chang got up off the snow and collected his equipment. Shaking off the hit, he snapped into his skis and continued down Headwall stopping where his opponent waited.

The Jet looked back at The Flyin' Hawaiian and yelled to be heard over the cheering crowd, "We've still got some course left. Let's finish the show!" He nodded down the hill, and he and Brian took off at full speed, no longer performing for the judges, but rather for the fun of skiing side by side as good friends. They crossed the finish line at the same time, both flying high in the air. Neither of the racers wanted to be the first to release from their airborne positions, and both held on too long. They crashed simultaneously in front of the judge's table and picked themselves out of the snow smiling and laughing deliriously.

The loudspeakers blared with the announcer's voice. "We've never seen a final like that here at Squaw Valley! Wow! Let's give these two one more big hand. Your runner-up today is Brian 'The Flyin' Hawaiian' Chang and your King of the Hill champion, showing old age and treachery will win out over youth and skill," the announcer paused for effect, "is Jake 'The Jet' Cohen."

CHAPTER 3

The last wave of hungry patrons was being seated when Jake arrived at Caples Lake. Bruno Kohl, the resort owner, was entertaining the guests with a story of a hibernating bear they had to evict from the substructure of the lodge earlier this season as he refilled wine glasses and passed out frosty mugs of beer. Bruno saw Jake and gave an upward nod with a furrowed brow toward the restaurant door.

Uh oh, thought Jake.

He'd joined in leasing the restaurant at the resort with a friend and fellow ski bum, D.J., who was pouring a twelve-year-aged Melka cabernet and schmoozing with a party of five when he walked in. Jake recognized the $290 bottle and smiled wryly at Deej, knowing with a group that size they'd order at least one more before their meal was through. Maybe two. *Keep it flowing. We need the money.*

Jake broke into a corny stance exposing the trophy he'd won earlier. D.J. completed the wine distribution, rolling his eyes toward the ceiling. His apron was streaked with remnants of the evening's fare. Jake's girlfriend, Janelle, was nowhere to be seen on the restaurant floor.

"Nice. I'm thrilled you won," D.J. said sarcastically as he passed by. "Put it with the others and get to work. Timmy crashed on a cornice jump and hurt his shoulder. He couldn't make it. The dish room is stacked to the ceiling. The five-top on table seven needs two New York's cut, we're out of scampi so peel me at least twenty shrimp and cut two more ahi steaks. Then start on the dishes. Janelle's done great, but she's near the end of her rope."

"Nice to see you too," replied Jake as he headed for the kitchen. On his way to the back, Janelle passed with the Caesar salad cart. Her long brown hair was up in a ponytail exposing her smooth neck. She was wearing a low-cut stretch top, and at 5' 7" with her hair pulled high she was stunning. He leaned and kissed her back just above the blouse as she passed. The salty taste of sweat, garlic, and olive oil told Jake that Janelle had been working hard.

"Not now. I'm busy!" She giggled, then saw the trophy in his hand. "You won Jake! This means you'll qualify for the world championships again! We'll celebrate later. Gotta go.

"Oh, your brother called early today and again tonight. The number's in the office. He said it was important." She headed off pushing the cart where she would prepare the salad tableside.

When Jake reached the kitchen, things didn't look as bad as anticipated. D.J. had organized everything, from dirty dishes to entrées. He immediately washed his hands, put on an apron, then cut the steaks and yellowfin tuna fillets as requested. He deftly peeled twenty shrimp, then started on the dishes.

Just a few hours ago he'd won the most prestigious mogul skiing contest in the Sierra Nevada mountains. Now he was scrubbing plates. Later he'd mop the floor.

Fame and fortune. The life of a freestyle skier, he laughed as he embarked upon clearing the goo from another stack of saucers.

Jake looked at the number on the message slip and felt the bottom fall out of his stomach. His brother had called, but the phone number was to the line at his parents' home. This could only mean one thing. The old man had finally had the heart attack everyone knew was coming. With the stress of surgery and the development company, the old man's ticker must have gone bad.

Closing the door of the office, he dialed. His brother answered on the third ring.

"Hello," Daniel Cohen said groggily. It was after 11:45 p.m.

"What's up, Bro?" Jake asked.

"Oh, Jake. How'd the contest go? I talked to Janiece, and she said you were gone. I didn't think I'd hear from you until tomorrow."

Dan, the psychologist… He lived in Beverly Hills and was establishing a thriving practice, charging $500 per hour to help the wealthy through the miserable burdens that inevitably came with being rich. Years before he'd slammed running backs into the turf as a linebacker at San Diego State. Now he wore bow ties and argyle sweater vests while listening to men and women moan about how unfulfilled their lives were while chauffeurs waited by polished limousines.

"Why are you at Mom and Dad's? What's up?"

"Well," Dan paused, "there's a problem with Dad. He was found in the parking lot outside the development office. He'd been beaten up pretty badly."

"Beaten up?"

"Yeah. He's in the hospital in intensive care. Broken ribs, a punctured lung, his cheekbone and jaw are shattered, and his face was severely lacerated. They thought he might not make it at first, but now his doctors say he has a good chance."

"What do you mean 'a good chance?' He might die?" Jake swallowed hard.

"Now they're worried about pneumonia. But he's getting stronger. Today was much better than yesterday. He won't be able to talk for a while. His jaw is full of wire and screws. But he did look at us and gave us a little eye roll with the uncovered eye."

"Better today than yesterday? When did this happen?"

"Thursday night. The sheriff's department got an anonymous 911 call from a woman saying she found a man beaten and bleeding. He'd be dead if she hadn't called."

Two days ago…His father had been at death's door, and he was just finding out.

"Why didn't someone call me sooner? It's been two days!"

"Mom didn't call until he got out of surgery on Friday morning. I canceled my appointments and came out. As soon as he got out of recovery, the sheriffs wanted us to go to the development office for questioning. We went from there back to the hospital. Mom slept on a cot in his room Friday night, and I didn't get back to their place until after midnight. I called first thing this morning, and Janiece said you were gone."

"Have you thought of getting your own phone that rings at your house? With no cell service up there reaching you through the lodge is problematic."

Jake ignored the suggestion. "So, what happened? Who'd want to beat Dad to a pulp? And how's Mom doing?"

"Mom's okay. It was a shock. She's finally resting upstairs now.

"At first the sheriffs thought it was a robbery, but Dad's wallet was there. They could have taken the Suburban too but didn't, so the cops checked a little further. The entire development office and escrow company were cleaned out. All office equipment and the funds in the company account are gone.

Three million, six hundred and fifty thousand dollars. Dad's partner and two company employees have vanished.

"Mom didn't know about the money. They were trying to get $2,000,000 from a construction loan for disbursement to the subcontractors, suppliers, and to pay off Wojicki's IRS lien. They planned on getting started on Phase II of the project with the balance. The bank funded the loan and she and Dad never knew it. All the funds the buyers had on deposit for the homes were in that account too. There was a wire transfer of over $3,400,000 to a bank in the Cayman Islands on Tuesday from the company accounts. The authorization for the transfer was signed by Dad."

Jake was stunned as he sat in silence in the tiny office. The door opening popped him out of his trance.

"Are you almost ready to eat?" Janelle asked. "Everyone's gone. I put another log on the fire."

"Sorry Jan; I need to finish up this call. Family crisis, it'll be a few more minutes."

Janelle nodded and eased the door closed. Jake continued talking with his brother. "Unbelievable. Dad's partner is gone, and so is the company money? Those numbers don't add up. Dad's never been a financial wizard but if the bank funded two million why was there over 3.6 mil in the account? And how did Dad end up getting beaten up?"

"Yeah, I pondered that too. The sheriff's investigator found a file at the office with a trust deed for another $1,500,000 payable to a man named Nicholas Stinnetti. He lives in Carson City, Nevada. Near Reno. I have a copy of it here."

"So, there are two loans totaling $3.5 million. They only transferred $3.4 mil. There should be $100,000 left, plus the home buyers' deposits."

"We thought so too. But Roger Scott, their banker, arranged for $250,000 in cash. It came from the accounts; he said he gave it Wojicki."

"You're kidding…" muttered Jake. "Tell me about the trust deed for the 1.5 million."

"Dad's notarized signature is on it along with Wojicki's, and Roger has verified the arrival of the incoming funds on Monday. Dad had made numerous requests of their bank for $2,000,000 in the prior few weeks, and Roger approved those funds on the previous Friday and funded the account Monday just before the $1.5 million arrived. With the loans and buyers' deposits on the homes, $3,650,000 was in the account at the beginning of this week."

"Interesting," said Jake. "So, what did Mom have to say about all this?"

"She was aware Dad was working on getting funding. Believe it or not, Jake, they were out of money. I guess Wojicki had massive IRS liens that prohibited the bank from loaning to the company. Dad was working on the $2,000,000 as a construction loan from their bank. Mom was completely unaware of the second note for the one-and-a-half million."

"What about Roger?" Jake questioned. "He's a family friend. He authorized the transfer to a Cayman's account and rolled together $250,000 in cash? Without verifying the signature?"

"Jake, he did what was instructed. The IRS had no order to freeze the account, but Roger said that could come any day. He thought he was doing Mom and Dad a favor."

"Hmmm." Jake's mind was processing. "What about the beating Dad took?"

"Until Dad can talk, or maybe write, we won't know. But the investigator was asking Mom some tough questions. 'Were you planning any trips out of the country?' 'Are there problems in your marriage?' 'Could your husband have been leaving without you?' 'You own a home in Mexico, don't you?' Whatever happened, the detective thinks Dad was in on it. I'm sure of that."

"That's ludicrous! Dad's laying in a hospital bed close to death and some jackass from the sheriff's department is pointing fingers at him as a criminal? Tell him to look at Mom and Dad's accounts. There would be no reason for Dad to bolt with the money."

"That's exactly what I told the detective," Dan said. Then he added, "But Mom told me it won't look good if the sheriffs start digging into their finances. The entire development at Vineyard Meadows has been funded out of their personal accounts. They've borrowed all they can against the house and Dad's retirement account, along with investing almost all their cash. There's no more money to finish Phase I, and she says no one will do another loan with the tax liens and the 3.5 million now owed on the property. On top of it, all the subcontractors have piled-on mechanics' liens until they get paid."

After a brief silence, Jake said, "They'll be wiped out. The retirement account and house too. Every loan probably has personal guarantees, Dan."

"Personal guarantees?"

"I remember from my business law classes that most loans other than home mortgages carry personal guarantee language. It means that if a borrower defaults, the lender can go after personal assets to satisfy the debt. The friendly neighborhood banker won't be so chummy after the payments stop.

"And the IRS will come around like vultures after fresh road kill. They'll consider those loans as taxable income. Once interest and penalties are tacked on, they'll never get out of the whirlpool of a huge debt to the IRS."

"Wow. I hadn't thought of any of that." Despite the problems at hand Dan couldn't help but think… As a pre-law student at USC Jake had made the honor roll. On the football field, he was all-Pac 12 as a sophomore. What a pity he was wasting his life as a ski bum.

Jake went on, "Mom probably doesn't know about any of this yet. You said she's holding up pretty well, but what I'm about to tell you could put her over the edge.

"You mentioned the buyer's deposits for the homes at Vineyard Meadows were in the company account. That's where the extra $150,000 came from. Law requires those deposits be kept in a separate account. Many developers combine funds. It's called commingling. It happens all the time, but it's illegal. As long as no one is damaged, the governing entity will just give a small fine and move on. And that's only if there's an audit, which almost never happens. With those deposits being stolen there will not simply be a slap on the wrist. Even if it's proven Dad had nothing to do with the theft, he'll still likely be prosecuted for commingling and in the worst possible scenario spend some time in jail. Hell, Dan, he *is* guilty of mishandling of the funds.

"Then a scum-sucking lawyer will contact all the buyers who lost deposits. A class-action lawsuit will be filed. Think about some poor housewife in tears on the witness stand telling the terrible story of how her life was shattered. It'll get ugly. Once the lawsuits are filed, the legal fees will mount and cripple any chance of cleaning this up.

"I've probably missed at least ten other actionable occurrences that might arise."

Wiped out might be an understatement, thought Dan. He asked, "Jake, what can we do?"

His mind already in gear, Jake answered, "I suppose making sure Dad recovers and that Mom is okay are most important right now. Finding Wojicki before he spends all the company money is next on the list. The police will work on that, but they'll give up quickly if they start to hit dead ends. You said the holder of the second trust deed lived in Carson City? That's less than sixty miles from the lodge here. Give me the address where payments should be sent, and I'll drive down and talk to this Stinnetti fellow if I can find him. Maybe he knows how we might find Wojicki, or at least where to start looking. If he wants to get paid back, I imagine he'll help. He probably doesn't even know the funds are gone."

"All right. Jake, maybe you should come home for a while. Just until Dad's condition stabilizes. I need to see patients next week. Marilyn and Brenda will be around for Mom. They're getting here tomorrow, but they won't do well with the sheriffs if they start asking accusatory questions. You'd do better with the cops."

It wasn't a request. It was more of a directive. Dan naturally assumed that he didn't have anything important going on. He almost said, *'Dan, I'm skiing in the world freestyle championships in three weeks at Vail,'* but he stopped himself. A sense of shame engulfed him.

"I'll be there tomorrow, late in the day. Let me have Stinnetti's address."

Dan gave him the information and told him everything would be all right. He assured Jake God would watch over their family. When they finally said goodbye, it was after 12:45 a.m.

Jake didn't exit the office immediately. He picked up the phone and punched in a number pulled from the archives of his mental Rolodex. His fingers hadn't dialed the line in years.

"H'lo," the voice on the other end half whispered.

"Good morning Fred. It's Jake. Sorry to call so late." He heard the rustling of sheets and light footsteps, then a door closing gently. Fred was leaving the room where he'd slept.

"Holy shit! Did hell freeze over? If Barb catches me talkin' to you, I'm a goner. Lauren ain't here, and if she was, I'd lie to you, and tell you she wasn't anyway. I got no problem with you, Jake, but the women of this house, well that's another story. You ain't the first man to try to get some extra honey on his stinger, but Barb's little girl suffered 'cause of it and your name ain't worth shit 'round here."

"I don't need to talk to Lauren. Someday maybe, but not today. It's you I called for, Fred. You know a man named Nicholas Stinnetti up the road in Carson City?"

Fred Asaro was the sheriff of the once-small town of Gardnerville, Nevada, which was now practically a suburb of Carson City. As sheriff, Fred knew everything about anybody in the Carson Valley worth knowing.

"Nicki Stinnetti? Jake, if you need some money, I'll float you a loan myself, as long as Barb don't find out about it. For God's sake, stay away from Nicki Stinnetti."

"So, this Stinnetti fellow makes loans for a living?"

"Yeah, you might say that. He's a loan shark, Jake. I should say *allegedly*. He's never been convicted. His borrowers are always too scared to testify. After they file a complaint, they usually have an accident. You know, a broken finger or two, or the nail gun slips on the job site and our witness gets a sixteen-penny framing nail in the thigh. Suddenly the complaint is withdrawn, and Nicki Stinnetti is back in business."

Jake was startled. "I need to talk to him. My father was just found beaten up in a parking lot outside his office. There were loan papers with Stinnetti's name as lender inside. Dad's signature is on the note. He's in bad shape, but they think he'll be okay."

"How? Your pop is a surgeon with a successful development company. I haven't seen him since you and Lauren split, but we hunted and fished together more than a few times. Always thought we'd be kin. How'd he get mixed up with Stinnetti?"

"I'm bewildered. That's why I want to see him. You know how I might find him?"

"Can you come down here?"

"Yep. I'm heading to my parents' house tomorrow. Or today, I guess. Leaving first thing in the morning. I can be in Gardnerville by six. Want me to meet you there?"

"Hell no! Not at the house. Meet me at the Nugget. I'll tell Barb something came up, and she'll have to go to church without me. Stinnetti will be the excuse so I won't be lying. It won't be the first time. Even though he lives outside my jurisdiction, he makes loans in town here. I'll see you in the morning. Make it eight. Stinnetti won't be up any earlier."

"Hey Fred, thanks. I know you don't have to do this; it's greatly appreciated," offered Jake.

"Oh hell, don't worry about it. Like I said, I've got nothing against you. I think my daughter overreacted. But stay clear of Barb. She'll make anything Stinnetti has done to his pigeons seem tame if she gets her hands on you."

"Okay. I'll see you in a while. Nugget parking lot. Eight." Jake hung up.

Jake found Janelle sitting in front of the fire on a blanket over the rug in the lodge. The lights were off, and the flakes of snow danced as they fell outside the window, illuminated by the firelight. Otherwise, the glow from the fireplace was the focal point in the big room, casting a soft red-orange hue on the rustic furniture and bar.

"I thought we'd eat out here, instead of the restaurant. I've seen enough of that place this weekend," Janelle laughed. "I went ahead and cooked while you talked to Dan. D.J. coached me. I hope it's okay."

"It smells great Jan," Jake said listlessly as he settled in beside her. The plates were meticulously arranged with the prawns and pasta, and the Far Niente chardonnay was on ice on the coffee table. She'd put a cloth on the old pine table that had been beaten by so many ski boots over the years. The setting was gorgeous, and so was she, both enhanced by the dancing flames.

"Something wrong?" asked Janelle as she lit the two candles on the table. "You don't seem very excited about the prospect of the romance at hand."

"Sorry," he said. He sipped the wine she'd poured. "Yeah, something's wrong, Jan."

He told her of the entire conversation with his brother, leaving out only the fact that Dan couldn't remember her name.

"How long will you be gone?" she asked after he'd finished the recounting. "It's disappointing, this being my week up here for spring break. I know you have to go."

"A week. Maybe two. Or three." He shook his head. "Honestly, I have no idea. Longer, or maybe shorter if my dad dies."

CHAPTER 4

SUNDAY

The sea below was not the deep blue Tom Wojicki had expected but a lighter hue, nearly the color of a swimming pool. The pilot explained the channel was shallow, less than twelve fathoms deep in most places, so the sunlight reflecting off the sandy bottom gave the ocean the color of sapphire.

Wojicki, dressed in plaid shorts, a mismatched Hawaiian print shirt, and black stretch knee socks above Top-Sider loafers had reluctantly stepped off the dock into the odd craft with the engine mounted backward above and behind the cockpit. Mike, the pilot, told him it was a Lake Renegade 250 Amphibian and could land in or out of the water. The lettering on the fuselage announced it as the *Flying Frog*.

The flight was arranged by the man Tom was to meet, ostensibly to avoid the possibility of getting mugged en route. The jewelry broker's business manager had explained that pirates still lurked here, but today cruised the streets of these islands instead of the sounds in between. Carrying valuable goods to trade or sell, travel to and from the meeting by air would be safest for Tom.

As they flew across the channel, he looked down on the chartered sailboats full of tourists from frigid places lazily drifting across the light blue Caribbean Sea. His stomach lurched when the plane bucked in the swirling winds as they rounded the leading edge of a tropical rainsquall. His white complexion turned mildly green, and Mike tossed his passenger an airsickness bag.

Despite the beauty of the scenery below Tom barfed up his breakfast.

Good, thought Mike. His employer for the charter, Amir Mojabi, didn't really care if those he did business with got mugged on the way to meet him. He had a deal with Amir; if he could make the passenger puke en route, he'd pick up an extra two hundred bucks. Amir was a tough negotiator and knew a buyer or seller weakened by the sickness on the bumpy flight and the bouncing of the landing on the water would crumble and give up thousands of dollars at the negotiating table. Mike was already spending the extra money.

Soon the *Flying Frog* was preparing for a landing in Hull Bay on the north side of St. Thomas, only fifteen minutes from their point of takeoff on St. John. Here Amir Mojabi had an estate carved out of the jungle on the wind-protected side of the remote inlet.

Mike put the seaplane down in the smooth waters of the bay without a bounce. He'd earned his bonus, there was no need to make a rough landing.

He pulled the plane up to a huge private dock below a grassy slope. At the top of the gentle rise was a beautiful island-style home comprised of white plaster and a clay tile roof. It was single level, and Tom guessed it to be over 5,000 square feet.

His legs were bandy as he picked up his valise and started up the gangway toward the house. A Middle Eastern looking man held what he guessed was a fully automatic rifle in his right hand and motioned Tom toward the dwelling with his left. The sight of the gun made Tom uneasy.

Do the deal then get the hell out of here, he silently told himself. He looked back at Mike who was headed for a shaded hammock to wait for the return flight, then wiped both sides of his mouth with the back of his hand to remove any remnants of the sickness.

"Hello. You must be Tom Miller." The soothing voice came from a darkened doorway at the entry of the structure. Without his sunglasses, mistakenly left at the hotel, Tom Wojicki's pupils were fully contracted in the bright sunlight. He could only see the outline of the man standing in the shaded foyer.

"I am Amir Mojabi. Welcome to my home. Can I get you something to drink? Iced tea? Rum punch? Or maybe our island specialty, the Pain Killer? Anything you'd like. The bar is fully stocked. Please, come inside out of the sun."

Tom walked into the home, clutching the valise tightly. His eyes hadn't adjusted to the darkened interior so he couldn't immediately discern what Amir Mojabi looked like. His stomach gurgled as he answered, "Bitters and soda on the rocks if possible.

"You have a beautiful home here. I've just retired from the construction business in the United States, so I recognize craftsmanship when I see it."

"Thank you. I've tried to create a pleasant environment."

"You've succeeded. Should we get down to business, Mr. Mojabi?"

Amir's smile showed brightly as Tom's pupils opened in the lowered light. Mojabi knew the bartender's cure for an upset stomach was soda with bitters. He barked in Farsi, and a woman across the room went behind a massive hardwood bar and began preparing the drinks. When Amir returned to the conversation in English, the pleasant timbre had returned.

"I hope your jump across the channel was enjoyable. Few people actually get to fly in a seaplane. I trust you have the merchandise we discussed? Come, let us look it over together."

Amir stopped at a large teak desk and motioned for Tom to sit in a white rattan chair on the opposite side. He spread a black silk cloth across the oiled hardwood top.

Tom guessed his age at near fifty. The dark hair was receding, and the eyes were an opaque brown. The body wasn't muscled but at the same time wasn't fat. The clothing was island casual—a pair of impeccably pressed sand-color slacks and a polo shirt. On his feet, Amir wore white canvas shoes. Tom was under the impression the man had never seen hard work or any serious stress.

The woman set Tom's drink on the corner of the desk on a coaster and left an iced tea for Amir on his side. Tom picked up his concoction and hastily gulped the entire thing down.

"Thirsty? May we get you another, Mr. Miller?"

"No thank you. Not yet."

"Very well. Let us see what you have in your satchel. Hopefully, we shall come to terms for a purchase and have a light lunch while my banker wires the money to your account. You'll be back at your hotel in time to enjoy the afternoon on the beach with your lovely lady friend."

Tom didn't like the fact that Amir knew he was with a woman at the hotel. What else did this man know? Did he know his real name?

Don't worry about it, he told himself. *Do the deal and get out of here.* This place scared the hell out of him.

He opened the valise and withdrew four items, each wrapped in black velvet. Inhaling deeply, he unrolled the packages on the silk Amir had laid out. Looking up as he presented the collection, he noticed another guard had silently appeared when he withdrew the contents of the bag. The sentry held a gun identical to the one held by the man on the dock.

Thankfully, the bitters had settled his stomach somewhat. Otherwise, he might have been sick again.

"Be assured, Mr. Miller, my guards are here for *our* protection. You have nothing to fear from them. If we cannot come to terms, you'll be free to go. I can even suggest two other possible buyers, one here on St. Thomas and one on Tortola Island to the east. It may take a few days to arrange a meeting and a few days more to transfer payment, but often my associates will pay higher prices for the same goods. I can simply offer a more expedient transaction."

Amir's statement calmed Tom slightly. *Ali Baba didn't intend to rob him.* But at the same time, he told him quite bluntly he wasn't going to get a good price. Additionally, he seemed uninterested in the collection of jewelry. The bastard hadn't taken a second look at his wares.

Was this camel trader the only buyer he could find? Maybe he *should* contact Amir's associates and get a second or third offer. It made good business sense.

No. While he was staying at the hotel under an assumed name, he was still on American soil. He didn't feel safe waiting a few hours more, let alone a few days. Nonetheless, he planned on bluffing Amir with his own attitude of nonchalance.

"Actually, I *had* planned on getting a second opinion. The collection appraised at over $2,500,000. We disbanded our company recently; I took it as part of my equity. In the United States, I'd get at least $1,750,000, but the IRS would take nearly half. My price is $1,125,000. Take it or leave it."

Tom Wojicki thought he sounded tough. It was a fair deal, and he was certain Amir would take it.

"Mr. Miller, people do not tell me to 'take it or leave it' in my home," Amir said calmly, yet with an underlying tone of vehemence. "It was you who sought me out, not vice versa. It is customary for a man in your position to present your product and wait for an offer. Or if you prefer to be bold, you should state your price and wait for a response. 'Take it or leave it' is so abrasive.

"Let me tell you what I think is happening here, that we might negotiate more openly." Amir sat up and put both hands on the table.

"I believe this collection of jewels is *stolen*. I don't believe your name is 'Miller.'" Mojabi projected an air of ambivalence, yet something changed as he spoke. Now his eyes remained locked on the collection, and he leaned forward to hawk over the jewels. His lack of pitch belied an increasing enchantment with the ornaments.

"The substantial sapphires on the necklace, pin, earrings, and ring are exquisite, and the added diamonds optimize the beauty. The collection as a whole would indeed bring your high-end 'United States' price. However, this collection will have to be broken down and reset to avoid recognition. I will sell it well below market, and I assume your risk. You have *zero* bargaining power. You're on the run, and you're scared. If I told you I would give you $250,000 you would take it and pack up your American slut and fly away."

The guileless words put Wojicki's already twisted stomach into further spasm. Yet at the same time, he saw in-depth concentration now in the eyes as the man stared down at the collection.

Mojabi continued. "But, Mr. Miller, I am a man of integrity. I will pay you what I think this collection is worth to me, taking into consideration the delicacy that must be used in liquidating it."

Finally breaking his gaze from the items on the velvet, Amir sat back in the alligator-hide chair and appeared to be mentally calculating. After what seemed an eternity he announced, "A figure of $500,000 sounds fair, I think. And I must add, *take it or leave it.*"

Tom was again about to be ill. A drink would be helpful right now. He wanted to tell Amir he'd find another buyer. Maybe he *should* keep the collection. Cindi had looked beautiful wearing the set the night before. The immense sapphires rimmed in diamonds lying on the black silk was fabulous. Truly, the set *was* one of a kind.

He looked across the desk at Amir, wanting to say, '*Fuck you, dune-coon*' and leave, but with machine-gun-toting guards nearby, he stifled his tongue.

Yet the eyes of Mojabi had become less steadfast; he was transfixed by the collection. Years of playing poker told Tom desire was on the other side of the desk. The man *wanted* what he had.

One more shot, Tom decided. He stated, "Mr. Mojabi, we both know this set is worth five times what you've offered. I can't let it go for $500,000. I think $900,000 is a fair figure."

"Thank you for coming today," Amir said as he abruptly stood. "Enjoy your stay at the hotel. I will take care of the bill through tonight. I'm sorry we could not come to terms."

Tom stood too. He began wrapping the jewels in the velvet pouches but kept a sideways eye on Mojabi. He didn't see fear or panic in the eyes. It was something else. Curiously, it appeared to be *longing*.

Finally, as Tom was about to place the velvet pouch in his valise, Amir held up his hands, palms out, and said, "Wait, Mr. Miller, please sit down. I'd like to have my gemologist examine the collection before a final decision is made."

Unwrapping the set again, Tom answered, "Only if the jewels don't leave my sight."

"Done. The jewels will remain on the table. My expert will be called from the store on the other side of the island in Charlotte Amalie. His arrival here may take thirty minutes or so. Then only a few minutes to evaluate your product. I assume you have the time?"

"I do. I'll take that drink you offered while I wait. Scotch, over ice."

The middle-aged man examining the stones was short, balding, and wore a hawkish expression as he studied the sapphires through a high-powered jeweler's loop. As he worked, the little man held the pieces brought by Tom side by side next to an item Mojabi had produced from the rear of the home.

Silence, broken only by the mild hum of a ceiling fan and the occasional squawk of a seabird outside, took hold in the room.

Finally, after nearly thirty minutes of intense examination, the gemologist spoke. "The cleavage planes and striations are similar; I would say identical. In my professional opinion I would say yes, they are a match. I'd stake my reputation on it.

"Amir, you have found the stones you seek."

Mojabi stared down at the desktop. Next to the collection of gems rested a dagger. The knife that had come from a gold-inlaid hardwood box was beautifully crafted with a shining platinum blade and gleaming golden handle. Inset on the ornate grip were two huge sapphires, complemented by shimmering diamonds as a background. The dagger by itself was exquisite;

resting next to the collection there was a natural match of color and brilliance.

"They seem to fit together. To complete one another," said Tom.

Mojabi reached down and gingerly picked up the necklace. He stretched it across his left hand and gently touched, one by one, the five stones making up the piece. The largest sapphire of the set was centered in the band, with two sapphires of nearly equal size set approximately an inch apart on both sides. Perfect diamonds were spaced equidistantly along the chain, but they paled in comparison to the shimmering blue stones.

Setting the necklace down, his fingers moved across the rest of the jewels. The earrings were simple in design yet gaudy in magnitude, each offering two shimmering diamonds with a larger sapphire in the center hung vertically. The dress pin carried two of the blue stones mounted in the center of a cross of still more diamonds. The most brilliant sapphire of the set was mounted high in a platinum setting on the ring.

Amir picked up the dagger and rotated it between his fingers. He bit his lip and said to no one in particular, "Ten stones that match the two in this blade." He looked now at his gemologist. "They are a match?" he quizzed again.

The man nodded. "Yes Amir, I believe them to be. I must say, too, the work on the pieces is exquisite. It rivals my own."

Mojabi looked at Wojicki, who now wore a smug expression of victory. "What is the name of the family from whom these were stolen?" he asked.

"Mr. Mojabi, this set was not stolen. It was part of a settlement of the—"

"The name of the family!" Mojabi barked as he cut him off. The ornate dagger flipped in his hand, blade outward, now an inch from Wojicki's throat.

Tom stepped back but found the chest of a huge guard blocking his retreat.

"The name!" Amir demanded again.

"Cohen! Victor and Anne Cohen," offered Tom weakly, pressing his body into the guard to avoid the knife. The ice cubes in his second scotch rattled as his hand trembled.

They stood for a moment, Mojabi's blade at Wojicki's throat as his eyes bore into the American's. "The woman's maiden name. Do you know it?"

"I don't!" implored Tom, eyes crossed upon the blade leveled at his jugular vein.

The brown eyes went from wide open to squinting as the blade was finally

44

lowered. Amir set the dagger on the bed of red silk in the box and turned back to Tom.

"My offer to buy your wares is retracted. I will not *buy* what I believe to be rightfully mine, and my family's. When you depart, you will leave the jewels here."

"But you said I had nothing to fear!" protested Tom.

"Mr. Miller, let me be frank with you. I find you a distasteful man, as I find most Americans. Yet I am a man of my word, and you shall not leave empty-handed. I will pay you a *reward* for the return of this property, which I believe was stolen from my ancestors nearly a thousand years ago.

"I will pay you $500,000. I assume you brought the wiring instructions for your bank?

"The jewels are mine. By birthright. I'll order some lunch for you while my banker wires the money to your account. And you can have the next drink which your body is craving."

Tom bit his lip, then answered, "All right. I'll take the half million. Another scotch would be nice too. Not that I need it."

"Good. You've made a wise choice. The money will be wired. Please wait on the patio overlooking the bay until verification comes in. I'll have your scotch and food delivered." He motioned with his hand for Tom to depart. Amir stayed with the collection.

Tom Wojicki was beginning to feel remorse as he waited. This set of jewels meant more than just the money he'd get from the sale, or now as Mojabi termed it, *reward*. It was the last piece in the crushing of Dr. and Mrs. Cohen. By now they had discovered all the company assets were gone, and soon they would find that their coveted collection of sapphires was gone too. To keep the set would be a constant reminder of how he'd set up the doctor and his wife. It was a pity to have to give it up.

The return flight to his hotel in the *Flying Frog* was smooth, but Tom threw up again.

45

CHAPTER 5

Traveling northward on Highway 395, the steep eastern slope of the Sierras looms above to the west. The home of Nicholas Stinnetti was located on the alluvial plain at the base of the grand mountain range. It sat on a narrow, paved road well off the highway west of town.

Carson City had boomed with jobs and housing developments over the past thirty years, but Nicki Stinnetti wanted his privacy, so he had a home built outside the range of the developers' reach. The property appeared to be about ten acres with a two-story pueblo-style home. The construction was log beams protruding through Navajo-white stucco. Smoke billowed from three of the five chimneys.

Sheriff Fred Asaro and Jake sat in the front of Fred's crew-cab Ford pickup outside of an iron gate in a low stucco wall. On top of the wall, wrought iron twelve feet high gave a view for the inhabitants but provided protection at the same time. The wall ran around the home, isolating the structure and about one-half acre of land from the rest of the property. A few other homes were also located on this road but none within a half mile.

Jake asked if they should call first. The sheriff told him it would be better if they just paid an unannounced visit. Now they sat outside the gate in the heated cab of an unmarked truck.

"What do we do now?" asked Jake.

"We'll sit a bit. See what happens."

"Don't you think we should let someone know we're here?"

"They know we're here. Trust me." The sheriff pointed to two small video cameras neatly tucked under the high arch of stucco over the gate. He continued, "Right now his security company, or maybe a cop he's got on payroll, is runnin' my plates. He don't recognize this truck, but he'll know who's here in a few minutes. If he's not along soon, I'll go hit the bell."

"You think he'll be scared off by you being a cop?"

"Maybe. But you've got a much better chance seeing him with me than without. An unknown face and name likely wouldn't get you through the gate. If you needed a loan, you'd contact his office. And that would have to be tomorrow. He don't work Sunday. Probably wouldn't get to talk directly with him unless you needed a big loan. He does have a somewhat legitimate lending business too."

They'd already waited fifteen minutes and waited ten more. Finally, the mammoth knotty-pine door on the home opened, and a youngish man in a white crew neck sweater and khaki pants crossed the driveway and approached the gate. Jake guessed him to be about six foot two and probably two hundred and fifty pounds. His shoulders and waist were likely the same size. Over the sweater was a herringbone sports coat that looked too small. From the size of the shoulders it was obvious he pumped the iron, but his thick middle announced he did little conditioning otherwise. His dark hair was long and pulled into a ponytail, and his face showed disdain for being sent out in the cold to greet the visitors. When he reached the iron bars, he motioned for the window in the truck to be rolled down.

Before doing as bidden, Fred said to Jake, "That's Eddie Lawton. He was a high school football hero around here a few years back. Went to Colorado on a scholarship but washed out of the program. Now he collects payments for Stinnetti.

"When he got back from getting dumped by the college, he busted up a few guys in bars around town. We arrested him on assault charges a couple of times, but he's been clean since he started working for Stinnetti." He looked Jake in the eyes before continuing, "Let me talk to these guys first, okay? You'll know when to jump into the conversation. Be patient." Fred rolled the window down.

"Mornin' Eddie. You're lookin' sharp today. I'd like to talk to Nicki for a few minutes. Think you could arrange that?"

"Got a warrant?" the large man grunted.

"Oh Eddie, lighten up. I used to bust you and your friends for tryin' to buy beer on phony IDs. Let Nicki know I want to talk. It might be worth a lot of money to him. I'm not here as a lawman. This is a personal visit."

Eddie nodded, then gave Jake a quick once-over before turning to go back into the house. He returned less than two minutes later, and the wrought-iron gate rolled open. Fred and Jake got out, and Eddie led the two of them through the entry of the house into the living room.

The home was open to the rafters, with a striking view of the pines in the hills to the west. A stairway rose from each end of the room toward the bedrooms upstairs. The center of the living room was sunken two steps from the entry floor, and the far wall facing the steep rise of the mountains was complete glass, except the doors, which had knotty pine frames and glass centers. A fire burned in a massive pueblo-style enclosure.

"What brings you out my way, Sheriff?" asked Nicholas Stinnetti as he trotted into the room extending his hand to meet Fred Asaro's. He was all of five foot six and one hundred and fifty pounds, and not an imposing figure in any physical way. But he carried himself with total confidence. It was obvious he didn't fear anyone in this room and seemed amused by the sheriff's presence. He wore black wool pants and a buttoned-down white shirt with Rockport loafers. Jake noticed the shoes had been re-soled with an extra thick layer of rubber, probably to add as much height as possible to the short man. Another man with a slight build followed Stinnetti into the room. He wore an impeccably tailored dark suit and black tie.

"Nicki, nice to see you this morning," Fred greeted. He gave all three the once-over. "What occasion are you boys all duded-up for?"

"Lunch at the sports book up at Lake Tahoe. Besides, it's Sunday ain't it? You never know; maybe we'll end up in church somewhere. My wife's there now," Nicki laughed. He cast a quick glance at Eddie and the other man, signaling that they should laugh too. They did.

"Who's the new guy, Nicki?" Fred looked at the man in the suit. His dark hair was gelled and combed back with a touch of gray at the temples, and he was smallish, although not as short as Stinnetti. "I ain't seen you 'round here before. What kind of rap sheet follows you?"

"Ah, Fred, don't be so caustic. His name's Bennie Temple. He's from the Midwest. With a flawless résumé. He works in my risk evaluation and loss mitigation department. Very good at what he does, too." Stinnetti laughed again.

"Let's see, we've got Edd-ee, Ben-ee, and Nick-ee," said Fred, accentuating each syllable, and holding the 'ee' mockingly. "Wow, what a boys' club. Can we join? I'll be Fred-ee, and this is my friend Jake-ee."

Stinnetti wasn't laughing now. "If I wanted comedy, I'd go to a club in

Tahoe. Besides, you're not funny. You told Eddie your visit could be worth some money. Let's hear what you got to say. It's snowing hard at the lake, and the drive might be long. Time, while meaningless to a meager-salaried civil servant like you, is a valuable asset to me."

The sheriff looked at Jake and gave him a quick nod. Wearing a pair of button-fly Levi's jeans, a baggy 'Racor's Edge' logo sweatshirt, and cross-trainer tennis shoes, Jake wasn't sure what to say. Something about the irreverent air of the three men made him uncomfortable.

"Mr. Stinnetti, my name is Jake Cohen," he said as he stood to his full height, just a shade under six feet. "I need to ask you a few questions about a man named Tom Wojicki, and a trust deed you hold on one of my parents' properties in Southern California."

The room was quiet for a moment. Then recognition hit Nicki Stinnetti.

"Cohen, huh? You must be the 'yid doctor's kid. How the hell did you get here so fast?" Stinnetti asked. Not waiting for an answer, he continued, "Yeah, your old man owes me 1.5 mil on a first loan on his development."

"I'm here about Tom Wojicki. He's gone, along with two company employees who may have come from here in Carson City. When he left he cleaned out the company account. My father was beaten nearly to death in their office parking lot. There is no way my father can pay you back if we don't find Wojicki before he spends all the money."

"Hmmm." Nicki looked thoughtful, but not concerned. "Did you come all the way up here from Southern California since Friday just to see me?"

"No. I live up at Caples Lake. About twenty miles south of Lake Tahoe. Fred brought me out here."

Sheriff Fred joined the conversation. "Surprise, surprise. Jake, if you had mentioned your dad's partner was Tom Wojicki, I would have requested Nicki come to the station for questioning. They know each other alright. Let me guess, the two employees that disappeared with Wojicki are Monk Phillips and Cindi Light?" The question was directed at Jake.

"Sorry Fred, I don't know their names. One was an escrow officer. Pretty, they say. The other a site worker," Jake said.

"What do you think Nicki? Was it them?" questioned the sheriff.

Stinnetti didn't seem so cocky now. Having the lawman in his home had seemed whimsical until a tie had been made between Tom Wojicki and him.

"I think I don't need to answer any of your goddamned questions without my attorney present, Sheriff," retorted Stinnetti.

"Which sports book you going to? I'll need to know when I come with a warrant to take you in."

"Fuck. What a way to kill my Sunday." Nicki rolled his eyes, then continued, "Yeah, I knew Tom Wojicki when he was here, but he's gone now. He called me up and said his company needed some dough, so I loaned the Polack and the Jew the 1.5 mil. That's it. What they did with the money ain't my concern. I don't care if they wiped their asses with it. Maybe Wojicki and the doc paid it all to the whore for services rendered. It don't matter. If it don't get paid back, I take the property.

"You assholes never give up. I'm a legitimate businessman, Sheriff. Go bark up someone else's tree."

"What about Dr. Cohen getting beaten up? Any ideas?"

"This is too fuckin' much! Every time somebody gets their ass kicked or has an accident you cops think I got somethin' to do with it. Now some jerk gets pounded five hundred miles from here, and I'm involved? Monk left here with Wojicki. If someone gets thumped and Monk's around, I'd suggest you talk to him."

Jake's patience was wearing thin. He stepped forward toward Stinnetti. He didn't see the movement behind him, but Eddie Lawton took a few steps closer too.

Jake looked directly into Nicki's eyes. "You and Wojicki are in this together somehow. No one mentioned exactly when my father got beaten to a pulp, but you knew about it on Friday. You also said my 'old man' owes you a million and a half. Wojicki doesn't owe you anything, does he?

"If your note isn't paid, you foreclose and take a development with the first phase nearly completed and paid for. Phase I was built primarily with cash. There are nine homes there that will probably sell for $800,000 each on average. So there will be $7.2 mil waiting for you upon foreclosure. It'll probably cost you $250,000 to a half mil to clean up the outstanding debts and get a final inspection on Phase I. Then whatever Wojicki owes the IRS to remove that lien. I don't know the amount yet, but I'd bet my ass you do.

"And the twelve ready-to-build lots in Phase II are worth—why don't you tell me? I guarantee you've already calculated it—but my guess is $200,000 each minimum. That's another 2.4 million. You'll never build out Phase II. You'll just cash in for almost two and a half mil more. The worst thing that could happen is my family puts together the money to buy dad's way out of the problems, and you make the whatever exorbitantly high interest rate you have on the note, plus the return of the principal. You win big either way."

"Smart fucker, aren't you?" snickered Stinnetti. "When I made the loan, I couldn't *possibly* have known Wojicki would take the money and run off. I heard about the beating of the doc on the news; that's how I knew about it Friday. The IRS was bearing down on Wojicki. He owed them a bundle!

"You see, kid, Wojicki hates your parents. Blames them for his woes. When he came here, he bitched continually about losing a fortune 'cause of a Jew doctor and his wife. Said they wouldn't declare bankruptcy years back and it cost him.

"Damn good construction guy though. He made a lot of money for developers around here. Too bad the idiot gambled and drank his tax payments away. If he's gone, it's a safe bet he ain't comin' back."

"Any chance you'd consider waiving payments on the property until my family can get reorganized?" asked Jake.

"Let's see? I can make eighteen percent deferred interest on a note in first position and maybe never get paid, or I can foreclose and make almost seven mil in profit. Bennie, you're my loss mitigation manager. What should I do?"

"Looks like you're fucked kid," said Bennie in a low raspy voice. The three well-dressed men laughed in unison.

Nicki looked at his watch. "Fred, as always, a pleasure to see you. Can't wait to do it again. Now if you don't mind, take this Jew kid and get out of my house. We gotta get to the lake. Jake Cohen, good luck!" He turned to leave the room.

"Wait, Mr. Stinnetti, I have one more thing to go over," said Jake.

Nicki Stinnetti turned back, and Jake took one quick step forward to close the gap between them. He let loose a hard kick with his right leg, snapping the foot at the end of the motion. It caught the unsuspecting Stinnetti square in the balls and lifted him off his feet. He landed in a fetal position on the tile floor, gasping for air.

"I've had enough of your 'Jew' crap," said Jake, standing above the loan shark.

After a brief period of immobility caused by utter disbelief, Eddie Lawton was now heading toward Jake. He knew Nicki, once recovered from the voice-raising kick, would be royally pissed at the failure to protect him. He cocked his right arm back and let his fist fly. Jake rolled to his right just as Eddie's hand grazed his face. The punch itself would have done little damage as Jake moved away from it, but Eddie wore a big square gold ring on his middle finger. The edge of the ring ripped open a gash in the center of Jake's left eyebrow.

He continued moving away after the roll and came up to his feet behind a couch in an open space between the living area and dining room. Eddie was on the other side of the couch, with Stinnetti still scrunched-up clutching at his testicles and coughing.

"You want me to kick his ass, Nicki?" asked Eddie.

Stinnetti couldn't speak but managed a cough that sounded like "fuck yeah" and bobbed his head up and down slightly.

"Your ass is mine!" screamed Eddie as he jumped over the couch and landed in front of Jake. He noticed Lawton's jacket had ripped at the shoulder when the man had thrown the roundhouse punch, torn by the flexing of his huge biceps and lats.

Fred Asaro stood silently, now with an amused look on his face. Bennie also stood, but his hand had crept under the lapel of his dark jacket. Fred's own hand went under his denim coat and snapped out holding a pearl-handled Colt .45 revolver.

"Leave it! I saw the bump when you walked in," he said sharply to Bennie. "Fair fight! At least if you don't count the seventy-pound difference between 'em."

Bennie calmly withdrew his hand from his coat and watched.

Eddie Lawton was accustomed to his victims being scared witless when he administered a beating. As he approached Jake, he was taken aback. The guy simply stood with blood running across the side of his face from his lacerated eyebrow, waiting. His hands weren't balled into tight fists but were half-open and held about waist high, each making small circles in the air. Then the left hand lifted and made an inward waving gesture.

"You coming, pussy?" taunted Jake.

The bigger man stepped forward accepting the challenge. Again, the big right arm cocked to deliver a thunderous blow.

Whack, whack, whack! Jake shot in with a lightning-quick left jab followed by a short right and another quick left. The three blows were completed before Eddie's grapefruit-sized fist ever got loose. Each punch snapped the head, and Jake stepped quickly back out of range, hands again relaxed at his waist. Then he shot in again delivering another series of five quick punches before Eddie could get his guard up. After the flurry, Jake again retreated out of range.

Now the bigger man was not on the offensive. Rather than preparing to swing, he started holding his hands at chin level to protect his face. Jake moved lightly around him then feigned another attack to test his opponent, easily sidestepping the man's slow left jab followed by a looping right. Each of the two missed punches pulled Eddie off balance with his elbows raised. The opening did not go unnoticed. Jake again faked a left jab and gave a head bob to the right. Eddie's response was to punch back with his right hand hard where he anticipated Jake's head would be waiting.

It wasn't. Jake continued moving to the right and was now bent at the waist, allowing Eddie's punch to sail above his head. Lawton's midsection was exposed as the punch missed, and his elbow flew high. Jake unleashed a right hook upward from his bent position, turning his body and driving all the force of his leg, shoulder, and arm behind his now tight fist. He caught Eddie directly under the left pectoral muscle in the ribs and heard the expulsion of air with the impact. The shot doubled the man over, and Jake came down from over the top with a left, delivering a crashing blow to Eddie's right ear. He went down to all fours on the tile.

"Just tackle him! Use your size, you fucking idiot!" The coughed command came from Stinnetti who had pulled himself to a sitting position.

Fred thought the bigger man was done, but to his amazement, he shot from his position on the floor and wrapped himself around Jake's midsection. The two went down behind the couch as one ball of flesh. Jake was able to spin himself around in Eddie's grasp and made it to all fours as his assailant tried to knock him flat by working higher on his body.

When wrestling competitively if an opponent gets his head too far to one side when trying a takedown, the flying elbow is an illegal but effective weapon. The key in competition is to make it look like an accident. The two elbows that hit Eddie Lawton in succession were clearly no accident. They both caught him hard in the nose and started the blood flowing.

But he didn't let go. He centered his head on Jake's back to protect himself and tried lifting Jake to pile drive him to the tile floor. As the weight of the man came off with the attempted lift, Jake kicked both legs out in front of his own body with such speed and force that Eddie's grip was broken for a split second. The meaty arms slid up high above Jake's waist, and he rolled to his right. But instead of rolling away to escape he continued the rotation inward and hooked his left arm under Eddie's right armpit as he came free, leaving the big man's arm wrapped around his back.

The underarm hook is known as a whizzer in the wrestling world. There are at least ten effective ways to counter a whizzer, but Eddie Lawton didn't know any of them. He was in big trouble as Jake quickly sprawled his legs out for balance and took hold where the ponytail was gathered, using his left hand coming up from under the armpit to get a solid grip on Eddie's locks. With the grasp on the hair and the whizzer underarm hook, Eddie's face was exposed. He had to use his left hand as a support to keep his face from smacking against the tile. Jake put his own weight on his toes and down on Eddie, hammering the exposed face three times with his right fist, then shouted directly into Eddie's ear, "Did you beat my father up?"

"Fuck you!" was Eddie's response. He received three more hard blows to his face. The vision in his right eye was starting to blur. Blood flowed from his nose and his mouth. He wasn't even trying to escape now, just waiting for the nightmare to end.

"Talk! Who beat my father up?" Jake snarled.

"Wasn't me, man!"

Three more devastating blows came down on the already battered face.

"I swear, it wasn't me!" Eddie cried. "Stop! Please! It had to be Monk. I was nowhere near there! I can prove it."

"How's little Nicki over there involved?"

"I'm not tellin' him nothin' Mr. Stinnetti! God, please don't hit me again," pleaded Eddie.

Wham! Wham! Two more solid punches landed on Eddie's face.

"Jake, that's enough!" the sheriff ordered. "Any more and I'll have to take you in. This ain't a fight anymore. It'll be a beating if you keep it up. Anything he says now would be inadmissible anyway."

Jake stopped. He looked at Fred and then at his right hand. It was covered in red. Blood. Eddie Lawton had no fight left to give. "These assholes know where Wojicki is," Jake said. "A few more pops and he'll talk."

"They have legal rights. Eddie chose to take you on, so his whippin' was his own choice, and your battery of Nicki is weakly justifiable considering his barrage of ethnic slurs. I'll testify to it if necessary. It's over. C'mon, let's go get your eye stitched up."

Jake pushed Eddie away roughly as he got to his feet. He walked to the couch and picked up a white pillow, using it to wipe the blood off his arm and face. When he was done, he threw it to where Nicki sat, still trying to recover.

"Wow! That was the coolest fight I've ever seen," came a shout from the top of the stairs. It was a boy's voice. "Just like the MMA fights on TV!"

All in the room looked up. A boy of about ten bounded down the stairway and stopped in front of Jake. He exclaimed, "I've never seen anybody whip Eddie, except Monk, and he doesn't count 'cause he's so big. It only took Monk two punches. He used to work for my dad, before Eddie."

The boy looked closely at Jake for a moment. "Wow! You're The Jet. I saw you ski at Squaw Valley yesterday. I thought Brian Chang would beat you for sure, but he blew up. You and Brian are good friends, aren't you? He's the best! Someday I'll be as good as he is!" said the boy. He added, "Oh, you're good too, for an old guy."

The loan shark stated, "This is my son, Nicki junior. He wants to be a freestyle skier. I guess that's what you do when you're not makin' my life miserable, huh?"

"It's what I used to do. I'm just about retired," said Jake

"Hey Jet! You think you could take care of an autograph on a poster for me?" Nicki junior asked Jake.

Odd, thought Jake. He was bleeding and standing in the home of a man who planned on stealing his family's remaining assets. He'd just done battle with another man who wanted to unscrew his head, and a gun had been drawn in the interim. Now a kid wanted his autograph? Life had changed in the past twenty-four hours.

"Sure kid, no problem," said Jake.

"Great. Thanks." Nicki Junior took off up the stairs.

The senior Stinnetti looked up at Jake from where he sat. "This ain't over. We'll meet again. Maybe Bennie will deal with you next time. He's faster than a speeding bullet if you know what I mean."

Jake and Bennie locked eyes for a moment.

"You got a permit for the piece under your jacket, Bennie?" asked Fred Asaro.

"Absolutely Sheriff. I'd never violate the law," answered the nattily dressed man.

The sound of the boy's feet running halted conversation. He took the stairs two at a time and came to a stop in front of Jake. He held out a rolled-up poster. "Can you make sure the signature goes right across the open space in the blue sky next to the skier?" asked the boy.

"No problem," said Jake as he started to unroll the poster. "Does somebody have a pen?"

The boy blurted out quickly, "No Jet, you don't get it. I don't want *your* autograph. I want you to get Brian Chang's for me."

Opening the poster completely Jake shook his head and smiled. It was a shot of his friend Brian flying through the air with sparkling crystals of fresh powder snow blowing off his boots and skis. He tucked the poster under his arm. "I'll see that this gets back to you. You ready, Sheriff?"

"Washed up at, what, thirty, plus or minus a little? Now you're an errand boy for my kid. Maybe after I break your family, you could come to work for me. You could have Eddie's job; you can see he ain't worth a shit," Stinnetti said scornfully.

"We'll see how this plays out. As for being 'washed up,' I'm not sitting on the ground gently coddling my huevos, am I?" asked Jake. He added with a nod, "I too anticipate our *next* encounter. Perhaps the sheriff will not be along to provide protection for you upstanding citizens. For the present time, I bid you, adieu." Jake picked another of the white pillows off the couch and again wiped the blood off his face. He replaced it on the couch, wet blood side down.

Fred Asaro led the way as they headed toward the door.

Before reaching the entry, Jake turned back to face Stinnetti with a look of revelation. "You said 'first note.' That means you don't know about the two million recorded on the property just before your loan funded. Stinnetti, you don't have a 'first'. There's someone ahead of you for two mil. Interest accruing daily.

"Oh, by the way, we're not Jewish. Dad accepted Jesus when he married my mom. Wouldn't hurt you to do the same. But your insults still earned you a trip to the floor."

They closed the door behind them and stepped out into the light snowfall.

From his sitting position, Nicki Stinnetti barked at Bennie Temple, "Find Wojicki! And get me a title report on that property! Two fucking million! On top of my mil and a half? Who knows what else that son of a bitch has carted off?" The language wasn't softened for his son's benefit.

Other than a look of disgust, he paid no attention to the battered and bleeding Eddie Lawton as he rose from the tile and gingerly stepped out of the room. Stinnetti's enforcer was on his own in finding medical help, which he needed badly.

Nicki had other, more pressing problems to deal with.

CHAPTER 6

"Who are Monk Phillips and Cindi Light?" asked Jake, trying to remain as still as possible. At the mention of the names, the doctor administering the sutures cast a questioning glance at Fred.

"No Doc, this ain't Monk's handiwork. Remember, a loose piece of baling wire did this at my ranch."

The doctor smiled. "Sure it did. Along with the cuts and swelling on this young man's right hand. Will I see the other guy in here too, with an equally silly bullshit story?"

"Naw, the other injured man probably went to Carson City. Remember, it's Sunday, and you're puttin' me on the spot. The good Lord might not approve of my answers."

"I find my excitement living vicariously through you, Fred," laughed the doctor. "Without your escapades, it would be boring around here. Although we haven't seen you in a while. Been a little slow?"

"I'll work on upping my visits," Fred said. He turned to Jake and continued.

"Monk Phillips we don't know too much about. He worked for Stinnetti for a few years but was crazy. Nicki had to dump him. The debtors started getting hurt so bad they couldn't work to pay up. One disappeared completely. Nicki didn't want no killing and Monk probably went overboard.

"He's a huge son of a bitch, and fast. Once in town, he started a brawl in the Nugget, and it took me and three deputies to restrain him."

Jake looked sideways at the sheriff, being careful to not move his head. Fred wasn't a giant man, but he was big enough and thick. As a former rodeo rider, he was tough too.

It took four men, one of whom Jake knew was mean as hell, to subdue this Monk?

Fred continued while Jake got sewn up like a rag doll.

He wasn't sure why, but Monk had taken up with Tom Wojicki. Wojicki was a gambling idiot, constantly in debt to bookies and had the distinction of being well known at most of the area casinos. Unfortunately, he was well known for losing. After binges at the tables where the liquor flowed free, Tom would wind up drunk and he'd be taken down to the station for detoxification. He'd vow never to gamble again when sobering up. He'd stay sober and away from the casinos for weeks but never months; the lure of the big win always took him back to the tables.

Monk and Tom disappeared about a year ago. Fred wasn't sorry to see them go.

Cindi Light was a whore. Not a hooker or cheap call girl, but an ultra-high-dollar pro. She was a local girl who'd wanted too much too early in life and found a way to make big money as a teenager. She'd actually been a friend of both Fred's daughters as kids, riding horses and skiing together. In her junior year, she was class princess. She offered that 'country girl' innocence so many men craved.

Sometime during that junior year of high school, Cindi figured out that what she was doing in the back of her boyfriend's pickup was worth more than the burger and the bottle of cheap rum he'd buy to get her into the mood. An escort service in Reno provided her a fake ID, and she drove the forty minutes to the big city on Friday after school and came home on Sunday afternoon with more cash than she'd make in two months working at any local minimum-wage job. Cindi's mother was a single parent, and a "fine-lookin' lady" by Fred's recounting. She let her daughter run wild while she looked for 'Mr. Right' at the local watering holes on weekends. So when Cindi came up with a story of having a great job in Reno on weekends and staying with a friend there, she never once questioned her daughter.

She continued high school but never dated, never went to the prom, and left for home or the gym immediately after school. After a few years in the business, she'd made enough to buy a home in a new subdivision and took a job with a property title insurance company, where she crossed paths with Tom Wojicki. Being an escort had run its course, and she wanted to settle down.

But one couldn't easily return to life in the suburbs after years of providing high-priced sex to those willing to pay for it.

Soon neighbors found out about her past from the 'good' folks in town. The wives shut her out of neighborhood gatherings. Husbands were verbally chastised for casting too long a glance in her direction as she unloaded groceries or worked in the yard. Jealousy bubbled over in her community. Eventually, rocks broke her windows, and she began receiving hate mail, suggesting she leave the neighborhood. Fred had consoled her as she cried on his shoulder when she filed a complaint over the heartless vilification by the neighbors.

She was trying to change her life, and the good Christian folks of suburbia just wouldn't accept her.

Finally, Cindi Light put her home up for sale and left for parts unknown. But not before getting even.

On the day her home closed escrow, three women who were her most vicious tormenters received envelopes in the mail. Each contained digitally printed photos and actual video on jump drives of the husbands of the bitches engaged in different sexual acts with Cindi. She'd seduced all of them and brazenly sent the candid still shots and movies to their wives, making sure that all received shots of the others' husbands in action. She wanted to be sure the neighborhood had something to gossip about after she left, Fred guessed. Cindi had moved in with Wojicki after being forced from her home by social condemnation.

When he disappeared from the valley, she must have gone with him. Two of the three marriages of the recipients of Cindi's envelopes ended in divorce. She'd left destruction in her wake.

With the suturing finished, the doctor told Jake to have the stitches removed in a few days to reduce scarring. He gave him a bottle of antibiotics. Fred Asaro told the hospital receptionist to bill the department for the visit. He drove Jake to the Nugget Casino to get his car, and they exchanged farewells. The snow was falling harder now and beginning to stick.

"Thanks, Fred," said Jake as they stood in the cold parking lot.

Fred replied, "Oh hell, Jake, I should thank you. It was great fun. Like the old days…" He nodded his approval. "You handled yourself pretty good today. Eddie needed a whoopin'. He's not a bad guy, you know. He just wants respect and doesn't know how to get it."

The sheriff took a deep breath and took on a contemplative look. "Before you go, let me give you one last bit of advice.

"I've seen a lot of bad folks in thirty-five years as a lawman. Some you can turn 'round but some you can't. And sometimes there's a thin line between good and bad. Today when we was at Nicki's house, I watched as you grew more pissed. If I hadn't stopped you, I think you might have killed poor Eddie.

"You reached that point today. Crossing that line.

"I always hoped you and Lauren would patch things up. Havin' only girls, you're kinda like my adopted son. But I don't think I want my little girl with anyone who's capable of crossing that line. So maybe it ain't such a bad thing you two split up."

Jake stood silently, listening. Fred drew a circle in the thin covering of snow on the asphalt with his boot. "I'm rambling. I've been told I do that as I get along in years.

"Here's some advice. You're goin' after Wojicki and his crew. I can see that in your eyes. You probably won't find 'em. If I took millions, God knows you wouldn't find me. But if you do, remember the line between good and bad is thin, and sometimes very gray. You'll probably cross that line. I know I've crossed it myself more than I care to remember.

"Salvation is on the right side of the line. I ain't talkin' about heavenly salvation." He paused before adding, "Shit, this must sound like a sermon."

"Well Fred, I could use a little divine intervention about now. Although a crusty old cowboy like you isn't where I thought it might come from," chuckled Jake.

Fred laughed too. "Divine, I ain't. Just ask my wife… Anyhow, the salvation I'm talkin' about is peace within yourself. I ain't the fuckin' Dali Lama, but I think your gonna run across plenty of spots lookin' for these folks where you'll have to choose which side of the line you want to be on. Sometimes you're gonna cross over. Just remember to come back. Otherwise, you'll ruin your life and maybe the lives of those you touch."

"Thanks. I'll keep all that in mind."

"Good. Well, I need to get back home. Barb will be waitin'. Sunday is brunch and a movie after church. You should be goin' too. You'll likely have a foot of snow between Bridgeport and Mammoth headin' south."

"Again, you have my thanks, Fred. Say hi to Lauren when you see her," offered Jake as he extended his hand.

Fred took the hand, but instead of shaking it, he pulled Jake in for a hug. "Don't be such a stranger. Call or stop by when you can. Not at the house though. The station would be better," he said with a wink. As he hopped into the cab of the big Ford pickup, he added, "And don't trust no one you don't know. It's a lot of money. I've seen people kill and get killed for a lot less."

Jake boarded his Forerunner and started the engine. As the sheriff began pulling out Jake gave a quick toot of the horn, motioning for him to roll down the window. Fred did.

"What was the name of the escort service Cindi worked for in Reno?"

"Image Escorts, I think," replied Fred after thinking for a moment.

Jake tapped his fingers on his forehead in a quick salute. Fred watched him roll the window up and drive out of the lot. The Forerunner turned right. Fred Asaro had expected to see the SUV turn left.

Jake wasn't headed south toward his parents' home, but north instead. *Toward Reno.*

CHAPTER 7

Jake found a room at a downtown casino hotel. This was not Las Vegas or Lake Tahoe. Prices were low, which suited him, and he paid cash for one night.

A quartet twanged out country music just slightly off-key. He felt better now after a meal at the cheap buffet and a decompression period. A web search on his tablet in the room was no help in finding Image Escorts, but Jake did find Imagine Escorts locally.

One of the featured escorts was a Cindi. Most of the ladies on the site were pictured in skimpy negligees or swimsuits, but Cindi was pictured in a backless evening gown with her sandy-blonde hair done tastefully in a thick braid. The tight black dress clung to every curve offered underneath, and the slit up the side revealed just enough leg to make any heterosexual male want to see more.

However Jake knew that Cindi Light was likely far away. The company probably left her bio up on the site to make the phone ring.

He'd called the service and talked with the receptionist. The story he told was semi-true. He was a professional skier in for a contest yesterday and would be in town overnight. Jake stressed he wanted an *experienced* escort, someone who had been with the service for a few years.

The receptionist suggested three ladies, now on the way over. He would choose the one with whom he would spend the evening. It was clearly understood that Imagine Escorts was not providing sex as any part of this service. The disclaimer rambled on, then Jake agreed, with the final verification that he was not a law enforcement officer or working with law enforcement.

For $800 he had a date. He would be expected to cover all expenses. The only hint the receptionist gave him was that the ladies preferred men who paid for their entertainment in cash, so he should carry at least $2,000 for the evening.

A nearly full regular Coors bottle sat in front of him as he waited. He wore camel-colored cotton slacks and an olive turtleneck under a navy sports coat with Top-Sider lace-up loafers, dark brown to match his belt. The sports coat was the only one he owned, and Janelle had insisted he have it tailored to fit his physique. A size forty-four at the shoulders with a thirty-two-inch waist was impossible to fit off the rack.

When packing, he'd included the jacket and pants in case he might need to attend his father's funeral.

The ladies from the service were easy to spot walking across the casino floor. Each was slim and attractive but had too much hair going in too many different directions. Two were blondes and one a brunette.

The brunette appeared to be the oldest of the three, Jake judged at first glance. She was also the one who looked the most prudish. *Or perhaps serious*, on second thought. She was stunning. There was a sophistication about her, and her brown eyes sparkled in an evaluating gaze. As much as he was sizing her up, she was evaluating him. The message was clear… *Was he worthy of her?* Obviously, she chose her business partners carefully. Jake doubted he'd get what he needed out of this one. She'd be sent packing. He needed information, and the two blondes seemed more apt to provide it. He'd choose one of them.

They were accompanied by a beefy man who looked to be in his mid-forties. He wore double-knit flare-legged pants of dark navy, a white polo shirt with an alligator, and a tan Member's Only jacket buttoned only at the waist. The look screamed 1990. Except for the crew cut. That screamed ex-military. He had the same extra tissue build up around the eyes Jake had seen on some of the older boxers at the gym in Lake Tahoe where he worked out. At about six foot one and two hundred- and thirty-five-pounds Jake guessed this fellow could wear whatever goofy outfit he wanted. He looked at the man's knuckles as the foursome stopped at the table. Thick and scarred.

"You Cohen?" the man grumbled.

"Yes, I am." Jake stood and offered his hand. The man took it after looking at Jake for a few seconds. He released it after a half shake. He didn't offer his name.

"I'm here with the ladies until you choose your date. The service sends me for a few reasons. First, I make sure you're okay. If I don't think our lady is safe with you, we leave. Second, I'm supposed to get a good look at you in case something happens to one of the ladies. You know, just in case I need to find you later. You capeesh?"

Jake smiled as he answered, "Yes. I capeesh."

"You got nothin' to smile about yet, stud. Laugh it up with the gals if you want. I got no sense of humor."

Jake stifled his grin.

The ladies were smiling and turning slightly from side to side. Jake realized each was posing, trying to get his attention. This was an audition.

"Now Cohen, you and the gals can talk for a few minutes, and you can pick out your date. Unless you've already decided."

Jake shook his head and put up one finger to signal he wanted a moment to talk with the trio.

"I'll take a walk for a few minutes. Then you choose and give me a room key. Standard with new customers."

"Last question. How'd you get whacked above the eye?"

"I'm a professional skier. Yesterday I crashed at the finish line," Jake answered. The thick man nodded his satisfaction and disappeared into the casino.

Jake gestured for the women to have a seat. "Ladies, would you like a drink?" he offered as he sat.

A cocktail waitress descended immediately upon them. He still had his beer. Each of the women ordered wine. The brunette asked for a Stonestreet cabernet, and the blondes had house chardonnay. As they waited for their drinks, the women introduced themselves.

Renee was the youngest, Jake guessed. Probably barely eighteen. She was attractive but lacked style. She'd done too much to the blonde hair, and her eyes were glazed. Stoned. Useless for Jake's needs.

The brunette was Amber, certainly the most interesting of the group. She was probably thirty, maybe a year or two older. Her arms were toned, and her black dress clung to her curves and plentiful bosom. Long hair framed a face with smooth features and plump, inviting lips. She was stunning. However, her initial look of business stuck in his mind. She might be a company girl, and Jake was certain they had rules about not being too talkative.

But her wide brown eyes now beckoned him, and her movements were more seductive. A pro. Just as Jake could ski smoothly through a field of treacherous moguls, Amber could negotiate this sort of selection process.

She made deep eye contact, and her mannerisms didn't say 'pick me' as the other girls did, but rather she was forming a bond with the paying male. She rolled the red wine that had been delivered in her glass, tilting her head slightly back to expose her silken neck as she took small swallows. She was quickly becoming captivating.

The hair that he initially thought too wild was now provocative. Jake was starting to wonder how that hair might look on a pillow.

Company girl, he reminded himself.

With reluctance, he again mentally dismissed Amber.

That left Jill, the older of the two blondes. Through the small talk, Jake determined Jill had been with the service for four years. She wore a tight, dark, denim skirt and a cream-colored, mock-suede blouse with silver stars fastened to it. The skirt showed thin hips and thighs, and the blouse was tight enough to reveal ample breasts underneath. She carried a brown leather jacket. Her blue-green eyes twinkled in the lights coming off the casino floor. Probably mid-twenties. Her wineglass was already empty. She'd be the one. He'd buy her dinner, a bottle of wine, and if she had any information on Cindi Light's whereabouts, hopefully, she'd blurt it out.

They chatted. At one point he turned the conversation to the service website. Jake asked, "Do any of you ladies know the featured escort? Cindi Light?"

The air got thick when her name came up. *Yes, they knew her, but she only worked with her own clients.*

The chaperone returned to the table. Jake confirmed that Jill would be his date for the evening. He thanked the other two ladies for coming. Renee became slightly pouty. Amber showed a hint of surprise at not being chosen but recovered quickly and thanked him for the wine. Jake and the chaperone stepped away, where Jake handed him a room key-card.

The only conversation was when Jake asked, "You a fighter?"

"A bit," was the answer. Nothing more.

Jake and Jill headed out on the town for the evening.

He traded cash for $500 in casino chips. They strolled through the gaming area and occasionally stopped at blackjack tables to place a bet, never sitting. The drinks were free for the gamblers, and Jake wanted to get his date sauced. Jill had a second glass of wine then switched to greyhounds. Jake stayed with the Coors and sipped lightly.

At random tables, he placed $10 bets, and asked Jill's advice as to decisions with the cards. She wanted to *win*. The concept of winning by letting the house bust was foreign to her. They were behind over $200 after forty minutes.

He needed to get out of here quickly, or he'd be broke.

Jill made slow advances toward him as they strolled and chatted. Soon one of her hands was constantly on him. She was a sure thing. The price would be determined later.

The two glasses of wine and two greyhounds had no visible effect on the woman. Jake realized that she probably drank regularly, and she might be able to put him under the table.

To cut his losses, he suggested they have dinner. Jill knew of a cozy Italian restaurant a short walk down the street. He said that would be fine; 'cozy' sounded inexpensive.

The restaurant was classic Italian. No pretense in the front. The dining area was concealed behind two partitions covered in tuck-and-rolled black leather. No bell or chime went off, but a tuxedoed man appeared and greeted them. He showed them to a table in the center of the dining area. Sound was absorbed by the decor, and lightly gurgling fountains covered private conversations going on nearby. A busboy in a red waistcoat poured them water.

Jake looked at the menu. The average entrée was forty to fifty-five dollars. Everything was ala carte. He picked up the wine list. They offered well over two hundred selections, many of which were also offered by Jake's tiny establishment up the hill. But at more than double the price. Knowing the wholesale cost of each bottle, he just shook his head and smiled.

"What's so funny?" Jill asked as she hung her jacket on an unused chair.

"I'm getting a kick out of this place. It looks like a set from *The Godfather.* I don't think I've ever eaten in a restaurant so dark."

"You'll love the food. It's the best Italian anywhere!"

And the most expensive, Jake thought. He wondered what was being served at the casino buffet down the street. Too late now. He ordered a Chianti Classico and explained to Jill that he wanted something light, yet with a strong body. He gave her a wink with the uninjured eye. She blushed slightly. Had he been with Janelle, he would have consulted her on the selection, but he had a feeling Jill might order a vintage older and more expensive than she. And with the speed she guzzled it, he'd likely be stuck for two bottles.

He ordered a bruschetta appetizer with the wine. They'd order dinner after they nibbled the starter course. As thin as Jill was, she couldn't eat too much, he decided, and perhaps a few sliced baguettes with the olive oil, garlic, tomato, basil, and mozzarella would be enough to satisfy her. Maybe he'd get out of here for under a hundred bucks.

"You keep yourself in good shape. And single too," Jill commented. "Most of my clients are pudgy middle-aged men passing through town. Married. Guys who all think they're high rollers. By this time in the evening they've usually dropped a thousand or two at the tables."

She reached over the table and placed her hand across the top of his. Under the table, she slipped off her shoes and caressed his ankles and calves with her bare toes.

"What's it like, being an escort?" Jake asked. "Do you have a boyfriend outside the business? Might make me jealous if you do."

Jill's smile became tight. She tilted her head while her wine glass was filled by the waiter. Jake suddenly felt sorry for her. She was pretty yet had a tired look.

When the waiter departed, she answered caustically, "No Jake, it won't make you jealous. A guy like you will take me out and spend some money, then he expects to get laid. Most do, just so you know. That's what it's like being an escort."

Taking a substantial pull from the glass, she continued, "I don't even know if I like men anymore. They're all so stupid. Including you. What a dumb thing to say, 'might make me jealous…' You can have your way with me, but don't tell me you're jealous. It's condescending, and it pisses me off.

"I may be a whore, but I'm high-dollar. After dinner you'll find out how high," Jill said softly, holding her head high with all the pride she could muster. "And you're no better than me. You're buying what I'm selling, so we're in the same business, at least for tonight."

Thank God for the sound-deadening qualities of the place, thought Jake.

The waiter served the bruschetta, took their orders then departed.

"I'm sorry. It wasn't meant to be demeaning," offered Jake.

"Yeah, apology accepted. I'm sorry too. You paid the service for a perfect date, and I went off on you. Please don't tell them about the meltdown. I've been having more lately. Maybe I should do something different, but what? My job isn't great, but I make over a hundred and fifty grand a year working three or four nights a week."

Jake quickly did the math. She probably made about eight hundred bucks a pop. Maybe he should talk to Janelle about a second career...

"When I have these lapses, I usually solve them by taking a solid whack of coke. Most clients don't care, but if you do, I'll hold off. I doubt you have any, but I'm always stocked. I'm going to the ladies' room for a moment, and when I return, I'll be the perfect date. As long as you don't mind?"

Jake shook his head.

She rose from the table. "Want some?"

He shook his head again. He'd tried cocaine while in college, and then for a short period after Lauren left him. He never enjoyed it. The drug only numbed life's pains temporarily.

Jill's outburst had given him an idea for an opening. He feasted on the appetizer as he awaited her return. There would be plenty. From firsthand experience, he knew she would not be hungry after the coke took effect. And she *would* be talkative.

CHAPTER 8

"You know, you're easy to talk to," Jill offered upon her return. She reached across the table and took Jake's hand.

No, Jill, I'm not easy to talk to, thought Jake. *The coke and booze are making it easy for you to talk. Keep going.* He poured her more wine.

"Thank you, Jake. You asked about being an escort, so here you go.

"I find that by being open about the sex I can raise the price. I've already decided I like you and you're gonna get it for $900. Nobody usually gets it for less than a grand. It's gonna cost 'em, and it's gonna be the best they ever had." She slowly nodded and smiled.

Jake saw the opening. He pushed.

"What about Amber? She wouldn't do it for $900, would she?"

"Hell no!" Jill laughed, "She'd want ten grand or more! Usually gets about fifteen. Assuming she felt you were worthy! We—the other girls and me—don't know how she does it. She can be bewitching. Probably only does thirty gigs a year and makes triple what we do. She never allows more than four clients on her schedule, and all are filthy rich."

Jake was thankful he hadn't chosen a partner for the evening who was well beyond his budget. He continued to probe, "What about the poster girl from the site?"

"Cindi? Five grand wouldn't get you head. She's long gone anyway. The service thinks we'll get more calls if her photo is left up on the site. That's bullshit!" She took a deep swallow of the wine and continued, "We don't need that witch's photo to make the phone ring." She was visibly jealous. Or envious?

"Long gone?" he asked.

"Yep. And good riddance."

The waiter dropped dinner off. He had chicken marsala, and thankfully Jill ordered a shrimp cocktail. The remainder of the wine was poured, and Jake shook his head when asked if they'd like another bottle. Jill showed slight disappointment, looking at the half-full glass in front of her. Jake poured the remainder of his into the goblet and her look of mild panic diminished.

"Well she's gone now, and that gave me the opportunity to meet you." Jake decided to continue in the direction of Cindi's whereabouts. "You said she left. Does that mean she quit the business? Or did she leave the area?"

"Hell, who knows? I never liked her, and we seldom talked.

"Cindi thought she was better than us. She would stay with Amber when she came to work, but she lived south of here in a hick town. She wasn't unfriendly; she just didn't associate with us. She and Amber were a pair," offered Jill.

Damn! Jake felt the sting of stupidity. Out of his price range or not, he'd been sitting at the table with Cindi's roommate and ended up with a coked-up lush. The Bolivian marching powder and the alcohol kept her talkative, but she had nothing to offer. She'd eaten one shrimp.

"She didn't tell anyone where she went when she left? Would Amber know?" asked Jake.

"Why all the interest in Cindi? You couldn't afford her even if she was still around. I have no idea what happened to the bitch. Let's drop it and enjoy the evening, okay?"

He decided to give up with her. He nodded and worked on the chicken sautéed in marsala, garlic, and mushrooms. It was excellent.

Jill made one additional trip to the ladies' room then babbled for ten minutes more about cars, clothes, food, and the weather while he finished his dinner and her shrimp. He just sat and nodded. No dessert was ordered. The bill was just under $180. He left the waiter a $36 tip. When they left, he headed toward the casino where he was staying. She caught on immediately.

"You're about to get the best two hours of your life!" she promised as they walked. She didn't know she'd be dismissed at the elevators. "It'd be better if you'd take a line of blow first. On me, no charge."

"No thanks. How do you know I'm not a cop? Maybe I could put you away for that stuff," laughed Jake.

"No chance. I've felt all over. No gun, and I know where to look. Waist, shoulder, ankle, under the arm… A lot of our clients are cops. They don't pay much, but they're helpful at times," Jill answered. "Besides, Cliff searched your room after we left. My phone would have buzzed by now with a text if you were with the fuzz. It's not standard policy, but something about you made Cliff nervous."

Jake continued walking, but his stomach felt suddenly empty, even after the huge meal.

After his nap, he'd started jotting notes into the word processor of his tablet computer. Just names and how they were connected. Tom Wojicki, Cindi Light, Monk Phillips, Nicki Stinnetti, Eddie Lawton, Bennie Temple, Imagine Escorts... Under each name, he'd made a few notations outlining all he'd discovered and their connection to the others. When he'd left the device was asleep, but he hadn't exited the word processing program. One touch of the 'on' button and the information would have popped up.

"You okay? You look sick. Too much rich food probably. You eat a lot," said Jill. "You must have a high metabolism or get a lot of exercise. Otherwise, you'd be two hundred and fifty pounds. My guess is you go one seventy-five."

"You're close. Good guess," Jake mumbled absentmindedly.

They'd reached the casino, and he pulled Jill close and kissed her neck gently. He'd been fading from the beers and wine, but adrenaline spiked when he found his room had been rifled. There was a good chance Cliff had discovered his outline.

Jill giggled with the kiss and put a hand under his chin to pull his lips to hers. He stopped her before they made contact. Smiling, he said, "I'm ready. How about you?"

"I could go all night. But that'll cost extra. You're in charge. It's okay with me if we move to your room for a private party," she answered.

"Great." He reached into his pocket and pulled out $100 in casino chips. Holding them out to Jill he said, "Keep yourself busy for a few minutes. I need some cash, and I want to order something special for the occasion. A little bubbly. I'll have it waiting when we get there."

"Yummy! Look for me at the set of tables we played earlier."

"Make a million for us while I'm gone," Jake said. He kissed her lightly under the ear then headed toward the front desk.

CHAPTER 9

He decided against calling hotel security. Wanting to get an early start tomorrow, complications with the casino or the local police would cause delay.

Jake decided; room service would be sent up with a bottle of champagne. He'd wait in the hall and ask if anyone was inside or if the interior was in disarray. If necessary, *then* he would summon security.

As he walked toward the desk, he saw a striking woman with dark hair in a ponytail moving gracefully in his direction. The black silk dress had been traded for a pair of jeans and a full, but loose, white turtleneck. She carried a black leather jacket.

There was no doubt in his mind. It was Amber walking toward him.

"What a pleasant surprise," Jake said as she reached him.

"Mr. Cohen, how nice to see you again," greeted Amber. "How's your evening going with Jill?"

"I find her shallow. Perhaps I made the wrong choice a few hours ago. She's not really what I'm looking for."

Amber feigned surprise and offered, "She's a coke fiend. But then I didn't think you'd be the type looking for depth of character. I thought the two of you would work well together."

"We must make the best of our choices, mustn't we?" Jake said. "Now if you'll excuse me, I have matters to attend to."

He turned to leave. Getting out of town was his priority now.

"Mr. Cohen?" Amber said boldly. He turned. Her head was tilted, and the incredibly bright eyes squinted. "What 'matters' need attending to, Mr. Cohen? And what *are* you looking for?"

Looking her directly in the eyes, he answered, "Cindi Light. The poster girl on your company website. Your old roommate. Isn't she what every man is looking for?"

"Last names aren't posted on the site Mr. Cohen, so let's drop the bull-shit," said Amber as she crossed her arms and stood defiantly. "She's long gone. I doubt we'll ever hear from her again." She paused, then continued, "Let me offer some advice. You seem like an okay guy.

"In my business, I have to make instant judgments about people. Sometimes I'm wrong, but mostly I'm right. You're not a pro. At least not in this line of work. You're out of your element. Running around trying to be a super-sleuth will get you into trouble. You shouldn't have ruffled Nicki Stinnetti's feathers. I must admit I was impressed when I heard that you throttled his collector. So was Cliff—the man you met with us earlier. He's waiting in your room right now. I think he'd like to test you to see just how tough you are. There's a smallish fellow with slicked-back hair up there with him. He doesn't look very tough, but he does look scary. Are you interested in what I'm telling you?"

"You have my undivided attention."

"Why don't we move to the bar where we met earlier?"

Jake nodded once.

"Good. Now go find Jill and get rid of her. Meet me there in five minutes," ordered Amber.

Jake found Jill flirting with a man dressed in all black at a $100-minimum-bet blackjack table. Her new friend had high stacks of chips neatly arranged in front of him for all the world to see. His diamond-bezel watch flashed as he nonchalantly flipped five chips at a time out to be swept away by the dealer. *A wise investor.* Winning or losing didn't make a difference. How cool you looked while doing it was what mattered.

"Hi Jill," said Jake as he approached from her blind side. She jerked her hand off the man's shoulder.

With a palms-facing-out gesture, he said, "Don't worry. It's okay. Something's come up, and I have to go."

The gambler clad in black looked Jake up and down and returned his focus to the table without saying a word.

"You're certain? Can't whatever it is wait an hour or two longer?" asked Jill.

"Unfortunately, no. I think you'll do better here anyway," Jake said as he nodded toward the high roller. "Thank you for having dinner with me. It was a pleasure."

"I'm sorry we couldn't finish the evening off properly. Thank you, Jake. Call for me next time you're in town." Jill gave him a wink. Her hand returned to the man's back.

His girlfriend for the evening was fickle. He wanted to ask for the hundred bucks in chips he'd given her. Or maybe he should ask her new boyfriend for the money he'd blown on dinner. This guy could afford it; the preliminary investment for a night with Jill had been paid. All the new man had to do was finalize the deal.

Amber sat in a darkened corner of the bar. Jake thought she might be setting him up and almost had a note delivered to her to change the meeting to another location. He planned to tail her and see who else might follow. Real cloak-and-dagger stuff... Then he realized his plan was stupid. Nicki Stinnetti wouldn't try anything inside a public area of a casino. This was as safe a spot as anywhere on the planet right now. He walked up to the table. She had a glass containing bubbly clear liquid, ice, and a lime in front of her. Jake guessed it was gin or vodka and tonic.

"Have a seat, Mr. Cohen. I'm sorry your evening was interrupted. Jill take it okay?"

"Heartbroken," Jake said, "but she'll bounce back. As a matter of fact, I think she's already found someone to help ease the pain of our breakup."

Amber shook her head. "Jill's going downhill fast. It's a pity. She really is nice. I've seen it too many times. She's a goner. Having Cliff around and the backing of the service is a valuable safety net for us. Freelancing, she'll get busted or beaten or both."

Jake really didn't care about Jill's problems. "Tell me about Cliff. And the little guy up in my room. What's going on there? I should call security or the cops and have them hauled off."

"You could do that. But then you wouldn't find out *anything* about Cindi Light. I'd get into big trouble too, and I just saved your ass. So as a return favor to me, you won't call anybody, and we can talk about Cindi. Deal?"

"We'll see," answered Jake tentatively.

"No, goddammit, we won't see," snapped Amber. "I'm doing you the favor

of your life, asshole. Nobody kicks Nicki Stinnetti in the balls without paying the price. He's got the hounds out now. There's a five-grand bounty for
whoever busts you up. Cliff is foaming at the mouth to collect. Hell, he'd do
it for free. He didn't like you when you met and finding out you lied to the
service pissed him off even more. The money is added incentive."

"It's nice to know I'm loved universally," Jake said. "So he entered my room,
activated my tablet and read my notes, then called Stinnetti."

"Riding back to the office with Cliff I overheard the call to Stinnetti. The
voice was muffled, but I heard Cindi's name mentioned a few times. It's funny
that I was there; they page me when I have a client. Lucky for you I was
hanging around, Mr. Cohen. Those guys would have pummeled you."

Jake didn't mention he'd already heard about Cliff's intrusion. The cocktail waitress approached, and Jake ordered a coffee. It turned out that Amber
was drinking sparkling water with lime and asked to have hers freshened.
The band was gone, and a deejay played music for the nearly empty bar.

Jake was tired and without options. The prospect of meeting Bennie
again without the sheriff along didn't appeal to him.

"I'm calling the police," he said defeatedly after the waitress departed. "I
ski, run a restaurant, and keep a broken-down resort running. You're right.
I'm not a pro. I'm not as much scared as I am worn out. Last night I didn't
sleep, and it's catching up to me. My car keys are up there along with most
of my cash."

Amber shook her head. "No. You can't call the cops. This is against my
better judgment, but I'm going to help you out. If you called the police,
the service would get involved, and they'd fabricate something making you
appear to be the bad guy. Solicitation, assault, battery… You'd end up being
the one held by the police.

"I'll help you, but you've got to promise—no cops. We still need to discuss Cindi and what you want with her. You want my help or not?"

In the trailer hitch of his car was a magnetically mounted spare key. He
had an extra remote to disable the alarm in the console. The tablet computer
was top of the line two years ago but was now antiquated technology. His
money was most important. With tips and patrons paying cash, he always
kept a few thousand dollars tucked into the pocket of the tablet case. He
wasn't sure how much was there now. Including the casino chips, he had

about $1,400 on him.

He decided to abandon the items upstairs. Fatigue was coming on, and he needed sleep. He'd park the Toyota out of sight and catch a few hours of rest. Amber seemed to be very interested in who might be looking for Cindi Light too. Jake would get to that later, but for now, getting out of here was paramount. He'd trust her, for the time being.

"All right, no cops. What's your plan?" Jake asked.

"We'll go to my place and put your car in the garage. You can stay there tonight. Do they know what you drive? If they don't, they'll figure it out. Cliff has a few friends who are local cops. I'll get my car out of valet; you can follow me. We'll chat about Cindi when we get to my house."

Intuition told him she wanted information from him as badly as he wanted it from her. Her place seemed like a good idea.

Or, was she setting him up to get him away from the hotel, so they'd have a free shot at him?

The plan they worked out together was simple. They'd get into his car and drive away. He wanted to stay together. Jake didn't want her out of sight.

He went to the bar and chatted with the waitress while he paid the tab, then walked over to the deejay and talked to the young man spinning the tunes for a moment. He handed him a few of the five-dollar casino chips and returned to Amber.

They walked to the cashier's window and exchanged the remaining chips for money. As they headed out of the building, Jake stopped and asked Amber, "Do you have a cell phone?"

"Sure," she answered, "in my purse."

"Is the number restricted?"

She laughed, "In my business? I'd be crazy if it weren't."

"Mine's not. Let me use yours." He thrust his open hand at her.

"Say please. Goddamn men! Everything has to be an order. Ask again, nicely."

He rolled his eyes and offered, "Amber, may I please use your phone?"

Her eyes twinkled with mild triumph as she handed him the phone, "Certainly Mr. Cohen."

As he dialed, he said, "Please, call me Jake."

The ringing room phone startled the two men. Bennie had been lightly napping while Cliff watched sports highlights with the volume low. The television remote was in his hand to shut the box down the moment they heard the door rattle. They looked at each other, then at the phone. After five rings it was silent. For ten seconds. Then it rang again. Five times. Then silence for another one-sixth of a minute. Then five more rings. The sequence continued for five minutes until Bennie got up from his chair and walked to the nightstand where the phone sat. When it rang again, he picked it up.

"Hello?"

"Hi, there! Bennie? Or Cliff?"

After a few seconds of silence, the response was, "Who wants to know?"

"Bennie! I recognize your voice! How's Nicki? Singing a higher tune?"

"Naw. He's okay. In fact, he wants to make a deal with you. You shook him up pretty good telling him his loan was in second position. He wants to work with you. Maybe help find Wojicki and the whore together."

"Really? Let's talk. I'm in the cabaret lounge. Meet me here in five minutes."

Bennie covered up the phone. "He wants to meet," he whispered.

Jake heard a muffled, "Meet him then. I'll wait outside to kick his ass when you're done."

"Okay. Which bar?" Bennie said.

"The one with the deejay. Find it. See you in five."

Ending the phone call with Bennie, Jake walked out into the parking structure. Amber chided him about being too cheap to pay for the valet. He explained he was frugal, not cheap.

As they drove toward the exit, Amber asked him, "You called the room to make sure they were there and not waiting to follow you, didn't you?"

"Yep," Jake answered.

"You don't trust me. I've risked a lot for you," sighed Amber. She continued as Jake drove, "Make a right when you get to the road. You don't suppose the waitress will tell them you were with me, do you?"

"She was going off shift along with the bartender. I checked when I paid the bill."

"You talked to the deejay. What was that about?" questioned Amber. Jake smiled. "I made a request."

"I don't see him," said Cliff over the screech of an old disco tune on the crappy sound system. He and Bennie had cruised the outskirts of the bar for ten minutes.

When they didn't spot Jake, they'd taken a seat in the lounge. A buxom young woman approached their table in the traditional casino cocktail waitress garb, showing a lot of leg and bosom.

"Scotch," said Bennie without being asked, "about two inches in a tumbler. No ice."

"Nothing," said Cliff. He got up and started pacing.

When the current song finished a spotlight snapped on and swung to the table where Bennie sat and Cliff patrolled. Bennie squinted in the bright light.

The deejay barked through the microphone, "And now here's a special request for the birthday boy! Bennie, how old are you today?"

Bennie glared and waved for the spotlight to be moved away with one hand. It remained glued to him.

The music started playing. The melody was familiar even through the tin-sounding bar audio system.

"What the fuck is this all about?" asked Cliff over the music.

"Relax and enjoy the music. There ain't gonna be no ass kickin' tonight. Sit down and shut up. It's one of my favorites," replied Bennie.

Cliff wasn't accustomed to anyone talking to him that way. But something about this little fellow made him nervous. He took a seat and listened.

Bennie forced a smile while the spotlight burned his eyes. The irony was lost on Cliff, but not him.

Elton John's "Benny and the Jets" rang out over the speakers.

Jake 'The Jet' Cohen was gone.

CHAPTER 10

The garage was nearly empty, and Jake backed in, then moved back and forth to position the SUV on the opposite side from where he entered. Amber asked, "What was that all about?"

"If I were trying to trap somebody here, I'd pull in tight, directly in front of the spot where the tracks in the snow entered the garage. No one would be able to get a vehicle out. This way I'm on the opposite side and hopefully can scoot right around if anyone tries to block the drive."

"Jake, nobody is coming!" she said with exasperation. Then she added, "It's not a bad idea though. So, what if your mystery pursuer pulled in straight across the whole driveway in the street? You'd still be trapped."

"No. I'd make a hard right and drive across your lawn. That picket fence wouldn't stop a Smart Car, let alone a four-wheeler," laughed Jake.

"If you drive across my lawn, Cliff will be the least of your worries."

"Amber, nobody is coming. Remember?"

"Well, you're a little trigger happy. I don't want the neighbor's cat meowing setting you off to play off-road racer across my front yard!"

Jake put his hands up in a gesture of surrender. "Easy there, little filly." He walked to the rear of the vehicle and opened the hatch. His gym bag was there, and he withdrew a pair of sweat pants and a dry-fit long sleeve shirt. He left the bag and followed Amber into her home.

"Shoes off," she commanded. He slipped off the Top-Siders and carried them.

The decor was perfect; a decorator must have done it all. Jake was certain the other folks in this suburban community didn't live like this. Amber was not a typical middle-class American working girl struggling along.

He walked to a set of French doors and flipped on a patio light. No footprints could be seen in the coating of snow in the yard. Jake saw a covered pool and deck with a gazebo and a portable spa. He opened the door and slipped the Top-Sider loafers on then walked out and looked around the sides of the home. The snow sat undisturbed; no unwanted visitors lurked. He went back in and removed the shoes.

"So where do we sleep," yawned Jake.

"*We* don't sleep anywhere. *You* sleep on the couch or the floor in here. You're not a paying customer, and I don't like you enough to share my bed. Men! You always assume you're going to sack out with us! I'll bring you some blankets."

"Don't flatter yourself," smiled Jake, "I just want to keep an eye on you. I don't want you making any calls. For all I know after I fall asleep you might sneak off and find a baseball bat then try to collect the $5,000 yourself from Stinnetti."

Amber smiled slyly, saying, "I hadn't even thought of that. But the prospect sounds appealing." She paused then continued, "Okay, you can sleep next to me as long as you keep your sweats on. C'mon, the bedroom's back here."

Jake followed her down the hall. They passed three darkened rooms, one of which had a computer. Amber noticed he stopped to glance.

"I leave it on all the time. The service e-mails and texts when I have a client call. I'll show you. Listen."

She walked to the desk and jiggled the mouse. The monitor screen activated. She double-clicked the 'Amber's e-mail' icon, then went quickly through the file menu for the program until she reached a 'test alert' command. *'Am-ber! I have a message for you!'* came from the speakers. The phone in her small purse emitted a few low-volume beeps.

Jake nodded his approval at the speed of the system. "Insta-sex, delivered in thirty minutes or less. Guaranteed."

With a head-tilt and smile, Amber said, "For those who can afford it, yes. For you—not a chance."

He followed her down the hall to the master bedroom. She had a king-sized maple sleigh bed with matching nightstands and a dresser. The bedspread was tan silk with a golden tassel fringe. Overstuffed pillows sat against a carved headboard. A massive mirror with a carved maple frame sat atop the dresser.

Expensive.

Jake checked the walk-in closet and found freshly dry-cleaned garments on plastic hangers evenly spaced. Pricey shoes sat on a rack. Lace lingerie and silken teddies hung in scores from hangers in one section. *Tools of the trade.*

The vanity in the dressing area had a countertop of granite. A white toilet and bidet sat polished side by side next to the shower. It was all so clean Jake was afraid to use it.

He walked down the hall and checked the other two bedrooms. The closets held more clothing Amber had stashed there, along with a pair of top-of-the-line Rossignol skis and Nordica boots. The fourth bedroom had the computer he'd already seen and a sit-up/tummy crunch device along with a cross-fit training machine.

He roamed the house looking for phones. Finding none, he realized she had no landline. Locating her handbag, he snagged the cell phone. Pressing the power button until it was off, he stashed it behind one of the overstuffed pillows on the family room couch. Satisfied no one was skulking about, he returned to the master bedroom.

Amber had disappeared into the cavernous closet and Jake could hear hangers being moved and clothes ruffling. *She must be changing for bed,* he thought. He wondered if she slept in one of those sexy nighties. While he was committed to another woman, the prospect of seeing what Amber looked like in skimpy silk and lace appealed to his masculine nature.

Oink, oink, Jake chuckled to himself as he waited for her to emerge.

The door to the closet opened, and she stepped out wearing baggy gray sweat pants and an oversized T-shirt.

Darn…

It was nearly 1:00 a.m., and he was tired. Amber explained that this was early for her and she was going to have a nightcap. She offered him a libation, but he opted only for a glass of water. While she was gone, he changed and hung his clothes up. He used the head and noticed Amber had put out a new toothbrush for him on the counter.

He brushed his teeth, then washed his face and cleaned the cut above his eye. He found Band-Aids under the sink and applied three over the stitches to keep blood off the pillows, then went back into the bedroom.

"Where's my phone?" demanded Amber, "You have no right to come into my house and take my belongings!"

"Sorry," he answered with no sincerity, "I'll give it back in the morning. You told me I'm not a pro. I'm eliminating chances."

After taking a sip from the snifter, she said with resignation, "Whatever. I won't need it until tomorrow anyway. You can play your silly games."

"Thanks for indulging me. And thanks for the toothbrush.

"Now since nobody's chasing us, can we talk about Cindi?"

"Sure. Tell me why you're looking for her."

One of his law professors in college had taught him about using a line of dialogue to get information—answer a question with a question. He saw no harm in telling Amber the truth; he'd just do it in stages.

He replied, "She was involved in the theft of a substantial sum of money from my family. Jill called her 'the bitch.' Why?"

Amber took a moment, then answered, "Professional jealousy, I suppose. She made ten times what Jill makes per client, almost as much as I do. Men *wanted* her more. Women too. She is incredibly alluring and made beaucoup bucks. Where are you from?"

"Southern California. What happened that made her decide to quit?"

"She was done with this. Had enough money to buy a house and tried to get a job in the real world. But the real world wasn't overly accepting of her."

He nodded, "I heard the same sentiments. Where's she now?"

Amber smiled. "Jake, a lot of my clients are attorneys. They do what you're doing. It's so deeply ingrained, they *can't* stop asking questions. It's annoying as hell. You tell me everything, then I'll tell you all I can. I think that's the deal we made."

She was a bright woman. He rolled both shoulders in wide arcs to relieve some of the tension in his back as he thought. What harm could it do?

"Sure, I'll tell you the story." He sat on the edge of the bed.

"Take off your shirt," Amber commanded, "I'll rub your back while you tell your tale. You've had a rough day."

Jake hesitated.

"C'mon. Take it off. Don't worry, I do this shit for a living, remember? Most men pay fifteen grand for this. But then, most men get more than a back rub," she laughed.

Jake tiredly peeled off the long-sleeved shirt. Amber gave him an appraising stare. He plopped onto the pillow with his head to one side, leaving his stitched eyebrow up off the silken case. Amber set her drink down on the nightstand and started kneading the muscles across his shoulders. He could smell the contents of the snifter. Remy Martin, he guessed. Aged. An extravagance he couldn't afford.

"You've got a set of shoulders, Mr. Cohen. It might be fascinating to watch you and Cliff exchange a few punches. I still think he'd kick your butt, but you'd likely go down swinging. His extra weight would be the difference, I think." She worked in silence for a moment, then continued, "So, tell me your story. From the start."

She had very good hands. Jake talked while she worked. He rambled about Tom Wojicki, his parents, the beating of his father, and how he came to be here. He never mentioned the exact location of his parents' home. He simply referred to Southern California.

As she rubbed the tired muscles and he told the story, his voice became dull and monotone. Then the recounting stopped as sleep took hold.

CHAPTER 11

MONDAY

Opening his uninjured eye wider than the other, he saw the clock next to the bed showed 7:40 a.m. He rose gently and walked into the bathroom. Next to the Band-Aids he'd used sat a bottle of Excedrin. Perfect. Pain relief and caffeine. Salvation was not far off.

After brushing his teeth in the kitchen sink so as not to wake Amber and taking three of the pain relievers, his next quest was coffee. A pot sat on the counter, with the display flashing the 'auto' setting. Punching the buttons, he found it was set to go at 8:45 a.m. Carpe diem was obviously not Amber's motto. He rolled through the menu to the 'on' position and was pleased to hear bubbling in a few seconds. Rifling through the cabinets, he located a cup and set it on the counter. The cup had a quote emblazoned on the side. '*A woman needs a man like a fish needs a bicycle.*' Below the maxim was a cartoon of a fish on a bike.

He chuckled then pulled his phone from his sweatpants pocket. The battery was dead. Checking behind the big pillow on the couch Amber's phone was where he'd left it. Remembering the passcode from last night, he performed a quick web search then called the hotel, giving instructions to pack up his room and store his stuff. Next, he called his parents' home. There was no answer, but the machine had his mother's voice telling the world that Dr. Cohen's condition was improving rapidly. Jake left a message; he'd be there early tonight, and he was happy about the news of Dad's condition taking a turn for the better.

He ambled up off the couch and headed into the kitchen for some coffee. He'd heard the perking, but something was missing—the aroma of freshly brewed joe. When he reached the pot, he found a brown-green liquid. *Tea.* Shrugging his shoulders, he filled his cup. Janelle wanted him to cut out

85

the coffee; she would be pleased. Except for the part about sleeping next to another woman. He'd omit that if this story was ever told.

"What are you doing up in the middle of the night? It's barely eight," mumbled Amber as she staggered down the hall. "Don't look at me. This isn't my best time of the day." She scratched the back of her head then filled a cup full of tea. Half of the hair had fallen out of the ponytail. She reached into the pocket in her sweats and pulled out a small handgun. It clanked as it hit the granite top where she dropped it. Jake stared in disbelief at the weapon.

Amber smiled sleepily and said, "Only an idiot would sleep next to a stranger unarmed. It's just a pea-shooter, a .22-caliber Colt, but it would sting plenty if I had to use it."

"Thank God I kept my sweats on," kidded Jake. He turned to her and said seriously, "Amber, thank you for taking me in. I owe you. Sometime I'll make it up to you." Looking around at her lavish furnishings and decor he added, "Although I don't know how. You seem to have everything a girl could want."

"I'm not a 'girl.' I'm a woman. 'Girl' is a term you'd use for an adolescent or a female in puberty. Men use the term to keep women from being recognized as equals. We're not little kids," she corrected.

Jake smiled and replied, "Feisty little filly, aren't you?" She looked damn good for just rolling out of bed.

"Yes, I am. Believe it or not, I've managed to do quite well without a man."

"Good for you. I'm impressed," he said sipping his tea. The pounding in his head was subsiding thanks to hydration and the painkillers. He went on, "Now, I think I fell asleep after I told you all I knew. Our deal was that you'd tell me what I wanted to know afterward. So where might I find the elusive Ms. Light?"

"I'm not sure. But I have ideas," offered Amber. She turned and looked directly at Jake. "You just said you 'owed me' for saving your ass. I know what you can do.

"I want to learn to ski better in moguls. Take me skiing today, and I'll spill my guts as we ride the lifts. Just here locally. That's how you can pay me back. I'll tell you all I know. I have an idea how we might work together. We'll make this a win-win deal. I can be ready in twenty minutes. What do you think?"

His mother had said in the outgoing message that his father's condition was improving. Another day wouldn't hurt. Amber might tell him something valuable. This woman was full of deals though. What would she want next?

Mt. Rose Resort just outside of Reno is small compared to the mega-mountain ski areas around Lake Tahoe. The accumulation of snow is never as deep, but the mountain is well run, and the trails are kept clear and groomed. The Monday crowd was light, and Jake parked the car within two hundred feet of the lodge.

Amber emerged from the SUV wearing a lime green and black one-piece powder suit that immediately turned the heads of those arriving in the lot. The top was loose Gore-Tex that was drawn at the waist by a wide elastic belt. The bottom was so tight it looked as though it had been applied with a paint sprayer. If it hadn't been flexible fabric, she wouldn't have been able to move. Men nearly tripped over their tongues and women were fraught with envy as the shapely brunette started a routine of stretching while Jake unloaded the car.

"Ready?" he asked.

"In a sec. I've got an audience here. My motto is 'never waste a crowd.' I work hard to stay in shape," Amber said as she threw one leg up on the tailgate of the Toyota, further tightening the stretch fabric across her shapely rump. "I'm not getting any younger, so let me have my moment in the sun. Besides, after I hit the slopes, no one will notice me, unless they're laughing."

Instead of the main lodge, Jake took her through the race department where he was able to obtain two complimentary passes. "Perks of celebrity status," he told her.

Amber proved to be a solid skier. She crashed a few times but showed incredible resilience and desire to learn. Rather than try to master all the movements and techniques at once, Jake worked with her on practicing individual steps, repeating each over and over until the desired action became automatic.

She didn't want to stop for lunch, so they ate two granola bars each with bottled water on the lifts. By 1:30, she'd adapted the basic steps to her skiing style and was moving smoothly through the mogul fields with confidence. They kept skiing up to 3:30 when Jake reluctantly announced it was time to go. He was enjoying the time they spent together.

On the last run of the day, they skied by the Mt. Rose photographer. Amber insisted they have a shot taken together. Removing their helmets, she had him pose, leaning into each other and smiling. Except for the bandage over his eye, it was picture perfect. Amber ordered an 8x10 for her wall.

They headed toward her home as the sun settled low behind the mountains. He was behind schedule, but with a few cups of coffee he'd cover all the needed miles and arrive at his parent's house early tomorrow morning.

"My end of our bargain is settled," Jake announced as he drove. "It's time for you to tell me everything you know about Cindi Light."

With a sly smile, Amber answered, "Why don't I tell you over dinner. I'll take you to my favorite Thai restaurant. I'm half-starved. Skiing bumps all day is a lot of work. After dinner, we can go to my place and warm up in the spa. I think you need another good night of sleep before you start driving. I don't have any clients scheduled. You can stay over one more night." She added nonchalantly, "And you won't have to sleep with your sweats on."

Jake pulled down the vehicle's sun visor and withdrew a photo of Janelle and him taken on a beach last summer. They were in swimsuits dripping wet and laughing. He handed it to Amber and said, "She wouldn't approve."

As Amber looked at the photo, she sucked on her cheeks, pursing her lips. Jake wasn't certain, but he thought he detected a pout. She stared for a moment then tossed the photo on the dash. She remained silent. Jake drove on. She picked the photo back up after they'd covered another mile and looked at it briefly, then again tossed it on the dash. Arms crossed. Silence. She pulled her lime green headband off and put her hair back into a ponytail.

"She's pretty," Amber finally announced. Then more silence. Then added, "Built well too."

"We've been together a few years. We're committed."

"Tell me about her. Does she ski well? What does she do?"

"She skis very well. So do you. She's stronger than you are, but you're more aggressive. When she graduates with her masters, we'll discuss marriage."

"I'm a whore, and she's a graduate student," she said flatly. "But I'm still a woman, and I have feelings. Occasionally I need to feel the closeness of a lover who's not a paying customer. You'll never hear from me again. Stay with me. She'll never know. You're not married yet. It's not a crime."

What an odd turn of events, he mused. Last night he would have had to pay thousands for this woman; now she practically begged him to stay. *A night in the real world for Amber.* Maybe this all-business beauty had a heart and a soft side after all.

Jake said, "But I'll know. And I gave her my word."

She laughed and shook her head. "A fucking moralist. How in the hell did I end up offering myself to the only good man in the world?"

"That's not true, Amber. There are many good men. And women. You just don't run into too many in your line of work. You're somewhat jaded. But maybe that's your protectionary mechanism," Jake said. "Let's change the subject. Cindi. What about her?"

"Yeah. Good idea. You're not much for my ego. I don't get turned down often. In fact, never."

Amber thought for a moment. "Hmmm… Cindi. The last thing she told me, she was moving to Southern California with some guy for a great opportunity. The relationship was more business than personal. And it carried the prospect for a big payday. I guess the payday was the theft from your parents.

"Cindi enjoys good food and wine but doesn't drink or eat to excess. Her body is fabulous; we'd work out together. She was just naturally toned. Most ladies at the service have fake boobs. Hers are real. We used to joke about it. I told her when she was growing up the tooth fairy didn't come to her house. It was the 'tit' fairy." She laughed, then added, "Mine are real too, in case you wondered. Wanna check?"

"Yes. I want to check. But I'm not going to. Keep going. There has to be more. Anything at all, even if it seems meaningless."

"Okay. Don't go to my house. We need to pick up my car and your stuff too.

"We shared an apartment three or four days a week until I got the house. She was a good roommate. Paid the bills on time and was gone half the week. Always had to have a boyfriend, but only on a peripheral basis. Men don't last long with us. They can't handle the fact that we're not exclusive to them. At first, they think it's cool. You know, the '*I'm dating a pro*' thing. But it doesn't last. Men are just plain stupid."

"There are always women as an alternative," Jake joked.

"Yuck. I charge double to have sex with a woman. Cindi hated it too, but for the money, either of us would rise to the occasion. Call me old-fashioned, but there are some things I'm just not comfortable with."

"I seriously doubt that I would ever call you old-fashioned, Amber."

"Oh. Sorry. Probably more info than you needed. Anyway, I don't know what else to tell you. We exchanged e-mails and texts while she was in Southern California. She said she liked it there. It was warm. No snow. She did mention she was getting close to the payoff. I can't really think of anything else."

"You save the e-mails and texts?"

"No. I delete them after I read them."

He drove for a while then asked, "How often do you clear your trash or deleted items folder?"

"Never."

"I'll bet you a million bucks the stuff is still there," said Jake. "Can I look at your computer?"

"Where on this earth would you get a million bucks?" she chided. With a shrug she agreed, "Okay, I guess."

"I'll stay for dinner then, but when it's done, I'm on the road."

They drove on to the hotel and casino, then he followed her home. Jake worried the casino might be watched but claimed his belongings with no trouble. He took an overdue antibiotic. Amber located her car, and they met in front. At a red light, he checked his laptop case. He found a note.

'You're a smart fucker. Your money is all here. I ain't a thief. See you around, Jet. Thanks for the song. Very original.' It was unsigned.

The Thai restaurant deliveryman was waiting when they arrived. Amber had phoned ahead. Jake parked in front this time, and Amber pulled into the garage. After dropping her ski equipment, he headed through the open door straight for the computer while Amber paid for the food.

"Shoes off!" she yelled as he shot past.

With a snap of each ankle, the Top-Siders flew off in the entryway.

"It's okay to use my computer. I appreciate you asking first," she called after him sarcastically. She carried the bags of warm food into the kitchen.

Jake activated the screen and opened Amber's e-mail. It contained seventeen items. The 'deleted items' folder contained over 1,500 e-mails. About half had been read, then dumped. Drive maintenance was not her forte.

Amber called that dinner was ready. He ignored her.

Sifting through the computer storage file was a painstaking process. It took Jake nearly an hour, and Amber had called two other times for him to come and eat. Finally, she brought him a bottle of Corona beer and sat in a chair nearby as he worked. He'd mumbled thanks and continued as the printer sporadically spit out a page or two.

With a stack of papers, he pushed his chair back.

"Done?" asked Amber.

"Done searching and forwarding," he responded. "I'll have to read this stuff. You don't have any other messages stored here? Any possibility others have come in?"

"If new messages had come in the computer would tell us. It's pretty smart," she laughed. "All right, enough computer nonsense. Let's eat."

"You haven't eaten?"

"No. That would be rude. I waited for you."

"You should have said something."

"I did. Three times. Finally, I gave up and put the food in the microwave. C'mon. The flavor will still be there, but the chicken and seafood will probably chew like rubber. You can read that stuff later."

The small table in the kitchen was set with gold-trimmed white china. Plates for the food and bowls for soup. Candles, half-burned, glowed on the table. Others twinkled on the granite counters. Long-stemmed wine glasses were in front of the plates, with a bottle on ice between them.

Jake expected take-out Thai eaten out of the boxes. He looked at Amber questioningly.

Escort, high-dollar call girl or whatever he might call her, Amber was a beautiful woman, and the mix of candlelight and wine could be troublesome.

Of course, he realized that was her plan. A game of cat and mouse. The key was to be the cat, if possible. But Amber had already taken that role and reversal didn't seem likely.

Be an elusive mouse, he told himself.

They ate, and Amber chatted about the day. He was only half-interested in the conversation and scanned the printed pages as she initiated the dialogue. Most of the information in the first e-mail chain was useless. But the later messages had a few things of interest.

Cindi was learning to speak a new language, explaining she'd need it when she and Tom took off. The exact language wasn't mentioned, but he assumed Spanish. A large swath of the world spoke Spanish. At least it was something. He put the pages aside and returned his attention to the meal and the lady sitting across from him.

She refilled his glass. The wine was a four-year aged Mer Soleil Silver un-oaked Chardonnay, and the mild zip in the taste was refreshing. Janelle preferred the heavy buttery flavor of the same grape but aged in oak. Amber's offering was unique. A rejuvenation of the taste buds with a little mischief thrown in for added spice.

He was weakening. Perhaps he should act on her proposal. Janelle would never need to know. He reluctantly squashed the thought and decided to bring the conversation back to Cindi. There was still something bothering him.

"Amber. Why are you helping me? I thought Cindi was your friend?"

"She is. When I met you last night, I saw something in you. Resolve. With my help, I think you'll find her. This way I may be able to retain some control of the outcome. If I help you, I'll need your promise on two things. Okay?"

As Jake stared across the table the candlelight playfully reflected from her dark yet sparkling eyes. She had changed into a pair of olive-colored pants and a white, sleeveless, button-front blouse of fine cotton. Her long hair fell in soft curls onto her shoulders. She had applied lipstick, a touch of makeup, and a subtle perfume. Jake, still in his ski pants and mock turtleneck, suddenly felt hot. He realized she'd lit the fire.

The setting was too perfect. Food offering just the right amount of zest, candlelight, a glass of flavorful wine with just the right amount of bite, a warm fire, and a woman who was becoming more alluring by the second.

"What two things?"

"Well, I think Cindi's fallen in with some bad people. She's not a thief. She's just confused." She paused and sipped her wine, then continued. "So, first and foremost, I want a promise that whatever happens, Cindi gets no jail time."

Shaking his head, he replied, "I won't likely have any control over that. If I ever get close to her at all... I plan to hand this information over to the investigating officers. Right now, the police or IRS or maybe even the FBI are all looking at my father as a prime suspect. Someone else has to be found at fault, or the cops need a trail to follow to take the pressure off my folks.

"Winning the contest on Saturday, I qualified for world mogul championships in a few weeks. I have almost no chance to win, but it's probably my last shot. When I get to my parents' house, I'll do what I can to help, but someone else needs to track these people down. A professional, or a group of professionals. I need to dedicate at least four days a week to training. Chasing crooks is *not* my forte."

"I don't know, Jake, you've done a pretty good job so far. You may have more talent than you think for this sort of thing," she commented.

"I could have been beaten or shot or both. No, Amber, I've ridden Lady Luck's back enough. I'll turn this over to the authorities."

She appeared to ponder his response. "No chance your father was involved?"

"None," Jake said firmly. "He's an honest man and a pillar of their church."

She laughed. "A deacon at one of the local churches is one of my best customers. He embezzles thousands from the offering, then spends it on me. That way his wife doesn't find out. Pillars can crumble... Think maybe your pop wanted to take a whack at Cindi? She can be persuasive, especially when an older man is involved."

Jake thought a moment, giving Amber's scenario serious consideration. "Nope. Taking off with a young beauty wouldn't be his thing. Dad's committed to home and family.

"He wants to leave his mark on this earth when he's gone. I think he initially planned to do it in the medical field, but the beast of centralized medicine is too big to tackle. So Dad turned to development.

"Sometimes he'll go to his developments and walk up and down the streets and watch the kids playing. It's a little of a God complex... At the clubhouse where he lives, people acknowledge him as Dr. Cohen, the developer. He likes it, even though he tries not to show it. Development is the mark he'll leave."

"Four children and a medical career isn't enough?" she asked.

"No. The old fart is driven. Running away with a sweet young thing wouldn't be a part of his plan."

"She's not a 'thing'. She's a woman," bristled Amber. "Women are not 'things.'"

"Sorry. Slip of the tongue.

"I can't promise Cindi Light will get no jail time. It'll be out of my hands. So that's my answer to your first request. What's the second?"

She shrugged her shoulders. "Doesn't matter if you're not willing to work with me on the first one. Forget it."

Jake waited. He picked up a scallop with his chopsticks and munched. She pushed some rice around on her plate.

As he studied her across the table, his gaze rested briefly on her chest. The buttons of the blouse were open to the center of the breasts, revealing the fringes of a black lace bra covering ample roundness.

Were the buttons open a moment ago? He didn't think so.

"Okay," she said, the awkward silence broken, "the second thing I wanted was a percentage of whatever you recover. You don't think my communications with Cindi are done, do you? She stopped texting and all her social media is off, but I have her e-mail address. So do you now, but she'll shut it down in a minute if she thinks someone is after her. All I have to do is keep a dialogue open, and something will come up. Hell, she might even tell me point-blank where she is. Maybe I'll suggest I come for a visit. I can lead you to her, and you can attempt a recovery. My thought was I'd get ten percent."

Jake considered the possibilities. He finally asked, "Amber, I'm confused. If Cindi is a friend, why would you help me find her?"

"Cindi *is* a friend. That's *why* I want to help you. She's crossed over the line. Stealing and ruining someone's life is shitty business. That's just not her... She's going to get caught sooner or later, and she'll end up in prison. If we track her down, we'll have a chance of saving her, and maybe recovering what she took. But if you want to involve the law, I can't help."

Crossed over the line. Where had he heard that sentiment recently?

"What about the reward you're asking for?" questioned Jake. "That doesn't sound much like the request of a friend. It sounds mercenary."

"My main objective is to save Cindi's ass. But if you find her and get some money back, a reward on my end would be fitting," she said. Then she locked eyes with him and added in a sultry voice, "Remember, above all else, I'm a businesswoman. So, what do you say, Mr. Cohen, shall we do some business together?"

Amber stood and slowly released the last button on her blouse. Without ever breaking eye contact between them she allowed her shirt to slide off, revealing a pair of round grapefruit-sized breasts held neatly in place by the black lace. Her body was everything he expected, toned and tanned. He wanted to tell her 'no' and make a run for it but was transfixed like a rodent caught in the gaze of a cobra, to be devoured at the snake's fancy.

She walked around the table and began rubbing his shoulders, allowing his head to rest between the perfect mounds on her chest.

The combination of the candles, wine, warm fire, and the willing beauty was too much. While skiing they hadn't worked up a heavy sweat but had perspired just enough to get their pheromones pumping. Now the sensory chemicals were thick in the tepid room, pushing them toward a union. He was in an infidelity nosedive. Janelle would never know. Sliding his left hand along her back, he found the bra hook. Pinching with the thumb and forefinger, he popped it loose with one quick motion. As he moved his hand up toward the shoulder to pull the top strap down over the arm, a voice coming from the hall broke the silence.

"*Am-ber, I have a message for you!*" The digital call came from the computer. "*Beep-beep-beep-beep!*" answered her phone in the kitchen.

"Not now, you stupid machine!" cried Amber.

The room went silent.

The spell was broken. Jake was suddenly in complete focus. The candle flames no longer danced, and the musty fog of lust had cleared. Almost failing in his promise of fidelity, he'd been saved by the divine intervention of Microsoft and Apple. He made a note to buy some stock if he ever had any extra cash.

Jake removed his hand from her shoulder and leaned away from her chest. "It would appear you have other matters to attend to. So in answer to your question, no, we will not do business together. Cindi Light will pay the price for her actions if they find her. If she contacts you again, you really should alert the cops; it would be the right thing to do. I do appreciate your help, Amber. I'm just not in the business of tracking down crooks and saving..." He stopped himself.

"Whores! Just say it!" she spat. "That's it, isn't it? Neither Cindi nor I are worth wasting your time with because we're whores. Get out! You ungrateful son of a bitch! I should have let Cliff and that other guy kick your ass! I don't want to see your sorry face around here again. Ever! Leave! Now!"

The eyes had sparkled with mischief moments before. Now they glowed with fury. He quickly collected his belongings and picked the e-mail pages off the table. As he headed out the door, she called to him.

"Oh, Jake! Here's what you missed." She stood tall and removed the black lace bra, exposing an exquisite bosom. "You'll never get another chance to touch these, you fucking jerk."

From down the hall, the computer called again, and the pager beeped.

"Looks like someone else will have to finish up tonight. More profitable for you anyway. Goodbye, Amber. And thanks again," said Jake as he ducked out.

"Pig!" was the last thing he heard her scream before a wineglass broke against the inside of the wooden door.

That ended badly, Jake thought as he drove away.

CHAPTER 12
SPAIN, 1495

"Inquisitor Torquemada, it is a pleasure to see you again." Astride his magnificent steed, Cristobal DeCorto spoke with all the sincerity he could muster. The carriage in front of him was flanked by the dozen uniformed men-at-arms who accompanied the Grand Inquisitor.

"I thought your visits here in the south had finished upon our last encounter. Two years ago, if I am not mistaken."

The tonsured priest leaned out of the carriage and stared directly at DeCorto. Cristobal saw bottomless hatred in the eyes. The spotless robes and diadem of the church could not belie the insatiable cruelty in this man.

Appointed Grand Inquisitor of the Inquisition, Tomás de Torquemada's acts of brutality while obtaining the confessions of heresy and blasphemy from those he interrogated were unparalleled. No junior inquisitor could match the ruthlessness and sanitary efficiency with which their leader went about his task of purification of the Spanish State.

Pleas for mercy went unheard as he tortured his victims to confession, with the blessing of the Pope. Torquemada carried a one-hundred percent record of producing affirmations of sacrilege against the Catholic Church.

Upon confession, each accused soul would be forced to offer names of others who practiced acts in violation of Catholic doctrine. Those accused would suffer the same torment and in turn offer up the names of others guilty of witchcraft, blasphemy, heresy, or sacrilege. The cycle was repeated until all the heretics in a town or region had been rounded-up, proven guilty by their own declarations.

Then the burnings would take place.

Entire families perished together in the flames, tied to stakes. A lucky few avoided the inferno and were sentenced to the prisons, where death was certain from plague, malnutrition, abuses of the guards, or the ultimate wasting away of the body.

The possessions of the guilty were, of course, seized by the Inquisitor to be dispersed between Church and State.

While Queen Isabella was credited with the rise of Spain as a power, few knew that her tutor in youth was none other than Tomás de Torquemada. From childhood, he had instilled in the girl the need for one religion to unify the country.

The ability to order death and seizure of property with the blessing of both Church and State gave him absolute power, and Cristobal DeCorto knew exactly how dangerous the man he now addressed was.

Perhaps the appearance of the Grand Inquisitor meant nothing more than a sale of mounts to his party. Every nobleman and knight in the country wished to be seen on a steed with a DeCorto brand upon its hindquarters. Even the King and Queen rode in carriages drawn by the horses bred on their rancho. Cristobal prayed silently this was the reason for the visit.

As his eyes panned the landscape, the Inquisitor answered, "Ah, such a beautiful country you inhabit. The Lord has created a second Eden, and you have claimed it."

His tone changed as he added, "I must be frank with you. We have word of heresy on your lands, Sir DeCorto. I am here on business of the Church and Crown."

Cristobal's eyes narrowed, and his chest tightened at the words of the Grand Inquisitor. His being here on "business" could only be troublesome.

"You need not address me as 'Sir', Inquisitor. I am Cristobal. You mistake me for my father, Juan Pablo, who perished at the King's side from a crossbow strike while fighting the Mohammedan El Zagal, or my brother Roberto III, who died here a year ago after service to the Crown on the march to Granada. Both were knighted many years ago for their heroism in the war."

"I am sorry for your losses. Meeting so many in my travels, sometimes I become confused." The offer of condolence was shallow, without conviction. Torquemada's head turned to one side as he asked, "You did not join in the campaign against the Moors?"

"My wishes were to join the march, yet my father contested, saying I was too young. My father and brother were gone from our valley the better part of four years in service of the King. I stayed to tend the herds, manage the vineyard, and run the rancho."

A few of the guards in Torquemada's contingent snickered.

"There is no levity in my father and brother's deaths," Cristobal stated. "Their reconnaissance in the mountains of Andalusia may have saved our King and nation. While I respect your position, Inquisitor, I will not have your men making light of the passing of two true heroes of Spain. It is disrespectful."

The captain of the guard spoke out, "Archbishop Torquemada, you may assure young Señor DeCorto we mean no insult. Many of us served on the march to Granada. We simply have little regard for those who chose herding and farming, while we risked our blood and souls in the service of Spain."

Edging his horse closer to the guard, Cristobal sat straight in his saddle. His light brown eyes bore into those of the sentinel. "Sir, you have made your last insult on my land. If you wish to test my mettle, I would gladly unseat you with sword or lance, or any weapon of your choosing." The back of DeCorto's gloved hand snapped out, catching the man under the chin. He nearly lost his seat with the impact. As the guard straightened in the saddle, the glove again hit him in the face, this time thrown by DeCorto's hand. It bounced squarely off his nose to the ground, where it lay for the entire entourage to see.

"I *beseech* you to pick it up, sir, that your insolence might be rewarded."

Torquemada's stern voice was heard. "We will have no dueling! Captain, you should be advised that the males of the DeCorto family are rumored to be undefeated in tournament. You may have an opportunity at redemption later in our visit."

The captain sat upon his horse with a look of both anger and relief, and said, "Yes, Inquisitor. You are right, it would be beneath a knight of my stature to engage one with manure on his boots."

"At least, Captain, unlike you, I have the good sense to keep the manure on the *outside* of my boots," Cristobal taunted. A few of the men snickered at the insult. The captain seethed silently.

The Grand Inquisitor addressed DeCorto. "We will need to examine the house and outbuildings, and question your hands and servants living on your lands."

"What do you expect to find?"

"We have been notified by a guest at your home that your wife continues to light the candelabrum of the Jews seasonally. Also, you slay the lamb and feast with the children and family in a reclined position once annually."

"My wife has accepted Christ as her savior. This fact was verified by you personally upon your last visit. Her lighting of the menorah and celebration of the Feast of Passover are not subversive in any way to Church or State."

"Those acts pay homage to the religion of the accursed Jews," said the Inquisitor.

"The Lord Jesus Christ himself was a Jew. My wife simply pays homage to him as the Son of God and King of the Jews. She, along with all of our hands and servants, have accepted all aspects of the Catholic faith," protested Cristobal. "Additionally, we have paid the 30,000 ducats on my wife and each of our servants to the Crown for the right to practice certain aspects of their prior religion."

"Judas Iscariot sold Christ for thirty pieces of silver; his Highness cannot sell him for 30,000 ducats. That edict has been repealed by the King, upon urging of the Queen."

"Then you carry with you a refund of our family's tribute to the Crown? The duty was paid at the King's request."

"He has asked forgiveness of the Pope for the lapse, and the Pope has granted him absolution. Funds paid in blasphemous pursuits cannot be returned."

"I expected nothing, Inquisitor. I simply wished to remind you of our total compliance with the laws and requests of Crown and Church."

"Your compliance, and that of those under your control, will be determined upon interview and interrogation over the coming days."

Cristobal DeCorto's eyes narrowed once again. "I trust you have brought the accuser along that we may cross-examine this person?"

"During the interview, she confessed acts of heresy of her own. Along with her family members, she was purified at death by fire."

Fighting to speak through clenched teeth, Cristobal stated, "The DeCortos have been loyal to the Church for centuries. Our family has been instrumental in the emergence of Spain as one nation. We have supplied horses for the armies of the Crown, and we have lived and died in this valley for five hundred years. Why does the King now bring this suspicion upon my wife and our ranch hands?"

Torquemada nodded as he looked up at Cristobal and offered, "If you are truly righteous, God will be with you, and your family will show their purity of faith in the interviews."

Cristobal pondered for a moment before saying, "I shall ride ahead and prepare for your arrival. Our dwelling is a half-hour journey on a swift steed, yet at least two hours in your carriage. There is one wide, shallow river to cross."

"Alas, I grow old in the service of God and Crown. My days of galloping are over. My captain and a guard will accompany you. Please make ready food and drink for our entourage. We often grow hungry in the work of the Lord.

"Be advised; all exits from the valley are guarded by many men. Please do not attempt flight," Torquemada stated, then added in a sinister tone, "Prepare your wife. She will be questioned."

DeCorto nodded curtly. "Of course."

He started to turn his animal in the direction of his rancho but spun back to face Torquemada. With squinted eyes, he said, "Inquisitor, it is said you make your lodgings in a castle constructed of the headstones from Jewish gravesites."

Torquemada nodded. "To let such fine masonry go to waste marking the rotting body of one of Christ's murderers would be to squander one of God's many gifts. I have put many of these stones to work in housing a servant of the Lord."

The two men locked eyes for a moment as if testing the will of the other, then Cristobal reined his beautiful Arabian stallion to one side. Leaning out of the saddle by pressing his right foot against its top, he deftly bent to the ground and retrieved the glove with his left hand. With a flick of his heel against the animal's rib cage, he was gone.

The captain of the guard hurriedly ordered another man to follow, and together they pursued DeCorto, but they would not catch the expert horseman on his exquisite steed.

"Dear Father in Heaven, why hast thou brought this cross to bear upon my family?" Cristobal wept as he prayed on his knees at the edge of the river where the road crossed. "If these men truly are doing your work, let me fall in the water and have my body carried away before I raise arms against them. Forgive me, Lord, if I err. Please accept the souls of those I am about to send to you, that you may make the final judgment. Amen."

Wiping away the tears he mounted his horse and turned back to the river he'd crossed only a moment prior. The cobble rocks his workers placed in the water every spring after the runoff made tricky footing for horses, yet abated erosion and allowed passage for wagons without deep pools. Horses, like people, become more sure-footed with practice on uneven terrain, and crossing the cobble-bottom of the riverbed was a daily occurrence for DeCorto's stallion.

Yet the mounts of the captain and guard sent to escort him were not sure of foot as he watched them crossing the river. They struggled as their hooves slipped on the cobble, the riders unsteady in their saddles.

Trotting his animal off the bank, Cristobal moved toward the men in the center of the rushing body of water. He said nothing as he approached. The two exchanged looks of amazement at the ease with which DeCorto and his horse moved in the river. Their expressions shifted quickly to confused fear as they saw him unsheathe his blade and raise it high above his head.

The specter of the curly-haired man clad in black knee-high boots, tan rider's pants, and loose-fitting white tunic coming at them with water splashing and weapon raised high was overwhelming. The brown eyes showed the grim determination of a man prepared for battle. The intent of the rider was clear. These men were not just enemies; they were a threat to his family and would perish here.

Rather than drawing their own weapons, they turned to flee, hoping to reach the safety of the opposite bank where they could fight on even terrain.

Yet their attempted flight was useless. As their horses struggled for footing on the round stones of the river bottom, DeCorto caught them from behind.

Each man wore a breastplate and helmet, so Cristobal's first blow was to the leg of the guard in the rear, laying open a gash in the meat of the upper thigh. Instinctively the injured man's left hand shot to cover the open wound as his right went for his weapon. DeCorto's second sword blow caught his left arm at the elbow. The guard watched in horror as his severed hand and forearm floated away and sunk in the current. Cristobal pulled his animal close and kicked the guard out of his saddle with his right foot. The man tumbled in the rushing water for a few yards before catching his footing and coming erect. Downstream of him, in the eddy created where his legs blocked the current, the water's color turned to red as blood freely flowed from both the leg wound and stump of his arm.

"I will come back for you," said DeCorto as he whipped his horse around to begin chasing down the other man.

The captain knew his sole chance for salvation was reaching the bank. As he reached the smaller rocks in the shallows, his mount became steadier, yet as he turned to check behind his eyes grew wide in horror as he saw Cristobal bearing down upon him, his steed seeming to float over the cobble of the river bottom as if it were soft turf.

Just as Cristobal reached him, the guard rolled out of his saddle and evaded the swipe of the sword passing mere inches over his head. He ran for the trees as his aggressor passed him by, but only made a few steps before the horseman reined his mount around and gave chase.

Looking back, he saw the wide eyes of both horse and man above with the cover of the thick only a few feet away. The sword came down upon him; he sprawled to avoid the blow. The hooves of the animal, however, found their mark on his back. The metal of his armor protected his spine and ribs from being crushed as the weight of the great animal pressed against his torso. Only the wind was knocked from his lungs. In desperation, he rolled as the horse passed over and the mass of the beast came off. From a sitting position he scrambled to unsheathe his blade, yet as it rattled free, the sword was hammered to the ground by the blade of DeCorto, who had leapt down from the saddle. The black boot stomped hard on the flat of the steel, and it snapped, leaving only a stub as a weapon. The soldier now sat at the feet of Cristobal, with a sword leveled at his throat.

Gasping to regain breath the captain begged, "Let me live, sir, and I will see to it the interviews are mild for your family!"

Looking down, with his blade at the captain's throat, Cristobal answered

the plea. "I assure you, as long as I breathe there will be no interviews or torture on my lands! How many men are guarding the two passes into the valley?"

The captain knelt silently. His refusal to answer was met with a vicious
kick to his face from the boot of DeCorto, knocking him over backward. The
helmet flew off with the impact. Eventually, he rolled onto all fours, his knees
underneath him. As he tried to gain his feet, he felt the cold of steel behind
his left ear. His movement stopped.

"How many men? Truth might save your life. Remain silent, and you will
die."

Between gasps, the captain answered, "Twenty men at each pass. They
converge upon your home from all directions. There is no escape. Let me live,
sir! I speak the truth, and I can lessen the pain of the interviews for those
you love."

"You've heard many pleas for mercy. How many have suffered through
interrogation, only to be burned alive in purification?" Cristobal grilled him.

There was no answer from the man on his knees. Cristobal knew well
that thousands had perished in the flames to date.

"Tell me, soldier, why has the King turned his eyes upon my family?"

The request was met with silence. DeCorto yanked upward on the blade,
cleanly severing the left ear of the captain from his head.

"Please let me live!" The plea came from the man as blood flowed through
his fingers where he clutched the side of his head.

Cristobal looked down the road in the direction from which Torquemada's
band would come. He knew they were at least one-half hour ahead of the
company, yet time was fleeting. Placing his blade under the chin of the captain he again asked, "Speak. Why has the King turned disfavor upon us? We
are loyal subjects."

The officer's voice rattled in fear and pain as he answered. "You have many
who are descended from followers of Islam living on your lands. Ferdinand
fears one might rise among them and incite war, as in years past. We are
ordered to remove these threats."

So, it has come at last, thought Cristobal. Looking down he asked, "Are
there reinforcements beyond your fifty-two men?"

"Not for many days' ride, sir!" The captain looked up at Cristobal. "Surely
you don't plan to engage an army of the King? Sources tell us that the men

of your rancho and outlying casas number less than a dozen. You and your family will surely die if you engage in such a foolish act. Surrender, sir, that you may live! Our orders are to interrogate and remove only the Moors."

Lowering his sword from the captain's chin, he stepped away. This morning he spent leisurely time with his wife and children. His son and daughter had practiced their horsemanship in the arena after breakfast as he, his wife, and the children's grandmother looked on. All wore smiles, and laughter filled the moment. Yet now, only hours after the delight of the morning, he faced an army of the King.

Should he give up his Moorish hands to this force? The families were descended of the two who had come from the East with Roberto I well over four hundred years ago. In the years when the battles for these southern lands were fought, not one Muslim from this valley had taken up arms with the Moorish forces. They were as loyal to Spain as his own family.

But what could be done? If Ferdinand wanted them removed, they would be removed. The valley could not be held against the forces of Spain.

"You would give them an opportunity to accept banishment?" he asked the captain. "And my family would live on here?"

A wave of relief came over the soldier who had faced certain death only a moment before. The blade had been lowered, and negotiation had taken the place of combat. "Yes, Señor DeCorto. I can arrange that," said the man as his right hand slid down inside his boot to the hilt of the dagger sheathed there.

"What of the guard in the river? He will likely not survive his injuries. And you. Can you forgive my actions? You will be disfigured for the remainder of your years."

The captain rose slowly to his feet. His left sleeve was bloody where he'd pressed it against the stump of the severed ear. His eye was puffy where the boot had caught him, and his nose bled. As he rose, his right hand gripped the dagger pressed against his buttock and leg to be obscured from Cristobal's sight.

"You are a man who fought to protect his family. I can forgive under that noble act. I will tell Torquemada we had our duel and the injury was sustained during the fight. The guard...," the captain took a step closer to DeCorto as he feigned a look toward the river, "we will let him sink into a deep hole downstream and tell that he fell from his saddle in crossing."

Cristobal's gaze followed the captain's to the river. As his eyes wandered, the captain shot forward, hooking the sword arm of his opponent with the bloody left hand, and driving the dagger upward. A quick sidestep by Cristobal kept the blade from finding its mark in his heart, but he was not fast enough to avoid the stroke completely, and the steel found an opening between the ribs where it entered his chest.

Pain shot through his body as he grasped at the hand holding the dagger. He was able to force the blade away. Yet even as he pushed, the captain was able to wrench the sword from his right hand, expertly grabbing the hilt as it came free. Stepping back quickly, Cristobal faced an opponent who now held a dagger in his left hand and sword in his right. Blood spread across the front of his tunic from the wound in his chest as the captain advanced upon him.

Cristobal silently cursed himself for allowing his vigilance to falter.

"Ahh," laughed the captain, "After I kill you here, I shall have the pleasure of watching your wife and children burn!"

He lunged at Cristobal with an overhead sweep of the sword. The horseman deftly moved backward and sideways with a false step. As the longer blade went by, he shot behind its arc to tackle the captain, yet the trained soldier was ready with the dagger and brought it upward with his left hand. The smaller blade tore a hole in the tunic and sliced a fresh gash in his chest over his ribs.

Retreating quickly, Cristobal ducked and rolled as the sword whisked above his head.

Sustaining another wound, Cristobal realized the man he faced was skilled with both dagger and sword. Now unarmed, he'd been lucky to avoid a mortal blow. He hastily decided to make a retreat. Still down, he scampered on all fours toward the cover of brush and trees. The captain pursued, but the faster DeCorto made the safety of the thicket and disappeared.

"You crawl like an animal to escape!" the captain yelled into the brush. "I will not forget the wound you inflicted. We will arrive at your rancho soon! I will enact retribution upon your family tenfold!"

Only silence came from the bushes as the captain stood by.

"Come out, coward!" Again, the call was met with stillness.

The captain called once more, "Well then. We shall continue our true orders—to remove you all. The King sees the nobles as a potential threat. I shall personally deliver to the King the jeweled breastplate of the DeCortos as he has requested!"

"Ferdinand's avarice is legendary, but it shall not be satisfied today. Nor by you at any time."

The strong voice caused the captain to spin, where he saw Cristobal standing tall in the road twenty yards away.

How could he have moved through the thicket so silently? the astounded captain wondered.

With sword and dagger, he began to advance upon the unarmed DeCorto, who did not move but rather stood high. Rage drove him forward, and a slight deviation in his path put him in position to cut off another escape into the woods. Once between Cristobal and the thicket, the soldier's gait increased.

Cristobal began taking backward steps, and his pursuer quickened his pace. Seeing the distance between them closing he turned and began to run. The man clad in light armor gave chase and DeCorto fought the pain under his ribs as he measured his gait so as not to outrun his follower. Backward glances showed the captain's pace slowing. Soon the man's legs stopped churning, and he slowed to a trot, then a walk.

No more than twenty-five yards separated the two, yet the winded captain could not close the gap. Cristobal stopped and placed his hand over the wound in his chest. Fresh red blood covered it as the two men stood staring at one another in the open road.

To the surprise of the captain, Cristobal put his fingers to his lips and let out a shrill whistle. From the thick emerged Cristobal's black stallion, answering his call. The horse galloped to the side of its master, where the rider winced only slightly with pain as he smoothly mounted the steed.

From the saddle, Cristobal called to his pursuer, "We have both run a good distance from the thicket. My horse can cover that span in twenty seconds. You are winded, Captain. It will take you four times as long."

The officer turned and began running at the same moment Cristobal kicked with his heels at the great animal's ribs. The earth shook as horse and rider neared and the captain realized, too late, that flight was useless. Stopping and turning to fight he tried to raise sword against the onslaught, but the blade was caught as the horseman reared the beast above him and the hooves beat downward mercilessly. The first blow caught him on the shoulder of his sword arm, driving him over. The second and third beats of hooves found their marks on the captain's head, knocking him senseless, so he saw only blackness with the initial impact. The final strike of hoof crushed his skull to end his life.

Cristobal dismounted and stood over the still-quivering body. He loosened the rope tied to his saddle and secured it around the dead captain's feet. He dragged the body into the river where the first guard was still stumbling over the cobble trying to reach the bank. Cristobal said nothing as he cut the rope off his saddle. Both men watched as the body of the captain was taken by the current to sink in the deeper pools downstream.

The remaining guard looked up at Cristobal and slowly reached to unsheathe his weapon. The blade was drawn, but the arm could not hoist the weight of the steel. The sword fell to the man's side, and his eyes rolled back into his head. He had succumbed to the loss of blood, keeling over and falling. His body was taken by the swift waters.

Cristobal wished he'd been able to capture the mounts of the fallen guards as the rider-less horses would alert the oncoming squads to danger if found. He thought briefly of rounding up the animals but realized he had too little time. Mustering the men of the valley was of most immediate importance.

Not taking the time to wrap his rib cage and stem the bleeding, he left the river and galloped toward his rancho.

The first stop was the home of trusted friends. When Cristobal came riding up to the portico, Bushra, the woman of the house, was carrying water from the well. Her two young girls played nearby as the horse stopped, towering above.

She was at first taken aback that Cristobal would ride in so rudely. When she saw the red spread across his tunic, she gasped, realizing trouble was afoot.

"Cristobal, what has happened? You must dismount and let me tend your wound!"

"There is no time, Bushra. The Inquisition is upon us. The Grand Inquisitor himself is on our lands. He approaches now. We must act to save ourselves."

The clay pitcher she held fell to the ground and shattered. She knew well what the Inquisition meant, especially to a family of Middle Eastern ancestry.

Her eyes were moist as she asked, "Cristobal, what shall we do?"

"Where is Nassih?"

"He is in the barn, fixing a wheel on our carriage," she stated in a hollow tone.

"Tell Nassih to ride to the other homes to the west and north. He shall summon the men to my rancho. Immediately! We have only an hour, maybe less. The men must come at arms. Swords, bows, and crossbows. Any male old enough to ride and draw a bow or swing a blade must answer my call."

She nodded.

"Make haste, Bushra. While your husband rides gather your children and make way to my home. Do not remain here. The lead band of soldiers is close behind me. Go on the back trails; do not travel on the main road," instructed Cristobal. "Take only portable items of wealth and the clothes on your back. You will need money for your journey, wherever you may end up."

She shook her head and muttered, "I..., I... cannot believe what you are saying. Our time here has ended?"

Cristobal looked down at tears streaking her face. "It is true. The Inquisition has been pushing toward us for years. I was blind to think it would pass us by.

"I will stop at the ranchos to the east and north. There is no time for grief, Bushra. We must act! As lord over these lands, I have never once given an order. That changes now; the men *must* come, and you must flee."

She nodded up at him. He wheeled his horse and was gone at a gallop.

The call through the countryside brought fifteen men together. They waited at the well as Cristobal's wife cleaned his wounds with boiled water then wrapped his ribcage with clean linen.

"Rebekah, you must tie the bandage off," said Cristobal. "It is time I address the men."

Slitting the cloth's ends and cinching them together she implored, "Husband, do not go. Your wound hissed as you breathed. Your lung has been pierced. You must be still if you expect any chance at healing."

"The soldiers approach. I will not see my children, or you, tortured while I am able to draw a bow or swing a blade." He flinched at the sting as he pulled a clean tunic over his head.

She didn't cry as he'd told her the story. Her face became stern, and resolve began to form within that her family would survive. Nonetheless, she feared her husband's injuries were too serious to allow him to join in the coming skirmish.

"Let the other men handle this. We need to make ready our departure," Rebekah again beseeched.

Shaking his head as he tucked the tunic into his bloodstained pants, he turned and looked at her. She was beautiful. Long, dark hair framed her wide, brown eyes. He wished he'd packed up long ago and moved far away to protect her.

"Ready the children. We will have to go on horseback, and we must travel with a light load. If we are successful against this force, we will gain a few days' start on the reinforcements they send. We must be out of Spain quickly," Cristobal said as he pulled the jeweled breastplate of the DeCorto clan over his head.

More than one of his ancestors, including his father, had breathed their last breath while wearing the shell. Yet many more family members had been spared as the armor had protected them from mortal blows in combat. The family coat-of-arms was ornately worked across the chest, featuring a horseman galloping to battle with sword drawn. Ornately set in the polished metal were ten jewels, all huge sapphires making up the blade of the warrior on the breastplate. It shimmered blue, and the hooves and eyes of the horse were radiant with diamonds.

Cristobal held his arms up, and as Rebekah laced the sides of the breastplate she asked, "Do you regret taking a Hebrew woman as a wife?"

As she finished, he pulled her close and said with a reassuring laugh, "As I hold our children in my arms, I cannot fathom any other as their mother. Feel no guilt in this matter, Rebekah. The soldiers would have come in any case."

Releasing her, he turned to go out to the men. She called after him, "Live, Cristobal. Your children and I need you."

The low murmuring of the men stopped as Cristobal stepped up on the wall of the well. He looked over them. Some were older, graying but stout, and some were not yet teenagers. He knew each one by his first name, and they knew him. He spoke to them in a solid voice.

"Today marks the beginning of the end of our time together here. An army rides against us, under the guise of the direction of the Church. I tell you truly, we cannot stand against the army of the King in any sustained battle. Our lands are lost, and we must escape, lest our families face the Inquisition and the punishment of death thereby.

"Yet this force that approaches has made an error; they have divided their numbers to cut off our escape routes. In doing so, they have weakened themselves.

"Three squads of soldiers now converge on us from the three passes leading into our valley. If these forces are allowed to merge, we are outmanned, and we will fail. My plan is we will never allow these smaller divisions to meet and become one stronger force. We ride faster mounts, we are lighter, and most importantly we know every path, rock, and tree in our valley.

"Deadly arrows will rain upon them fired from the thick of the forest or from placements behind boulders above, and when they pursue us, we will run like the wind on horseback, leading them into another volley of our arrows. To engage this force directly will cost us; they are too strong and are clad in armor. Have no shame in turning to run from the fight today, for your flight will save the lives of your family and the families of all. We will attack, run, regroup, and attack again.

"We are sixteen versus fifty, yet they ride in groups of twenty, twenty, and ten. After each of our volleys, their forces should be diminished by two to four. By sundown today, there should be no soldier of the King left alive on our lands. It is my wish that the years of terror initiated by Tomás de Torquemada and his Inquisition shall end here."

Cristobal quickly outlined his plan. They would ride in groups of four, engage the enemy for two volleys of arrows, then run away, slowly enough to be easily followed yet fast enough to not be caught. As the soldiers pursued, they would encounter another hidden force that would again rain arrows upon them, and again would run. Once the troops were depleted, the forces of the valley would engage them directly. There would be no prisoners.

With adrenaline coursing through their veins and certainty in their quest borne of the passionate words of their leader, the band of men rode out from the rancho to engage forces of King Ferdinand and the Catholic church.

By sundown, true to the words of Cristobal, forty-eight soldiers lay dead on the DeCorto lands. They had been ambushed, gave chase, and found death in box canyons with no exit. As the soldiers died many cursed Torquemada for the folly of dividing their force and underestimating their foe. The smaller force of DeCorto's men used their knowledge of the landscape to defend their families. Fourteen of the sixteen riders tiredly returned home; two had died during the fighting.

To the dismay of the men of the valley, they had been told by a dying soldier Torquemada's carriage had turned away when the mounts of the captain and accompanying rider had been found. The Grand Inquisitor had retreated to continue his reign of terror until his death by failing health three years later.

At sunrise the following day, the people of the valley set out for other lands. Many of the followers of Islam turned to the south and east. Some went to the Mediterranean seaports where they found passage to North Africa and joined groups of other Moorish descendants who had been banished by the Spanish monarchy. A few even found their way back to the lands of the Middle East, where the story of the routing of the Spanish army in their escape was told and retold.

The DeCortos, too, set out on horseback from their home at sunrise. They took with them a string of ten horses to use as breeding stock wherever they might settle. Their chests of ducats were emptied, with Cristobal's family carrying all they could while still maintaining their speed. The balance of their riches was distributed among the people to help with their journeys. The extra mounts were saddled to make quick switches if they needed fresh legs under them to escape. With tears in their eyes and lack of understanding, the son and daughter of Cristobal and Rebekah left the rancho with the family. His mother wept too as they trotted away toward the Pyrenees mountains.

For over five hundred years the DeCortos had been lords and masters in this place; in less than twenty-four hours they were uprooted, running like criminals.

For days they rode driven onward by Cristobal's words and actions. He forced them to rise before the sun and ride into the dark. Nights were spent in the open woods where they ate sparingly and slept fitfully. Cristobal only dozed in short naps with crossbow drawn and sword unsheathed, ready to defend his family from robbers and road agents.

His cough grew deeper with a greater tone of gravel in his lungs as the days passed.

Food and supplies were purchased from farms they encountered, but offers of lodging were turned down as they pushed to stay ahead of the force that would most surely be following. Often, they ran into bands of Spanish soldiers who had no news of the routing of their comrades to the southwest. Pleasantries were exchanged, and they went their separate ways.

A week of frigid nights and blistered backsides from long days in the saddle had passed when they stopped at a farm to purchase some food. They were joyous to hear the farmer say hello to them. In French. They had made the border and were free of the tyranny of Spanish rule.

After purchasing supplies and continuing for a few miles Cristobal, now gaunt and haggard, had a coughing fit. He fell from his saddle as he hacked up blood and mucous, spitting the repulsive mixture out in large wads.

With his quest of delivering his family from Spain complete, he died there on the side of the road, his head in the lap of his wife as his children and mother looked on.

They dug the best hole in the ground they could. Rebekah and his mother took knives and pried the ten sapphires and diamonds off the breastplate he wore. After laying his body in the pit and all of them crying during the prayer his mother offered over her son, they pushed the dirt in and piled rocks on top. Then the remaining DeCortos moved on to resettle to the north and east.

CHAPTER 13
TUESDAY - LATE AFTERNOON

Studies have shown commuters who travel more than twenty minutes to work have a lower instance of heart attack than those with jobs close to home. The theory is travel time offers a 'cooling off' period, allowing the commuter to relax from the workday before the rigors of home and family life take over.

Jake wasn't buying it. The seemingly unending line of cars inching along only a few feet apart was *not* relaxing. *The people who did the study are morons,* he decided. He wondered if studies had been done on how many of these folks died of lung cancer or other ailments caused by the inhalation of exhaust fumes.

After leaving Amber's home last night, he hadn't stopped until he reached the town of Bishop, far enough south he felt he was beyond the tentacles of Nicki Stinnetti's reach. He'd pulled off on a side street and slept for a few hours under a sleeping bag he kept in the rear of the SUV, then resumed his journey into Southern California at first light.

The hospital where his father was recuperating was only a few turns off the freeway. He'd decided to stop there first, guessing his mother would be bedside.

As he parked the Forerunner, a sense of responsibility engulfed him. Had he accepted his father's generous offer years earlier to run the development company, the old man wouldn't be in a hospital bed. Tom Wojicki wouldn't have been needed to run the housing project.

The chubby young woman at the reception desk directed him to the fourth floor. A quick elevator ride and a few turns in the hallway later, he was surprised to find a uniformed guard outside the door. The man looked at Jake questioningly.

Jake returned the stare. "Who are you?"

"Deputy Brad Logan. Sheriff's Department, Riverside County," answered the man. He was above average height with a solid build with short-cropped blond hair. He questioned, "What business do you have here?"

"It's all right, deputy. He's our son." The answer came from inside.

"Oh, sorry Mrs. Cohen." He stepped aside and allowed Jake to enter.

"Hello, Jacob," said Anne Cohen as she rose from a chair and gave her youngest child a hug. She released him and smiled, offering, "Your father is doing much better. He can't talk yet. His jaw is screwed together. Two ribs are cracked badly, but they're stabilized, and the lung is fully re-inflated. Pneumonia is not such a worry now. He's going to be okay.

"A plastic surgeon was called in to sew up the cut on his face during surgery. It helps to have clout here. The surgeon said it may require a few more procedures to have him looking perfect again, but when he's done your father will look years younger. I always wanted a younger man." She laughed.

While she was talking Jake surveyed his sleeping father. His face was heavily bandaged, and he had a tube with dark liquid flowing coming out of his nose. An IV tube was inserted and taped to his left arm while his right arm was immobilized across his chest. The right eye was completely covered with gauze. The left eye was uncovered but closed as his father slept. Various monitors fed information about his vital signs to the nurse's station outside.

Jake fought to control his emotions. Sadness. Helplessness. And again, responsibility. Slowly, the feelings merged into one reaction. *Rage.*

"My, it's good to see you! Daniel left yesterday, but he'll be back tomorrow. Marilyn and Brenda are at the house now making dinner. I've spent almost all my time here since Friday. I may seem somewhat dingy, but I was a wreck until Victor started improving. I'm giddy now that he's doing better.

"What happened to your eye? Black and blue with stitches! No wonder Deputy Logan didn't let you right in. They're worried that whoever did this might come back to finish the job! Can you believe this? An armed guard! What a mess!"

Jake looked at the deputy sheriff outside the door and their eyes locked. He wanted to say, 'No Mom, they're not worried about anyone coming back. Deputy Logan is here fishing.'

"That's *very* nice of the department," Jake said coldly but loudly enough for the deputy to hear.

Anne Cohen continued, "Did Janelle come with you? What took you so long to get here? Didn't you leave Sunday?"

"I had a few stops to make. Janelle offered to come, but I told her it wasn't necessary. The eye was just an accident. It'll be fine."

She seemed to accept his explanation. "Well, let's wake your father up. He'll want to see you."

Moving to his bedside, she gently shook her husband's left arm. The head jerked slightly, and the uncovered eye popped open. She said softly, "Victor, Jacob is here."

Jake leaned down and looked at his father's face. The left eyebrow raised and then the face pulled into what Jake thought was a quick grin, followed by a wince of pain.

"It hurts him a little when he smiles," Mrs. Cohen said. She added reassuringly, "He's fine. His doctor says that's good pain."

"Hi, Dad. It's good to see you."

With his left hand, Dr. Cohen motioned for his son to come closer for a look. The unbandaged eye appraised the cut over Jake's eye and the spreading dark purple around the socket. He motioned for a legal pad sitting on the stainless-steel hospital tray. Anne Cohen handed him the pad, and he propped it against the bed rail to secure it in place. Using the pen clipped to the paper he wrote. Victor Cohen was right-handed, and the left-handed scrawl was hardly legible.

Good to see you son. Mother was right. Wojicki was not to be trusted. What happened to your eye? Daniel said you'd talk to this Stinnetti fellow. Did this have anything to do with that? He pointed to the injured eye.

"Indirectly, yes, this scratch is a result of meeting Stinnetti. We didn't hit it off well." Jake looked toward the door. The guard was safely out of earshot. He continued in a low voice, "Stinnetti is in on this. He and Wojicki knew each other up in Carson City. Stinnetti is a loan shark. I think Wojicki owed him some money and they set this deal up."

"Jacob, this discussion can wait until your father is stronger. I have to put my foot down," protested Mrs. Cohen.

While exchanging looks, they heard the pen rapping loudly on the pad. The doctor began writing.

No - important. Rest later. When Tom came back, he had IRS liens. Those

116

were later recorded against the property.

Jake cut him off. "I know all about Wojicki and the first and the second loans. How'd they get the money?"

I guess the bank approved the 2 million and funded it just before the 1.5 million was wired. We'd already signed the papers on the 2M pending bank approval. Your mom and I went to Palm Springs for a long weekend—we never knew the bank had funded the larger loan. I went to work on Monday and didn't check on the office until later in the week. I signed a mountain of paperwork before we left for P. S. They must have slipped the transfer order in the package. They got it all...

The writing had been an effort. Victor Cohen was exhausted when he finished and his one unbandaged eye closed as sleep found him. Jake's mind churned in thought. "Anyone talk to Roger Scott yet?"

"Yes," answered Anne in disgust as she walked to the window.

"This whole thing is a nightmare, Jacob," his mother continued, looking out at the parking lot. "The police think your father is involved. They've tracked Tom Wojicki, Cindi Light, and Monk Phillips as far as Lindbergh Field in San Diego. Wojicki flew out a few days earlier, and the other two boarded a flight to Cabo San Lucas on Friday morning."

She paused. With hesitation, she said, "There was also a ticket reserved in the name of Victor Cohen on that flight."

"Mom, surely you don't think Dad was involved?"

"No." She shook her head. "The signs do make you wonder. But your father wouldn't run off like that. Oh, he might leave me. I'm not as young as I used to be..." She laughed tiredly. "It's the development he wouldn't leave."

"He'll sleep for a while now. I suggest we head home. You must be exhausted. I'll leave my car here and ride with you, okay? We can catch up on the way."

"That's fine, Mom," Jake said in a monotone voice.

She collected her belongings, and they began walking through the intensive care unit toward the elevators. Jake looked back at the guard outside the door. He said to his mother, "I'll catch up in a minute. I'm parked near your Tesla, just outside the doctors' parking. I need a moment alone with Dad." Without waiting for her response, he trotted back to the room, exchanging looks with the guard as he went in.

He went to the notepad and pulled off the scribbled pages, folding the papers into his pocket. Turning to leave he heard a tapping on the bed rail. Victor Cohen was clicking his wedding band against the stainless steel. Jake saw the eye was again open and his father's left hand motioned for the notepad. After handing it to his father, Jake watched while he scrawled.

Where is your mother?

"On her way to the car."

I need you to do something. Mother doesn't know it, but I had to hawk the jewel collection to cover costs. I need you to check—make sure the collection is still there. I have a feeling Wojicki cleaned it out too. Your mother will be destroyed if the jewels are gone. Don't tell her if they're missing.

"All right Dad, I'll check on it. Where do I go?"

San Diego. Bayview Jewelry. It's a high-end pawnshop. The amount to get the collection back is 250K. I know you don't have that much money—I just need to know if the set is there. If it's not there, come back and tell me. I'll hire a bounty hunter to find it.

"All right, I'll go tomorrow." Jake looked at the guard. He was still facing out toward the hall. "Dad, is there anything else I can do?"

The open eye closed, and the pen rolled with the hand on the paper. Jake caught it at the wrist and removed the writing instrument then gently placed the arm against his father's battered body. He tore the page off the pad and folded it into his pocket with the others. Before leaving he doodled quickly with the pen on the notepad then snapped off the page, folding it one time down the center. He dropped the page in the trash then left the room.

At the car, his mother asked what had taken so long. He told her he stopped to use the head, then they started toward the family home.

Inside an unmarked van parked in the hospital lot, Detective Chip Collins took off the headphones and hit the 'transmit' button on his radio. Logan got the beep and responded.

"All clear up here. I couldn't hear what was said in the room. Anything valuable? Over."

"Maybe. The kid's been to see the Stinnetti fellow in Carson City. He has the second loan for 1.5 mil. We'll check out this Stinnetti character.

Kid says he's a loan shark. That's interesting. Good work planting the bug. Everything's been loud and clear. Is the old man asleep? Over," replied Chip.

Logan peeked into the room. Dr. Cohen was resting and breathing evenly. "He's out. Over."

"Any hospital types skulking about? Over," asked the detective.

"All clear. Want me to go in and check what the doc wrote? Over," replied the deputy.

"Yeah."

The radio was silent as Logan walked into the room and looked at the notepad. Finding a blank page, he went silently to the trash and withdrew the yellow sheet left there. Unfolding it his face flushed with anger. He crumpled it and threw it back in the garbage container.

After waiting too long for a response, Collins broke the radio silence, "Find anything? Over."

"No. Nothing," Logan barked.

"Brad, you sound pissed. What'd you find?" asked Collins. He waited, then added, "Don't forget, I'm your superior, even if we do drink together. Tell me what you found. Over."

"The doctor's kid drew a dick."

"A dick? You sure?"

"Yeah. A penis. With testicles for feet. And little stick arms. And a badge. On the shaft of the dick, he wrote 'Deputy Brad Logan. Riverside County's Finest.' He put eyes and a sheriff's hat on its head. What a jerk!" he finished and waited for a reply. When it didn't come, he hit the 'transmit' button and asked, "Chip. Are you there? Over."

"Yeah. Sorry! I was laughing so hard I couldn't talk! Save the page! That's an order! I'll place it in the file as evidence," chuckled Collins.

"Right. It'll go straight from the file to the squad room bulletin board. Then someone'll take a pic of it and text it through the department. Sorry. Order disobeyed. Over."

"Insubordination won't get you that promotion to detective," Chip joked. "Okay. Let's take a break and get a bite. I'll put the bug on voice activated."

"Let's walk to the Mexican place on the corner. I want a margarita. Too bad you're in uniform, or you could have one too. Ah, the life of a detective!" Collins sighed. "No one will try to move the doc. Let's pull you out of there and put you in the van tomorrow. I'm going to follow the son and see what he's up to. I like his style. A penis-cop! Can I at least see the artwork?"

"No. You wouldn't think it was funny if it was a picture of you."

"It's not a picture. It's a caricature. Forget about it. Meet me at the restaurant in five minutes," Collins ordered. Then he added, "And Brad, try not to be a dick! I'm out."

CHAPTER 14

WEDNESDAY MORNING

Jake wore an extra-large Bamboo Cay shirt he'd borrowed from his father's closet and a pair of loose-fitting, faded, navy blue Dockers. Whenever he returned to his parents' home, he'd conduct a raid on his father's wardrobe. A week or so after leaving, he'd receive a call from his dad asking the whereabouts of certain garments. Jake would blame the disappearance on a mix-up in the home laundry. Dr. Cohen would clarify that all his shirts were sent out for cleaning and his son was a larcenous, thieving devil.

He sipped coffee while sitting in the Forerunner outside the Inland Savings and Loan building. The scoreboard-style thermometer in front of the bank flashed the time and temperature as Jake awaited the arrival of Roger Scott. He'd seen the temperature climb ten degrees to sixty in the forty-five minutes he'd waited. It was 9:15, and the bank president had yet to arrive. Jake thought about going into the building and reading the paper while he waited, but a voice inside told him to stay here and take the man by surprise.

So, he sat with the tinted window slightly open pretending to enjoy the last few sips of his now cool coffee as he listened to a San Diego-based morning sports radio show.

At 9:25 a.m. a burgundy Jaguar convertible pulled into the space next to the Forerunner. The top was raised, then a man in a charcoal gray suit climbed out with a laptop case. The suit was exquisitely tailored to fit the physique of the banker. The tie, shoes, and belt matched the Jaguar. It would be difficult to make any clothing look good on this rotund man, thought Jake. The tailor should be commended for a fine effort.

With his computer valise in hand, Jake met Roger Scott as the banker walked out of the gap between the cars. They were just about the same height, but Roger was much narrower in the shoulders and vastly larger in the middle. When his eyes rose to meet Jake's, Jake saw surprise with a flash to fear. The banker clutched the case to his chest as if it were a shield. Jake remembered Roger Scott wearing thick glasses and having a bald spot in front. The man before him had a full head of dark hair and no spectacles. Looking closely at the scalp Jake could see the plugs where the hair had been placed.

"Jake Cohen! You startled me!" gasped the banker. "It must be six years since I last saw you. I thought you were in Lake Tahoe."

"Hello, Mr. Scott. I was in Lake Tahoe, but my father was beaten nearly to death last Thursday night. I'm sure you heard about it. Now I'm here for a week or so to help."

Roger Scott shook his head in disbelief. "I've checked in twice a day on his condition. I can't tell you how relieved my wife and I were when we heard he was out of danger. I just hope they catch the thug who did this. It's absolutely abhorrent."

"Yes, it is. The police aren't doing much though," said Jake. His eyes bored holes in the banker as he spoke. "If we can figure out what happened to the money you transferred, we might be able to find the people responsible. Any ideas?"

Roger Scott looked down at the ground and moved a pebble around with his polished burgundy tassel loafer. "None whatsoever," he answered without looking up. "I really don't know anything. I've already told the police that."

"Yeah, I understand," Jake replied. "But I don't understand why you transferred the money so quickly without talking to my father first." He waited for a response.

It didn't come quickly, but finally, Roger Scott replied. "Jake, let's go into my office and catch up. I'll get you a cup of Kona-blend coffee." He put his hand on Jake's back and started walking. Jake went along with him.

Inside, Roger greeted a thick-necked security guard at the door as he and Jake walked toward his office. To the left, tellers handled transactions for customers and in the open center of the building desks sat for new accounts, loans, and other bank business. Roger escorted Jake into his exclusive glass enclosure and offered him a seat. As soon as Jake's backside hit the chair, Roger excused himself and headed into the men's room. In less than five minutes he returned with his face still damp. He sat behind a massive desk of bleached teak.

"Would you like coffee?" he asked as he turned on his computer.

Jake accepted the offer with a nod. "Sure, thank you."

Roger pushed one of twenty buttons on his console phone and spoke, "Betsy, could you bring us two cups of my private blend?" He looked at Jake and asked without taking his finger off the button, "You take anything?"

"No," Jake said as he leaned forward and spoke into the speaker. "And thank you, Betsy."

"No problem sir!" the perky voice responded.

The banker released the button. He placed his hands behind his head and leaned back in the high-backed black leather chair. He was in his element now, like a captain on the bridge of a ship. The flustered look from the parking lot was gone. Jake waited in silence.

Roger inhaled deeply, then with the release of air said, "Where were we? Oh yes, the transfer...

"Jake, I had no choice. I've done fifty transfers like that over the years. Tom Wojicki brought in the paperwork and funds were moved. He said it was imperative the money go out that day. We do it all the time."

"I'm sure you do. But never nearly that amount. And never to an offshore account. And two hundred fifty thousand in cash?" asked Jake incredulously.

"Well," Roger said as he thought for a moment, "We knew about the IRS liens. Tom told me that the IRS was planning to attach and freeze the company accounts immediately. With the money offshore, they'd clear the liens up in less than a week, and the funds would be wired back. He said the company needed the cash for working capital. Jake, I tried to call your dad twice. And I even authenticated the signature on the transfer slip. Your dad had told me during the prior week he'd be making a large transfer soon."

The coffee arrived, and so did Betsy. She was a shapely bottle-blonde who towered at least six feet with the three-inch heels she wore. Jake noticed the other women in the bank wore business attire, but Betsy wore a crêpe dress of yellow and white plaid. The dress itself was not overly revealing; it didn't carry a high hem or a low neck or back. It did, however, cling tightly to the ample curves underneath and the long, tanned arms and legs protruded proudly from the shoulder straps and hemline. Her face was cute, not beautiful but girlish. Jake had seen at least ten other women working in the bank as he'd passed through and couldn't recall what any one of them looked like. He would be able to evoke a complete description of the woman who set his coffee in front of him later, starting at the powder-yellow colored pumps and ending at the blonde curls cascading from the top of her head. In the company of men over beers, he might even elaborate on the curves and bumps the dress generously displayed.

"Thank you, Betsy," said Jake as she set the cup on a coaster on the desk. He looked directly into her twinkling green eyes.

"You're welcome, Mr.…." Betsy stopped and looked at Roger Scott.

"Betsy, this is Jacob Cohen. He is the son of Victor and Anne Cohen, who I'm sure you remember. Jake is a professional skier."

"Very nice to meet you, Mr. Cohen," she offered. "I love to ski. I try to go once a week in the winter. I tried snowboarding last year, but I always fell right here and got terrible purple bruise patches." She stuck the right side of her rump and thigh out and pointed at it. Jake appraised the landscape.

"You better stick to skiing. Not as many bumps and bruises. But injuries on skis are usually more serious, so be careful." He pointed to the stitches above his purple eye. "Swimsuit season is coming, and you wouldn't want this area to be black and blue." Jake didn't touch her leg but moved his slightly cupped hand gently over the hip an inch above the dress. She smiled.

"That'll be all, Betsy." Roger's voice carried a firmness that sounded more like a father talking to a daughter than a boss talking to an employee.

Or did it carry a hint of jealousy? Jake wondered.

"Okay. If you'd like a little more just buzz me." Her eyes sparkled as they caught Jake's upon leaving.

"Betsy's interesting," said Jake after the door closed.

"She's a diamond in the rough. Just turned twenty. Came in about a year ago looking for a teller's position but got flustered behind the counter. She'd be wasted there anyway. I'm keeping her on as my personal assistant for a few years until she matures, then I'll move her into real estate lending. It's no sin to use the gifts the good Lord gave you to open doors. Between you and me, I plan to use the gifts the good Lord gave Betsy to make some money for the bank.

"If I were a single man twenty years younger, I'd figure out a different use for those gifts," he said with a wink.

Jake evaluated the man sitting behind the desk. Convertible Jaguar, hair implants and dyeing the gray, eye surgery to shed the glasses, and the attractive young assistant. Father Time was chasing, and Roger Scott was running. Fast.

Jake shook off the tangential thoughts and sipped his coffee. It was excellent.

"So, Roger, I understand you attempted to talk to my father. Why didn't you call my mother at the house?"

The banker fidgeted before answering, "I didn't think it was necessary. Wojicki was a partner in the business. Everything was done under bank guidelines." He looked at the floor as he spoke. Then he looked up. Staring directly at Jake he said, "I did try to call. I'll show you the records of the two phone calls if you'd like, Jake. In retrospect, yes, I should have called your mother. But a phone call is not required. This is not my fault."

His head shook vehemently in absolution as he spoke. The banker's bases were covered.

The two were quiet for a moment as Jake set his coffee on the coaster. Picking up the small leather valise he'd carried in, he reached in and removed photographs.

"What have you got there?" asked the bank president.

"Just some pictures," answered Jake.

"Roger, you're in this up to your eyeballs. No friend would let loose over 3.6 million bucks of their friend's money without some sort of verification. And two hundred and fifty thousand of it in cash? I'm not buyin' it.

"I don't think you did it for money. Mom says you're thinking of selling out to a national banking power. As the major stockholder, you'll have tens of millions after the buyout. Rumor is maybe over twenty million. So, what's your angle?"

Roger rose from behind the desk with a look of fury. "How dare you accuse me! It's not my fault your father and mother got mixed up with a crook. Or maybe your dad was planning on running off to Cabo. Your father is a criminal, or he did something stupid. Either way, it's not my fault. I don't appreciate you coming into my place of business and making accusations. Get out of here!"

Jake saw the bank staff and customers look toward the glass walls. "I'll leave when I'm ready. Those aren't kind comments to make about a loyal bank customer and friend of yours. You're awfully quick to pass the buck on this.

"You know this woman?" He flipped over the photographs and tossed them on the desk.

Roger recoiled at the sight of the first image. Regaining composure, he picked up the pages and looked at the pictures. He swallowed hard twice before answering. "I've never seen her before in my life."

"Why Roger, you're trembling. She's a captivating woman, isn't she? Her name is Cindi Light. Does that ring a bell?" asked Jake. He'd downloaded the photographs from the Imagine Escorts website and printed them last night at his parents' house.

"No. I've never seen her and never heard the name. And I've had enough of you. You've been trouble since high school. Dropping out of college, in and out of jail for brawling and lascivious behavior, being nothing but a ski bum when your father tried to hand you the world on a silver platter. I don't need to put up with this nonsense, especially from a loser like you." He pushed a button on his phone and spoke, "Betsy, ask the security man to come to my office and escort Mr. Cohen out of the bank. Tell him to see that Mr. Cohen leaves the premises."

"Right away, sir!" Betsy answered with a shocked tone. Jake watched through the glass as she rose and quickly walked toward the entry. Their eyes met for a moment, and hers rolled upward. Jake remained seated in the office.

"Can I have my photos back?"

"I have no use for them." He pushed the pages to the edge of the desk. Jake placed them in the worn leather valise but did not rise.

"You need to get up and start moving, Jake. Friend of the family or not, I won't hesitate to have you forcefully removed."

Jake was leaning on the armrest of the chair. "What made you do it, Roger? Selling out my parents... You know where Wojicki and Cindi went? Probably not. Your role was just to send the money, wasn't it?"

"You have about twenty seconds left to babble. The security guard is heading this way, and I have work to do. I'll forget this conversation so the relationship with your family won't be damaged. The one bad apple off their tree won't spoil things." He turned to his computer and started tapping at the keyboard.

Jake stood as the burly guard reached the door. Upon entering, the thick man grasped him by the left wrist. Jake quickly twisted his arm away toward the thumb of the security man and easily broke the hold. The guard stood motionless in surprise.

"Don't try to hold my hand. You're not my type. I'll leave, but without you as my escort. Otherwise, we're going to have a situation here. Okay?"

The guard looked at Roger Scott. The banker didn't look up. "Let him walk out. Just follow him to make sure he goes." With a wave of his hand, he dismissed them.

The guard gave a head motion toward the door. "Let's go, sir."

Jake snatched a business card off Roger's desk and started walking. The banker called out, "One more thing, Jake. Keep quiet about this. If you don't, I'll have to file suit against you for slander and defamation."

"It's only slander if it's not true. Thank you for your time today." Jake said.

As he walked past Betsy's desk with the security guard in tow, he winked at her. She blushed.

In a far corner of the parking lot, Detective Chip Collins looked up from the sports page. Jacob Cohen's appearance in the doorway was a welcome sight to relieve the tedium of scanning NBA box scores. What piqued Collins's interest most was that a uniformed guard followed Cohen out of the door and to his SUV. He pushed the button on the radio.

"Brad. It's me. You read? Over."

After a few seconds, a reply came back. "Yeah. Whad'da you got? Over."

"Our boy's been busy. He stopped by the Cohens' bank and ambushed the bank president in the parking lot. I thought the guy was going to pee his pants. I followed them in and went through the teller line. The bank pres and the Cohens' kid were in his office. I didn't want the banker to make me. So, I've been sitting here, oh, maybe twenty minutes. Now the kid just got kicked out by security.

"We need to find out what happened in the bank while the feathers are still flying, but we need to stay on the doc's kid, too. If we lose him, we likely won't pick him up again until tomorrow. Over."

Logan replied, "Okay, nothing is happening here at the hospital. This bug ain't doin' us any good cause the doc can't talk. We'll leave the recorder on voice actuated. Over."

"Right. Go talk to the banker. Plain clothes. Just flash your badge and tell him you're my partner. Ask him if he's seen Cohen. Tell him we got word the kid is running around town causing trouble and we wanted to find out if he's been to the bank."

"I'll follow the doc's kid. Over," Chip reported.

"Roger that. I'll be at the bank in ten minutes." The radio went silent.

Collins started his unmarked Ford the second the Forerunner pulled out. A metallic-tan Mercedes coupe pulled out in front of him and turned in the same direction as Jacob Cohen. The detective used the car as a buffer to stay behind the SUV without being seen. Fortunately, the car was going the same direction and made for natural cover.

To Chip's surprise, the Forerunner went a few blocks then stopped in a florist's parking lot. The greater surprise, however, came when the tan Mercedes abruptly pulled over to the side and parked along the road a half block before the shop.

A coincidence?

He continued past the shop for a half a mile then doubled back and parked in a grocery store lot across the street. Pulling out a pair of small but high-powered binoculars, he focused on the license plate of the Mercedes. He radioed headquarters with the plate number. The query would take a few extra minutes as it was a Nevada license. He waited.

Less than ten minutes later, Cohen emerged from the door of the shop carrying nothing. *He must have had something delivered,* Collins thought. Maybe flowers to the hospital...

Word had come in; the Mercedes was owned by a corporation in Carson City, Nevada. They were now checking to see who owned the company. As Cohen pulled away, the Mercedes again fell in behind at a distance.

Interesting, Collins thought as he moved in line with the other two cars. He maintained a considerable gap between him and the members of the newly formed caravan.

He followed the two for a few more minutes. The SUV stopped at a coin-operated car wash, and the Mercedes stopped too, this time a block back. Collins parked a quarter of a mile away. He decided the man in the coupe was good, maybe a pro. Cohen hadn't seen him, but the third guy never looked in Chip's direction, and the detective was certain he hadn't been picked up. He'd increase his distance and watch.

Good things happen to the one who waits. Good detectives knew it.

Jake washed the road grime off the vehicle and towel-dried it with rags he'd grabbed at his parents' home. As he cleaned, he noticed new dents from the rocks and other hazards of the mountain roads he frequented. He'd need a new ride soon. With well over 200,000 hard miles on her, this one had about a year left.

At 11:30, he wiped away the light perspiration on his forehead and arms with a clean towel. He hopped in the Forerunner and headed back in the direction of the bank. He didn't notice when a tan Mercedes and another nondescript Ford fell in behind him.

Jake parked at a Mexican restaurant. He went inside, and the hostess seated him at a shaded table on the patio where he could see the entrance. It was 11:50, and the lunch crowd was not yet thick. A waitress brought water with chips and salsa and offered a margarita or a beer. Jake declined and scanned the menu.

At seven minutes after noon, a tall blonde in a fetching yellow dress walked in. Jake rose and gave a two-fingered wave. She spotted him and returned a smile of recognition, moving in his direction. When she reached the table, he rose and pulled her chair back. She hesitated. He motioned for her to sit by opening his hand toward the chair. She planted her shapely bottom on the seat. Jake thought (even hoped) the tight dress might burst but the fabric stretched across her thigh and rump to accommodate the young lady's new position.

"Sorry," Betsy giggled, "I'm not used to a man pulling out my chair for me. At first, I thought you were taking it for yourself. Most men I know haven't got much in the way of manners."

"Then you're associating with the wrong men," Jake said with a smile. "You need to train them to pamper you. But not too much. You'd be spoiled."

"Fat chance of that. The only thing my boyfriend spoils is his car. Five hundred horsepower, polished lacquer finish, and I'm the requisite blonde in the front seat," she sighed.

Her voice carried a mild twang as she spoke. It immediately made Jake think of stock cars and country music.

"I'm honored you'd share lunch with me. I wasn't sure you'd come."

She shook her head. "This isn't a date. When you called my first thought was a 'no.' You sounded sincere, so I switched to 'maybe,' but I really had no intention of showing up. Then the flowers came. Bobby, my boyfriend, would *never* spring for a dozen roses. Any spare cash he has goes to car parts and beer. But I'm committed to him; you need to know that up front.

"I guess you can afford it though, your family havin' all that money and you being a pro skier," added Betsy. "The flowers did it alright. I decided I'd meet you and tell you I wasn't interested face to face. I won't tell Bobby though; he'd come lookin' for you."

When he'd phoned Betsy at the bank, he could hear her hesitation about joining him for lunch. Eighty bucks and a dozen roses later he had a date.

"What's it like, Mr. Cohen, being a professional skier?" she asked excitedly.

"Please Betsy, call me Jake."

"Okay, Jake, it is. But tell me. It must be a dream life. I'd just love to live in the mountains. Clean, crisp air and beautiful scenery. Skiing every day and getting paid for it!"

"It has its moments. But life in the mountains can be tough. Fighting snow all the time... And there's no good Mexican food," laughed Jake. She laughed too.

The waitress came and took their order. Jake wanted a carne asada plate with rice and beans but instead opted for a chicken salad. He still had the world championships in a few weeks and wanted to stay in shape even if he wasn't training. Also, the lunch he'd selected was four dollars cheaper—not a huge sum, but his bankroll was limited and shrinking fast.

Betsy ordered a salad too with vinegar and oil dressing. She drank iced tea. Jake was thankful for the inexpensive choices of his lunch date. When the waitress departed, they continued chatting.

"Do you always eat like a sparrow?" he asked.

"God no! I can put it away at times. But Bobby dudn't like it...," she stopped her speech. Continuing, she corrected, "Bobby *doesn't* like it when I put on weight. Please excuse me. Mr. Scott is helping me with the grammar and other stuff. Anyway, I've been gaining a few pounds, and I want to watch my figure. I don't want to be a fatso!"

Jake gave her a sideways look and asked, "Mr. Scott is helping you?"

"Oh my, yes. You see, I come from a farm just up the road in Chino Hills. Not really a farm, but my daddy is a dairyman. I know the smell of a hunnerd milk cows on a hot, windless day.

"Daddy and Mom wasn't—excuse me—weren't big on grammar and etiquette. They expected us all to get good grades but didn't do much to train us in the ways of life outside the farm. So, Roger is helping. I want to be a businesswoman, a loan representative. With Mr. Scott's help, I'll do it."

She sat erect with her back straight and her left hand resting on her left thigh midway between her knee and hip as she spoke. The elbow of the right arm never touched the table, but the forearm rested on it. Her napkin was folded perfectly in her lap. Jake noticed she chewed gum, but very gently, almost imperceptibly.

Other than the gum and the occasional slip to the country speech, she looked like an illustration from Emily Post. Or on second thought, with the long frame and curvaceous figure under the tight yellow dress, a cross between Emily Post and Victoria's Secret.

"What does Mr. Scott get out of this?" Jake asked.

Her eyes gleamed as she said, "He says I'll make money for the bank someday. A lot of money. So I'm worth investing time in."

"Does he spend a lot of time with the other loan representatives? Or did he when they were training?"

She thought for a moment. "No. Most of them come in trained, though. Loan reps make great money. Especially those working for our bank. The best in the business come to Mr. Scott for a job. He's got the top reps lining up at the door."

"Betsy, if Roger Scott has the top loan reps in the area coming to him begging for work why do you think he's spending so much time with you? Please don't be hurt, but it doesn't seem to me that the time he's spending cultivating your talents is necessary."

She looked down at the table and fumbled with a tortilla chip before answering. "It is a little odd. Daddy said it was inappropriate, and I thought it was weird at first. I know I'm built pretty well. Maybe not a super-model but I've been picked to be trophy-girl at the track more than once.

"I thought Mr. Scott was just another old pervert trying to score with a young babe too. As it turned out, he's been a perfect gentleman. He hasn't tried to touch anything he shouldn't. I like the attention, too. I feel as though someone's investing time in me as a person, not just an object. Without Mr. Scott, I'd probably have just married Bobby and started havin' kids. I plan on at least three, but there's things I want to do first. It's a ten-year plan." She spoke with commitment and certainty. Jake admired her. He'd never really committed to anything further than three months ahead.

"Sounds like Mr. Scott is a modern-day Henry Higgins," laughed Jake.

"Who?"

"Never mind, Ms. Dolittle," he laughed, "Someday you'll figure it out."

She blushed and smiled.

The waitress brought their lunches. Betsy gingerly put a piece of the napkin over her mouth and pushed her gum onto it with her tongue and set it aside.

"Don't tell Mr. Scott I was chewing gum," Betsy giggled. "He says gum-chewers are never seen as contenders in the business world."

With a sideways tilt to his head, he said, "Betsy, when I left the bank did you notice that a guard escorted me to the door? I don't think I'll be telling Roger Scott anything. The man won't let me within fifty feet of him."

"Well, I wondered about that. I thought your family and his was—excuse me—*were* close. I asked him about it when you left, and he said you were like a black sheep and had been a problem for your family since high school. In jail a few times for this and that. That's really one of the reasons I came to lunch. This is all so sinister—a stranger with a shiner and stitched-up eye ruffling the bank president's feathers, and the cops coming by the bank all the time. Another one came in just after you left. Deputy Logan was his name, I think. Kinda handsome and strong. I don't watch soap operas, so I have to get my excitement where I can. What's going on? Mr. Scott says it's none of the bank's business. He's involved though, isn't he?" Her eyes twinkled with excitement.

Jake laughed. "I've never been called sinister. I'll admit I've spent a night or two in the slammer, but the only thing I was guilty of was having too much fun. Waking up with a bunch of drunks and hoodlums does wonders to calm a wild young man down. Trust me."

"You've never been to prison? Or long-term at the County?" she asked expectantly.

"Sorry, no."

They had nibbled as they talked. Now a quiet came over them as is apt to happen when strangers meet. They ate for a few minutes during the void in conversation. Jake broke the silence by tossing the photos of Cindi Light on the table, hoping for some kind of reaction.

"Betsy, do you know this woman?" he asked directly.

Her body language changed. She lost the smile she'd worn since her arrival and stopped working on her salad. "She's a bank customer," she said flatly.

"Was she ever friendly with Mr. Scott?"

She hesitated. Fidgeted in her chair. Cleared her throat. Then she picked up her fork and took another bite of her salad without answering.

"She was friendly with Mr. Scott, wasn't she? And you don't like this woman much?" probed Jake.

Betsy turned her head sideways and focused her eyes on nothing. Finally, she said, "Not exactly dislike. The air in the bank would change when she'd walk in. She's got… What would you call it? A 'presence' about her. Kinda like when a mean dog joins a group of others playing. They get along fine, but you know you have to watch the one 'cause it might latch on to the throat of one of the others any second. There's just something not quite right.

"Very pretty though. Stylish. Like I said before, I know I'm built well, but I don't have that sophistication she carries. She's drop-dead beautiful. Men hit on me all the time. I guess that's 'cause I look approachable. Miss Light gives the impression she's unattainable. But there's something else. She's rock hard. Only another woman would pick it up.

"So, it's not that I don't like her. She's scary. It's more fear than dislike. Or maybe even pity. To be that beautiful but not happy…"

Jake was quiet for a moment, then asked, "You only answered half my question. What about her relationship with Mr. Scott?"

"You'll have to ask Mr. Scott about that."

"I did. When I showed him these photos, he said he'd never seen this woman before. Then he called security and had me tossed out of the bank."

"It didn't look like you got tossed to me. That security guard has hands like a vise. You popped out of his hold like he was a child. It surprised him," she offered as she smiled.

Her expression changed. She looked troubled as she asked, "Did he really tell you he'd never seen her before?"

Jake raised his eyebrows, stitches included, and gave an affirmative nod.

She suddenly slumped in her seat, left elbow on the table. The perfect sitting posture was gone. The image of her mentor had been shattered. He'd lied. "Well I'm not going to be the one who rats out Roger Scott, but I'll tell you he knows her. Anything more you need to figure out on your own."

"Betsy, do you remember my father and mother?" asked Jake.

"Sure. Your dad at least. I'd probably recognize your mother too, but your dad came in all the time. Closed-door meetings with Mr. Scott. He's handsome, for an older man."

"Why don't you stop by Memorial Hospital today after work? Room 412. You can see firsthand what Roger Scott is involved in."

Her perfect posture had returned. She replied, "Jake, I appreciate the lunch and the flowers, but I'm not getting involved with you or this. Mr. Scott has given me a great opportunity, and I'm not about to screw it up. I'm sorry." Her statement carried finality.

"I understand," said Jake. He changed the subject.

The final fifteen minutes were pleasant, filled with laughter and mild flirting. He paid the bill and walked her to her car.

"I enjoyed lunch today, Betsy. Shall we get together again?" he asked as she slid into the driver's seat.

"Nope," she smiled and looked him directly in the eye. "Jake, most men who chase me want me for my body. I'm workin' to change that so they see me as intelligent first. But you don't want me for either my mind or my curves or anything in between. You want me to be a spy inside the bank, and I won't do that.

"Thanks again for lunch. Maybe I'll see you around town sometime. I'm truly sorry I can't help you." Betsy closed her car door and drove away.

Jake looked at his watch, then trotted to his car. Betsy was pretty sharp. She'd do well in business.

He'd swing by the hospital then run for San Diego and hopefully arrive before closing time at the jewelry store.

CHAPTER 15
WEDNESDAY AFTERNOON

"Nicki, calm down! You have nothing to worry about. The doc's kid can poke around all he wants. He won't find us. No one will find us," said Tom Wojicki into his GlobalStar phone. For the first time in weeks, he was relaxed. The trio was thousands of miles from Southern California, and they hadn't told a soul where they were going.

"Don't tell me to calm down, asshole! You told me the worst-case scenario was Doc Cohen would find some way to bail himself out and pay back the loan with interest. Now I got $2,000,000 more in front of my loan! Within a week, his kid shows up on my doorstep with that fuckin' country bumpkin sheriff. This ain't been easy so far. Where the hell are you? I got a right to know," Nicki Stinnetti barked into the phone.

The reception on the satellite connection was remarkably good, Wojicki noted as he sipped his scotch. In the past, he would cower and whine when Nicki yelled. Now he was calm and in control. The coming days would be warm and the nights pleasant. He might live here for a few years, or he might stay for good if he could master the local language. That would be decided later. For now, he was content. The IRS and his creditors were far behind. He hadn't felt this much freedom in years.

Cindi Light slept on a nearby couch. They hadn't made love in weeks, he suddenly realized. The stress of pulling this caper off had taken its toll on both of them. She was beautiful while sleeping, and he decided to start making up for lost opportunities tomorrow. Only Monk had seemed unfazed by the whole affair.

"Answer me you fuckin' idiot! Where the hell are you?" Stinnetti's rasping snapped him out of his musing.

"Sorry Nicki, I can't tell you. I know that wasn't part of our deal, but everything is going to be okay. You're going to make millions on this even with the two million more in front of your note. Vic Cohen won't be able to pay it back. The only trails we left have dead ends, and they'll spend months chasing those if the cops bother to look at all."

"It ain't the law I'm worried about. This kid snoopin' around has me spooked. You told me there'd be questions asked. I was prepared for that. But this son of a bitch already made a connection between me and Monk and you and the whore. You sure that tramp you got with you didn't tell any of her girlfriends where you was headed? Cohen's been to Reno and talked to one of the broads from the escort service. Paid for a date and didn't boff her. Just asked a bunch of questions. Now he's ruffling up the banker. He's putting things together too fast. I don't like it."

Tom looked across the great room of the hacienda he'd leased for two years. Cindi still dozed. The derogatory comments made by Nicki Stinnetti about her annoyed him, but he let them pass. That part of her life was history. Nicki was a hood. It was his nature to be crass.

He took a pull of scotch and answered, "Cindi couldn't have told anyone where we are. Monk either. Both of them were kept in the dark about our destination until we got on the plane. I've met Jacob Cohen. He's a ski bum. When he'd run out of money, his daddy would give him a job working on our projects. He was smart and worked hard, but as soon as snow fell in the mountains or big waves started breaking on the coast he'd be gone. Every time he left, it broke the doc's heart. He'll give up quickly."

There was a moment of silence on Nicki's end. Finally, he said, "You're wrong. If it were just the money, I'd agree he'd quit. But it's more. Why the hell did you have to beat up his dad? I saw it in his eyes; he's pissed as hell and he ain't gonna quit."

"Monk got out of control; you know how easily that can happen. It won't make a difference. Don't do anything rash that will get the law more involved than they already are. I know you're not accustomed to working like this, but the foreclosure will give you the biggest payoff of your life. This time the law is actually on your side."

"You got away with two fucking million more, you bastard. I wish I'd never let you talk me into this!"

"That two million is your guarantee of close to five mil. You should be thanking me, Nicki," chuckled Tom.

"All right, I'll be patient. But if the doc's kid gets any closer, I'm going to have my guy ice him. He's on him now."

"Nicki, there's no reason for that."

"Oh yeah, there are a few. First, I don't want anybody finding you unless it's me. You owe me over two mil with the IRS shit I have to pay. Until that's paid back, you're on the hook. And second, in all my years of loanin' money to these deadbeats, no one has ever kicked me in the balls. This is personal. My developer friends say there's still big bucks in that project, but my patience has its limits."

Tom Wojicki said goodbye and hung up. Wojicki decided that the newly created Tom Miller would get a new number from GlobalStar. He never spoke to Nicki Stinnetti again.

CHAPTER 16

San Diego offers the best climate on earth, Jake reaffirmed as he drove down Rosecrans Boulevard toward the marinas on Point Loma. Someday he and Janelle might retreat from the snow-covered mountains and settle here, he decided as he watched the lengthening shadows cover the bay.

During his stop at the hospital, he'd reiterated the details of the conversation with Roger Scott while his father listened. When he finished, Victor Cohen scribbled his thoughts on the notepad.

The banker had *not* been told to expect a large transfer of funds. He was surprised to discover that Roger knew Cindi Light at all. He thanked Jake and offered to reimburse him for the flowers for Betsy, then he dozed off.

Ten minutes later Jake was on Interstate 15, headed south to San Diego.

He'd gone to Bayview Jewelry (which had no view of the bay at all) and met with the proprietor, Willie. He was thick and covered with more hair than Jake had ever seen on a human, like a six-foot-tall teddy bear in a silk suit. Behind his black-granite counter, Jake noticed the protruding butt of an aluminum bat, and he kept a handgun for the entire world to see under his old-fashioned cash register. The storefront was all windows so Willie could see who was coming long before they reached the door, where he buzzed them in after inspection.

The jewels were gone. Willie verified that Tom Wojicki paid the fronted pawn money back plus the fee in cash last week. With the proper paperwork, again signed by Victor Cohen, the jewels left with Tom. The jeweler apologized, and Jake had bidden him adieu. Willie, the consummate salesman, reminded Jake to return if he needed anything.

Jake headed next to Lindbergh Field, the international airport serving San Diego. He'd purchased a ticket on the Racor's Edge company credit card for a flight out tomorrow morning, then phoned his boyhood friend, Don Austin, to see if he could stay at his home overnight.

The two had grown up together, roaming the hills and skiing and wakeboarding at Canyon Lake for countless days as carefree youths. In high school, they battled together on the gridiron and wrestling mat. After graduation, their paths had gone in different ways.

Don Austin had a gift. He could gain instant rapport with individuals and crowds alike. While in college he'd started a small marketing company. His ability to charm others soon turned into large contracts, and his small company had exploded into a massive advertising firm. When he married three years ago, Jake stood at his side.

When Jake phoned, Don explained that he and the missus were having some problems. His incredible workload was burdening the marriage, and his wife was demanding more of his time at home. They'd been in counseling for almost a year, at least when he didn't have to cancel a therapy session for an appointment or other business crisis.

Don told him they were "working on it," and a houseguest might complicate things. Jake said he understood and would get a motel. Don told him that was nonsense. The Austins' yacht sat in a slip near the airport, and after a quick conference call to the dockmaster, Jake was set with a floating condo for the night. During their conversation, a call had come in Don had to take, so an assistant arranged a tab for dinner and breakfast at the yacht club, a shuttle to the airport, and parking for his car as long as he needed it. Jake protested. An Uber would be fine, but the assistant explained that the shuttle company was on retainer and Mr. Austin paid a monthly minimum whether the service was used or not.

The assistant was very efficient. Jake wondered if Mrs. Austin spoke more often with her than with Don.

He found the Kona Kai Yacht Club and located the dockmaster's office. With a gate card and a key to the boat in hand, Jake went directly to the yacht, *Another Page*. The fifty-five-foot custom sportfisher built by Viking Yachts was flawlessly maintained. He stepped inside the salon to find a crystal bucket with six Coors Light longnecks embedded in ice up to their tops. A folded note sat next to the bucket. Dropping his bag and tablet computer on the polished teak table, he pulled one of the bottles from the bucket. Grabbing the note, Jake climbed the ladder to the boat's flybridge wheelhouse and unzipped the Eisenglass entry flap. He settled into the captain's chair and twisted the top off the bottle.

The sun had retreated below the horizon, and the orange-yellow sky was giving way to pink and purple hues. The skyline of the city to the east was beginning to light up for the night's festivities. Downtown San Diego had been a decaying inner-city years ago, but with an aggressive redevelopment plan it was now the chic place for the up and coming. The homeless who'd controlled the area for years were still there. The city had no other place to put them, so the redevelopment happened around the indigent souls. It was now en vogue for the beautiful people to stroll among the rabble as they listened to jazz, rock, or reggae in the clubs on Fifth Avenue and B Street after a major league baseball game.

Jake unfolded the note. It was in Don's nearly illegible handwriting, and from the mild distortion of the printing, Jake surmised it was faxed. Probably to the boat's machine and the steward who'd delivered the ice bucket folded and left it. Jake read:

Ah, my friend, how our lives have changed. I envy you. Your freedom. Five more years, then I sell this monster of a business and retire. Then you and I will take the boat you're sitting on to the South Pacific and fish and surf until our arms grow weary.

I'm sorry to hear about your family and the jam they're in. Good luck. Call when you get back. I'll sneak away, and we'll paddle out for a surf session. Feel free to use the boat anytime for as long as you'd like. God knows we never have time.

Time changes us, but not our friendship. That shall endure. Don

---

Jake set the note down on the chart table and looked around him. The teak steering wheel on this boat probably cost more than his net worth. He *envied* Don Austin.

The view of the San Diego skyline from the flybridge of the boat was spectacular, and he decided to enhance the scene with a second, then a third Coors from the ice bucket.

His life was changing. He would soon no longer be a competitor or a ski bum. He could bear the burden if the yoke of responsibility were placed upon him gently. Janelle understood, and that was one of the things he loved about her.

140

Jake took the last sip of beer number three then collected the empty bottles and descended from the boat's bridge. He locked the cabin of the yacht and headed for the club restaurant.

————————————————————

In a municipal parking lot across the street from the Kona Kai Yacht Club Chip Collins dialed his phone. His call was answered on the first ring.

"Hey Brad, I need a favor. It's important to the case."

"Sure."

"Go by my house. There's a bag packed for me. I called, and Lashonda put together everything I need."

"Roger. By the way, when I talked to the bank president, he panicked. Told me he hadn't seen the doc's kid, but he'd call if he showed up. The man's scared. The guy started babbling about how he knew Doctor Cohen was turning into a crook. He went on about how sad it was the doc was running out on his wife and family. He really wants this to go away. Pin it on Cohen and be done with it."

"You think the doc is guilty?" Chip asked.

"Guilty as hell. He signed all the transfers for the money, and he had a plane ticket out of the country. Something just went wrong. Doc Cohen and the big guy probably got into it over money, and the guy thumped him," answered Logan. He added, "How about you? You think he did it?"

"Brad, I can't figure out the 'why' in the doc's case. And now the banker is scared and lying. Something's not right with this. I'm going to stay on the Cohens' kid."

"Okay. You're in charge. What next?"

"Get the bag. Come to the Kona Kai Club in San Diego. Google it."

"Roger. I should be there in less than three hours. You still have the third guy with you?"

"Yep. He checked into a hotel about a block down the street. Still hasn't spotted me. Tenacious fellow. The car is under a dummy corporation owned by Stinnetti Lending. Same name as the second loan holder on the doc's development. By the way, you should bring the van, so we have a place to sleep."

"We?" asked Logan incredulously.

"Yes, we. I need you to spell me watching these guys so I can get a few hours rest before I fly," Chip replied.

"All right, I'm on my way. Where are you going?"

"Cabo San Lucas. One p.m. flight tomorrow."

"Shit, Chip! The brass will have your ass if they find out you followed someone into Mexico!"

"They won't find out. I'll leave my gun and badge with you. Be sure my passport is in my bag when you grab it. I'm coming back in two days. They probably won't even miss me at the station."

"I'm gonna fry for this. I can feel it already," Logan said. "Okay, I'll see you in a few hours."

Chip got out of the car to stretch his legs. He walked down the street and into the yacht club driveway. Passing the empty guard shack, he moved to the club building where he entered and took a seat at the bar. Dressed in tan Dockers and a sky-blue polo shirt he fit right in, except for being the only African-American in the place. The bartender served Chip a Ballast Point Yellowtail Ale. A basketball game was just starting on the big screen, and the crowd was light. He positioned himself to get a view of the game and the gate to the docks at the same time, then ordered fish and chips along with the beer. Then he waited.

In a nearby hotel room, Bennie Temple phoned Nicki Stinnetti.

"Cohen is movin' around pretty fast," he reported to his boss. "The bank this morning, lunch with a broad, the hospital, a jewelry store in San Diego, and the airport. Now he's settled down on a boat. Big fucker. Must be sixty feet long. Wojicki say anything about his family havin' a boat?"

"Hell, who knows? You think he's finding anything?" asked Stinnetti.

"Can't tell for sure, but yeah, I think he's on to something. He went straight to the airport after the jewelry place. International departures. Looked to me like he bought a ticket on Alaska Airlines. Don't know where, but I'll figure it out. My guess is for tomorrow. Want me to follow him?"

"Shit!" Stinnetti muttered, "Yeah, follow him."

"I ought'a just whack him now. Pretty quiet here. I got a silencer with me. Just give me the go-ahead, and this kid won't be no problem to you no more," said Bennie.

Nicholas Stinnetti was silent for a moment. He'd ordered arms and fingers broken as he roughed-up debtors when they couldn't pay. But he'd never ordered anyone's death.

He rubbed his groin. It was still sore and inflamed from Jake's kick a few days ago. And he'd never had so much money riding on one deal. This was the big one... The decision was made.

"Go ahead. Whenever you think it's best," said Stinnetti hesitantly.

"I'll try it tonight. If I don't get him, I'll follow him until I get a chance. I always carry my passport, so if he leaves U.S. soil, it won't be no problem. In my line of work, you never know when you might have to leave the country in a hurry," Bennie stated with a graveled laugh.

"Keep me updated. You sure I ought'a do this?" Stinnetti swallowed hard after speaking.

"No problem. Just relax and leave this to me," offered Bennie as he screwed the silencer onto the barrel of his small handgun. It lacked range, but he was an expert. It would be no problem. He checked the clip, then the action of the gun. Up to now working for Stinnetti had been boring. Finally, he'd get a chance to work his craft.

The two men hung up. Stinnetti headed for his bar and Bennie Temple headed for the yacht club and the docks.

CHAPTER 17

Jake wanted a burger and fries, but the waitress explained something else had been arranged. The meal started with a spinach salad with hot bacon dressing flambéed tableside, followed by succulent seared diver scallops in garlic, sherry, and butter sauce. Jake downed two glasses of four-year-aged Hopper Creek chardonnay with his feast. No bill arrived, and the waitress explained that everything was covered by Mr. Austin. When Jake tried to leave a tip, she followed him into the bar and returned the two twenty-dollar bills.

A Lakers game was on the television and Jake felt a desire to stoke the embers of the fire. The stress of the last few days had mounted. Tonight, he decided to relax. He'd watch the game and have one, or maybe two more beers then retire to the yacht for needed sleep.

When the bartender had asked what he'd take, Jake's mouth betrayed his common sense.

"Double Patron on the rocks with a splash of Gran Marnier and a lime squeeze." When the bartender raised an eyebrow, Jake had added with a salty growl and a smile, "Don't worry, I'm not getting behind the wheel tonight." The bartender smiled back and poured a heavy-handed double shot of the blue agave tequila into a snifter half full of ice, then added just a few drops of the orange liqueur and the concoction was topped off with the lime. Jake slid onto the barstool, swirled the mixture around a few times in the glass, and took a sip. He smiled and nodded his approval to the bartender.

Before the evening was over Jake had one more. When the crowd had thinned the bartender joined him, placing his cocktail in a coffee cup in case management happened to stop by.

The Lakers played their typical lackadaisical game of basketball, managing to keep the game close through three quarters. In the fourth, they fought back from a nine-point deficit to hit a winning shot as time expired. Were the glory days returning for the team? Time would tell, but tonight's game was a welcome diversion.

He bid the bartender goodnight shortly after the end of the game. They'd traded jokes and stories and assured each other they'd do it again sometime. When he stood, he experienced an unfamiliar dry mouth and a brief loss of balance. He forced himself to stand straight and gave a final wink to the barkeep, then headed for the bunk on his friend's yacht.

In the shadows between the boats, Bennie Temple crouched. Waiting. Initially, he'd been worried about the task. While he'd killed many men (and one woman) in the past with relative ease, this one might be different. The speed at which the young man moved had astonished him at Stinnetti's home. Bennie's tension lessened as he'd observed his prey through the window at the bar. It looked as though Jake was feeling no pain. In the man's current condition, it would be easy to walk up behind him as he boarded the boat. The silenced weapon in Bennie's hand would make dull coughs as it delivered its shots. First a slug upward through the ribs, destroying the lung and maybe getting a piece of the heart. The .22 caliber pistol probably didn't have the wallop to push a bullet through his victim's chest, but the lead would do enough damage to take Cohen down if it didn't kill him.

Bennie smiled as he looked at the small gun. In the movies, killers carried massive firearms that resembled small cannons. A gun this size was the only truly silenced weapon made, and ballistic testing was inconclusive on these peashooters. A quiet second slug to the back of the head would finish the job. He'd take the wallet to make it look like a burglary then throw the gun off the end of the dock far out into the bay. A smart killer never kept the murder weapon. They probably wouldn't even find this punk until the seagulls began to pick at his unblinking eyes in the morning. Or maybe even the afternoon.

He'd waited until Jake had drained about two-thirds of his drink, then he moved near the marina entrance until a boat owner approached from the dock below. Timing his advance to coincide with the arrival of the yachts-man, he put his phone to his ear and fumbled in his pocket as if looking for a key card. When the security gate was opened by the man on the other side, Bennie had looked away to hide his face and mumbled a "thanks" as he caught the galvanized steel frame. He'd walked onto the dock as the gate clanked shut behind him. The boat owner said nothing and continued on his way.

Before heading to the slip where the boat was moored, Bennie checked the exit to be sure that he didn't need a card key to get out. He was relieved to see that the handle simply turned on the inside of the gate's steel mesh. He walked casually down the dock until he reached the boat Jake had boarded earlier. Taking one last glance to see that he wasn't observed, he slipped in between the boats and took refuge in the shadows of the high bows.

Now he waited…

He heard the metallic sound of the gate squeaking open then clanking shut a few times over the muted music that drifted across the water. Maybe the kid would have another drink… While it meant a longer stay here in the shadows, the extra alcohol would make his job easier. Bennie had learned patience was an asset in his business.

He'd been careful to handle the silenced .22 only with gloved hands. Rather than flying where he'd leave a record, he'd driven to Southern California on the heels of his target. He paid cash at service stations, and his car was registered under a dummy corporation owned by Nicki. The calls made from the cell phone wouldn't be a problem; it was a burner, and he planned to toss it along with the gun. If the cops ever quizzed him about the death of Jake Cohen, he was sipping scotch in a bar in Reno tonight. He'd have friends to back up his story.

The sound of footsteps approaching snapped him to attention. He held the weapon in his gloved hand and crouched deeper into the shadow under the bow of the yacht. As he waited, adrenaline pulsed in his veins. This was his favorite part of this business. Not the killing, but the stalking and the hunt. Outsmarting his prey.

A shadow came into view, followed by the man who cast it. He turned down the same finger of the dock where Bennie crouched and stepped onto the swim platform of the correct boat. The big yacht listed slightly under the man's weight. Bennie rose silently and moved toward the stern. Unseen, he raised the gun and took aim as the man stepped up from the platform less than six feet away. He almost gave the trigger a squeeze but noticed a glint of light off the man's hair. Straight *blond* hair. Not the brown curls he remembered for Cohen.

This was the wrong man. Bennie slowly lowered the hand holding the gun and stepped silently back toward the shadows.

Sensing a presence in the darkness, the man on the boat spun and dropped behind the solid fiberglass rail with surprising quickness. With equal rapidity, the guy was up off the deck and using the rail as cover. The gun in his hand pointed square in the center of Bennie Temple's chest.

"Police officer!" he shouted. "Step into the light with your hands up!"

A small splash was heard from the space between the dock and the yacht.

"Jeezus officer, you scared the hell out of me," answered Bennie as he stepped from the shadows. "I'm just in from out of town, looking at these big boats. Boy, I wish I could afford one."

"Please, step completely into the light. What did you throw in the water? It looked like metal."

Bennie raised his palms and stepped out into the better light of the open dock. "I picked up a fishing weight back there." He motioned to the darkened end of the dock. "When you spun, you scared me so bad I dropped it. How come you ain't in uniform? You got a badge?"

Using his free hand, the officer reached into his jacket pocket. He flipped open a leather case containing his badge.

"I'm off duty. I watched you walk in without a key, so I followed. Took a while to find you. It's obvious you don't own a boat here, so I'll have to ask you to leave," said the officer as put his gun back into the holster under his jacket.

"Yeah. Right away. I was just takin' a walk before bedtime. You know, you Californians are wound a little tight. G'night, officer," said Bennie as he walked toward the gate.

Brad Logan wanted to ask more questions of the man, but he knew he was out of his jurisdiction, so he let the matter pass. When he'd arrived and found Chip's car, it was empty. He started looking for his partner on foot.

He'd first seen the smallish man slip onto the docks and disappear into the shadows. He decided to follow. Whatever the guy dropped gave only a glint of metal as it hit the water, but he surmised it was a weapon of some sort. Maybe a gun or a pipe, or perhaps the shine was the polished leather of a sap. Regardless of what was dumped, Logan was certain it was meant to do harm. Most honest people reacted with more fear when a gun was pointed at them; this man didn't seem flustered at all. And why did the fellow have gloves on? The temperature was cool but not cold.

He pondered as he waited five minutes, then headed toward the parking lot himself.

As he walked along the last leg of the dock before the exit gate, another man approached from the other end. Logan had seen enough intoxicated men to know when an individual's step was forced. The person approaching him was bombed, but still managed an erect stance and walked a straight line. As they passed one another, he looked away and thought he hadn't been recognized, but Jake Cohen stopped and smiled as he stepped in close.

Their eyes locked for a moment.

"Good evening Deputy Logan," said Jake with a thick tongue and breath heavy of alcohol. "Aren't you out of your jurisdiction?"

Logan answered, "Technically, yes, but—"

He never got the chance to finish. With shocking rapidity for a drunken man, Jake gave him a two-handed shove to the chest, and the deputy flew backward into the bay. When Logan caught his breath and tried to tread water, he looked up and saw Jake looking down at him. Then the weight of his Kevlar vest and the heavy steel-toed shoes and weapon began to take him down.

Rolling his eyes, Jake muttered, "Shit!" then jumped off the dock. He caught Logan by the collar just as his nose went level with the water, and with a few strong kicks dragged the deputy to the bank. When both men found their footing on the muddy bottom, Logan loosed an angry roundhouse punch at Jake. The blow was slowed by the heaviness of the wet jacket he wore, and Jake easily blocked it with his forearm. He rolled with the impact into deeper water and swam back to the dock. Hoisting himself up he turned at looked at the officer standing in the shallow water.

"I don't know how you found me, but I'm telling you right now—stop hounding my family. You'll be sorry if you keep this up. I promise you."

Dripping wet, Logan answered, "Are you threatening an officer of the law?"

"You bet. Now dry your sorry ass off and go back to Riverside. Hand out some speeding tickets and bust a jaywalker or two. Do cop stuff but leave my family alone."

"When your father recovers, he's going to jail. The only question is who will send him there—the Feds, IRS, or us?" said Logan. Then he started climbing the rocks below the boardwalk but turned to add, "I'd have made it to shore without your help."

Jake turned and walked toward his floating home for the night, not knowing that the man he just dunked in the bay had likely saved his life.

CHAPTER 18

It is said that only three things on earth last three days—a holiday weekend, a pet goldfish, and a tequila hangover. Jake was a victim of the latter.

He woke up early to a throbbing head and a mouth tasting like sawdust, so he decided to borrow Don's surfboard and wetsuit. After two hours in the waves at Sunset Cliffs on the ocean-exposed side of the point, he was winning the battle of the three-day proverb. The cool salt water crashing over his head and the exertion of paddling and riding the six-foot waves pushed most of the fog of the hangover from his body. Two cups of coffee and a liter of water also helped. He'd be ready for some food in an hour.

The typical early spring marine layer covered the San Diego sky as he hosed the salt water off the wetsuit and the nine-foot longboard. Jake was looking up trying to decide if the sun would emerge today when the phone in the salon chirped. "Hello!" he answered.

"Hello, Jake?" asked a familiar voice.

"Oh, hi Janelle. God, it's great to hear your voice. I've meant to call, but just haven't had a chance. How did you find me here?"

She hesitated before she spoke. "Well, it's been four days since we talked, so I called your parents' house. You're not answering your phone or my texts. Your mom said you went to San Diego for a few days. I called Don's office this morning, and he told me you were on the boat. I've been worried sick. I thought you'd at least call to update me on your dad's condition. Your mother told me he's going to be okay, but I thought I'd hear that from you on Monday. She said you didn't get there until Tuesday afternoon."

Her tone at the end signaled a question. Or was it a challenge?

"Jan, I'm sorry. I just got caught up in things. When I went to see the man in Carson City about the loan, I ran into some problems," he said without elaborating.

"Is that how you cut your eyebrow?"

"Yeah. Turned out the guy's a loan shark. I got out of line, and his collection goon popped me. It's really nothing. Did Mom tell you it was serious?"

Janelle answered flatly, "She never mentioned it."

Jake thought for a moment about possibilities. Janelle's voice carried an unfamiliar coldness. He asked sheepishly, "How did you find out about the cut?"

"From the picture, Jake." Now her voice carried an acute snap.

"What picture?"

"The one on the web. Mt. Rose was so honored to have last year's Far West mogul champion at their mountain that they posted your picture on their website and Facebook and Twitter and Instagram." She went silent after dropping the bomb.

The hangover symptoms he thought he'd whipped surged back into his head and stomach. Only one photo had been taken of him at the mountain. Janelle had seen him with Amber in a very chummy pose after a day on the slopes. He had two days and nights to account for, and he hadn't called her. Now he understood her chilly disposition.

He paused as he tried to encapsulate the tale of his travels. Janelle remained silent on the other end. Deciding to hit only certain points he continued, "I'm assuming the photo you're talking about is of me and a woman. She knows one of the people who ran off with my parents' money—the company bookkeeper. I thought she might be able to help. Her name is Amber. I took her skiing to spend the day asking her about her old friend. As it turned out she was no help."

"This 'Amber' woman doesn't look like a bookkeeper to me. What did she and her friend do together?"

Jake danced around the subject. "They were in business together in Reno," he answered.

"What kind of business?"

"Well, sort of what you do at the mountain. You know, they showed people around Reno and Lake Tahoe. Out of towners mostly. Kind of a hostess business."

"Really? My job is to familiarize people with Kirkwood Meadows and introduce them to the amenities of the resort. I can't imagine that position in Reno. Who do they work for, the Chamber of Commerce?" Janelle asked sarcastically.

Jake swallowed. His stomach churned as he answered, "Well Jan, to be exact, they were professional escorts."

"You spent two days with an escort! Remember Jake, I was a Kings cheerleader for two years. I saw plenty of 'escorts' meeting the players after the games or sitting courtside with the bigwigs. 'Escort' is just a politically correct term for a hooker!"

"I asked her some questions. That was it," said Jake. He left out the information about his sleeping arrangements at Amber's home and his near fall from the fidelity pedestal at dinner. He added to the story, "I slept in the Forerunner. By myself. And I only spent one day with her. Not two." It was the truth; partially. In total, he and Amber had spent less than twenty-four hours together.

She was quiet for a few seconds and when she finally spoke the softness had returned to her voice. "You can tell the whole story when we're together. I've got a nine o'clock tour so I'll have to run. Are you sure you're okay? The bandage over your eye looked pretty big."

"It's going to be fine. I'll take the stitches out later. The cut is centered in the eyebrow, so when it grows back, you'll never see the scar. I've got a massive shiner though," laughed Jake.

"You should have a doctor take those out," she protested. "Okay, Jake. Thanks. I'm over-reacting, I suppose. The whole thing with your family sounds traumatic," she said. In a more upbeat tone, she asked, "What's next?"

"Everything points to Cabo San Lucas, so I'm flying there at 12:50 today."

Janelle protested, "Jake, don't you think the police should take care of this? You're not a detective or anything like that."

"I know my way around Cabo. The gringos have their little enclaves, and I might be able to ferret something out."

"Great. The man I love is taking off to the Third World to chase crooks," she laughed. "You might as well put on a suit of armor and go fight dragons."

He joked back, "I'll stay away from the fire-breathing ones. Love you."

She sighed. "I've got to run for my tour. Call me as soon as you get back. And be careful. I love you too."

He hung up the phone and placed it back on the receiver in the boat's salon.

Curiosity nagged him into turning on his computer. While the machine booted, he hung the wetsuit off the fishing rod rack in the stern to dry and wiped the beads of water off the custom surfboard. After putting it away, he returned to the tablet. With a few quick keystrokes, he had the Mt. Rose website on screen. By clicking on the icon for 'Recent Photos,' he quickly found the picture. The bandage over his eye was clearly visible, but he hardly noticed. Rather, the woman in the photograph captivated him. Her powder suit clung to each bounteous curve, and her shiny black hair blossomed out from under her lime-green headband as she pulled in close to him for the camera.

Too bad I'll never see her again, he thought as he logged off the site and shut the computer down. He picked up the phone and dialed his mother's house for an update before heading south.

CHAPTER 19

The gate for the flight to Cabo San Lucas was crowded with one of the most diverse groups of people Jake had ever seen. Golfers, fishermen, tennis players, surfers, coeds, senior citizens, and entire families all waited patiently or impatiently for transport to the northern fringe of the tropics. Bloody Marys flowed freely from the bar as the open room sizzled with the anticipation of a long weekend or even a week or two in the sun.

The attendant called for the pre-boarding passengers. Buying his ticket only yesterday, Jake's group was the last to board. As he waited, he smiled as he heard a group of surfers chattering nearby.

"Dudes! I'm not gonna make the flight," said one young man loudly as he walked toward his friends. "I was using the head, and some crazy fart on standby offered me a thousand bucks for my seat! The flight sold out yesterday, and he said he has family there. He didn't look like the Cabo type to me, but a grand is a grand!" He fanned out ten $100 bills and held them up for his friends to see.

One of his compadres answered, "Flea, you gotta make the trip! We'll be jones'en without ya', bro!"

Flea answered, "No prob' man! I'm on tomorrow's flight. We fixed it with the lady at the counter. With the extra thou, I'll pick up a new stick. I'll meet you tomorrow by five. We'll all be shreddin' *olas grande* at the green flash glass-off!"

"Damn Flea, you're always droppin' into the killer deals. All right, we'll see ya' tomorrow bro! The Pacificos will be cold. Adios!" said one of the gang.

Jake understood the language they spoke. He smiled to himself and suddenly felt older. Not over the hill, but a certain level of the vitality they possessed had passed him by.

Eventually, his group was called. As he settled into his seat, he was relieved to see that his traveling partner in the next seat was an African-American man who looked to be in his early thirties. Still nursing the fading hangover,

Jake had feared the prospect of being stuck with one of the yammering surf rats for the flight. He placed his pack on the floor next to the man's bag of tennis rackets. They exchanged the brief hellos that travelers often do then each went about reading the utter nonsense the airlines provided in the seat-back.

Neither raised his head as a smallish fellow passed in the aisle with his back to their seats, but with a sideways glance, Chip Collins recognized the man who'd been following Jake for the past few days. With a quick flash of the badge, the deputy had arranged to be seated next to Cohen for the flight.

A few rows back in the plane the shrill voice of one of the surfers could be heard giving advice to a first-time voyager to Cabo San Lucas.

"Dude, take it from me, you gotta lose the wing tips at the airport! You'll need shorts too; those wool pants will be way bogus in the heat. Don't worry man! I'll tell ya' everything you need to know on the way, bro! We gotta look out for each other. You got Flea's seat, so it's like you're one of us now."

Bennie Temple looked at the kid seated next to him. He suddenly wished he hadn't left his other gun in the car, but the Mexican authorities frowned heavily on travelers carrying weapons. Bennie knew that one could obtain a gun in nearly any country with a little effort.

The reward of popping Jake Cohen would be worth the agony of two hours next to this kid.

CHAPTER 20

The sun danced atop the now black mountains to the west as Jake walked to the Rancho Buena Vista bar and ordered a Pacifico beer. The nearby pool surface glistened muted gold under the fading sunlight while small waves breaking on the beach one hundred feet away rhythmically clapped on the sand. With last night's bender lingering he felt a Coke or water would be better, but as he planned to ask a few questions, he thought the beer might help him blend in with the crowd of gringos.

The stories overheard from the resort guests were all the same, with one of two endings. Either the 'big one' was fought and landed as a result of the incredible skills of the angler, or the subject fish got lucky and escaped to fight another day. Jake smiled as he listened to the thin midweek crowd tell their tales. He remembered his father joining in similar narratives many times in this same bar.

After taking a few small sips of beer, Jake motioned for the bartender. As the man approached Jake placed two photographs from of his valise on the bar.

"Amigo, I'm looking for some friends of the family." He motioned toward the pictures of Tom Wojicki, Cindi Light, and his mother and father together at some black-tie function. Next to that photo, he laid a picture of Monk Phillips, Tom Wojicki, and his father his mother had taken at an informal groundbreaking ceremony on the job site.

"I heard they were in the area. Any of these people look familiar?" He watched the bartender's face, catching a hint of recognition.

With a coy smile the bartender replied, "Señor, it seems we always have one gringo looking for a friend or two here. We never know why. Would these be resort guests?"

"Maybe. Arrived here about a week ago. Any ideas?"

"I cannot be sure. So many gringos come and go," he muttered with a shrug. "Pardon me; I have drinks to pour. I'll think about it while I make cocktails. You think about it too; how important this information is to you." He walked away.

Jake knew from experience; everything in Mexico came with a price tag. He guessed something between $10 and $20 would do the job, so he laid a $5 bill on the bar to open negotiations then sipped his beer. Soon the bartender returned and pretended not to notice the bill on the polished hardwood as he washed glasses and cut limes into wedges.

The sun disappeared from the sky, and a gentle breeze off the Sea of Cortez blew through the bar. The conversations from the few occupied tables melded into a singular din broken only by the occasional cackle of a laughing fisherman, all of them brushing off reality for a few days. The temperature was perfect. Jake wished Janelle was here.

"*Una mas cerveza, amigo?*" asked the bartender upon his return.

The beer in Jake's hand was clearly two-thirds full. "No, gracias."

The bartender leaned on the bar and casually studied the photographs. He picked one up and examined it in the lights hung from the palapa roof. "Five dollars does not go far in Mexico anymore, amigo." Smiling at Jake, he placed the photo back on the hardwood and walked to where a waiter had approached to place a drink order.

Jake took the cue, placing $10 where the $5 had been. When the bartender returned a few moments later, he picked up one of the pictures.

"Staying at the hotel, señor?" he asked without taking his eyes off the photo.

"No!" laughed Jake. "Too rich for me. I am a poor gringo. In the United States, I do what you do. *Un cerveza* and *no mas.*"

"I see. I think I've maybe seen one or two of these people here before, but I'm not sure," said the bartender as he laid the photo of Monk Phillips in front of Jake. He pointed to the big fellow in the picture. "Is this the man who hit you?"

Jake lightly touched the area where the wound was healing. He smiled, "No. It was a friend of his. I should have ducked."

The bartender smiled too. "Yeah, maybe you should have!" He leaned in closer and said, "You look, maybe, a little like this man, no?" He pointed to Dr. Cohen.

"We are related. He's my father."

"*Caramba!* I've seen them many times. One time every year this man comes with a truckload of medical equipment for our local hospital in Los Barriles. He has helped there in emergencies too. He knows the owner of the hotel very well. The woman... Your mother, yes? She is well known for her help with the local school. She brings computers for the kids. Last year the owner had a dinner in their honor here. All the local hotel and business owners came. I worked that night—we all took no tips. Every peso went to the school or hospital. They have a house somewhere nearby, yes?"

Jake knew his parents often came to dinner here along with the other resorts on the East Cape (his mother regularly said it was too hot to cook at the house), but he'd never heard about a dinner in their honor. He knew, too, of their donations and that his father had treated many of the locals for different injuries and illnesses in the past. Did these people know that all those items were discards from the United States?

"Señor!"

The bartender's voice snapped Jake out of his musings. "*Lo siento.* I was thinking about something else."

"I can tell, señor. I smell the wood burning," laughed the bartender. In a more serious tone, he asked, "Is there trouble with these people in the pictures?"

Jake wasn't certain how much to disclose. If the three were staying nearby, they might have people on watch for inquiries as to their whereabouts. The wrong words might be reported and send them into hiding. On the other hand, silence would get him nowhere.

He answered, "This man almost killed my father." He pointed to the photo of Monk Phillips, then touched the images of Wojicki and Cindi. "These three stole a great amount of money from my parents. I believe they may be somewhere in the area."

"*Lo siento, amigo,*" offered the bartender. "I have two niños, both boys. At school, they use the computers your parents have provided. They will be educated and become businessmen. They will not tend bar as their father must. My wife, she almost died giving birth to the second boy, but the doctors saved both their lives at the hospital. Because of your parents' donations, the hospital is better equipped."

He studied the photos. "The skinny one; he was here maybe eight or nine days ago. Then the big man and the beautiful lady joined him. The skinny man, he likes his scotch. The lady is *muy bonito!*" He whistled softly and moved his hands vertically in a serpentine motion. "A man does not easily forget a woman like that.

"The three had dinner together. They seemed to be celebrating. I have not seen them since that night. I'll ask the other bartenders and waiters if they have seen them since."

"Did they stay here?" Jake asked excitedly. He couldn't believe his good fortune, meeting someone who'd spotted the trio at his first stop in Mexico.

"No, I don't think so. I never see any of them by the pool or on the beach. Just the one, one time before, and then all of them for dinner only. Say, amigo, you hungry? I can order something from the kitchen for you."

"No *gracias*. My next stop is Palmas de Cortez. I'll get something in the town there. Anything else you remember about them?"

"No señor. But my cousin works at Palmas as manager. I'll call and see if he can talk to you. It should be no problem. Midweek is slow. I can ask around other places too. Maybe you come back tomorrow night, and I have more information for you."

Jake handed him the photos after writing his cell number on the back. "You keep these, and here are the names of the three I'm looking for. I have other copies. If you help us find these people, my family will be very grateful. What is your name, amigo?"

"Freddie." He extended his hand. Jake took it in a high shake with thumbs wrapping. "I will check around. Most people here know of your mother and father. Very few gringos do much to help us here. It is appreciated. Come back tomorrow. Ask for Martín at Palmas. I will phone ahead. Who should I tell him is coming?"

"My name is Jake Cohen. Freddie, thank you. It has been a pleasure sitting at your bar," he said as he rose from the stool. He laid another $10 bill next to his half-full beer and picked up his valise and pen then he turned to walk away.

"Adios, Mr. Jake. Good luck!" offered Freddie as he picked up his cell phone.

At a table in the shadows by the pool palapa, Chip Collins sipped a beer and watched with unease as Jake walked out into the darkness. He'd bummed a ride with Cohen from the airport, concocting a yarn that he happened to be staying at this resort. He'd told Jake he'd pick up a rental car at the hotel. He was aghast to discover rentals had to be ordered and delivered from the airport, fifty minutes to the south. He would not get a car until tomorrow morning.

Chip knew the smallish man tailing Jake had obtained a car; he'd seen him following them through the desert.

With no transportation to follow along, the detective felt a tinge of guilt. If something happened to Jake, he'd be responsible. He quickly decided to level with Cohen and tell him he was being followed.

Rising from the table, he trotted to the cobblestone driveway of the hotel. When he reached the parking area, he saw the taillights of the rental car at the top of the drive. When the red lights disappeared around the corner, Chip heard another engine rattle to life in the lot. The car was parked facing forward. Before Chip could act to stop the driver, that car was gone too.

CHAPTER 21

After adjustment to the down-haul line to remove the wrinkles in the sail, Jake decided the rig was ready. A few hours of sailing on the speedster sailboard he kept here might help clear his mind. More to the point, he really had nothing else to do until this afternoon.

The wind had built up to twenty-five knots during the evening, common to the East Cape of Cabo San Lucas during fall, winter, and even early spring. In another month there would only be light breezes from the southeast, Jake knew as he waded into the water to rinse the sand off the base of the sail before attaching it to the board. He wore a 'shorty' wetsuit, named so for the short sleeves and legs. The water was cool but not cold, and Jake knew the minor wind chill on his wet bare legs would be quickly forgotten once he was bouncing along at thirty-plus miles per hour over the ocean's surface.

With the sail firmly joined to the board, Jake left the combination rig in the sand and walked up the beach toward his family's vacation home. Every civilized day began with a cup of coffee, and the pot he'd started earlier would be ready by now. The sun had not yet climbed above the ocean to the east, yet the purple-gray of first light had transmuted to red-orange at the horizon.

As he walked over the mixture of white sand, driftwood scraps, and crushed seashells, Jake thought about last night's discoveries. After leaving Rancho Buena Vista, he'd gone to Palmas de Cortez a few miles to the northwest in the town of Los Barriles. Martín had been as helpful as Freddie. Perhaps even more so.

Tom Wojicki had stayed at Palmas for a few days, where he'd been joined by a woman and a huge man with longish blond hair later in the week. His records showed they'd checked out on the previous Saturday and took a resort shuttle to the airport. No one knew where the group had gone from there. Martín said he'd do some checking; he had friends at the airport. Even if they traveled under assumed identities, Martín guessed he'd be able to track their destination, as the three were not an inconspicuous trio.

He'd assured Jake he'd have information for him tomorrow afternoon, which was now today. Jake knew from years of traveling in Mexico that nothing here was assured, but he had no other leads. He doubted he'd be able to track them any farther with limited time and dwindling finances, but maybe Martín's information would be helpful to the authorities back home.

On his way out to the house last night Jake had stopped at the Playa del Sol resort and the hotel at Rancho Leonaro. Employees at both resorts remembered seeing Wojicki at some point during the previous week, but no one had any information other than the fact that he'd been there.

Mexico was a country of waiting. Nothing happened quickly here, and Jake resigned himself to the fact.

The beach here was deserted at this hour of the morning. A few gringos were staying at their homes, but it was not yet high season for fishing and the development was primarily empty. As Jake opened the door to the house, he smelled the aroma of the fresh-brewed coffee. Off in the distance, he heard the sound of a car engine approaching muffled by the whoosh of the gusting wind. He walked to the kitchen and poured himself a cup of the brew, then went back to the door. The engine was abruptly shut off a few hundred feet away.

The only sounds were the howl of the breeze, the breaking of the waves on the nearby beach and the rustling of the palm fronds on the palapa roof shading his parents' patio. He closed the door behind him and with coffee in hand walked across the yard and out the gate in the lath and plaster wall toward the Sea of Cortez. Instead of moving in the direction of the ocean he turned to the north, into the wind, disappearing into a set of low sand dunes. Only footprints were left behind.

Restrictive gun laws made it more difficult to get a firearm in some places in the world. However, with a bit of effort, a handgun could be procured in most countries. Benny Temple had begun arrangements the previous evening at a liquor store outside Rancho Buena Vista.

After following Cohen from the airport to the resort, Benny had watched him enter the bar and guessed he had a bit of time to start scavenging for a weapon. He'd stopped at one small *mercado*, but that seemed to be a mom-

and-pop store, full of families, and he'd quickly moved on. At his next stop, he'd detected the faint smell of pot smoke. A few men were seated outside at a stained white plastic table with cans of Tecate and a tin coffee can they used as an ashtray. Benny had gone in and purchased a beer, lingering while he took a few sips.

Looking at the clerk, Bennie held out his forefinger with the thumb up. He brought down his thumb in the motion of a firing hammer of a gun. The clerk had pursed his lips slightly, then gave a slight nod.

The storekeeper disappeared out the front door. In a few moments, he returned and pointed to the door with his finger. Benny thought that the man was telling him to leave. He stepped out of the door. Immediately he heard a voice from the shadows.

"Amigo, come sit with me," requested a man now sitting alone at the discolored table. He wore cotton pants that had once been light tan but were now multicolored with stains that even the most aggressive laundering wouldn't remove. His shirt was Western style, the sleeves rolled to the elbow. The small scars on the forearms and hands told of hard labor in this man's younger days. Reptilian cowboy boots covered his feet. The face was tan and weathered. On his head, he wore a starched cowboy hat above coarse graying hair hanging a few inches below the rim. This man's skin was a testament to what years of outdoor toil in this inhospitable environment would do to a human.

With a smile that revealed yellow teeth intertwined with gold fillings, the *vaquero* spoke as Benny approached, "I speak a little English. Sit down. Maybe we do some business together, huh?"

Benny had hesitated as he looked at the plastic chair soiled with grease, dust from the road and God only knew what other substances. He reluctantly slid into the seat, and as the day had receded into darkness, a deal was struck.

He was instructed to check back at this spot about 11:00 p.m. and if no one was here, check back at 5:00 tomorrow morning before the opening of the store.

After the transfer of the hundred-dollar down payment, Benny had returned to the hotel. The Toyota driven by the kid was still there, and he waited.

During the evening and into the night Benny had followed Cohen from hotel to hotel over one dusty road after another. At about 10:00 p.m. Cohen had left the last hotel and traveled down yet another dirt road for a few miles, coming to a small town. There, he'd stopped at a *mercado* and picked up some groceries. The streets had been dark and empty, perfect for a kill. Bennie wished he'd had the gun.

Tomorrow he would have the advantage; tonight, the kid got a reprieve.

He stayed back about a quarter mile and was beginning to think that Cohen was catching on to the fact he was being tailed. The area outside of La Ribera (he made a note of the town's name to use as a reference point) was desolate. Theirs were the only vehicles on the road, so he dropped back nearly one-half mile behind and kept the tail lights barely in sight. In the darkness, they'd made so many turns the cerebral compass heading was indefinite, but at least they now traveled on a paved road. That quickly changed when the lights on Cohen's car flashed as he'd hit the brakes and turned left. In the short time it took the hit man to reach the spot, the other rental car had disappeared.

Bennie stopped at the corner and saw a real estate sign in English advertising Lighthouse Point Estates six kilometers down the road. It was now 10:50 p.m. and he'd realized he couldn't get back to the *mercado* by 11:00 so he was in no hurry. He'd figure out where the kid was staying, go back and pick up the gun at 5:00 a.m., and finish the job before Cohen would wake the next morning. By noon he'd be in a bar in Cabo San Lucas, sipping a drink and checking out the señoritas on the beach.

Finding the development was easy enough; the real estate signs were well placed to guide him through the darkened landscape. By the time he arrived, Cohen was parked outside a white plaster and red-tile-roofed building with a light on inside. He guessed the kid was in for the evening. Bennie headed back into the desert. He'd be back tomorrow.

Returning to La Ribera had been simple, but from there the trip became unpleasant. He hadn't eaten and assumed he'd grab a bite at the little *mercado* where Jake had stopped. Upon reaching the store, he'd found the lights off and a 'Cerrado' sign on the door. He was tired and hungry, but the worst of the night was yet to come.

Starting up the unpaved street in the reverse direction the lights of La Ribera were soon left behind. Bennie came to a fork in the dirt road. He followed the track he felt reasonably certain would return him to Buena Vista, but he quickly came to an intersection. Here he made another choice he thought would be the right direction, yet he came upon still more forks and intersections.

For the next two hours, Bennie Temple drove in circles and figure eights through the scrub cactus and brush of Baja California's East Cape desert. Three times he passed the same small group of emaciated cows nibbling on brown tufts of grass, and with each trip past the herd, his anger at his predicament grew.

He blamed Jake Cohen.

The first shot might be to a knee or shoulder when he found him. Let the kid writhe in pain a while before finishing him off. The development had looked empty enough that he might have a few extra minutes to enjoy the fruits of his efforts.

Eventually, he reached the paved highway and found his way back to the *mercado*. Sleeping in the driver's seat of an economy sedan proved to be impossible. Thankfully, the temperature was neither too warm nor too chilly. At 4:00 a.m. he switched to the passenger's side of the car and dozed fitfully until tapping on the window stirred him.

The old *vaquero* stood outside the car in the darkness. Bennie got out, and the transaction took place. From the look of the man, Bennie had expected a Colt or some type of long-barreled Western-style pistol, but instead, the cowboy handed him a snub-nosed Saturday night special. The Röhm RG 14 had been cleaned and freshly oiled but showed signs of oxidation. Bennie opened the revolving chamber and checked the action of all mechanisms. Satisfied the firearm was serviceable, he handed the black marketer the additional three hundred American dollars.

With a fully loaded gun in hand and a small brown paper bag containing six extra rounds of ammunition, Bennie had headed out into the gray light of morning to finish his job. He'd traveled back down the main highway and soon turned at a well-posted sign for La Ribera. From there the local Realtors made the job easy by advertising Lighthouse Point Estates as the 'Jewel of the East Cape' with prominent signs and directions in English. As he'd reached La Ribera, he saw a few people stirring in the morning light. Bennie caught the scent of breakfast being prepared in the *casitas* as he passed by, and his stomach ached.

Turning to the south (he now knew the direction with the orange glow on the horizon to the east) he headed down the road toward Cohen. At the turn-off to the development, he stopped the car and took a few steps into the desert. Satisfied no one was nearby, he squeezed off two shots to be certain the old gun would fire. The desert boomed briefly, but the sound was gone as quickly as it had erupted. He expelled the used shells and reloaded the chamber, then started on his way again.

Bennie felt tired, dirty, and hungry. He couldn't remember the last time he'd been this strung out. During missions in the Middle East as a marine sniper, for certain, but not in many years.

Jake Cohen had gotten lucky two nights ago when some bozo cop had interrupted things. *Today will be different,* Bennie told himself as he approached the development of beach houses and shut off the car.

Maybe the door will be open, and I'll pop him in bed while he's asleep, he silently voiced to himself as he exited the vehicle. He left the door open to avoid the noise of closing and walked toward the house.

When Victor and Anne Cohen had built the home, they'd oriented the structure to face the ocean and capitalize on the cooling summer breezes from the southeast. This design also protected the structure from the fierce winter winds out of the north. The layout of the home made great cover for an assailant approaching from the rear. Only small, high windows were in the wall in back to limit penetration of the afternoon sun.

The wind-protected side the home offered a palapa that shaded the family fishing boat, an old Jeep CJ-5, and quad-runner. A stone and plaster wall surrounded the property with a large iron gate on steel rollers. Jake had left the gate open the night before. His rented Toyota sat motionless as Bennie approached.

The howling wind and distant breaking waves muted the already-soft noise of his footfalls.

The curtains hung still as he rounded the boat and jeep. Working his way past the structure, Bennie peered around the corner to the front of the house. He saw only a vacant front patio and an additional palapa for shade. His heart raced as he softly stepped across the yard, staying low to avoid being seen through the front window. As he crept along his nose picked up the slight aroma of coffee on the breeze.

Cohen was awake. Bennie slowly dropped lower and gently thumbed the hammer back on the gun. After surveying the yard area, his eyes moved to the beach beyond. Seeing no movement, he continued in his crouch, and with ever-increasing stealth, Bennie moved to the front door. He stood outside for a moment listening, hearing nothing save the wind and waves. The burnt-orange corona of the sun peeked over the ocean behind him. Pulling gently on the knob to put pressure on the mechanism to avoid a 'click' of the latch, Bennie turned the handle slowly. Despite his effort, a minute 'click' came and went as the strike plate and latch separated. He stood motionless for thirty seconds.

Hearing no movement inside, Bennie opened the door a crack to peek in. Seeing adequate space, he thrust the door open and dove into the room. He too was known for his quickness, and although not physically imposing, he was an expert marksman. By going past the opening into the room, he'd get around Cohen if he were waiting behind the door and fire before his adversary could reach him. Spinning instantly to his feet, Bennie gyrated in the room, leading with the revolver. Seeing the living room and kitchen empty, he ducked behind the couch and peered at the open doors to two bedrooms. He waited for some noise and hoped for a groggy Cohen to emerge from one of the rooms. Hearing nothing and seeing no movement for an entire minute, he rose and sprinted to the section of wall between the bedrooms. From here he could see into the kitchen and watch the front door.

With a slow, careful inspection of the interior, Bennie was satisfied the structure was empty.

Waiting for Cohen to return might be the best strategy. Staying low so as not to be seen through the windows, he poured himself a cup of coffee. After the long and unpleasant night, the fresh brew smelled as good as anything he ever imagined. Up in the States, he never would have taken such a risk. Surgical gloves would have been worn into the house, and still, he would have touched as little as possible. Yet he was certain forensic investigators were nonexistent here, so he helped himself. He opened the refrigerator and removed some tortillas and cheese. Fresh. Must have been purchased by the kid the night before. Positioning himself to keep an eye on the approach to the front door through the window, he ate and sipped the coffee in the kitchen. If he saw movement, he'd drop below the breakfast bar and surprise Cohen.

Again, he promised himself that he'd soon be by the pool at a Cabo San

Lucas hotel with a scotch in hand, but his arrival time might be delayed until 1:00 or 2:00 p.m.

With the food and two cups of coffee, he began to feel human again. He used the toilet to take a pee without flushing and washed his face in the sink. A wet toothbrush sat on the Saltillo countertop, and he wished he had his own. Toweling his face dry and checking the mirror, he noticed the graying stubble of two days' growth. His eyes were dry and red after the night on the dusty road.

He went back to the kitchen and paced. He dared not sit as sleep might find him.

After fifteen minutes more, he began to wonder if Cohen was coming back. He checked outside through a window, being careful to move the shade as little as possible. The car still sat behind the house. The kid would come back.

Another twenty minutes passed. After thumbing through a *Golf Digest* and a sportfishing magazine, the staying power of Bennie Temple began to wane. Through the windows, he could see footprints in the sand heading off down the beach with a set of prints marking what he assumed was a return trip. A solitary set of marks went off in a different direction into an area of small sand dunes. After surveying the landscape to make sure his exit would be unobserved, he walked out onto the beach. Before leaving the house, he donned a San Diego Padres cap he'd found, and he pulled the collar up on his light jacket. Even if he was spotted, he guessed the kid wouldn't recognize him until it was too late.

With the snub-nosed revolver in his jacket pocket, he headed out into the low dunes.

As he trudged through the sand into the wind, he again felt the fatigue. His unprotected eyes suffered the sting of airborne sand carried on the stiff breeze. When he walked up the faces of the head-high sand dunes, the sun shined directly into his eyes. The combination of the dust and sunlight was nearly blinding, and he wished he'd picked up his sunglasses from the car before trekking out after Cohen. He almost turned back to continue his vigil at the house but doggedly moved on following the tracks in front of him.

After an exhaustive ten minutes of laboring through the heavy sand, Bennie was huffing. The morning air that had been cool was now feeling hot. The combination of the sun and exertion caused him to break into a low sweat. He realized he was slightly dehydrated, and his eyes burned as he continued into the unrelenting push of air. Ambling up the face of the largest dune he'd yet encountered, the footprints he followed looked slightly fresher. He was no expert at reading tracks, but the sand had a recently broken look about it. With his hand on the cocked gun, he withdrew the weapon from his pocket and concealed it under his jacket. When his head neared the top of the rise the wind whipped sand from the lip of the dune into his already irritated eyes, and the sunlight bit at his unprotected corneas. He stopped and blinked, attempting to clear his vision.

Again, anger welled up from within. *Why does this guy make things so difficult?* he asked himself. Who in their right mind would take a morning jog directly into the teeth of biting wind and blinding sun?

Suddenly Bennie realized—Cohen *wanted* him to follow in this direction.

Instantly the revolver was out of the jacket. Simultaneously the lip of the dune in front of him surged upward, the wind carrying the fine sand in an unabated path to his eyes. Completely blinded, Bennie's free hand never went to clear his vision, but rather grasped the wrist of his gun hand. He quickly squeezed the trigger four times, moving the barrel slightly to fan the shots in the direction where the onslaught of the windborne grit had originated.

Then he waited. There was no sound save the whoosh of the wind. With the hammer back and the gun raised into the breeze, he removed his left hand from where it steadied the wrist to scrape away the crusted sand first from one eye, then the other. He tried to open his eyes. Initially, he saw only a fiery orange color. Blinking a few times, the hitman felt the sting of the particles that found their way under his eyelids, but his vision cleared slightly. He looked down and shook his head with more wiping of his left hand. The gun never dropped.

As Bennie looked up slightly, the sunlight again bit into his eyes. Once more he was forced to drop his gaze, only for a second. But in that brief instant, he was hit from behind. He tried to bring the barrel of the gun around as his assailant tackled him, but a vise-grip lock on his right wrist prevented the motion. The gun went off, and the grip never slackened, so Bennie knew he'd missed his mark.

As the two men grappled for position and control of the other, they tumbled down the sand. In the struggle, the final shot was discharged. When they hit the bottom of the dune, one man gasped to catch his breath. The other lay motionless as his blood seeped into the sand, his skull opened from the impact of the last bullet in the revolver.

CHAPTER 22

It was near 10:00 a.m. as Chip Collins reached the seventh of the 'X's on his map. After greasing the concierge at the hotel an extra hundred bucks to get the first rental car sent out from the airport, he'd headed south to the spot on the highway where Jake had pointed to the east yesterday and said, "Our vacation home is over there a few kilometers."

That was all he had to begin a search.

Turning to the east, he'd found the small town of La Ribera and at a little *mercado*, while holding out a map, asked the proprietor, "*Gringos aquí?*"

"*Mucho gringos,*" he'd affirmed with a nod. The storekeeper took the map and with a red Sharpie drew eight 'X's.

Chip bought a large bottle of water and some fruit, then took off. He'd hurriedly visited the beautiful locales of Los Frailes, Cabo Pulmo, and the four other spots the shopkeeper had marked. Given time, he would have picked up a case of cervezas and relaxed on the picturesque tropical beaches.

There were plenty of gringos in the noted locations, but not the two he sought. Now, traveling down a twisting washboard dirt road, he came upon a low plaster wall with an arched gate and a sign—Lighthouse Point Estates. Entering he spotted an economy Toyota parked away from the homes, the color of the one driven by the man who pursued Jake. Parking next to the car, he looked about. There was no movement in the development, and he heard nothing but the wind across the desert and waves breaking on the distant beach. A few dusty cars were parked by other *casitas* and Chip guessed that folks were inside to hide from the gale.

The sand told the story of the driver's path with footprints heading from the Toyota toward one of the houses. As he followed the prints, he rounded a corner and stopped abruptly, seeing Jake's rental parked near the beach house. There was no movement outside and no sound from within.

He walked along the side of the structure and saw a low stone and plaster wall dividing the front yard from the beach area. The absolute quiet, save the whoosh of air rushing past his ears, unnerved him as he surveyed the *casita*. He walked to the door and tried the knob. Locked. Walking to the windows and peeking through the sheer outer curtains Chip saw no sign of life inside. A wave of guilt engulfed him as he thought he might have arrived too late.

A distant 'pop' broke the silence and Chip spun toward the sound on the balls of his feet. Where the low sand bluff sloped toward the beach, the ocean was visible. Over the water's surface sped a windsurfer, catching air off every third wave.

With a short walk to the beach, the detective spent a few moments watching the sailor. The pilot seemed to launch the board and used the sail as a foil to gain altitude as he jumped the waves. Twice on the outward-bound pass of the windsurfer, the sailor looped the entire rig, board over sail, landing perfectly upright. When riding back toward the beach the man at the helm flew off the wind-ravaged crests of the waves and skipped out in front of the breakers in the shallow water over the sand. Then the board spun, and the sail rotated, snapping into position with the same 'pop' heard a moment ago. In an instant, the board and sailor were off through the choppy ocean. This time, however, Chip got a good look at the sailor. It was Jake Cohen.

The relief at seeing him alive and unharmed was quickly replaced with curiosity as to the whereabouts of the other man. Jake appeared to be content to thrash about in the waves, so Chip started surveying the beach. He spotted footprints leading off into some small sand dunes to the north. As he followed the tracks, he noticed there appeared to be two sets heading off into the mounds of sand, yet only one returning. Now more curious as to what happened to the pursuer, he started trotting into the wind.

In five minutes, he reached a low spot in the sand surrounded by higher dunes. Here the tracks disappeared, and the sand was neatly raked, the surface texture resembling a bunker on a golf course.

The sand told a story. Chip was no Native American tracker; however, it was plain to see two people had walked or jogged to this spot and met. Only one set of tracks returned toward the row of beach houses. Another set of prints showing someone coming and going went off at ninety degrees to the west. Following these for less than one hundred feet, he found the knobby tracks of some sort of all-terrain vehicle. Those marks told of a trip to and from the housing development on a motorized vehicle.

Scratching his chin Chip walked back to the raked area. With the toe of his loafer, he started pushing the sand. Soon, using the shoe tip as a plow, he'd furrowed troughs in the soil. He bent down to examine his work. In his duties, he'd seen plenty of blood, and he was fairly certain the heavy dark, matted chunks were a mixture of sand and human plasma.

Was there a man buried here? Did Cohen whack this guy and hide the evidence? As he wondered, a voice startled him.

"You're a long way from Buena Vista."

Chip stood and looked at Jake Cohen standing on top of the low dune. The tight wetsuit revealed arms and legs that were cleanly muscled. The left hand hung loosely, and the right hand rested just behind the hip, out of sight.

Chip hadn't heard him approach and was caught off guard. Slowly he let the sand held in his hand slip through his fingers and blow in the wind.

"This sand is heavy. Like somebody spilled syrup in it. Or maybe blood. Any ideas?" replied Chip.

"When the wind blows here it usually lasts three or four days. In the spring, sometimes less. But it will hold up long enough. That sand will be bone dry, and all these tracks whisked away by tomorrow morning.

"Odd things happen on a deserted beach in Mexico, my friend. Gringos have been known to disappear without a trace. Now, why don't you tell me what you're doing out here? It's been a tedious last few days, and I'm worn a little thin." As he finished Jake exposed the revolver held behind his back.

"You're not going to buy the story I gave you of looking for a honeymoon spot, are you?" Chip answered with a smile.

"No. I didn't buy it yesterday," answered Jake. "It was lame then, and it still sucks. That's why I left you up the road without a car. I realized then, you were in the bar at the yacht club in 'Diego too."

"It was the best I could come up with on short notice. You move around fast. It's taken two of us to keep up with you over the last few days."

"Well, your partner's not going to give me any more trouble. The question now is what to do with you. Should I get melodramatic and mail one of your fingers back to Stinnetti?"

He slid the fingers of his left hand an inch into the right sleeve of his wetsuit and pulled out four heavy-duty tie wraps. Tossing two of the fifteen-inch plastic bands to Chip's feet, he continued, "Put these on. One on each wrist, bring your hands behind your back. I'll finish them off. But before you do it, empty your pockets. Turn the front inside-out and drop the contents of the back pockets in the sand. Do it! Now!" He brought the gun to bear on Chip's chest as he gave the order.

The detective slowly inserted his hands into his pockets as he explained, "Jake, you're mistaken. I'm a cop. Riverside County Sheriff's Department. I had nothing to do with the man following you. The last time you saw my partner was when you shoved him off a dock in San Diego. He probably saved your life a few moments before, I might add. You were drunk and probably staggering into an ambush. Deputy Brad Logan chased the assailant away."

"Empty the pockets and show me your badge. Then do the wrists, as I asked.

"Forgive my skepticism, but a man tried to kill me here today. Then you materialize out of the desert. I've only had a gun pointed at me one other time, and that was by a jealous ex-husband who had no intention of pulling the trigger. Scared me so bad I almost wet my pants though. Well, the fellow today did pull the trigger. At first, I was scared. Now I'm just pissed. I'm not accustomed to the whiz of a bullet passing within inches of my ear."

Chip turned the pockets inside out. Rental car keys and a few pesos fell to the ground. Reaching into the back pockets, he withdrew his wallet and a folded map. "I don't have a badge; it's with Logan back home. My cards too. You can check my identity off my license and call the station if there's a phone that works anywhere nearby. I'm not armed so don't get froggy with your Röhm. With that snub-nose, you'd have to be lucky to hit me from there, but I'd rather not take the risk.

"The name I gave you yesterday is real. Chip Collins. I left out I'm investigating the battery of your father and the matter of the missing funds from his company's trust account—"

"Yak all you'd like," interrupted Jake, "but keep working on the tie wraps. I'll put the gun away when your hands are secure."

Chip slowly nodded. He worked the thick plastic wrap around his wrist and slid the end through the locking mechanism, pulling it tight. He started working on the second one. "The man following you is not my partner. He's been on you for a few days. I picked him up tailing you outside the banker's office.

"By the way, what happened to him?" Chip let the question hang as the second tie wrap clicked tight.

"Put your hands behind your back. I'll hop down and loop them together with the other wraps," Jake ordered. "If your story is true, you'll be free in an hour. Maybe less."

Collins did as instructed. When his hands were behind his back, Jake placed the other two tie wraps in his teeth and came down off the dune. Chip banished any thought of escape. As unnerving as being cuffed was, especially as a cop, he'd already decided to go along to allow Jake to verify his story.

Jake, now behind, reached out and took the wrist. He gave a rough push, and the natural reaction of the other fellow was to push back to avoid falling forward onto the sand. At the exact moment he felt the pressure come back at him, Jake hooked the elbow on the free arm and placed the ball of his foot against the heel of the man in front of him. Using the momentum of the push backward and the leverage of the hooked elbow he instantly spun the man to the ground. Once down, Jake inserted two wraps through those on Chip's wrists and secured the ends tightly with 'zip' sounds.

Chip spat out a mouthful of sand. "That was so unnecessary," he said angrily.

Jake took his knee off the middle of the deputy's back and stood. "If you are a cop, of which I have doubts, you have no authority here. If the man I met earlier has indeed been tailing me for days, you're delinquent in your duty. Somebody should have taken him in or notified me of the situation. Your action, or inaction, placed me in grave danger.

"I don't know what to do with you exactly. Maybe I'll wait until dark then put you in your rental truck with this gun. I'll throw what's left of the other fellow in the back and park you both outside the police station in Los Barriles. The local cops will have a field day with that one. A gringo with a gun and a man shot in the head. Usually, it takes a few months to go to trial here, so you'll spend that time in a prison in La Paz. You'll probably go to trial in August. You've never been to La Paz in August, have you? There is no place hotter on earth. It's arid desert and sits almost smack dab on the Tropic of Cancer. You'll pop and sizzle like a strip of bacon in a frying pan while you wait for your day in court.

"After they find you guilty, who knows where you'll end up? Maybe a prison on the mainland. If you're lucky, they'll let you out to work as a plantation hand during the day. Your diet will consist of moldy tortillas, soupy beans, and greasy rice. Your honeymoon in Mexico story will come true, but Pedro or Juan will be your new love interest. But it won't happen on a white sandy beach with a piña colada in your hand. It'll be in a hot, block-walled cell that smells of sweat and piss."

Chip had rolled first to his rump and then to his feet as Jake spoke. He wanted desperately to wipe the sand off his face, but his hands were now securely behind his back. Trying to remember this was temporary, he spoke to Jake with as friendly a tone as possible. "That's the same speech I give the hoods and punks I pick up. Trouble is, in the States they're back out on the streets in a few hours.

"You're right Jake; I should have let you know the man was following you. You mentioned a fellow named Stinnetti. We've determined the man is likely working for him."

"Start walking back in the direction of the house. I'm not discussing anything until I know for sure who you are. You're welcome to tell me what you know as we merrily stroll along. My folks have a satellite phone there, and I will check up on you."

As they trudged together through the sand, Chip gave an update.

There was little doubt Monk Phillips had been the one who had mercilessly beaten Dr. Cohen. Department staff was currently investigating the history of all three.

IRS investigators had contacted the sheriff's department regarding swapping information, but they had little to go on. Realistically, all they were looking for was evidence of a taxable event anyway. The IRS was sometimes helpful, especially in white-collar crimes, if one could tolerate the pricks.

Chip's recounting of his meeting with the banker sounded like what Jake had heard directly from the man. Roger Scott had taken the proper steps in the transfer of the money. The man in the makeshift handcuffs said the banker showed surprise when told that Dr. Cohen had a ticket on a flight to Mexico. He had said it was certainly unlike Victor Cohen, but he knew the doctor was under a huge financial burden. Things weren't going well at home for the Cohens, the banker had alluded during their meeting.

As they neared the house, Jake began to believe the story, but Collins would stay in the restraints until verification. Something Chip had said clicked Jake's mind into gear. He spoke for the first time since their walk had begun.

"When you met with Roger Scott, did you tell him my father had a ticket on a flight to Mexico, or did you specify Cabo San Lucas?"

"Mexico only." Chip knew Jake was coming around. They were now corroborating information. He'd be free soon.

"That fat little fart told me he knew my dad had a ticket to Cabo San Lucas, specifically. You're certain you said only Mexico?"

"One hundred percent. The plot thickens."

They now stood at the front door of the house. "Wait here. I'm going to make a call to the Riverside County Sheriff's Department. I'll be right back."

"The number is—"

"I'll get my own number." Jake cut him off and walked inside.

He looked around the house for a phone book. He knew his parents kept one here for Riverside County in case they needed to call in an emergency. After two minutes he gave up the search and pushed the power button on the satellite phone. The twelve-inch antenna was folded out, and thirty seconds later he had a strong enough signal to make a call. He dialed the country code for the USA, then the area code and number to his parents' home.

CHAPTER 23

"Hello. Cohen residence."

The phone was answered on the second ring, with a remarkably clear connection for a satellite handset. The female voice on the other end was slightly familiar, yet not that of his mother or sisters.

"Hello. This is Jake Cohen. Who am I speaking with?"

"Jake! It's so good to hear your voice. When are you coming back?" came the answer from a thousand miles away.

"Who is this?"

"Why Jake, I'm hurt you don't recognize my voice. It's Amber! Down to visit from Reno."

He was too stunned to respond immediately. He checked the phone display to be certain he'd dialed the correct number.

The confusion was quickly replaced by fear. Amber worked for a business that cooperated, at a minimum, on a peripheral basis with Stinnetti. He was certain the twerp was behind the attempt on his life a few hours ago. Amber was motivated by money. Could she have sold out and arranged a similar event at the Cohens' home?

"Amber, where is my mother? If anything has happened to her by God, you'll pay. Just so you're aware the man, or men, sent here to kill me failed. I'm alive, and I'll follow you to the end of this earth if any harm has come to her," said Jake coldly.

Amber answered, "Well, that's news to me. It's great to hear you're doing well. Your mom and I are busy; we're baking cookies. Oatmeal chocolate chip. She says they're your favorite. Her hands are covered with dough right now, so she asked me to grab the phone."

"I want to talk to her."

Jake heard a muffled, "Anne, it's Jake. He wants to talk to you."

The reply was barely audible in the background but sounded cheerful enough. "Tell him I want to finish this sheet, then I'll wash my hands and

178

talk to him. You kids chat for now."

"She said—"

"I heard," interrupted Jake, "Put the phone to her ear. I want to talk directly to her."

"Okay."

The next voice he heard was his mother's.

"Jake, how are you? Your father is much better today. Amber and I went to see him this morning. Where on earth did you find this young woman? She is such a dear! She wanted to stay in a hotel until you got back, but I insisted she stay here. You can tell me the story of how you two met when you get back from San Diego. Right now, I'm up to my elbows in sticky dough, so talk to your friend.

"Just a hint, son, she'd look good in white!" chimed Anne Cohen in a slightly hushed voice.

"Mom, I'm not in San Diego. I'm at the house in Cabo. I wanted to check on a few things here."

"Cabo? That's where Tom and his friends went. I hope you're not chasing after them. They're dangerous. Leave this to the police," she advised.

"It's fine, Mom. Just snooping a bit. If I find anything, I'll pass it on. Speaking of which, I need a phone number for the Riverside County Sheriff's Department. Not a recorded message number, but a number where I can talk to a live body. Can you find one for me?" he asked.

"I think so. I have the deputy's card upstairs. Let me pop this sheet in the oven, and I'll get it. Talk to Amber for a minute while I finish up."

As he waited for Amber to come back on the line, Jake began to understand Sheriff Fred's warning. The breach in the line allowed people to flow in either direction. Since the contravention, he had mercilessly beaten a man. Today for the first time an attempt had been made on his life, and he'd been covered with the blood of another. A man he'd shot.

Now, the sanctity of his mother's world was compromised. On a particularly randy day, she might go see a PG-rated movie, but never anything with impiety beyond. He immediately decided the gap needed abrupt closure.

"Cabo San Lucas, Jake! What are you doing there?" Amber's voice brought him out of his musing.

"Amber, I want you to pack whatever you have there and leave."

"Oh, you want me to join you there?" she asked.

"No. I want you to go back to your cave and never contact my family again. My mother's world consists of helping the poor and homeless, Bible studies, hospice visits, and wholesomeness. Your existence is the antithesis of hers. Nothing good can come of you two being together."

"Well thank you, Jake! I miss you, too. After a long drive down here, that's sweet of you to say. I'll get the first flight I can," she answered.

"Based upon your subterfuge, I assume my mom can still hear you. But she can't hear me, and I'm telling you to get out. Do not come here. Neither I nor my family wants or needs you," he said sternly.

She answered, "Thanks! I'm beginning to feel the same way about you, too. Listen, I received an e-mail from our long-lost friend. Pictures and everything! We've traded a few back and forth since then. Coincidentally, she's down your way. Maybe we can visit her while I'm there."

After a moment of silence, Jake exhaled, "Criminy… Can't you just tell me where she is? I don't think you coming here would be productive."

"Do you remember the arrangement we discussed when we got together for dinner? It's a good idea. I think she'd love to see us too," Amber said warmly. With her voice directed away from the phone she called, "Sure Anne, I'll watch the cookies!"

She continued five seconds later. "All right, you self-righteous prick! Your mother can't hear me now. How dare you treat me as though I'm some two-bit tramp! You're like every other fucking jackass man! My profession didn't bother you in the slightest while you were starting to feel me up or when I saved your ass at the hotel. What? I'm not good enough to be welcome at the Cohen house?

"I'm not the one who's got my ass in a sling! Your perfect little family is in trouble, and you need me. So, tell me where you are and how to get there. The deal's the same—ten percent and no prison for Cindi. *I know where she is Jake.* While I find you to be a pompous pig, I can tolerate you for a few days. She won't talk to you, but she'll open up for me."

Jake's mind raced. Amber had been very helpful in Reno. Having her come here would get her out of his mother's house.

"All right, you've missed the San Diego flight, but if you hurry, you might make the flight out of LAX." He looked at his watch and continued, "Yeah, if you leave now, you'll make it. You have a passport?"

"Yep. I thought I'd need it. You'll pick me up when I land then?" she asked.

"No. I've got things going on here. Get a cab to Hotel Palmas de Cortez. I'll meet you there. Remember, Palmas de Cortez. It's on the East Cape. Any cab driver will know where it is. Just hang around the bar until I show up," he instructed.

"Got it! I'll see you in a few hours."

"I'm counting the minutes. Hey, how did you find my parents' home?"

"You called here from my phone. I had the number traced to this address and just started driving. I thought we'd team up again," she giggled.

Jake imagined the lively twinkle in her eyes when she laughed.

Bewitching... For a brief instant, he looked forward to seeing her.

In a more serious tone, she continued, "Your mom is great, by the way." After a pause, she asked, "So, if your mom knew about my occupation, would I still have been allowed through the guard gate?"

"Absolutely. She's always looking for a soul to save. Jesus didn't show favoritism between harlots and priests. Mom always tries to live by his example. I don't think the 'she'd look good in white' comment would have flowed so freely though," laughed Jake.

"Be nice," she retorted. "Hey, you said someone made an attempt on your life. Are you serious?"

"Serious as a heart attack. It was the guy who was after me in Reno with your muscle-head from the service. He's no longer a threat, but I don't know if he had a backup man here somewhere."

Amber gasped, "What do you mean, he's no longer a threat? Did you kill him?"

"He's no longer a problem. I'll just leave it at that."

"Yikes! Hey, your mom's back in the kitchen. I think she has what you asked for. I'll hand the phone off and go pack. Be careful until I get there."

"I'll see you soon. If the flight is booked, we'll do the same thing tomorrow," he finished.

Anne Cohen's voice was the next one he heard. "Okay Jacob, I found the card. The name of the deputy is Chip Collins. He's a fine-looking African-American man, by the way. Really a gentleman, more like a politician than a police officer. He was very helpful and stayed with me in the emergency room while your father was in surgery."

"Did you ever see him with another deputy? Anything to verify he was a cop?" Jake asked.

"Oh my, yes! Uniformed deputies were with him when we met, and the guard outside your father's room and he talked often," she answered. "Why all the questions about him?"

"Just checking details, Mom. I don't need the number now, but thanks."

She exhaled, "Jacob, be careful. Your father is going to recover, and I don't want our family torn apart by this mess." She paused. "So, Amber is joining you there? To meet a friend? She went straight upstairs after giving me the phone. What happened to Janis?"

"It's Janelle, Mom. She's doing just fine. Amber and I are barely friends. Nothing more. We just have a mutual interest in seeing someone here."

"Well Son, if things should change, I like this one. She's bright and pretty, and we've done nothing but laugh since she arrived. I needed that," said Mrs. Cohen. She added, "What does she do for a living?"

"She's a prostitute."

"Oh, Jake! Really, you must stop your joking. That's in bad taste. Now tell me what she actually does."

"Public relations, Mom. In Reno," he replied.

"That's better! I wouldn't dream of telling her what you actually said! That sweet young lady… She'd be mortified," she chimed.

"I have to go, Mom. It was great talking to you. I love you and Dad, and I'll be home soon."

"All right. Take care and make a list of whatever we need there. We love you too. Bye-bye."

Jake turned off the phone and went to the refrigerator. He withdrew two bottles of water and walked out to the front patio. Chip Collins sat on the edge of a plastic beach chair.

"So, did you make your call?" questioned the deputy.

"I did. Seems you are a cop. Although someone ought to take your badge away forever. That man had been following me for days, and you never detained him? Or notified me?" Jake shook his head as he spoke.

"We thought he was a private dick and didn't know he was dangerous. Hey, since you know I'm okay, how about cutting me loose?" his eyes darted down toward his bound wrists.

"Nah, I don't think so." Jake opened his water and took a sip. "We're in Mexico, amigo. Your badge, which I've yet to see, is meaningless here. Plus, I got an undeserved ticket last year that I'm still pissed about. You can sit for a while longer."

"I didn't give you the damn ticket! Now cut me loose," ordered Chip.

"You're guilty by association. When I look at you, I can envision the motorcycle cop. Polished boots, reflective sunglasses, helmet. Wouldn't listen to a reasonable explanation.

"Yeah, I've two reasons to be pissed at you. The ticket. And the fact that you almost let me get killed! When did you plan on telling me I was being followed? At my funeral?"

Chip could only apologize. "I'm sorry. What happened to the guy?"

Already standing, Jake motioned for Chip to follow. Rising from the chair, he stood and followed inside.

Jake ordered him to stop in the living room, then went to a drawer in the kitchen and removed a diagonal cutter. With a few snips, the hands were free. He placed the tie wraps in a trash can under the sink then returned the cutter to the drawer as Chip rubbed his wrists then flexed his arms. Jake's thumb pointed to the back of the house, and the detective followed.

As they reached the bedroom door Jake announced, "Chip Collins, meet Bennie Temple. Hit man for Nicki Stinnetti."

"Shit!" exclaimed Chip.

On the bed was a Mexican blanket. On top of it rested the man Chip had seen tailing Jake for the last three days. Initially, Chip thought he was dead, but he caught a slight rise in the chest. The man's head was heavily bandaged, and upon close inspection, the deputy noticed a thread-thin white line running from the man's wrists to the pine bed frame. The line wrapped around the wood and came back to itself with a huge fishing swivel tied to the end and fastened with the snap end back around the line at the frame. Each end around the wrists was tightly knotted. A matching restraint was placed around each of the ankles.

He reached down and checked the man's pulse. Slow, but steady. The breathing was rhythmic. Pushing the eyelid open he found the pupil of the man's reddened eye fully dilated.

"What's he on?" Chip asked.

"Full-strength surgical-grade anesthetic. My father keeps it here for emergencies."

Chip shook his head as he exclaimed, "How'd you know how much to give him? You might have killed him with an overdose! We need to get him medical attention right away."

Calmly, almost with clinical authority, Jake crossed his arms and explained, "Mr. Temple is recovering from a bullet wound to the head. The slug—I think that's the slang you folks use for a bullet—was meant to go into my head. Fortunately, I was able to twist the gun, before it fired, away from my cranium. The bullet deeply grazed his scalp down to the skull.

"Mr. Temple went down and was not moving. I got our quad-runner and towable dolly we use to bring fish that are too big to carry back from the beach and went into the dunes to pick him up. Just in case a neighbor or passerby saw my return trip, I covered him with a tarp. He has yet to regain consciousness. I cleaned and dressed his wound. The scalp was too far separated to suture, so I thought it best to let it heal over. I trimmed the hair back then shaved around the wound. Before applying the dressing, I rinsed the gash and his entire head, then disinfected the thing with rubbing alcohol.

"That line holding him may look thin, but it's four-hundred-pound test Spectra fishing line. If he tries to twist out, it will cut into his flesh. The harder he twists, the deeper it will cut. The swivel at the bed frame will allow me to release him to pee or eat. If he ever regains consciousness.

"But I really don't give a shit if he doesn't. And I don't give a shit if he dies from an overdose. I need to keep him quiet, and I injected what I guessed would do the job. I've watched my father do it a few times. I'll give him more when I feel it necessary. Frankly, I still may have to kill him. If I do, or if he dies, I'll wrap the chain and anchor from the boat parked next to the house around his body, and I'll use one of my parents' sea kayaks to tow his carcass out to the drop-off. It's a few miles offshore, and I'd prefer to wait for the wind to die, but that might be a few days, so I'll brave the trip in the waves. I'll have to leave the beach at night to avoid potentially nosy neighbors.

"I'll set him free to sink into a thousand feet of water, and he'll never be heard from again. That would be the best solution for me. And unless you want to spend the best years of your life in a Mexican prison, you'll keep your pie-hole shut about the entire thing.

"This man tried to kill me, and I'll bet he's been successful in the same pursuit more than once before. His death and disappearance would be a benefit to society. I'm not a killer but your action, or inaction, has left me little choice. I don't have time to hang around here and nurse this lowlife back to health. And who's to say he won't try to pop me again when he's recovered? He's better dead."

With a headshake, Chip spoke, "I can't allow you to kill him. I made a mistake, but I'm a sworn officer of the law, and I can't be a party to murder, even in a foreign country. We've got to do everything we can for him."

"Well, isn't that touching," Jake said sarcastically. "Let me tell you, I'm probably flying or driving out of here tomorrow, and this guy's at least a few days from being ready to travel. You want to keep him alive, you need to stay with him while his wound mends. It'll be your penance for almost getting me killed. Just be sure and lock the door when you leave.

"Or we can dump him in the ocean together. I'm leaving tomorrow, either way."

Chip turned away, into the open living area of the *casita*. Jake followed.

"I don't believe this shit. All right, I'll stay with the bastard."

With a smile, Jake offered, "There's a bottle of Vicodin for pain in the medical bag. I'll show you where the kayak and anchor are in case he doesn't make it. There are antibiotics in the bag you can give him. I'd go three a day. They're slightly out of date but use them. Otherwise, you'll likely have to handle an infection."

He added, "Smile Deputy, you're staying a week on one of the world's most beautiful beaches."

"Great. Just what I wanted to do with my week off. Sit on some wind-blown sandbar playing Florence Nightingale to a wounded criminal. Where's the gun? I might need it while I'm here."

Jake retrieved the revolver and handed it to him, barrel first.

Jumping to the side away from the barrel Chip cried, "Hey! Be careful with that!"

"Don't worry. It isn't loaded. Here are some shells." Jake grinned as he handed him the gun and the paper bag with the extra ammunition.

Chip examined the pistol and placed the four remaining shells in the chamber. As he worked, he said, "I ate a mouthful of sand, and you had an empty gun!" He smiled. "Come to think of it, I think you're bluffing about killing him, too. You wouldn't really have done it, would you?"

"Now that you're here I'm no longer faced with the choice. From crime stopper to nursemaid… Who knows, this might be your vocational fork in the road!" Jake laughed.

"Boy, you ain't scorin' no points with the Riverside County Sheriff's Department. When this is over, I'm turning Deputy Logan loose on you for a few minutes. He's still sore about your artwork and the dunk in the bay you gave him."

"Cops… You guys have no sense of humor!"

"Yeah, right." Exhaling, Chip asked, "Where's the phone?"

Jake tossed him the device. "Dial 001 for the United States, then the area code and number. Press send."

The deputy followed the instructions. "Brad, it's Chip. I need you to do me a favor. I'm going to be gone longer than I'd thought."

CHAPTER 24

After comparing notes with Jake through the afternoon, Chip was convinced Dr. Cohen was innocent.

At approximately three thirty, Bennie stirred. He told them he needed to take a pee and wanted water. He showed no surprise that he was a captive or Chip was there. Within minutes he was again asleep. Jake changed the bandage on his head and re-secured the wrists and ankles while Chip watched.

Jake made quesadillas and cut oranges into wedges for them, drinking water as he ate. Chip had a Pacifico beer with his late lunch.

He gave Chip lock-up instructions for the house, then packed his small bag and computer and loaded them into the car. When he came back into the house Chip was thumbing through an old *Golf Digest*.

"I might be back here tonight, but I doubt it. In case I don't return, let's rouse Bennie and chat with him."

The man awoke quickly with only a fleeting moment of disorientation as Jake shook his arm. He initially squirmed and pulled at his restraints, however he quickly gave up as the ultra-thin Spectra fishing line bit at his wrists. Once calmed down, Jake asked him, "Bennie, do you remember what happened today?"

"Fuckin' rat shit. That's what happened," he rasped. He lifted his head slightly and looked around the room. "Who's the schwartz?"

"I forgot to tell you. Bennie and company are racists," Jake told Chip.

Chip smiled. "Chip Collins. Looks like we'll be roommates for a few days. Unless we can't work out an understanding." He left out the fact he was a law enforcement officer.

"Whad'da you mean, an understanding?" questioned Bennie, his head flat on the pillow again.

Chip explained, "You're going to tell me why you've been following Mr. Cohen for three days, and why you tried to kill him in the dunes today. I'll leave you tied up for as long as it takes. No more water, no food, no trips to the john. This could be a very uncomfortable few days for you. So, who are you working for?"

"Fuck off. I'm an innocent tourist. I took a walk on the beach this morning, and this fuckin' punk jumped me. Threw sand in my face then clubbed me on the head. You're holding me against my will and without cause, so I'm ordering you to cut me loose so I can go to a hospital."

"No, Bennie, it's not a bump on your head. It's a gunshot wound. It came from your own gun. We can't take you to a hospital because all three of us might end up in jail for a long time. The best thing for Jake and I would be if you died. If you get out of line, I'll personally take care of it.

"So, let's have an understanding. You can be comfortable and talkative, or I'll keep you doped with the anesthetic Jake has you on. Only problem is, I don't know how much is safe to give you. That could be what kills you. Makes no difference to me. The choice is yours. You can talk about your employer and have a nice, comfortable recovery or you can be hungry, thirsty, and lie in your own excrement until you're ready to travel."

"Nice speech, copper. Yeah, I can tell you're fuzz. I ain't sayin' nothin.'" He turned to look at Jake and said, "How'd I get here? You bring me? You the one who bandaged me up?"

"The same," answered Jake. He reached down and unclipped the heavy fishing swivel that held Bennie's wrist to the bed frame, then walked around the mattress and did the same on the other side. Grabbing an overstuffed pillow off a pine chair sitting nearby, he helped Bennie sit up and positioned the pillow behind him. "More comfortable?" he asked.

"Yeah. Except for the fucker that crawled inside my dome and keeps hitting my forehead from the inside with a sledgehammer."

Jake picked up the bottle of Vicodin and showed it to Bennie, "This will stop the headache. Along with some water. But the officer says you can't have any until you get more talkative."

Chip and Jake exchanged glances. The deputy gave a slight head shake, signaling Jake to remain silent. They waited, and soon the injured man looked up at them. His gaze rested upon the painkillers and a bottle of water sitting nearby.

Bennie inhaled deeply, then spoke. "Nicki asked me to follow you. He's got over a mil and a half invested in Wojicki. He don't know where the fucker is either, but he wants to find him. Preferably before the cops or you do. That's the honest truth."

"That's it?" the deputy asked.

"Honest. I don't know no more. Only that Nicki wants to find this Wojicki guy real bad."

"Nicki tell you to kill Cohen?"

"Like I said for the record, the kid jumped me. Quickest bastard I ever seen."

Chip asked Jake, "Where does Stinnetti live? I'll send Logan up to roust him. Bring him back to Riverside for questioning."

Jake lightly rubbed his chin as he paced. "Stinnetti lives outside Carson City. Picking him up is a bad idea. He thinks Bennie has eliminated me, or that he will. Let's let him think Bennie is still at large. Stinnetti won't talk anyway. He'd be surrounded by attorneys and wouldn't say a word during questioning."

"Yeah, I suppose," Chip answered. "You think your parents are okay?"

"Yep. Stinnetti's desire to have me whacked is part ego. We had a little run-in; it's personal. My family's okay. Just ride this out here with your new friend for a few days," Jake said to Chip. "Now I'd like to talk to Bennie one on one. Take a walk on the beach."

He pulled a short aluminum bat from behind a pine dresser, then motioned with his head for Chip to leave.

The detective walked out with a headshake, closing the door behind him.

Jake reached out and touched the tip of the bat to a spot between Bennie's eyes then spoke. "When we catch fish that are too big to safely bring into the boat, we calm them down first with this. This little bat has cracked the skulls of three-hundred-pound tuna and seven-hundred-pound marlin. My guess is you weigh less than one seventy. Your skull is not as thick as a prehistoric ocean predator, and this bat doesn't care what it cracks."

With the bat still between his eyes, Bennie spat out, "Save the theatrics for someone else. Kid, I been worked over by professionals. I been shot at, and I been beaten so bad I wanted to die. If you was gonna kill me, you'd have already done it.

"Truth is, I *really* don't know shit. Knowing things leads to trouble. You know too much, and people like me show up to make sure you don't tell no one else what you know.

"Ignorance is bliss, my friend."

Jake pulled the club back, then took a half-swing into the man's shin just below the knee. Bennie didn't howl in pain, but rather emitted a low guttural growl. His eyes were unfocused for a moment, but when they cleared, they bore into Jake with utter contempt.

"That little love tap was double-purposed," Jake announced. "First, I owe you for trying to kill me. I should have left you to die in the dunes, but I didn't. So, like it or not, you owe me. Something tells me you're the kind of man who'll remember that.

"Secondly, that tap was a warning as to what I'll personally do to you one-hundredfold if any member of my family is harmed. You will become the prey, and not the predator. I *will* get you. You are now the official protector of the Cohen family where Stinnetti is concerned."

"Kid, in the Middle East I'd track and kill ragheads through the shithole cities. You got lucky today. If I'da been able to find a real gun, you'd have never gotten close to me. Maybe I'm gettin' older and slower. Who knows? Fact is I'm lyin' here, and you got that bat."

He rubbed his shin for a moment then leaned back again on the pillow. "You didn't have to save my ass, and I appreciate that. I ain't a saint, but I remember a favor. You got my word. That good enough for you?"

Jake studied the short-barreled bat. "If that's the best we can do… But be warned, I'll hold Stinnetti's entire network responsible if harm comes to my family. You may want to seek a new employer."

"Stinnetti's a pussy. You got nothin' to worry about. He don't have nobody else but me," snickered Bennie.

"Well that's just dandy," Jake said with a nod. "Here, take a few of these painkillers. Don't take more than four a day. They're addictive as hell. You're going to stay here with Deputy Collins until you're okay to travel without raising too many questions. Swim in the ocean once a day. It'll help break up the scabbing on the head wound, and it will heal faster, with less scarring."

"I planned to finish this trip with a broad and some drinks by the pool in a hotel in Cabo. Now I gotta end it on the most desolate beach I ever seen with some coon cop as my nursemaid." He stopped to swallow two pills with gulps of water.

Jake laughed as he spoke, "I'm leaving now. Please, be a good citizen and don't make him have to shoot you. By the way, I took most of your money. I left you a couple hundred and all your credit cards. I'm low on cash. Have Nicki reimburse you."

"Was Nicki's money anyway," said Bennie. In a more serious tone, he added, "Thanks for patching me up. I won't give the schwartz no trouble, as long as he don't fuck with me."

Reaching down to the bed frame, Jake unclasped the two swivels securing Bennie's feet. "You probably need to take a whiz, and it might do you some good to walk a little." He walked outside and left Bennie alone in the house, picking up the gun off the coffee table as he passed by.

Chip sat in a patio chair in the sandy front yard. The shadows had crept along the ground to the east and the fading day was turning cool. Jake approached and took a seat nearby.

"I don't think Bennie will give you any trouble, but in case he does…" Jake handed Chip the weapon. "He's loose and using the head. I'm leaving and likely won't see you for a few days. The person I'm meeting won't want to be seen by our friend in there. It could cause problems for her later."

"A lady friend, huh?" Chip raised his eyebrows.

"An acquaintance. I wouldn't even call her a friend."

The two sat in silence as the slackening breeze blew in over the water. Finally, Jake asked, "So, why the extra interest in this case?"

Chip looked out to sea. "If I can prove your parents' innocence, it will be a feather in my cap. Your folks don't have much political clout, but they *know* the people who do. Supervisors, the planning commissioner, the mayor, and even my boss, the sheriff, have played golf or been to parties with your parents. This might be a steppingstone to a political seat. They'll be indebted and may pay back the favor. That's politics, my friend."

"Sounds a tad mercenary."

"I didn't cause this mess. I'll help get to the bottom of it, and in the process, my career may be helped along."

Jake nodded and stood. "I'm outta here. Good luck with Bennie. Use anything you want. Just be sure it's rinsed clean of salt water and sand when you put it away. The quad-runner is full of fuel. The kayak and paddle are in the garage, and there's a spare anchor in there too in case you need them."

Chip smiled. "I won't need the kayak. We'll be fine."

"I'll need the satellite phone. You'll have to go to La Ribera to make calls; there's cell service there. Supplies too. Try to keep to yourself here. Be sure and throw that gun in the ocean when you leave, or even before.

"Adios, my friend." He extended his hand. Chip took it and held the grasp a few extra seconds.

When the Toyota was out of sight Chip tucked the gun into his waistband at the small of his back and let his shirt fall over it. He walked back into the house. Bennie was rummaging through the refrigerator.

"What the fuck we gonna eat for dinner? I ain't eaten nothin' substantial since yesterday, and all they got here is tortillas, cheese, and some mangy tomatoes. Don't you people need watermelon and fried chicken to keep you alive?"

It's only going to be a few days… But they're going to be long days, Chip decided as he closed the door behind him.

CHAPTER 25

The beach bar at Palmas de Cortez was teeming with life when Jake arrived shortly after sundown. The quiet midweek crowd had been replaced by the weekend throng of fishermen. Most had come to set new world records not only for the size of the fish they'd yank from the ocean but also for tequila consumption. A samba band played loudly in a wind-protected corner of the patio, and the guests worked diligently at depleting the local supply of distilled agave juice as they waited for dinner.

Jake scanned the bar. Those who'd been forced off the water by the wind today had an opportunity to start on libations early. The newcomers, who outnumbered them, were quickly catching up with shots.

Jake smiled as he walked through. The current filling the air was familiar; under other circumstances, he would have joined in the revelry. Yet there was work to be done...

Recognizing him from the night before, Martín caught his eye from across the bar. He waved for Jake to join him. In contrast to the shorts and tee shirts of the fishermen, he wore a buttoned-down white cotton shirt and finely pressed black slacks. Polished cap-toed black shoes completed the resort manager's outfit.

With the noise level too high to have a conversation, Martín made a thumb motion. Jake followed him out of the bar toward the office. On the way, Freddie, the bartender from Rancho Buena Vista, joined them, a bottle of Tecate beer in hand. They went past the reception desk to a private room where they sat around a conference table of hardwood. The adobe walls were adorned with colorful mounted fish.

"*Cerveza*, amigo? Or maybe a margarita?" asked Martín.

Jake answered with a nod, "Sure. Pacifico, por favor."

Martín looked at Freddie, who held up his bottle to show it was nearly empty, then he spoke in Spanish into an intercom and asked for a Tecate, Pacifico, water, and some food.

"Nothing for you?" Jake questioned.

"No, señor. The crowd tonight is restless. If any of these men choose to start trouble, they may go to jail in Los Barriles. It is the hotel policy to get them out before morning. Not really our job, but our guests remember the favor and return. It may be a long night for me.

"Señor Jake, a woman, *muy bonito*, is here looking for you."

"She's expected. No problem, I think. Did she come alone?"

"Sí. But a beautiful woman, alone in the bar with those drinking... This can be a problem."

Jake laughed, "You do not know this woman. She is not the one you need to worry about. Trust me."

Freddie and Martín laughed too. Freddie said, "*Señorita chubasco*, no?"

"*Chubasco grande!*" answered Jake.

"Shall I send word to have her join us?" asked Martín.

Jake answered, "No. Maybe later. So, what can you tell me that we didn't know yesterday?"

The door opened, and their drinks arrived. After the young woman passed them out and placed a plate of fresh ceviche and tortilla chips on the table, they continued. Jake's mouth watered after his meager fare for the day, but he decided it would be in bad taste to pounce on the food. Only when Freddie and Martín had each helped themselves did he load an ample portion of the lime-juice marinated seafood concoction on his plate. They had each eaten a few bites when Martín spoke.

"I believe the people you look for are in Manzanillo. Not Manzanillo exactly, but a little place north of there. Barra Navidad. It is a town of beautiful beaches and small hotels. When Americans come to Mexico, they go to the big resort towns; Acapulco, Cabo San Lucas, Cancún, Mazatlán, Puerta Vallarta, or Manzanillo. When Mexicans go on vacation, we go to places like Barra Navidad. Very quiet and very beautiful. And inexpensive."

He spoke with an air of authority, as though he was Hercule Poirot unwinding the plot at the end of an Agatha Christie novel. He was now the hero detective and Freddie his sidekick, the two eager to share their attained knowledge.

"Nice work, gentlemen," praised Jake. "How do we know this to be true?"

Freddie spoke. "Martín, as manager here, knows some of the airline employees. He asked them where this Thomas Wojicki went after leaving. They track him through the computers and find that he and the two other gringos leave here on a flight to Mazatlán, then from there they fly into Manzanillo."

"It was not quite so simple," Martín corrected, not wanting his accomplishment diminished. "None of the airlines had them on a manifest. However, with some digging at the airport, we find they left here on Saturday morning on a chartered flight."

"Excellent work. Anything else?" Jake asked.

Martín took a drink of water and then ate some of the seafood mixture. After dabbing his mouth with a napkin, he expounded, "Yes, señor. I pull the records of the phone calls from Mr. Wojicki's room while he stay here. Many phone calls to Barra Navidad. The hotel Grand Bay, and a few calls to a real estate office there. Here are the numbers." He handed Jake an envelope. "The real estate office is Playa Estates. They specialize in selling beach property to gringos. The agent there is Estela. I called and talked to her. When I ask her about his whereabouts, she say that all sales there are confidential.

"So, I make up a little story and tell Estela this Thomas Wojicki stiff the hotel on his bill, and we need to find him. One thing we Mexicans do not like is to be taken advantage of by gringos. Typically, we stick together on these issues, and Estela say she will have him call when she speaks to him."

Jake waited for Martín or Freddie to go on, but neither spoke for a few moments. He ate a few more bites of the appetizer then said, "*Nada mas?*"

"No señor, nothing more. Maybe this Estela can help you out if you go to Barra Navidad. I don't know though; she seems to not want to talk much about them. We have done all we can here, I think."

Removing his wallet, Jake placed four hundred-dollar bills on the table. He left it to the two to decide how it would be divided and said, "That's all I can afford for now. Thank you both for your work. It is appreciated by my family."

"Whatever you can give is enough. Your parents have helped our community, and we wish to return the favor. Good luck to you. I hope you find what you're looking for," said Martín.

Freddie stood and tipped his half-empty beer bottle toward Jake. "*Salud, señor.* May you be successful in your journey."

Jake stood and tapped his bottle against Freddie's. They drank a swig then

Jake said, "May I ask one last favor?"

"Sí."

"I need a room for tonight. Two beds preferably."

"No problema, señor. It will be taken care of. However, are you certain you want two beds? The señorita is *muy bonita*, no?" Martín raised his eyebrows as he spoke.

"Sí, my friend. Two beds. This señorita is loco!" laughed Jake.

"I think you make a mistake, my friend. Loco señoritas are the best kind!" barked Freddie. The three laughed in unison.

When Jake returned to the bar, the pitch of the crowd had increased two decibels. Spotting Amber was easy now; she'd managed to initiate a limbo contest in the middle of the huge room. The conga drums from the band had been brought in from the patio, and the drummers wailed on the skins as the mostly portly fishermen each tried to slither under the fishing rod used as a limbo bar. Amber stood near each one as he made his attempt and coached them by example. She wore a knee-length sarong and a tight black blouse that stopped just below the ribs. As she bent to go under the bar, she hiked the dress up just high enough on the thigh to excite the predominantly male crowd. The men called out loud bets as to whether or not she wore underwear, but the fabric of the sarong never rose quite high enough for anyone to be certain. The muscles in her stomach flexed as she demonstrated proper technique and her dark hair woven in a French braid dragged on the polished tile as she deftly slid under the bar again and again.

Jake was amazed at how Amber had the crowd involved in the contest. The few women present stood and howled as the men fell on their backsides time after time. None could keep up with the lithe woman nobody knew. Some men made attempts to single Amber out with an arm around her waist or embrace as she helped them from the floor, but she would deftly spin away to initiate the sequence again with the next contestant in line. As each man leaned back to start under the bar, a waiter poured a tequila shot directly from a bottle into his mouth. Judging from the wobbly knees, Jake surmised many of the men had gone under the bar more than once.

Seeing Jake standing near the back of the crowd, Amber went over and stood in front of him. Every eye in the room followed as she approached, and with her chin down and a sideways sultry look she beckoned Jake to join her at the limbo bar. His hands rose in protest, but an immediate howl of displeasure rose from the crowd. Amber looked him straight in the eye then leaned back and neatly glided under the bar held by the waiters. Upon completion, she stood and opened her hands in a challenging gesture.

Jake leaned back and easily navigated under without a wobble. None of the other men had completed a pass at this height, and the crowd bayed in approval. He gave a slight head nod and wave and tried to hurry off the floor, but Amber had already motioned for a lower setting. As he reached the interior perimeter of the horde, he found his exit blocked with bodies and was pushed backward toward the limbo stick.

Amber leaned her upper body backward to a point where Jake was certain she'd fall, but she surprised him with her agility and strength. Her knees were inches off the floor, yet the feet stayed flat, gripping the tile, and moving forward inch by inch, driven from the hip as she passed under the bar. When the pass was completed, she again stared at Jake, but this time winked as she offered the challenge.

He looked at the makeshift limbo bar and shook his head, putting his hands up in a gesture of surrender. The crowd again expressed its displeasure with taunting catcalls, and Jake quickly found himself back in front of the bar, which was now less than twenty-four inches above the tile. While Amber was certainly the more graceful of the two, Jake had the leg and abdominal strength to hold his own body parallel to the floor and make his way under the stick. Upon completion of the pass, he gave a pronounced bow to the crowd and again tried to make an exit. Amber, however, had already given a hand motion to the limbo bar holders for a lower setting. She caught his hand from behind. With the host beckoning the two took their positions in front of the bar, now no more than eighteen inches off the floor.

Amber again went first, this time not with her feet flat on the floor but rather folding them under her tight rump and shimmying forward on her shins. The outside air was cool, but in the wind-protected area with the body heat of over one hundred people, the temperature had risen to over eighty degrees Fahrenheit. The drums wailed at a fever pitch, and the crowd yowled in approval as she again slid under the stick. When she stood on the other end, she beckoned Jake to come to her.

It was near pandemonium now as the mass chanted in unison, "*Go! Go! Go!*" Sliding up to the bar Jake shook off his thongs and following the example set by Amber, he leaned back over his feet. This time the waiter with the tequila bottle stood over him and poured the golden liquid into his mouth. He hated cheap tequila and normally drank only ice cold, one hundred percent blue agave straight or mixed with Gran Marnier, but presently his choice was limited.

As the liquid burned its way down his throat, he too made the pass under the bar. The throng bawled as he stood. This time he realized an attempt at escape was futile and waited as Amber again motioned for the bar to be lowered to what seemed an impassible height.

A mild layer of perspiration shimmered on her skin as she contorted herself into an impossible stance to slide under the limbo stick. With her body parallel to the floor and her knees in front, she somehow was able to slip forward. When she reached the point where her ample bosom had to clear the rod, she arched her back further and managed to get the shapely appendages under the bar. The mostly male group was near hysteria as she finished her pass. She stood, crossed her legs, and gave a dainty curtsy.

Jake again held up his hands in a gesture of surrender, and this time refused to go. Better to capitulate than look like a fool. This was Amber's show, and she was basking in the limelight.

She came over and put her arms around his neck. Giving him a hug, she whispered into his ear, "Don't get any ideas. I'm still pissed at you, but I need to make these animals think we're together, so they'll leave me alone. So be a dear and hug me back."

He did and again smelled the musty scent he'd encountered at the dinner table in her home. With his arm around her waist, he retrieved his rubber thongs and escorted her toward the huge dining room where the waiting dinner had been delayed by the impromptu contest.

Once away from the noise of the bar, he asked, "You have the memory stick with the e-mail info?"

She spun out of his arm and faced him with her hands on her hips. "You calloused pig! How about a 'How was your flight?' or 'Sorry I couldn't meet you at the airport...' or just a friendly 'Hello, it's great to see you...' No, all I get from you is 'Give, give, give…' Men shell out big bucks for my company, and even though I'm paid for, they treat me better than you do.

"We'll get to the memory stick. But there are more important things on my mind right now. Like, where are we sleeping tonight? And are we eating here? If not, let's go now. I'm famished! I didn't have time for lunch."

Admonished, he answered, "I'm sorry. You're absolutely right. I've arranged for a room here for tonight. We can't stay at my parents' home. The man who tried to kill me today is recovering there from a gunshot wound to the head."

"My God! You shot him?" she gasped.

"Not exactly. We scuffled and the gun he was trying to kill me with went off. It grazed his head. Anyway, I didn't think you'd want to be seen with me by someone from home."

"Thank God you weren't killed. You're okay, aren't you?"

"Not a scratch," he answered. "Anyway, I think I know where Cindi and company went, and I'll try to fly there tomorrow."

"I know. They're north of Manzanillo. Tom Wojicki bought a beach house there. Cindi and I have exchanged a few e-mails. She's attached photos. Looks like she's having the time of her life."

"Yeah, living it up on my parents' money. Are there any pictures of the house, or exact locations noted in the e-mails?" he questioned.

"No. Well, maybe. One photo could be of the house. She just wrote that they have a beautiful spot out of the way, on a very secluded beach between Manzanillo and Puerto Vallarta. After dinner, we can look at the bunch. For now, let's eat," she said leading Jake into the dining room.

The tables were wrought-iron with glass tops, and each was set for four. Jake pointed to one in a far corner and quickly unfolded all the linen napkins, placing two over the backs of the chairs to give the appearance their table was full. As the other hotel guests meandered in from the bar, some of the men cast furtive glances at Amber, now seated with Jake.

"It seems you've made friends here quickly," he mentioned.

"Jealous?" she said with a smile and twinkle in the eyes.

He squinted at her and said, "No, not jealous. Just concerned that you don't get too friendly. The fishermen who were here today got skunked, and the others who've just arrived know they'll likely get the same tomorrow.

The windy weather's got them wound pretty tight. This could erupt, and an overly flirtatious, beautiful woman could be the spark that ignites it."

"Thank you, Jake," she said with sincerity.

"For what?"

"Telling me that I was beautiful. A lady can never hear that too much, you know." She paused, and they exchanged a long look that ended with each of them smiling.

"Don't worry about the crowd. I felt the tension in the room and was accosted by at least ten of these guys while I waited for you. I *know* how to handle men. The limbo contest allowed them to let off some steam and maybe built a little unity in the group as they cackled together. If I hadn't started that I'd have been pushing guys away all night. There was a method to my madness."

"Or perhaps it was madness to your method."

"Perhaps," smiled Amber as she spoke. "Either way it works for me."

CHAPTER 26

Jake placed the tablet computer in his valise while Amber peered out the window during the descent into Guadalajara. Between dinner last night and the flight, he'd reviewed the e-mail information at least ten times. Cindi had sent photos of her and Tom on a golf course, by a hotel pool, on a beach and lunching in a café. The one on the beach showed a house up on a bluff in the background. Jake guessed it was the hideaway they bought. Cindi was deeply tanned, with Wojicki white as paste. The e-mails told of nothing important, except that Cindi looked forward to the trips into Manzanillo for shopping. She'd gone on about the warmth of the climate, the freshness of the papayas, how she loved her morning dips in the ocean, and the slow pace of life. Amber had sent return communications with questions about possible visits, but Cindi had simply written it was impossible until things settled down. She didn't elaborate, and Amber had not wanted to press too hard.

At dinner last night Amber had imbibed in a few too many margaritas and had woken with a mild hangover. Jake had abstained from further alcohol after the involuntary tequila shot.

They'd fallen asleep quickly after retiring to the room, each spent from the rigors of the day. Jake woke early and went to the workout facility. He watched the sun rise over the Sea of Cortez as he went through a series of lat pulls, pull-ups, butterflies with twenty-pound dumbbells, squats, leg lifts, arm and leg curls, French presses, and calf-raises.

He stretched on the deck by the pool and finished the routine by seven. After a quick rinse in the health club shower, he returned to their room to rouse his new cohort. Amber groggily protested when he'd announced it was time for breakfast, then on to the airport. She showered while Jake removed the stitches above his eye, a task he'd unfortunately done more than once before. Upon completion, he fetched toast for the two of them, with tea for her and coffee for himself. By 8:15 they thanked Martín (who worked double shifts on weekends) for the hospitality and were on the way to the airport with Amber's hair in a wet ponytail.

They went from one airline counter to another comparing the most direct route and the costs involved with each. Jake was pleased that Amber had been willing to take a more roundabout itinerary to save $300 each by accepting a three-hour layover in Guadalajara. They'd be in Barra Navidad by sundown.

After a Bloody Mary on the flight from Cabo to Mazatlán, Amber was feeling better. The beaches and hotels looked inviting as they'd flown over the city, but they hurried to the next gate for the flight to Mexico's industrial mecca.

"There are beaches where we're going," Jake reiterated.

The airport at Guadalajara was like any in the United States. It offered fast food restaurants, bars, and upscale eateries. They arrived before 1:00 p.m., and with nearly three hours to kill, Amber wanted to go sightseeing in the city. Jake said no. In Mexico, anything could happen, and he didn't want to miss the flight. They'd see plenty of sights around Manzanillo. She sulked for a few minutes, then went to the gift shop and overpaid for a trashy chick novel. Jake pulled out his tablet and began adding to his notes.

After thirty minutes and five chapters, she announced, "I'm bored."

"How could you be bored? Those little books are full of enough sex and emotional intrigue to keep any woman occupied for hours. Janelle picks one of those up and can't put it down," he answered without looking up from his keyboard. Then he grinned and added, "Oh, I forgot. That storyline might be redundant in your case."

"Ha! Ha! At least I'm doing something that pays well. If you weren't so broke, we could have taken a more direct flight, and we'd be there by now." She let the novel hang loosely in her right hand, then rubbed her chin with the left. Fidgeting for the next five minutes, she finally rose from her chair and took a walk. In ten minutes, she was back, standing in front of Jake with her arms crossed and her head held sideways.

Eventually, he acknowledged her presence with a peek over the tablet's screen.

"Let's go have a drink," she said. "I usually make it a point not to have any alcohol before seven, but the tedium of waiting in airports will drive me to the bar every time. I've already broken my rule with the Bloody Mary, and I am on vacation."

Jake exhaled. "This is no vacation. Do you always get your way?"

"Mostly. I've been told I use a velvet hammer. Get off your butt and let's go."

He shook his head and rolled his eyes, then gathered up their luggage and followed. She'd already picked out the bar. They were quickly seated, and a woman came to take their order. Amber asked for a chardonnay and Jake a water.

"Not drinking?" she asked.

He shook his head. "I need to stay in shape. I'm skiing in what will likely be my last shot at a world championship in two weeks, and I've been drinking more than I should.

"You know, we might run into these people this afternoon or tonight. I want to be in a peak state, mentally and physically. A lapse in San Diego three nights ago nearly cost me my life, I think. A cop I shoved into the water may have saved my ass. I need to apologize to him when I get back."

She laughed, "How do you get into these things?"

"My mom calls it 'stirring the pot.' She says I have a knack for it." He laughed, too.

Their drinks arrived, and the conversation became more serious. "When we find them, what will you do?" she asked.

"I don't know. I've been thinking about it. I can't really call the local police or *federales*. Most can be easily bought, and Wojicki has a lot more money than we do. The U.S. government won't likely attempt to extradite them without proof of a crime, and even then, the stakes probably aren't high enough to have them hauled back home. Maybe if we can figure out where the funds are deposited, we can report it to the U.S. authorities and have the assets seized or frozen. But that will likely take months or even years to work through the system before we get the money returned."

They sat silently for a moment, each thinking about possibilities. Jake stared vacantly about the room, and Amber looked at her nails.

"Maybe I'll offer to split it with them," he said, coming out of his trance. "Let them keep half and send the balance back. That might be easiest. My guess is, we'll get about 1.8 million. With that amount, we can finish up enough of the homes to crawl out from under the financial burdens. Just getting *some* money is most important right now. Even if we could get a million, it would be enough to finish up Phase I of the development and tap the existing equity. Hell, it might end up being more profitable for Dad and Mom in the long run if they don't have to split proceeds with Wojicki, even after the legal trouble and paying off that crooked loan shark.

"Wojicki, Cindi, and Monk keep half, and live happily ever after."

"So that's our plan? We're shooting for half?"

"It doesn't feel right, but I think that's our best option. There's a bit more though."

"More?"

"Yeah. I haven't mentioned this yet, but they also made off with my mother's jewelry collection. The DeCorto family jewels. It is said to have been in the family for nearly a thousand years. I want that back, too."

Her eyes lit up at the mention of the collection. "What's it worth?" she asked with an eyebrow raise.

"Two, maybe two and a half."

She whistled then said, "Wow. Two hundred and fifty thousand!"

Shaking his head, Jake muttered, "No, Amber, not two hundred and fifty grand. *Maybe two million, five hundred thousand.*"

Her hand quickly covering her mouth stopped the sip of wine from hitting him as she coughed in utter shock.

He looked her directly in the eye and stated, "Amber, I'm not paying you on the collection. Only on whatever funds we recover."

"Hey, our deal is ten percent of *whatever* I help recover. Don't start backpedaling on me now that I'm down here and you have the information you need."

"Our deal was ten percent of whatever money we got back. You didn't even know about the jewels. Also, nearly everything you've given me was duplicate information of what I got from Martín and Freddie. But I made a deal, and I'm sticking to it. Ten percent of the money. That's it."

She was now standing in front of him with her hands on her hips. "When I signed on, we were talking about ten percent of about 3.65 million. Now based upon the figures you're throwing out, I might receive as little as $180,000. I can make that in a good six months! No, our deal is ten percent of *whatever* we get back. Otherwise, I walk off the plane when we land and find them myself and tell them you're coming!"

He closed his eyes and shook his head while exhaling. "All right, Amber, ten percent of everything. You're damn lucky there are witnesses here. Otherwise, the headlines in tomorrow's local paper would read 'Unidentified Woman's Body Found in Airport Dumpster.' With a crowd around, I'm forced to capitulate."

She hopped back up onto the chair and took a sip of the chardonnay. Squinting, she gave a circuitous grin and said, "You'd never kill me, Jake. First, you're not a killer. You don't have it in you." She took another sip of the chardonnay and was quiet.

Jake broke the silence. "You said 'first'..."

With the smile still in place, she said, "Secondly, you couldn't kill me 'cause we're too much alike.

"We're not so different, Jake Cohen. Somewhere under your indifferent veneer, you have a big heart, and in that heart, you know I'm right.

"We're both *bored* with our present lives. It's not the money we're after. Neither of us is fulfilled in what we're doing. It's the *adventure* we took off to chase. The money is a by-product, the dangling carrot, that's keeping us going. I haven't thought about anything but this hunt since I met you.

"You don't care about skiing anymore. You're good, but you're apathetic. Sure, you put in the motions and hours of hard training, but it's no longer what you want. Your life at that little restaurant and hidden resort is *too* quiet and uncomplicated. From an outsider's view, you've got it made—skiing every day, a small but booming restaurant business, living with a hottie of a girlfriend. But I'll bet it's *all* eating at you from within."

"You've been to the resort?" he asked. Suddenly he felt violated. Caples Lake, so far off the beaten path, had been his sanctuary. *Another of the consequences of crossing the line.*

"Oh yes," answered Amber. "I took a client there. We skied at the mountain, had dinner in the restaurant, and then stayed the night in one of those funky little cabins. I loved it! The seafood diablo was to die for, by the way, but my client probably didn't appreciate the severe garlic. The raspberry cheesecake with the Chambord sauce was by far the best I've ever had. Janelle served us. She's quite a looker, you know. Some incredibly handsome man was there wooing her with all his might, both during the dinner hour and in front of the fire in the lodge afterward. She sent him packing at closing time.

We talked for at least an hour. My client didn't seem to mind. I think he was more interested in her than me. Beauty and brains. What a package."

Any other week Janelle would have been at school, but it was her break, and she stayed on at the resort.

Amber gave him a thoughtful look. "You won't keep her, you know, if you stay at the resort and keep doing what you're doing now. It's not enough for her. She's outgrown it. She's waiting patiently to see if you're ready to do something else, but she won't wait forever. And even though you're tired of what you're doing, you're scared of the change and commitment she wants."

"Jan told you all this?"

Amber peered at him over the rim of the glass. "Nope. Woman's intuition. You've got six months, give or take, to show her you can make a change. Just for the record, I never mentioned you had your hands up my blouse at dinner. As a matter of fact, I never mentioned you at all. Your secret is safe with me."

"She didn't recognize you?"

Amber's head tilted as she asked, "How could she?"

"Our photo was on the Mt. Rose website. She saw it there."

"Guess not."

As he thought silently for a few moments, she twirled the wine some, seeming to inspect the consistency of the golden liquid.

Finally, he said, "You're wrong, Amber. This venture is to help my family. In a couple of weeks, I'll be skiing in Colorado at the world championships."

"Whatever you say," she said as she put the glass down on the table and pushed it away. "Wine just doesn't seem like the proper thing to drink in the tropics, does it? What should I have instead, a piña colada? Or maybe a mai tai?"

Jake didn't answer. He was lost in thought. Amber had hit a nerve.

CHAPTER 27

"Oh my God! This is so cool! We're landing right on a beach! How far do you think the ocean is from the runway?" Amber asked.

Jake glanced out the window. "A hundred and fifty yards, give or take. You seem overly infatuated by the ocean. Where are you from?"

"Nebraska. Look at the palm trees! And the plants! Are those banana trees? This is all so intriguing, isn't it?" she said as she grabbed his arm with both hands. "The two of us chasing villains through a third-world jungle."

He looked at her as she stared out the window. Her eyes sparkled with the excitement of a little girl at Christmas. "Is this your first trip to the tropics?" he asked.

"No. I've been to Hawaii and the Bahamas. But those trips were always to swank hotels where the outside world was hidden from us. We'd go to the Bahamas every year after football season. Daddy wouldn't miss a Huskers game. I've been to Hawaii three times with clients, but it's so touristy. I can't believe you're not excited by this."

"Maybe under other circumstances. Honestly, I'm nervous as hell. These people are dangerous. You've seen what happened to my father. They're not going to be thrilled to see us, you know."

She laid her hand on top of his on the armrest. "Don't worry," she offered, "Cindi would never allow me to be hurt, and you'll be with me when we confront them. Everything will work out fine."

"All right, I'll hold you to that," he whispered as the plane touched down.

The air was incredibly warm as they drove away from the airport at 6:00 p.m. in another rented car. The city of Manzanillo was to their south, but all the clues they'd picked up told them to start in Barra Navidad, which they'd learned was twenty to forty minutes to the north of the airport, depending on the traffic.

Amber proclaimed that speeding through the jungle in the convertible was a top-ten life experience for her. The banana and coconut plantations they passed were like monuments to the lower latitudes, and the two small towns they crawled through with a jerky stop-and-go motion oozed the storybook charm of old Mexico.

Jake deftly negotiated the cramped streets and as they drove he gave her a narrative of as much of the history of the area as he knew.

The Spanish, he told her, had settled here before the Pilgrims landed at Plymouth Rock. They'd used the area trees to build ships and launch expeditions farther to the north to California and to the south in Central and South America. Manzanillo had become the major port city for the western coast of the New World during the early years of European settlement. With the gold and treasures looted from the Aztecs whetting the appetites of the Spanish monarchy, the necessity for ships and further exploration and exploitation of the New World had arisen. Cross-wielding Catholic priests led the way, always backed up by a contingent of Spanish soldiers, enlightening the simple natives of their sinful ways while enslaving them and stealing everything they had. Only recently did the history books begin to tell the true story of the brutality of the early missionaries to the Americas.

As they started down the spit of sand on which Barra Navidad was situated, they caught a glimpse of the ocean, gray-green in the light of the fading day. A gentle breeze blew in off the water and Amber commented on how her skin had immediately become sticky once they got close to the sea.

"Welcome to the tropics," Jake said.

Jake wanted to begin the search for the real estate office right away. Amber had other priorities. Reluctantly he acquiesced that lodging would be first on their list of to-dos. Driving up and down the tight cobblestone streets they found a few hotels which Amber inspected while Jake waited in the car. After numerous stops they checked into the one she deemed most sanitary. When Jake saw the room, he proclaimed it a palace, stating he'd stayed in many worse places in his travels through the lower latitudes. Amber fixed her gaze on him for a moment standing in his cargo shorts, tee shirt, and thongs and declared she believed him.

While she freshened up in the bathroom, he called the desk and asked to be put through to the real estate office. He found the office phone answered by a machine with the outgoing message in English, then repeated in Spanish. The message stated they were open Tuesday through Saturday until 4:00 p.m., and Sunday and Monday by appointment. Jake left the hotel number and his first name, asking specifically for Estela. He said he and his wife were in the area looking for a second home. Preferably a beach house.

The prospect of a sale would arouse a real estate agent the way a steak on a backyard grill aroused a dog. The phone would ring soon enough, he knew.

He didn't leave the satellite number or that of his cell phone, knowing they might be traceable.

The sun was setting as they went off to survey the town. Jake exchanged a few hundred dollars for Mexican pesos at another of the many 'ma and pa' stores so prevalent here, and he and Amber walked toward the beaches and restaurants. Wal-Mart and Amazon had yet to engulf the local population and destroy the sole proprietorship economy. It was only a matter of time before it happened. Jake told Amber she should enjoy the vibe while she had the opportunity as they moved along.

Music wafted through the streets from the bars and cafés they passed. The scene was different here than the towns they'd traveled through. This was a *beach* town.

Interspersed with the host of Saturday night revelers were a few other gringos. Jake scanned the crowded sidewalks and open restaurants and bars as they passed by. Amber was taking in the sights and seemed uninterested in any individuals, focusing on the complete picture. A few surfers walked by them, boards under their arms and hair still wet. The cobble-rock streets were too rough to walk on, but the town offered crude concrete sidewalks. Buildings were made of poor-quality block, some without paint or plaster, all showing the ravages of the ocean winds and salt air. The shadows were long and only moments from disappearing altogether as Jake and Amber strolled toward the section of town the hotel clerk had told them was the gathering place for the Americans in the area. They could hear waves breaking on the sand nearby. The air wasn't hot, just warm and sticky.

As they passed a restaurant and bar, Jake stopped and stared in for a moment. It was crowded, but through the swarm of patrons, he could see the sun setting red over the ocean. Thin cirrus clouds stretched like ribbons across the sky, glowing auburn at the horizon and fading to gray streaks on a deep purple background. Amber gave him a questioning look, and he motioned with his thumb and forefinger they should go in. The name of the place was the Barra Bar, not where their hotel clerk had suggested they go, and she was confused.

Walking silently around the open restaurant, Jake noticed that many eyes, male and female alike, followed Amber. Focused on finding Wojicki, he'd given a cursory "fine" when she'd asked if she looked okay upon leaving the hotel. But now he realized she was stunning in the sarong dress from last night and a white sleeveless blouse. Her dark hair fell across her shoulders in random curls and her salon-tanned arms and legs flexed with a muscle tone unfamiliar to the local people. Her eyes continued to amaze him as they danced with the light from the candles on each table.

Bewitching, he was silently reminded.

Forcing the thought from his mind, he led her to the bar, where they sat on stools of jungle hardwood. The bartender came over, and Jake ordered a Pacifico beer and Amber a mai tai.

"I'd rather sit at a table by the water and enjoy what's left of the sunset," Amber stated.

Jake was looking slowly around. "One of the photos Cindi sent you was taken in this bar."

Looking for a thread of familiarity, she asked, "Are you sure? They all look the same."

"The palapa roof hangs lower here. And the chairs are the same as in the picture, leather-backed. Everywhere else we've seen so far has wood backs. The spacing on the hardwood rafter supports is right too. This is it."

With wide eyes, she said, "Wow! I thought you were whacko when you kept going through those pictures over and over. Okay, what next?"

"Give me a twenty. I'm going to see if the bartender has seen them. A little American green might jog his memory."

With squinted eyes, she said, "That's a fine idea, but use your own twenty bucks."

He cocked his head sideways. "If you want to split what we recover, you need to invest."

"Fine," she hissed as she pulled a bill from her tiny handbag. "But only ten percent. I'm looking for two hundred out of your wallet before I reach into mine again."

"Nope. We'll split expenses equally. Believe it or not, I'm just a poor ski bum," he laughed.

She rolled her eyes toward the palm-frond roof. "Should I ask the bartender for separate checks?"

"No, Amber. I'll splurge and buy you a drink."

"Boy, you really know how to impress a girl."

"I thought the term 'girl' was demeaning?"

"Only on an 'as needed' basis to scold a man. It's okay in certain instances."

Jake nodded, but in truth didn't understand.

The bartender arrived with the drinks and reached for the $20 lying on the bar, but Jake waved his left hand over it. With his right hand, he offered one-hundred peso note. He spoke in Spanish as he pulled the photos from his valise.

They exchanged names, and the bartender studied the photos intently after Jake had explained they were looking for the people in the pictures. Amber saw a few slight headshakes and then a nod of recognition as he shuffled through the prints. Jake and the man talked for a few minutes, then he went back to his duties of satisfying the thirsts of the crowd.

"Well?" she asked simply as he turned back to her.

"He didn't recognize Wojicki or Cindi, but he saw Monk Phillips here a few days ago. The photo I recognized of the lovebirds here was taken during the day though, and he said two others work that shift. He suggested we come back tomorrow."

She smiled and sipped her mai tai. "We're close," she said with a nod. "Exciting, isn't it?"

"Scintillating," said Jake as read the label on his beer.

Slapping his arm, she said, "Oh, it is! Cheer up! You're near the end of the chase."

They both sat quietly for a moment listening to the waves crash on the sand below the bar. Only gray-blue light could be seen on the horizon over a now black sea. "Finish your drink," he said finally. "We're movin' on."

"Where to?"

"Grand Bay Hotel. It's across the bay. The bartender says that's where all the wealthy people stay, Mexicans and gringos alike. And Wojicki called there from the hotel at Palmas."

"How do we get there? Swim? And I'm not going unless you guarantee there will be food. I'm beginning to see how you stay so thin. You never stop to eat."

"I don't know how to get there. I saw it on the map that came with the car. We'll figure it out."

"Shouldn't we ask for directions?" she asked, the fear of being lost in a foreign city past dinnertime obvious in her voice.

Tapping his forefinger to the side of his head he said, "Sense of direction. Like a penis. Another of the gifts God, in his acts of divine dispensation, singled out for men."

"Yeah, he, or maybe she, wasn't necessarily gender friendly in the endowing of favors upon the sexes. You don't get to enjoy the gifts God gave us. PMS, a monthly period, water retention, cellulite, pregnancy and childbirth, and totally unrealistic societal expectations, to recount a few. Oh yeah, and boobs that after twenty-five start sagging toward the floor. Gravity is not overly friendly to women. High heels and not being able to stand to take a pee are high up on my list too, especially down here.

"And a penis is not a compass. I've been with plenty of men who couldn't find their way out of the bathroom, so let's ask."

Smiling with his lone eyebrow raised, he said, "Lack of food has made you a tad cranky. Let's grab a table by the water and sample the fare of this fine establishment before moving on. Besides, I'm certain the cost will be lower than a swank hotel."

"I knew there had to be a reason you'd want to stay." Rising, Amber moved to a table on the rail just above the beach.

Jake carried their drinks over. As he sat, he said, "Being a woman couldn't be all bad. At least you get to have multiple orgasms."

"Don't flatter your gender. Most of my clients are good for five minutes. Ten tops, and that includes foreplay and obligatory cuddling. Multiple orgasms are right there with Santa Claus and the Easter Bunny; I stopped believing in them long ago," she said indifferently as she picked up the menu a waiter had dropped off. "What should I order?"

"I don't see any kind of 'cynic special' on the menu, so I suggest the seafood," Jake proffered, pointing with his thumb to the ocean. "I think it might

212

be fresh." He winked at her.

Looking up from her menu, the smile that he'd come to know and the twinkle in her eye were back.

They ate as the waves lapped the sand below their table. Her fish and his calamari were not the best they'd ever had, yet in the beautiful setting, they both deemed it more than passable. Amber had a second mai tai, and Jake switched to bottled water. His eyes constantly scanned the bar and street beyond throughout the meal.

When finished they split the bill. Amber was amazed at how inexpensive things were, and Jake reminded her that was probably why Wojicki and Cindi had come here. The money could last a lifetime.

After dinner, they walked in the direction Jake suggested and quickly came upon a series of docks. The town narrowed to a sliver of sand separating the ocean from the bay only a few hundred feet wide at the southern end. Here, they boarded a pontoon-boat taxi and had sped across the dark waters of the inlet to the Grand Bay Hotel. Amber immediately decided they'd move here tomorrow for the rest of their stay. She proclaimed it to be as beautiful as any hotel she'd ever seen, and she couldn't spend another night in the tenement they'd chosen across the bay. Upon notification that the rooms at this swank campsite cost ten times what they were paying she reluctantly conceded to remaining in their current quarters.

With a few more twenty-dollar bills selectively distributed among the staff, they'd determined Wojicki and Cindi stayed at this hotel at an earlier date, possibly six months' prior. Jake surmised they'd planned this caper long ago and were here on that trip to shop for a home and prepare for their escape. However, he and Amber had been told that Monk Phillips had been spotted on several occasions a few days ago. He'd been vocal about having moved into the area. A man his size stuck out from the crowd.

By 11:00 p.m. they'd found their way back to their small room. Waiting at the desk was a message from Estela, the real estate agent. The hand-delivered note said she would be happy to meet for coffee in the morning to discuss beach houses. She would call after eight.

So, Amber read her novel in her bed as Jake drifted off to sleep in his own, with the strong conviction that he'd soon be face to face with both the man who'd stolen over 3.6 million dollars from his parents, and the man who'd nearly killed his father.

CHAPTER 28

Amber awoke alone in warm, heavy air. The bed Jake had slept in was made. He was gone. With a quick inventory of his belongings, she discovered he'd taken the satellite phone and the tablet computer with him on his early morning foray. She wished he'd left a note as to his whereabouts.

After a quick shower and blow-dry, she descended to the lobby to look for tea. She found Jake sitting at a table with a woman, coffee set out before them. As she approached the table, Jake rose and gave her a warm hug.

"Honey, this is Estela from the real estate office. She's going over what she has available. It seems our best bet might be to buy an oceanfront lot and build. Other Americans have bought nearly all the existing homes."

"Whatever you think is best, dear," Amber said as she took a seat. Offering her hand to the agent, she offered, "Estela, it is very nice to meet you."

With a firm handshake, she said, "Sí! Likewise, Mrs. Cohen. It is nice to meet you, too. Perhaps we might find a nice place for you to have a home here."

Reaching over Amber took Jake's hand and said, "Well, that decision will be up to Mr. Cohen. I leave *all* the important decisions to him. As long as the place has a beach, I'll be happy."

Estela smiled and pronounced, "So then, we should get going! I'd like to have you back by noon. One at the latest. The sun is high here at this time of year. It will grow very hot soon. It would be best to get our traveling out of the way as early as possible."

Jake smiled and looked at the two women. "I think that's a great idea. But we'll need to find someplace to get Mrs. Cohen breakfast. She gets a little cranky if she doesn't get her three meals a day."

"To look at you, I'd think you ate nothing," offered Estela in a complimentary tone. "You must tell me how you stay so thin."

"Regular meals, but smaller portions to start. It's difficult when traveling with Mr. Cohen. He doesn't always stop to eat," Amber replied with a tilt of her head. "Exercise helps too. By the way, is there a gym or aerobics class anywhere in town? I'd love to get a workout or two in while I'm here."

"Sí Señora. At the Grand Bay Hotel, there is a gym. The facilities are reserved for guests, but no one ever checks there. They have exercise classes too. No one will pay any attention to you." Estela leaned forward and half whispered, "As a matter of fact, you look like you belong there, instead of here."

"My husband is far too frugal to waste money on the frivolity of a fancy hotel," said Amber in a mildly caustic tone as she rose.

"My prudent spending will allow you to have a beach house here, dear. Get what you'll need, and we'll be on our way," Jake said as he patted her bottom to start her up the stairs. Amber didn't move, shooting him a look through squinted eyes. Turning to Estela, he continued, "I'd like to see a list of the homes you've sold recently. Specifically, in the last six months. It will give us an idea of prices in the area. Perhaps we can even drive by a few."

"Sí! That is a good idea. There is a restaurant by my office. While you have breakfast, I'll run a list of recent sales for you. Then we will be off to see the beach properties." She turned to Amber and said, "By the way, calling you Mrs. Cohen seems so formal. May I call you by your first name?"

"Certainly, Estela. It's Amber. Amber Cohen."

Estela's chin rose slightly, and her lips pursed when she heard the name. She recovered quickly, but both Jake and Amber caught the wobble in her bearing. "Well then, Amber it is. Let's get going. It will be hot here sooner than you think."

Amber had fresh papaya and mango at the open-air restaurant across the street from Estela's office. Jake had eggs scrambled with chilies with rice and beans on the side, all smothered in hot sauce. He positioned himself to see what the agent worked on in the office as they ate. Looking through the glass, he was able to pick up she used a computer feverishly for a few minutes upon entering. Once she held her phone up in their direction. Then she ran a few pages off a printer.

The air carried a smoky, wet smell to it in the morning. Families strolled by on their way to the local church dressed in their Sunday regalia, and some shopkeepers opened their doors and swept their porches. Colorful bougainvillea blossomed mixed with the tropical flora everywhere, giving the scene a postcard-like effect. The little beach town of Barra Navidad was coming slowly to life.

"It's all so pure," said Amber as she cut a piece of papaya with her fork.

"Pure?" he asked.

"Yeah, pure. The people here. The pace at which they live. It's a little like the Midwest, but without the cold. Something's different though. They just seem more content. No one is in a hurry. No one is stressed. They all have very little, yet I get the feeling that they want only a little. Stress is contagious, you know. In the United States, it's an epidemic. Here, I think they treat it by rejection. We haven't even been here twenty-four hours, and I can feel the change."

"That's a very profound analysis, but right now we've got other things to think about. Finish up your breakfast, so we're ready to roll when Estela comes out," he stated flatly, almost like a father telling his daughter to stop daydreaming and do her homework.

"See. You've got it. The stress bug. Don't feel picked on. I've got it too, but the first step toward healing is realizing you're ill. I'm constantly focused on saving and wise investing and using every minute of the day to be as productive as possible. Business, business, business. And avarice. Work hard, then acquire. Then show the world how much you have.

"Jake, I think you've avoided it for years. That aspect of your life has made you somewhat of an outcast with your family and even your friends, hasn't it?"

Lowering his sunglasses on his nose, he looked over the rim at Amber. "Dr. Nelson, is my hour up yet?" he muttered. "You need to eat so we can go. We're not stopping for food."

She placed a piece of papaya between her white teeth and grinned at him. Tilting her head back she let the fruit fall into her mouth. After swallowing, she tapped her lips with her napkin and continued, "So you've been avoiding societal pressure for years. Until a week ago. Then you got caught up in it, but not voluntarily. Sure, you've been sucked in. But there's more going on here."

She pretended to examine a square of mango speared on the end of her fork.

"Your world was closing in on you. You were ready for this to come along. It's another escape."

Wiping his mouth, he said, "I don't need your dime-store psychoanalysis.

There was no one else to do this. I'd much rather be training right now than sitting here with a…" He stopped himself.

"Whore. I'll finish for you. It doesn't hurt my feelings. I've set my dealings up to be classy and businesslike, but I know I still sell sex. I'm ready to do something different. We're *both* trying to get away from what we're doing. It's just fun to poke at you about it."

"Well, it bugs the hell out of me, so knock it off."

Amber giggled. "I think it's my job to nag you since we're married now."

Jake closed his eyes and broke into a grin. He muttered, "Shit."

She went on. "Yeah, I guess I missed the ceremony last night after my drinking binge on the mai tais. The wedding night was kind of a letdown too, you know, with the separate beds and all. I guess these days wedding nights are overrated anyway. Is Mexico a 'community property' country? I wonder if I should have filed some sort of pre-nup. I have a feeling this marriage won't last, and I certainly don't want you getting half of my assets."

Jake smiled at her. "Your worldly goods are safe. The marriage is only for the duration of this voyage. We'll have it annulled by the bartender at the palapa bar before we get on the plane home."

"Oh, what a load off my mind," she teased, her eyes bright with laughter.

Suddenly he was no longer consumed with finding the trio, but rather was enjoying the moment. The flowers around the restaurant seemed to grow brighter in color, and the purity that Amber had spoken of in the town and people became clear.

"What did you think of Estela's look when she heard my name?" Amber asked, bringing him out of ruminations.

"It struck some chord with her."

"Yeah. Zero to bitch in two-point-five seconds. What do you think that means?"

He shrugged his shoulders and turned his palms skyward. "We'll see. Here she comes. You ready to ride through the jungle again?"

"Sure. Let's go."

CHAPTER 29

Estela's prophecy of heat came faster than Amber expected. The agent was prepared with an ice chest full of bottled water and beer. Amber drank two waters early on, then switched to a beer by midday. Although he thought the beer looked divine, Jake stuck to water.

They bounced across the dirt roads of the jungle in Estela's open jeep, moving from property to property. Both he and Amber were disappointed to discover most homes could not be seen through the tropical forest. The dwellings they did observe were oriented to face the ocean, obscuring any possibility of a good look at the structures. Jake asked about neighbors on each side of the potential building sites and who'd moved in recently. She rattled off names quickly and, as expected, Wojicki's did not come up. The property was likely purchased under an assumed name. Jake then asked about the occupations of possible new neighbors. Estela had quickly accorded the professions of many of the local American landowners. Computer company executives, attorneys, Hollywood producers, and so on. She went on and on about how *everyone* wanted to be on this stretch of the Mexican coastline. It was *the place* for Americans who wanted privacy and unspoiled beauty. And it was still a bargain, but prices were rising fast, so the Cohens shouldn't wait to decide.

Two of the owners mentioned had been developers in the United States. Southern California specifically. She was kind enough to point out their homes as the jeep sped past. Jake asked when they had purchased. One of the developers had just recently purchased and moved here permanently, she explained. The other had owned for nearly ten years and still lived in the States, visiting the home here only a few times a year.

By the end of their journey, both gringos looked windblown and frazzled, yet Estela looked ready to make the next sale. The tight bun kept her hair perfect, and the canvas dress was only slightly rumpled. She bid them *adios* and confirmed a time to meet tomorrow morning to "select" one of the properties they'd looked at.

By one thirty they were back at their hotel, having seen four potential home sites. Amber was amazed at how slow-going the process had been in traversing the jungle roads.

Jake had asked all the right questions as they viewed the properties. Prevailing winds, water availability, building costs, drainage, wave direction during hurricane season, waste disposal systems, and most importantly, the availability of power... All things had to be considered. And, of course, the availability of title insurance: important in the United States but essential in Mexico. He'd been extremely convincing as a buyer.

Amber was also surprised at the amount of dust they'd encountered, and quickly showered upon their return. She hadn't expected the rainforest to be so dirty. Estela had apologized and explained this was the dry season and they hadn't had any significant rain in four months. There would be plenty of rain in the rainy season—July through October.

The morning exploration gave them hope. Maybe the home of the recently expatriated developer would be the end of their search. After Amber's shower and a quick late lunch (at her insistence) they drove back up the road to the north.

While she was showering, Jake had formulated an elaborate plan of surveillance and waiting until one member of the trio was alone to confront them. Amber suggested they simply walk up to the door and knock. Hiding out in the jungle seemed silly. She'd learned the hard way that while some sort of mosquito control had been done in town, in the jungles the blood-suckers were thick. Standing or sitting still out in the tropical flora was an invitation to have her body become a living buffet for the voracious little beasts.

Jake bought bottled water at a local 'ma & pa' store and a can of Cutter's repellent, allegedly for Amber. While she wasn't watching, he'd secretly applied some of the stuff on his own arms and legs. Now, protected from the bugs, they followed the dirt road through the jungle that would lead them to the home where they hoped to find Wojicki and his cohorts.

Amber was astonished as Jake confidently made turn after turn at different forks in the road, but she didn't dare compliment him that he seemed to know his way. All the trees and bushes looked the same to her, and she was convinced they were lost more than a few times, yet he drove boldly on. He gave her a few oblique glances accompanied by a tight grin as he threw the convertible sideways at some corners and managed to get the entire vehicle airborne more than once on bumps in the dirt road.

The jungle shadows were lengthening as they parked above the drive to the house. Jake got out and surveyed the countryside. Unlike the flat sand spit of Barra Navidad, the terrain here was hilly. They were positioned on a small rise above the clay tile roof of the home, with the front of the property clearly visible. Nothing moved, save the branches of the trees and palms with the ocean breeze that had mercifully broken the heat of the day and kept the bugs hidden in their lairs. This home, like most they had encountered today, was completely open on the backside to the ocean, yet stretched across the lot to conceal the living area and beach.

As he stared down at the property, Jake felt a wave of energy course through his body. Adrenaline. He knew the slight tremble rising within his muscles was a good thing.

He trotted a little farther up the road for a different view of the property. Still not able to see into the yard or onto the beach, he turned back and asked, "You think we should just go up and knock on the door, huh?"

"Yes. But maybe I should go alone. You seem a little wound up, like you're ready to pounce."

"No, I'll be fine. Let's do it." He trotted around the car and hopped in.

Going up the drive, they passed rows of freshly planted mango and papaya trees. The drive itself was pea gravel, which also looked recently installed. The stalks of the jungle foliage that had been cut back to clear the path were clean and fresh. All signs pointed to someone who'd recently moved in and upgraded the property.

He pulled up in front of the house and did a three-point turn to position the little vehicle to face out toward the road. Amber gave him a questioning look.

"If we need to leave here in a hurry I don't want to have to turn around."

She nodded and reached for the door handle. He reached across the small cab and put his hand on her arm. "Wait. There may be dogs. If there are any, I'm certain they heard this little rattle-wagon pull up. If they're in back, it will take them a few seconds to get around here."

As they sat, Amber looked at the single-story Spanish style home. A dog appeared from around the corner. The animal was indeed large but hardly intimidating. It was a yellow Labrador retriever, dripping wet. The protector of the property carried a tennis ball in her mouth. She immediately ran over to Amber's side of the car and jumped with her front paws on the top of the door, tail flapping wildly. Amber rolled her eyes at Jake and opened the door.

After exiting the car, they both stood with the dog doing figure eights around their legs. Jake walked in mild serpentine to miss the pooch's unpredictable darting and rapped on the front door. When a minute had passed, he knocked again, this time with a harder thumping. There was no answer.

"Let's look around back," he said.

Amber nodded and spoke to the dog. "Show us the way."

Instinctively the beast shot off but stopped at the corner of the house to wait for her new friends. Amber led the way as they rounded the corner and headed toward the beach.

Stepping out from behind the shade of the structure, they were immediately bathed in the golden light of the descending sun above a green ocean. A boat bounced in the light wind-chop at anchor a few hundred feet off the beach. They walked on a clean path of rock that again looked to have been recently installed, each small boulder painstakingly dug into the soil to make the surface as level as possible. Looking at the edifice, Jake realized it was an older home. The edges of the adobe bricks were worn, and the grain of the wood in the eaves was uneven, almost as if it had been sandblasted. Yet everything about the place shown of fresh paint or new install.

When they reached the corner of the building, Jake stopped Amber with a hand motion. Samba music mixed with the sound of the small waves breaking on the beach and wind rustling the palms. The dog stopped about ten feet out from the corner of the home and stood staring back at them, her tail wagging and body undulating at the joy of having found new friends. Rolling his eyes, he looked at Amber and whispered, "There goes the element of surprise."

Leaning around the edge of the adobe to get a better look at the rear of the property, Jake was startled as he came face to face with a large man, pressed flat against the bricks a foot back on the other side of the corner. With startling quickness, the man's left hand shot up and grabbed Jake's shirt at the chest, yanking him out from behind the wall. Not looking at his aggressor's face, Jake focused on the aluminum bat he wielded with his right hand.

With the same motion that brought him from behind the wall, the man spun him toward the ground. Jake knew he was going down. He countered by rolling with the force, swinging his own weight in a wider arc than his assailant anticipated. As the two swung out into the open, Jake's left hand raised to ward off any blow that might come from the bat, and his right hand attached firmly to the aloha-style shirt of the other man and yanked downward and outward.

The man was large and thick, but using the force applied by this fellow and his own weight and momentum combined, Jake was able to avoid landing underneath as they hit the ground on their sides. A brief wave of elation came as Jake heard the aluminum clink a few times on the rock path; the bat had been dislodged and was not an immediate threat. The grip on his shirt loosened with the impact as he heard the air puff out of his assailant's lungs.

Jake felt the man struggling to throw his feet out of their human tangle and find a toehold. He didn't have a chance to see his attacker clearly, but from the ease with which he'd been yanked down, Jake knew this was a sizable opponent.

Was this Monk, who'd throttled his father? If this guy got his toes into the creases of the rock to create leverage and roll over on him, Jake conjectured it might be the end of his life. He released the grip on the shirt he held and rolled behind the man with astonishing swiftness, catching his attacker's right elbow in a chicken-wing hold between his own bicep and forearm. Practically in the same motion, he snagged the left arm in the identical hold. With his right arm pinning the man's right elbow back, he was able to slide the right hand across the man's back and secure the left elbow in a vise-like grip. Now holding both arms with his right hand, Jake had his left hand free. By using his toes for leverage and forcing his own chest into the secured twist of arms he had his assailant pinned, face down.

The brief scuffle was over. If his attacker continued to squirm, Jake could pound away on his head with his free left hand.

Coming to focus, Jake saw the dog barking wildly and spinning around the two of them. He looked for Amber. Finding her, he saw her lips move and heard her scream, "No! Wait!"

He wasn't sure whether he first felt the thud or heard the clink of the aluminum bat as it hit him in the back of the head, but he was surprised that for a millisecond he knew he'd been struck. Then the thought faded, and everything went to darkness.

CHAPTER 30

The ammonia mixture burned at Jake's nose. He yanked his head away to escape the horrible stinging odor.

"That's probably enough."

It was a male voice. Spoken with authority. From the fringes of consciousness, Jake thought it sounded like his father.

With the odor gone, the burning at his eyes and sinuses faded. Jake felt himself settling back into a state of slumber. He imagined he was floating on air and gently swinging on a breeze. Sleep beckoned, yet he knew sleep would be a bad thing. Nonetheless, he was losing the contest with the sandman.

"Better give it to him again. He's fading back."

The authoritarian voice again. Followed by the resuming inferno in his nose. It again permeated his sinuses and reached into his brain, biting and pinching from the inside out. He swung wildly at the unseen source of the smell. Shaking his head, he felt a wave of pain across the back of his skull.

"How hard did you hit him, Gayle?" the voice chuckled.

"I don't know. I just picked up the bat and swung. I thought he was trying to kill Bill," the woman answered. "My God, I've never done anything like that. Will he be okay?"

"Yeah, I think so. I felt the skull, and there were no evident fractures. Probably has a mild to moderate concussion and a hell of a headache. Might have a crack in his cranium, but he deserves it, sneaking up on you like that.

"You okay, mister trespasser?"

Jake, only halfway to coherence, realized what had happened. This was *not* the home of Thomas Wojicki. He'd scuffled with an innocent man.

"God, I'm so sorry," Jake offered, rubbing his hand across his face. "You probably didn't hear the car pull up over the wind and waves back here. We knocked at the front then came around back…"

"Amber told us the whole story." The voice belonging to the woman named Gayle cut him off. "It's our fault as much as yours. Bill overreacted. I told him to go see what the dog was barking at and he attacked you."

"Bullshit! If you'd just walked into the open instead of skulking along the wall like a criminal, this wouldn't have happened."

Squinting, Jake took in the surroundings. The feeling he'd had of floating on air came from being in a hammock on the patio. He was, indeed, swinging above the ground. The ocean emitted its rhythmic growl close by as small waves detonated on the sand. The sun was now gone from the sky with purple showing at the horizon with a distinct line of black where it met the sea. Gentle wind, now cooler than that of the day, blew across his body. Other than the headache, the scene was idyllic. Turning his head, he saw the faces of the couple standing together and another man. He guessed the owners of the home, Bill and Gayle, were in their mid to late fifties. Both were tanned and thick, yet not fat. Each held a glass with condensation on the outside. The other man was slender, with long sinewy arms exposed by a tank top. His hair was long and shaggy, and he sported a graying beard.

Where was Amber?

He blinked his eyes a few times and said, "Please accept my apologies, Bill and Gayle. It was certainly my mistake." His gaze shifted to the second man who stood alongside the couple. "From your bedside manner, I'd say you might be a doctor, sir. That, along with the fact that the common man doesn't carry smelling salts. My father keeps some at our place up the coast."

"Paul Herloss," he introduced himself. "Retired from the States. My wife and I have a winter house here. Next one over on the beach. Bill came running after they thumped you and your lady friend explained the faux pas. Damn sure brought a little life into cocktail hour around here. From the look of your eyebrow and the purple around your eye, this isn't your only scuffle recently." He chuckled in an appraising tone.

Amber appeared from the doorway to the home. In one hand, she carried a large Ziploc bag filled with ice. Her other hand held a glass with red-pink liquid, ice, and a large piece of pineapple on the rim. The sight brought a smile to Jake. Even with the wild events of this afternoon, she was still on vacation. She brought the ice pack over and placed the bag under his head with almost motherly tenderness.

Amber addressed the others. "Thank you for your help, Doctor. And thank you, Bill and Gayle, for your understanding. We're both very sorry for this." She looked at Jake. "If you're okay, we can be on our way."

"I'd recommend against it," advised Herloss in a doctor-esque voice. "Bill, Gayle, you may not be ready to double date with these two, but this young man should sit tight for eight to twelve hours. I know you have an extra room. A bumpy ride through the jungle could cause hemorrhaging. If you don't want them here, they can stay at my house."

"It's not a problem. I feel somewhat responsible for this anyway," Gayle stated. "We were just getting ready to grill some fish when you…" she cleared her throat and finished, "… arrived. There's plenty for everyone. You two will stay right here. I insist. We even have extra toothbrushes."

Amber looked at Jake who shook his head. The doctor caught the action and spoke, "No. Stay. And that's an order. Wake him up every two hours and have him walk a little. Then back to bed. He's probably fine, but let's use a little caution. No booze of any kind tonight." The orders were given to Amber. "I'll walk over and check on you in the morning. Have a nice, calm evening. Get me if there are problems."

With goodbyes said, Gayle settled into the task of cooking, as Amber assisted. They seemed to form an immediate bond. As a matter of fact, Jake noticed Amber made friends easily wherever she went, even in a somewhat strained situation.

Bill busied himself with little projects around the patio and said nothing. He was obviously miffed at having these intruders at his home and made no pretense about it. The sun couldn't come up too early tomorrow, allowing him to send these pests on their way.

Folding the ice pack behind his head, Jake closed his eyes. Their mistaken identity of the owners here bothered him, but the fact that time was slipping away ate at him even more. He mentally thumbed through the photos Amber had supplied as the hammock rocked back and forth in the breeze.

The gentle touch of the hand on his arm twenty-five minutes later roused him as Amber alerted him dinner was ready. Standing, initially he was wobbly but quickly found his legs as he walked to the outdoor dining table set beautifully with brightly colored plates and glassware.

As Jake sat, Amber took the Ziploc bag and went to refill it with ice. Bill came and sat next to Jake, but as he settled into his seat, he remained silent and noticeably slid his chair away a few inches.

Gayle and Amber carried plates from the kitchen. Each contained generous portions of fish, fresh papaya, and pineapple, and one-half a potato.

Bill finally spoke. "How come there's only half a potato?" he grumbled.

"I only baked two, dear. We have guests, and it's only right to share. There's plenty of fish and Amber was a help and cut extra fruit for everyone."

Bill grumbled a little more and began to eat. Gayle stopped him, reminding her husband to give thanks. He tapped his forehead and across his chest. Jake also performed the sign of the cross. Gayle recited a blessing. Finishing with a nod, her husband dove in.

Jake, still woozy, nibbled at first but found an appetite as he ate. The fish was excellent. He tasted a hint of lime and cilantro in the firm white meat, and of course the garlic and butter common to seafood cooked in Mexico.

While the conversation buzzed between the ladies, the men ate in silence. Finally, Jake decided to break the ice. "This wahoo is fabulous, Gayle. You must have caught it this morning. From the thickness of the fillet it must have been a big one; forty pounds or more." Jake knew that complimenting a man on the size of the fish he caught would always ingratiate oneself with the angler.

Bill's quiet continued. Gayle cleared her throat and said, "Well, we actually bought the fish from some local fishermen. When we purchased the house, the boat on the anchor out there came with it. We had it completely restored at a boatyard in Manzanillo, but with all the work around here, we haven't used it often. We've been out a few times but haven't caught much. Everyone says the fish are thick out there. We're planning on getting one of the locals to go out with us and teach us how to catch them."

Jake turned to Bill and said, "Bertram 29, right? Looks late seventies or early eighties. Probably twin in-line diesels side by side. Looks like she's rigged well, from what I saw before Gayle clobbered me."

Bill looked at Jake and nodded. "You know your boats. She's a '79. Runs twenty-two knots all day on forty gallons of diesel. Had her completely refurbished. Re-christened her the *Gayle-Force*."

Gayle smiled as Bill continued. "She's better than new. Someday I'll learn to fish after I get this place in shape."

"From all I've seen your landscape crew is doing fine," Jake complimented. He saw a crack in the hard veneer.

"Crew?!?" the host muttered incredulously.

Gayle smiled and patted his arm. "Bill's done all the work here himself. He toils tirelessly from sunup to sundown."

Jake's looked around the patio and offered, "Bill, this is truly amazing. I've never seen a gringo take on a project like this without any local help."

With the compliment, Bill's chest puffed out slightly, and he sat more erect in his wicker chair. "I worked more than forty years building things. I came down here expecting to relax. You know, sit on the beach. Fish. Pick up shells. Become a beachcomber.

"Well, after a few days seeing all that needed done I realized I wasn't ready to retire. I'm sixty-two, not eighty-two. The work keeps me occupied, and I know it'll get done right. Saves a few bucks too. When this is done, we'll build another one and sell it. After I realized I couldn't sit on my ass for twenty more years, we bought two more lots."

Jake was impressed with the man's spirit. While much younger, he too dreaded the day he'd be put out to pasture. He asked, "So you never use the boat?"

Bill answered, "No. We ought to, though. The thing came almost fully equipped, and what it didn't have, I had added. I love to fish, but I've always gone out on charters where everything was done for me by the skipper or a deckhand. All I had to do was reel them in." He smiled and raised his eyebrows. "I always thought it looked easy. Throw out some lures and wait for the reels to squeal. We've caught a few small dorado and skipjack that way but nothing else. Guess there's more to it than I thought."

"Why don't you let me take you fishing tomorrow? To make amends for the trouble I've caused?" suggested Jake. "We've had a house and boat down here for over twenty years. I'm not an expert, but we've caught a few."

Gayle jumped at the offer. "What a great idea! That boat hasn't been used for anything but short sunset cruises in a month. All the *pangaderos* say the fishing is crazy good! It would be perfect."

Bill gave Jake a sideways glance. He put his fork down and shuffled lower into his seat. His head moved from side to side. "I don't know. There's a lot to do around here. And no offense Amber and Jake, but Gayle, we don't know anything about these people. Lots can happen way out in the ocean. This young man has a scar over his eye from one recent altercation, and nobody's ever thrown me like that. He's quicker than a wet shit—"

"Bill! Please! Not at the table!"

"Sorry," he grumbled, "but I just don't feel good about it. We don't even know if their story is true."

Jake thought for a moment, then asked, "I saw a satellite dish on the house. Does it transmit internet data back and forth?"

"Yep. I can manage our accounts in the States from here, and keeps me up on the news back home," Bill said proudly.

"Well, with your permission, after dinner I'll prove what I'm telling you is true."

"If all this checks out will you take a day off tomorrow and take your wife fishing?" Gayle asked with pleading in her eyes.

Reluctantly he answered, "I suppose so."

"Great! I've been looking forward to getting out on the water! I'll pack lunch. Should we fix breakfast to go or eat here? What time do we leave? Sunup?"

"The earlier, the better for sailfish and marlin. They start hunting for food at first light. Sometimes tuna bite better midmorning to midday after they locate schools of feeder fish," Jake said.

Bill looked at Jake and with a sly smile said, "Fifteen years ago you wouldn't have landed on the top of our scuffle, you know."

Jake smiled and said, "Hell, I think I got lucky today. You're quicker than a wet shit yourself."

"That's enough!" Gayle protested. "We're eating dinner. Amber and I didn't work hard to listen to the two of you allude to disgusting bodily functions. You boys need to clean it up."

Bill smiled broadly for the first time since they'd met and said, "Sorry honey, but it just seems like the right analogy, being down here in the land of Montezuma's revenge. Why I haven't had to push on a—"

"Bill! No more!" Her voice cut him off. Trying to find an ally she looked to Amber and said, "You can't ever really take the boy out of the man, can you?"

Amber answered, but her gaze rested on Jake rather than Gayle. "Nope. But that's why we love them, isn't it?"

The light from the flickering candles danced in her eyes as she spoke, and Jake again felt himself get woozy. But this time the blow to his head had nothing to do with it.

CHAPTER 31

Jake sat in the tower next to Bill at the helm as the *Gayle-Force* rolled with a rhythmic rise and fall on the ocean swells. On the GPS unit, Jake had plotted points over an offshore structure. Seamounts and ridges, he explained to Bill, were areas where the upwelling waters forced nutrients and tiny sea organisms up from the depths. Small fish feasted on these in huge numbers, and bigger fish, in turn, feasted on the smaller fish. The food chain continued, and the fish they now hunted were at the top.

After about twenty-five minutes of running, Jake tapped Bill on the shoulder, pointing off the port side. After running another five minutes on the new course, Bill slowed the boat and Jake gave him hurried instructions. Jake then hopped down out of the tower and pulled one of the fishing rods out of the stainless-steel holder known as a 'rocket launcher'. He moved to the bait tank and used a hand net to capture a caballito he'd caught on the beach with a throw net at dawn, then quickly stuck the hook tied to the line through its nose. Gayle and Amber winced slightly at the sight of the razor-sharp hook penetrating the small fish's skin and bone.

The boat was now idling out of gear. Jake nodded up to Bill who pushed the transmission levers ahead.

He spoke to the ladies. "Sailfish. Two of them." He pointed.

Amber at first saw nothing, but after focusing she made out two gray-black sickles protruding from the water about seventy-five feet away. From this distance they were barely recognizable, so she asked, "How could you have seen those from a half mile away?"

"I didn't see the fish. I saw the birds." He pointed to the sky. Amber and Gayle looked up and saw two large fork-tailed birds floating on the air high above. "Frigates. They wait over the big fish until they chase bait to the surface, then they swoop in as the small baitfish try to get away by jumping into the air.

"Okay, Gayle, you're up first. I'm going to cast for you because you've never done this before, but the rod goes in your hands immediately."

"Bill," she yelled up to the steering tower, "You should do this!"

"No time, honey. The fish are right here now."

"The engine noise doesn't scare the fish?" Amber asked Jake.

"No. These creatures have almost no enemies in the water, so they fear nothing," answered Jake before swinging a wide arch with the rod. The eight-inch baitfish flew silently through the air and landed with a splash fifteen feet in front of the sailfish. He put the rod in Gayle's grasp with her left hand in front of the reel and her right hand behind it. With his thumb and forefinger, he placed her thumb on the spool and pulled on the line. "Use that much pressure on the spool," he said as he lifted her thumb slightly with his pinkie finger.

At first, nothing happened. The fish seemed to continue on their path, but the idling boat in gear moving slowly forward kept the bait just in front of them. Abruptly in tandem, the two sailfish shot forward in a contest to eat the helpless caballito.

Amber stood fascinated as the first sailfish to reach the bait raised its head out of the water and slapped at the caballito with its long sword-like bill. The other swam next to it and tried to steal the small fish slapping with its own rapier nose.

"Gayle, let's let the bait run a little now. When we release a little line, it slows down, and they'll think they've stunned it." He lifted her thumb off the spool to ease the pressure slightly, and the line began to unwind slowly.

Both fish ducked their heads underwater and disappeared. Amber thought at first they were gone, but Gayle yelled, "Uh oh!" as line peeled off the reel.

"Let him eat it for a few seconds. Bill, get ready to gas it for five to seven seconds after Gayle throws the lever. Gayle, keep your fingers clear of the reel after you put it in gear. And hang on to the rod!"

Gayle's body shook with excitement knowing the huge fish was ripping the line off her reel. After what seemed too long a time, Jake gave her the nod to engage the gear as he simultaneously gave Bill a hand signal to go. Bill pushed the throttles forward, and the boat accelerated. The rod bent immediately, and the sailfish shot into the air, now one hundred feet behind the boat. Putting on an aerial display, the beast seemed to float above the water with its tail touching down only long enough to re-launch the body skyward. After a few seconds, Jake signaled with the flat of his hand for Bill to stop, and Gayle held the rod end under her armpit, knees bent and back straight. The fish was now one hundred yards out and peeling line at will against the drag pressure of the reel.

"I'm running out of line!" Gayle yelled.

Jake examined the reel, and reassured her, "You're okay. He's got about one-third of it. They usually stop running after about a hundred yards. If he doesn't, we'll back down. Let's get you in the fighting chair." He smiled and winked at her.

They shuffled across the deck, and she sat, placing the rod butt in the cup on the base of the seat. As predicted the line stopped peeling off the reel before it ran out. Jake now coached her to pull slowly against the fish and wind down on the handle to take up the slack. When she looked like she had a good rhythm going, he reached into the cooler and pulled out three Pacifico beers. He used the line-cutter pliers to pop the tops and passed one to Bill in the tower and one to Amber who now sat on the gunnel.

"It's customary that the crew have a beer while the first fish of the day is being fought," he announced. "Here's to Gayle. And to the fish!" He raised his bottle high. Bill and Amber joined him, and everyone smiled, except Gayle who struggled against the sailfish in the tropical heat.

"That's not fair. You all get to drink cold cervezas while I have to sit here and sweat. Someone else take over now!"

"Nope," said Jake. "Keep pullin'. You'll have yours when you're done. This is your fish, and you'll feel better about it when it's landed if you do it yourself."

"It doesn't feel so great right now!" she yelled as she pulled back again on the rod.

"Remember, you're the one who wanted to go fishing!" Bill yelled back to her.

For the next twenty-five minutes, Gayle pulled, and Bill used the twin engines to rotate the boat to keep the fish off the stern. At first it jumped regularly, but in the end, it came down to Gayle pulling against the tired sailfish. When the fish was next to the boat, Jake instructed Gayle to come to the rail and with a few final pulls and some guttural emissions she muscled the beast alongside.

233

Leaning over the side and using a towel for abrasion protection, Jake grasped the fish's bill. When he had it secured, he unwound the leader off his left hand and pulled pliers from his pocket and worked the hook out of the hard mouth plate of the fish. He pushed the hook into the foam of the rod butt to stop it from swinging loose.

Jake lifted the fish out of the water briefly and spread the beautiful sail open. Amber was the photographer, and Gayle stood proudly by the creature, her gray-blonde hair stringy with sweat and a huge grin across her face. When done, Jake lowered the fish into the water and gently rocked the body to move water over the gills as the boat moved forward at idle speed. When the fish swam naturally, he let it loose and the creature darted away into the depths.

"I guess we don't eat those?" Amber asked.

Jake shook his head. "No. They taste like cat food. We'll keep looking." With a nod and hand motion forward to Bill, they again got under way. Jake passed a beer to Gayle who sat tiredly in the fighting chair, then began re-rigging the rod with a new leader.

The day went on, and they caught another sailfish and a dorado, known as mahi mahi in other parts of the world, before noon. Soon after lunch, they ran into other boats out of Barra Navidad that had found a school of huge tuna, and they hooked four of the beasts, landing two. They kept one for dinner and the freezer and released the other. At 2:00 p.m. Jake suggested they try some rooster fishing along the beach on the way home.

During the day they'd traveled west out into the ocean about eleven miles and south about twenty, which put them even in latitude with the town of Barra Navidad. Jake advised that the beach just north of the populated area looked good for roosterfish and they should try there first. As they traveled, Jake filleted the tuna and dorado, and the cooler was full of fresh fish on ice by the time they reached the shallow waters along the beach. They put out lines with live bait and they slow-trolled along the shoreline looking for the famous fighting roosterfish, or *pez gallo* to the locals.

After forty minutes of frustration with nothing but the razor-sharp teeth of long, slimy needlefish slashing through their lines over and over, they decided to call it a day. Jake suggested that he take the helm and Bill and Gayle catch a nap in the v-berth under the bow section as they headed back to the house. The heat under the tropical sun in combination with Jake's insistence they share a celebratory cerveza after the landing of each fish had the owners of the boat gratefully accepting the offer of a snooze. With the swell slightly abeam of the *Gayle-Force's* course creating a gentle rocking motion and a breeze blowing through the open hatch of the cabin, Bill and Gayle soon dozed peacefully in the shaded forward berth as Jake bumped the transmission into gear to head up the coast.

"That was quite a day of fishing," said Amber as she sat next to Jake in the tower of the Bertram. "You must be tired. Especially after all that beer. I know I'm exhausted, and you went nonstop all day."

Looking at her through his sunglasses, he smiled. She wore a borrowed pair of shorts and conservative bikini top, but she'd wisely kept her upper half covered from the sun most of the day with an old button-down dress shirt of Bill's that Gayle brought on board. Only now on the way home did she decide to allow the sun to bake her toned body. She put her bare feet up on the console of the helm and leaned back in the sturdy chair, exposing the length of her lithe legs. Her raven hair was in a ponytail under a baseball cap, and behind her sunglasses, Jake knew the bright eyes glowed with a touch of mischief. He was enjoying the view and found himself staring at her longer than he should have as he pushed the throttles down a little farther to cover more ground.

"I'd give it a seven and a half on a one-to-ten scale," he announced. "A ten would be all your blue-water fish at over three hundred pounds, topping it off with a few roosters on the beach at sixty to eighty. I'm glad you had a good time," he said with a smile.

The grin faded to a serious look of business as he continued. "But you and I didn't come out here just to fish. I needed Bill and Gayle to take a nap, so I kept the beer flowing all day. When you weren't looking, I poured the majority of mine over the side or into the bait tank. With limited sleep last night and a six-pack today in the sun I'd be sawing logs now too if I hadn't dumped the suds. I must admit I'm impressed with your stamina."

A thoughtful quiet came between them, broken only by the cadenced rumble of the engines. Jake's eyes alternated between the shoreline and the path of the boat, constantly scanning. Finally, Amber broke the silence.

"I'm having too much fun to sleep. This has been one of the best days of my life." As she spoke, he saw a serious (or was it sad?) expression on her face. As she stared toward the beach, she added, "This is real. I need real for a change." He thought she was going to expound on the declaration, but instead, she asked, "So if we're not *just* fishing what *are* we doing?"

"Looking." Reaching down into his valise, he pulled the photos out and flipped through the stack until he found the two he wanted. The couple stood on a beach in front of a home with a palapa roof in the background, Cindi in a thong bikini and Wojicki in baggy shorts and a mismatched Hawaiian shirt.

"In this boat, we'll cover two-thirds of the coastline between Barra Navidad and Chamela to the north in just over an hour. It would take us two weeks on land bouncing through the jungle in our rental car. The homes are almost all secluded and fenced, so getting close to them might be difficult. You can see these photos were shot from near the water up toward the house by the slope of the beach. Keep your eyes on the beach as we pass and look for this view."

"Ahhhh! I see now. The idea to come in to the beach for… what did you call them?… Roosterfish… was all just a ploy," Amber said with a nod. "You're a wily fellow, Jake Cohen. When did you concoct this plan?"

"Last night at dinner. I realized that we were spinning our wheels after our first day of running circles through the jungle. All we got was a dusty ride and a lump on my head. We needed a change of strategy, so keep your bright eyes open and look for the house."

"Aye-aye," she said with a mock salute.

They motored up the coast for about an hour, zigzagging their way along the shoreline as they scanned the homes along the beach. Some of the structures were almost palatial while other inhabitants lived in huts thatched of palm fronds and hardwood trees.

They didn't hear Gayle rise and take a seat in the chair at the lower helm station, and Bill's voice startled both of them when he climbed the ladder to the tower.

"No luck, huh?" he asked, his head at about knee level to them.

"Excuse me?" Jake asked.

"The house. You didn't see it on the way up the coast?" Bill bellowed over the hum of the engines.

Jake looked down from the helm and shook his head.

Bill's eyes scanned the beach as the boat moved across the water. "We're about three miles away. It's four o'clock now. When we get back, we'll off-load the gear, and you can use the boat to run the rest of the way up to Chamela. That's about seventeen miles straight, but probably closer to thirty if you follow the coastline. There's really nothing north of there. Lot of homes between our place and Chamela though. You'll have about two and a half hours of daylight. Stay in the bay there on the boat tonight. You can't make it back by dark."

Amber and Jake exchanged looks, but before they could say anything, Gayle yelled up from below. "We want to help you kids! I think it's a wonderful thing how you are trying to help your family. We'll get some food together for your dinner. There's a propane barbeque on board."

Bill nodded to Jake. "It was Gayle's idea. I can see that you can run this boat fine. Bring her back tomorrow. And without any holes in her, please. The fuel's on us. You won't use but twenty gallons anyhow."

"Thank you," said Amber with the utmost sincerity.

"Don't mention it. We want to help out."

Smiling, Jake asked, "So, when did you figure out what I was doing?"

"Soon as I saw the course you plotted on the GPS this morning. I spent years with employees plotting behind my back. Your conniving is amateurish compared to the shit they used to pull. But hey, it all worked out. We've got fresh fish, Gayle got out on the boat, and I escaped a day of work on the homestead. Plus, we get to be involved in some intrigue. This is the most excitement we've had in months."

As the boat bobbed across the last few miles of ocean, Jake felt the tender lump on the back of his head. Then his fingers ran across the nearly healed gash over his eye and felt the stubble of the hair growing back where his eyebrow used to be.

He wondered how much more excitement he could take.

CHAPTER 32

"Victor and Anne's son is in Barra Navidad. And he's with my old pal Amber Nelson. How on earth did they end up together?" proclaimed Cindi as she pushed the computer keyboard away in disgust. "Estela attached a digital photo of them eating in that little restaurant across the street from her office."

"Honey, don't get agitated. We planned for this. They won't figure it out." Tom walked over and placed his right hand on Cindi's shoulder as he read the contents of the e-mail. In his left hand, he held a glass freshly refilled with scotch and ice.

The touch made her wince slightly; Tom's hand smelled of nicotine and cigarette tar. When she'd been with the service that smell had always repulsed her. She'd tolerated it, writing it off as a temporary irritation and part of the job. Now, with Tom back to two packs per day and drinking heavily, he carried the stench of the jerks she thought she'd permanently left behind.

"This place sucks, Tom. The food sucks. The language sucks. The whole damn thing sucks. I feel trapped. Like a hunted animal. At least back home in prison they'd speak English," she huffed.

"They won't find us," Tom said with a reassuring pat. "Estela says she won't take them out again. They'll buzz around the area like idiots for a few days, but before long they'll give up."

Pushing his reeking mitt off her shoulder, she stood. "I'm sick of this already! You said at first we'd only be here a year, now you're saying two. And the ogre you've got staying with us is starting to scare me. He looks at me like a hungry dog staring into a butcher's window. He gets twenty percent? Will he be here the whole time?"

Wojicki sipped heavily. After letting the liquid slide down slowly, he spoke with his voice strained. "The two of *you* hatched that harebrained scheme of selling off the office furniture and equipment. You risked over three and a half million over a measly three thousand bucks worth of office crap. Now we *have* to stay longer because of the beating. We made a clean take on that money, and you almost lost it with a bungled burglary, like a cheap whore stealing from her john's wallet. Hell, you used to make ten grand a night!"

He regretted the words he'd used instantly. Cindi gave him a look of absolute hatred, then left the room. Tom made a mental note to apologize in the morning and take her out for lunch and some shopping at the marina tomorrow. Without Monk.

They'd all become edgy, and what she'd said about Monk was true. His actions were beginning to unnerve Tom too.

The giant was high-strung. He located a dealer for methamphetamine in town within a day of his arrival, and the speed gave him a sense of enlightenment and a feeling of invincibility. When he was high, he stated that he'd soon be cashing out his share and traveling the world. The thought of handing him a bag full of cash and letting him go was appealing for so many reasons, yet the reality was, having him here was much safer for all of them. This way he could be watched and controlled. Loose on his own, he'd probably end up drifting back to the USA with a load of drugs for sale or whatever contraband caught his fancy.

Sitting down on the sofa, Tom held his glass by the rim, rolling the mixture of booze and ice around with a mild clinking of the cubes. The plan was working out, and there was no need to panic merely because the Cohens' kid had followed their trail into Mexico and the quaint little town of Barra Navidad. That was to be expected. Planned, in fact. The search would hit a dead end from that point, and the tiny posse of Jacob Cohen and his hooker friend would soon disband.

The scotch was thin from the melting ice, and a final pull left the glass empty. He set it on the table next to the couch and fingered the remote for the big flat-screen television. Scrolling through the channels, he found SportsCenter, with updates on basketball and ice hockey. Not really his favorites, but there was nothing but soccer locally, and he had bets down on two of tonight's NBA match-ups with a sports book in Costa Rica where he'd opened an online account.

He looked around at the tiled floors and beamed ceilings of the villa and smiled contentedly as he listened to the announcers' banter in English. Looking to his left, he took in the view of the bay below.

Not a bad place to spend a year or two, he decided as he rose to refill his glass.

CHAPTER 33

Forty minutes north of Bill and Gayle's hacienda they saw the house. It was unmistakable on the low bluff above the beach. Jake maneuvered the boat into the little bay in front of the home and turned the bow out to sea as he held the photo.

"This is it," he announced to Amber, who sat reclined in the fish-fighting chair in her bikini soaking up the last of the afternoon sun. She lowered her sunglasses beneath her baseball cap and squinted at the shore and the beautiful home above.

"Yep. No doubt. Okay, what now?" she asked.

Swinging down from the tower Jake's feet never touched the rungs on the ladder. He quickly set the anchor. Once solid to the bottom, he turned the key, and all engine noise died away.

The beach was deserted. However, music wafted from the house above. Jake would have expected Mexican melodies, but the sounds they heard were more American pop than local tunes. Yet the vocals were in Spanish. Another boat, much larger than the little Bertram, bobbed at anchor closer to shore.

"Cindi a fan of hip-hop?" he asked after they'd listened for a moment.

"No. Sometimes she'd listen to country, sometimes jazz or classical, and every now and then rock or reggae, but never that stuff."

Jake seemed to ponder for a moment before speaking.

"That boat at anchor is a 48-foot Riviera convertible sport fisher. Late model. Expensive. And the house... Based on what Estela showed us, prices are low here compared to the States, but that one is extravagant."

Amber looked puzzled. "What are you getting at?"

Rubbing his chin, he said, "I don't know for certain, but I have a hunch. Let's put the kayak in the water and go ashore. It sounds like a party up there at the hacienda."

"No sneaking around this time. We go up, find them, and lay out our deal."

"Yes, mother," Jake replied as he untied the lines holding the kayak on the starboard rail of the boat. Amber wrapped the sarong around her waist and pulled a light sleeveless blouse over her bikini top.

In five minutes, they were paddling in tandem toward the beach. Jake had loaded the photos in a roll-top waterproof bag Bill and Gayle had provided.

A small wave lifted the craft and propelled it on whitewater for the last few yards before the little boat bumped on the shore. Amber grinned as she bounced out onto the sand.

After pulling the kayak up twenty feet above the waterline, he motioned toward a path that left the beach and meandered through the jungle. Jake took the lead as they moved toward the home. When they reached the base of the bluff, the beach gave way to a manicured jungle landscape, and they found stairs of smooth rock and concrete to help with the climb. Only fifty feet above them, music blared from the flat spot where the home was built.

Reaching the top of the stairway first, Jake found a large tile patio and finely manicured grass yard protruding onto the mesa of the bluff around a swimming pool. As Amber stepped up, she started to speak what would have been a "wow," but the vocalization was cut off when three automatic weapons swung from different locations around the yard in their direction.

The nearest armed man took a few steps closer and barked in Spanish, *"Deja caer lo que tienes y pon tus manos arriba!"*

Dropping the bag and raising his hands, Jake said, "He said raise your hands."

"I get the idea," Amber hissed from behind, hands already high. Slowly taking a step forward, she said to the man with the gun, "There's been a—"

"Shut up!" he snapped in English. "Step apart. You over there, hands against the wall of the house, legs spread." He motioned with his head at Jake.

After assuming the position as ordered, Jake was frisked by another man. Each wore olive pants, loose-fitting black polo shirts, and black tennis shoes. And each man carried an M-16 rifle. The outlines of bulletproof vests were visible under their shirts. He counted five men, all trim, neatly shaven with slicked hair cropped short.

Amber was led away through an open doorway in the house. Jake was instructed to remain against the wall. The lead guard rummaged through the dry bag. The guards conferred over the photos for a few moments, then the one who'd first addressed him approached and said, "This way," with a motion of his thumb. Two men took up the rear, weapons at the ready, with the man giving instructions off to the side to remain out of the line of fire should the guns be needed.

As he crossed the patio behind the house, Jake saw numerous shapely young women in bikinis on the other side of the pool. A large waterfall slide made of smoothed native rock sat unused as the ladies cast furtive looks at the stranger who'd interrupted the festivities. The music had been cut off, but the cook at the polished stainless-steel outdoor grill under the palapa continued flipping his carne asada and grilling vegetables. He wore a full chef's outfit, complete with the mushroom-topped hat. Upwind of him was a bar, fashioned out of jungle hardwoods with another palapa-style roof. The bartender wore black pants and a white shirt and waistcoat. A dozen men whom Jake guessed were between forty and sixty reclined in lounge chairs. Most were at least rotund with some being corpulent. Nearly all wore sunglasses, had dark hair slicked with gel, and were in shorts and shirtless.

He was led through the doors where Amber had been taken. Passing through a large room with vaulted beamed ceilings, he saw the entire rear section of the home was smoked glass etched sparingly with marine scenes. The fish and turtles cut into the glass were lightly illuminated by what he was certain were fiber optic lights set in the casement around the windows. After sunset, the display would glow beautifully, yet during the daylight, it would not inhibit the view of the ocean.

Very expensive, Jake thought as the guards pushed him past.

Down a hall, they turned into a room with an ornate desk. He was ordered to sit in a chair, and his hands were immediately secured with zip-tie handcuffs around the back supports. His sunglasses were removed and set on the bureau. The guards who'd escorted him in stood by the door, and the one who'd originally confronted him sat behind the desk. He looked at the pictures taken from the dry bag for a few seconds before speaking in English.

"My name is Francisco. I am chief of security here at the hacienda. You and your lady friend have made me and my men look like fools to our employer. Anchoring your boat out of sight behind the yacht then sneaking up from the beach. You have caused problems for me."

"Francisco, we pulled into the cove, diesel running, then rattled down an anchor chain. We paddled to the beach in a kayak out in the open water and walked right up a path to the patio. We were hardly sneaking."

Gritting his teeth and emitting a low growl he snarled at the guards standing behind Jake, "*Cavrones!* What do I pay you idiots for?" He shook his half-clenched fists at them, then relaxing only slightly placed his hands behind his head. Turning to Jake, he asked, "Why do you have pictures of this house?"

"We're looking for the people in the photograph. It's our understanding they live in this home."

"Tell me why you think they would be here. And if you do find them, what do you want?"

"It will take some time to tell you."

"I am in no hurry," Francisco said as he placed his feet on the desk. To the guards, he growled in Spanish, "You two. Go to your stations and see to it no one else walks casually up from the beach or in through the jungle. And stop gawking at the pretty señoritas by the pool!"

Francisco listened patiently, sipping sparingly from a bottle of water. When Jake was done, he rose and growled, "Wait here," as he left the room.

When he returned five minutes later, Francisco had Amber in tow. He ordered her to sit in the other chair, then left again, closing the door behind him.

"Jake, thank God!" she exclaimed. "Are you okay?"

He answered, "I'm fine. I guess he doesn't see you as any kind of threat or he would have locked you up too."

She rose from her chair and circled around behind the desk. As she rummaged in the drawers, she said, "I was petrified. I had no idea our friends would have a security force like this. Did they tell you where Cindi and Tom are? Here. Got it."

"Got what?"

She held up a paperclip. As she walked back around the desk, she bent the metal straight.

"They questioned me for a few minutes, then left me alone. I asked if I could see Cindi and told them she'd straighten everything out. I told them we're old friends."

"Amber, our *friends* are not here. I'm guessing these people are dope deal-ers or Mexican mafia. They may be involved somehow. Maybe they bought the jewels from Wojicki laundering money. They probably separated us to see if our stories were the same. In any event, we should get out of here as quickly as possible. Guns in the hands of the untrained have always made me a little nervous, but M-16s in the hands of professionals scare the shit out of me."

Silently she passed behind his chair with the bent paperclip. She bent down behind the seat and started to work.

Finally realizing what she was doing, he instructed her, "Just push it in until it won't go any farther and start moving it around. When you hit the right spot, you should feel a slight give, at that point, it might go in a little farther. Push backward on the cuff where it latches as you push forward with the tool."

Twisting the device she'd forged, she said, "Oh, Jake, you're making me *hot* talking like that."

"Jeez! Forget the jokes. Just work on the cuffs," he said shaking his head.

With surprising rapidity, the right side of his hand popped free from the plastic shackle.

"Wow, I didn't think it would work!" Jake exclaimed as he pulled his hand onto his lap. "Nice going."

As she moved to work on the left hand, she chuckled, "Do you really think this is the first time I've dealt with handcuffs?"

"God, I should have known," he muttered.

"I do this bondage thing, two thousand bucks extra. Sometimes things get a little wild, so I got pretty good at this. I could even do it while I was getting—"

"That's enough," he cut her off. "I don't need to know what you were doing."

"Just like all men… You want your women to have certain skills, you just don't want to know how they were developed," she said as the left side popped free. "Okay. Now, what makes you certain they're not here."

"There's *too* much money here. This house and property are worth a small fortune, even for Mexico, and the boat is a very pricey toy. The grounds are flawlessly maintained. Chefs, bartenders, girls… it all costs money. Tom and Cindi didn't get away with *that* much."

Jake had risen from his chair and was examining the window behind the desk. It was closed and secured from the outside by iron bars bolted into the block of the home. "Automatic weapons mean someone is very worried about people coming here and doing bad things."

"If this is where they fenced the jewels, maybe these people know where to find them. Although I've refined my clientele over the years, I've been around plenty of hoods in the past. They're kind of like rattlesnakes. If you don't bother them, they won't bother you. Let's wait a few minutes and see where this leads. This is as close as we've been, Jake."

Digesting what she'd said, he answered, "That door is the only way out. On the other side are at least five trained men with weapons that could cut both of us in half. So, I think your strategy is sound."

"Yeah," Amber nodded. "You better sit down and put your hands back behind you. At least make it look like you're still cuffed."

Jake sat down and grasped the shackles of the handcuffs behind the chair. Amber sat down next to him and leaned back to see that the ruse looked real and the ends of the shackles were not visible. "What now?" he asked with a half-smile.

"We wait."

After five minutes the door swung open. Francisco walked in followed by another man neatly dressed in pressed shorts and a golf shirt. He appeared to be in his mid-fifties. The legs were tan, and he wore expensive woven sandals. His build was heavy, not excessively fat but not in shape either. Based upon his thickness Jake surmised he knew fine cuisine but tempered his appetite so as not to become overly portly.

Francisco stepped briskly to the side of the room leaving the chair behind the desk to the man who'd followed him in. As he sat, Jake noted a slightly receding line of shiny black hair and a thick yet finely trimmed mustache. Warm brown eyes appraised Amber and him as the new arrival leaned back in his chair with his hands behind his head. With a smile, the man spoke.

"So, I have heard your stories. And your boat has been searched. I am certain you are no danger to me or anyone else here.

"I bought this isolated piece of jungle and sand to hide at times from the rest of the world." He raised his eyebrows and bobbed his head in Francisco's direction. "Francisco has been with me for many years. Despite the occasional slip in the vigilance of those he hires, he has managed to keep me safe from real threats on numerous occasions.

"Who can blame them? We have so many visitors coming and going. Some colleagues. Others adversaries. Sometimes our visitors are both!" He laughed. "A few out there by the pool would like to see me gone; my power stripped so they could replace me.

"Some come to enjoy the fishing. Others to enjoy..." his gaze shifted to Amber, and he smiled ". . . the other bounties my estate has to offer."

She smiled back with a nod. "The young ladies at the pool."

"Sí! They are all *nieces* of the men, in case any of the wives of my visitors should come to know of their presence here." He winked mischievously. "We share dark secrets, my guests and me. It comes in handy when we need favors from one another. Our business is certainly questionable and often dirty, but we have learned how to make it profitable by our counterparts north of the border. It is unfortunate that it has come to the point that we need guns and security, but there are those in both government and the private sector who might like to see me taken down. Not to mention tabloid photographers who'd like to get photos of me in unfavorable company for their seedy little publications."

"Well, Mr...?" Jake started, letting the sentence hang to become a question.

"Alvarez. Gregorio Alvarez."

"Mr. Alvarez. We mean you no harm and want nothing to do with whatever you're running or selling. You can rest assured that we're not going to report where you are or what you're doing to any authorities. We only want to know if you've had dealings with the people we're looking for. Maybe they've invested money with you? Contraband is highly profitable."

Alvarez exchanged a puzzled look with Francisco, then turned back to Jake. Placing his elbows on the desk and leaning forward he asked, "What is it you think I do?"

Jake cleared his throat and said, "My thought is you're in the business of drug running and sales, or something like that." Quickly he added, "But we're only looking for the people in the pictures. We don't care what you're doing."

Alvarez let out a deep laugh. After catching his breath, he said to Jake, "Señor, you have been watching too many American movies or too much television. Do you think that all *Mexicanos* with a little money are dope dealers or smugglers? Oh, and Mr. Cohen, take your hands out from behind the chair. There is no reason for you to keep up the ruse; we know you're loose. My compliments to the resourcefulness of the lady." He nodded in Amber's direction. She smiled back.

Jake's eyes scanned the room for a microphone or camera as he brought his hands out from behind the chair.

"The sound is picked up from a receiver under the desk, señor. And video cameras are in each of the light fixtures," said Francisco.

"Are you in the habit of spying on all your guests?" Amber asked.

"Oh no! My beach estate is for the enjoyment of my visitors. It would be horribly rude to invade upon their privacy. This is the only room in the house that is—how do you say it in America—bugged, I believe. To Francisco's dismay, I will not even allow cameras on the beach or the road in. Or anywhere else in or around the home. It makes his job more challenging, but it helps with the trust of my guests.

"I maintain a staff here after the rainy season, from mid-November through May. At other times the place is closed up tight, and the staff is relocated to a retreat in the mountains to escape the oppressive heat that comes in summer. I normally have guests staying here in-season. Businessmen and friends. And often with their nieces." Alvarez again winked at Amber. "Their wives pretend to turn a blind eye, yet we know that many of them have nephews dropping by for visits while their husbands are away."

"No, this room is used only for situations…" his palms opened wide, ". . . like this."

The man was warm and friendly, Jake noticed. His English was excellent, and his speech seemed to flow easily. While his eyes flirted with Amber, there was no lecherousness to the act. Yet his tone with Jake created immediate camaraderie as if they might enjoy lighting cigars and sipping tequila while swapping dirty jokes. He liked Alvarez and could tell Amber did too.

"So, Mr. Alvarez, you never did finish telling us what it is you do," she said as her bright eyes flirted back at him.

"Oh, sí! Our conversation, like so many, strays… I am somewhat humble, so I will have Francisco tell you."

Francisco looked at the man behind the chair with what Jake thought to be a combination of a longstanding friendship and admiration. The security officer announced, "Gregorio Alvarez, my friends, is the governor of this province, Colima, and is also the front running candidate to be the next president of the nation of Mexico."

Amber and Jake exchanged embarrassed looks. "Please accept our mutual apologies," she offered.

"Accepted. Now, may I show you the grounds and the rest of my estate?" He rose and offered his arm. She took it, and they went out of the room together.

Jake stood then looked at Francisco, offering the chief of security his arm as Gregorio had with Amber. With a roll of his eyes, he said, "*Caramba*," and pushed Jake's arm back down to his side, giving him a thumb motion in the direction out of the room.

CHAPTER 34

"Bill's right. We won't make it back by dark," Jake announced as they motored out of the bay. The sun was fading from yellow to orange as it marched toward the sea. "I can get us there without light. We'll swing outside and come in straight to avoid any coastal shoals or local fishermen's pangas. Probably will take about two hours."

"Oh, Jake, I've had enough bouncing around. When we get back, you'll want to drive back to town tonight, which means more bouncing in the little rental car. We won't get back to the hotel until well after midnight, probably without food, and you'll be up at six looking for the bad guys again. I'm tired. Let's go stay in the cove they talked about. The bunk down below looks comfortable, and Gayle packed a wonderful cooler for our dinner. Plus, I'll cook for you."

Seeing what he thought was pleading in her eyes, he turned the wheel of the cruiser to the north toward the little bay and town of Chamela.

The look in her eyes changed from supplication to the feisty sparkle he'd come to know immediately after she'd realized she'd gotten her way.

If he'd looked more closely, he would have seen that this time Amber's mien had a devilish quality.

Twenty minutes later they pulled into a protected cove behind a high point. To the south, a series of small islands offered protection from any swells that might assault from that direction. Up on the beach, Amber watched children playing fetch with mongrel dogs as a few men waded in the shallows and threw cast nets. She saw rows of white plastic chairs set around tables where a few people sat drinking beer and soda. A heavenly aroma drifting on the air suggested something delicious was being prepared on the grills up under the palapas.

Jake sniffed the air. "Shrimp. Fresh too. Want some?"

"Sounds yummy. But I thought we should eat some of what we caught today. You get the barbeque going, and I'll do the rest."

"Deal. Can you back the boat down to set the anchor after I drop it?"

"Aye-aye captain," she said with another mock salute and the ever-infectious smile. "But shouldn't we anchor closer to the shore?"

"We want to have dinner here, not *be* dinner. With the mangroves behind, the mosquitoes will get thick there on the beach. They love new blood. Especially that of cute brunette fisher-ladies. Better to stay outside a ways."

"Oh. By all means then. Go farther if you'd like."

They dropped anchor as the lights began to flicker on one by one on the shoreline. The sky's color swung from a deep red at the horizon to purple above and outright black to the east, and stars peeked out here and there. The actual view of the sunset over the ocean was obscured by the jungle-covered point to the west, but the changing color of the sky was magnificent, nonetheless.

A few other boats, mere nearby shadows now in the early evening, swung gently on their hooks in the little bay. As the diesels were shut down, silence, broken only by the laughter of the children and the occasional barking of a dog, descended upon the cove of Chamela.

Jake set up the barbeque and suggested to Amber they take a freshwater rinse to remove the stickiness of the day's salt while the grill heated up. Jake went first standing on the swim platform using the deck shower. He dutifully turned his back as Amber flung her swimsuit top and bottom onto the deck to get a full body rinse. He hung the small pieces of fabric on the rocket-launcher rod holder and went into the cabin to get towels. Upon his return to the deck, he saw only her silhouetted curves against the last vestige of the sunset as she squeezed water off her ponytail. He thrust the towel out with one hand as he turned his head away.

"I think I'll call Janelle on the sat phone," he announced as he dried off. "It's been a few days since we talked. She thinks I'm still in Cabo, come to think of it."

Amber said nothing as he went forward after retrieving the phone, but he couldn't help but notice her foot on the gunnel of the boat as she dried her leg exposing the roundness of her bottom. She heard his conversation from the bow as she flipped on the deck light and wrapped the towel tightly around her like a short dress, securing the end under the pressure of the fabric just under her armpit.

After a few minutes on the phone he returned to the stern to find cut squash on the grill, and fresh tuna steaks ready to go. Wasabi and soy sauce sat on the top of the bait tank with plastic bowls and plates at the ready. Amber was placing candles around the boat, bending over just enough so as not to expose her bottom under the towel.

Still bent but without turning around, she asked him, "How do you like it?"

Swallowing before he spoke, he answered, "Well, the candles are a nice touch, but I think the towel should be replaced by your shorts and blouse."

"No, that's not what I mean. My shorts have salt on them anyway. This is much more comfortable. I mean how do you like your fish? Rare, medium, or well? I love ahi rare, and this couldn't be any fresher."

"Oh, rare's fine."

"Couldn't reach her, huh?"

"No. Not at the restaurant or on her cell phone. It's snowed like hell today back home."

"Glad I'm not there then," she said as she lit the last candle. "I think I've had enough snow and cold. *This* is nice." She popped a beer open and handed it to him.

"Yeah, it feels pretty darn good. Probably about seventy-five, but it won't get too much cooler than that. Water is at 79.4, according to the fish-finder. Breeze will likely kick up off the jungle as it cools. Should be a very pleasant evening," he pontificated as he sat in one of the folding deck chairs he'd brought out from the boat's cabin.

"Yes, it should. Thank you for the detailed weather report." She flipped the vegetables on the grill. When she was done, she turned and sat on the gunnel, her long tanned arms and legs stunning in the candlelight. "You're so analytical. You take in everything around you, seeming to process and store it for application later."

"It helps to break things down to the parts and pieces. Like this cove we're anchored in. You see it as a laid-back spot to spend the night. I view it as the same thing, but you're right, I had to scrutinize things before setting the anchor. That action becomes an unconscious act, preparing for what is likely to happen and what could happen. Keeps the mind honed." Jake sipped his beer.

"See the cruise ship out there." He pointed over her shoulder. A brightly lit ocean liner had emerged, miles offshore but visible in the gap between the islands and the point.

"Yep. It's beautiful against the fading light. I've been on a few, you know. It's a very romantic getaway." She took a sip of her beer. "Yet as tempting as lobster at the captain's table sounds, I can't think of any place in the world I'd rather be than right here at this moment."

Jake nodded. "They think they're having fun out there, and they may be at their level. But their minds are turned off. They've surrendered to the processed life that society has arranged for them. Be born, parents see to it you go to the right schools and get the education to prepare you to fit into the prefabricated life that's been created, graduate, get a job with upward mobility, get married, buy a small house in the right subdivision, have a few kids, get a promotion or two, buy a bigger house in a better subdivision, and see to it that your kids get the education so they can do it all over again.

"And inevitably you end up on that cruise ship. Your fun, and life, prefabricated and processed. Wake up, go to a feeding trough of some sort where you eat too much, enjoy one of the pre-planned activities, eat again, start drinking, go ashore on a prearranged sightseeing excursion, eat and drink some more, have a ball in the totally contrived confines of the ship's casino or disco, and pass out to do it all again the next day. You might find ten or fifteen minutes to boff the old lady a couple of times during the trip, then the boat docks, you pile off, and some other couple boards and is plugged into your spot on the fun-factory assembly line. You end up nothing more than an interchangeable part, whether you're on that ship or on the job or in your subdivision."

Amber made a sour face. "Wow. That was a bit heavy."

Jake finished the beer with a long pull. "Sorry. I guess it's the letdown of finding the house in the photo and have it turn out to be the wrong one. Even though our chasing the clues has been low-key for the most part, it's had stressful moments. I don't much like guns, and in the last two weeks, I've been standing at the business end of a few. My concern is that sooner or later one will go off.

"So about now that cruise ship full of lemmings with their minds rotting actually looks pretty good. I've vowed never to ride one, you know. I would hope to be able to create my own diversions, and not have my leisure activities laid out for me."

"Or your life," Amber added with an understanding nod.

They were quiet for a moment. Music now wafted over the cove from another of the yachts anchored nearby. Occasional laughter drifted from the beach or surrounding boats as the glow of cocktail hour took hold. Jake reached into the cooler and popped open another beer, holding it out to Amber. She raised hers to show him it was still half full. He shook his head and said, "You don't need to hear my derisive dissertations on the subject of life. Again, sorry."

"Oh, I do! I enjoy these different sides of you. Philosopher, mariner, fisherman, restaurateur, ski bum, sleuth, loner. And you probably wear ten more hats I don't know about. You're a very complex fellow, you know."

"Yep. That's me. Jack-of-all-trades, yet master of none. At least nothing that matters. Just ask my dad." Jake smiled and shook his head. He took a long pull off the beer. "And the sleuthing I'm not doing so well at, so you can delete that from the list."

"I think you're doing fine," she protested. "In the last few days, we've sat in the same restaurant and stood on the same beach as they did only a few days ago. We're close, Jake. Tomorrow. Maybe the next day. We're gonna find them."

Jake rubbed his chin and grumbled, "Yeah. Maybe."

Amber reached over and turned the knob on the barbeque to off. Then she put the two beautiful pink-red tuna steaks back into the cooler.

"What are you doing?" asked Jake suspiciously.

"We need to change your mood," she answered. "Just sit back and relax. Dinner can wait."

Amber walked around behind him. She touched his head gently at his temples with the fingertips of both hands and stroked downward with a touch so light he wasn't certain whether her skin was in contact with his or not. He was shirtless, and she continued the motion to his waist. The act was repeated, this time starting on his cheeks and moving downward across his chest. When she'd completed the light-touch strokes over his entire front, she had him lean forward and repeated the process on his back.

After completion, she said, "That was to get you to the point of relaxation. Now I'll work out the stress, knot by knot." She began a kneading of the back of his neck, using her strong fingers to find the striations in his muscles. As she worked, she asked casually, "So Jake, tell me how you happened to learn so much about boats."

"Kinda grew up with them. Ski boats first. Then my folks bought a sailboat. An old Hobie 14 catamaran. I pulled the lines on that thing until my fingers bled. Then a 26-foot Columbia. Sailed that boat all over the Channel Islands off Southern California. We got pretty good at it—all the kids. Good enough in fact that another doctor who worked with Dad recruited my brother and me to deliver a boat to Tahiti in the summer between my junior and senior year of high school. That was an experience for a kid. Over a month on the ocean without seeing land."

"Relaxing?"

"Oh my God! There was *nothing* to do. One set of the sails and the trades blew us the whole way. Got to know my bro pretty well though. He's eight years older than me, so we never spent much time together before that."

"Sounds like a productive trip, then," Amber stated as she worked dutifully across his shoulders.

"Not really. We went our separate ways again immediately after. My brother had been drafted by the Lions as a linebacker out of college in the late rounds. He was tough enough, but twenty pounds too small. Never made the team, so he took off to grad school. Now he sits next to a couch all day."

"He's a shrink?"

"Yeah. All my siblings have some kind of title or professional designation."

"Ah, I see. So, what happened to you?"

"After high school, I had two seasons of football and two and a half years of pre-law at USC. I loved it... Football, that is. Law, not so much... Still not sure why I quit. We'd won the Rose Bowl my last year. It just didn't feel real to me. I knew my extra 0.2 seconds in the forty-yard dash, and the extra fifteen pounds of muscle wasn't mine, but rather came from injections and pills. We were a bunch of juiced kids performing for the school. And for the NCAA. The school made millions and the NCAA billions, and we got nothing. The thing that bothered me most was the coaches knew about the juicing. And expected it. The NCAA knew it too. I walked away at the end of the season seven years ago and went skiing."

He laughed. "So I ended up on a boat in a tranquil tropical cove with a beautiful woman massaging my shoulders. Not bad, huh?"

He pulled again on the beer and continued. "Trouble is, the boat's borrowed, the woman is only here to collect her percentage, and nearly every penny in my wallet was lifted from a man who tried to kill me. I have credit cards that belong to someone else, and my career in a sport that didn't pay squat is coming to an end. That's my life story, in a nutshell. If I'd stayed in college there's an outside chance, I'd have made the NFL, but likely would have ended up by now a second or third-year attorney working fourteen-hour days dreaming of my week or two off so I could be carried to manufactured euphoria on that blasted cruise ship out there."

He sat for a moment as Amber worked on his legs. After the brief break, Jake said to her, "So, enough about me. What about you? How'd you end up an escort?"

She now moved up to his pectoral muscles and abs. As she answered, her lips were inches from his ear. In a sultry whisper, she said, "You know. Same old story of every good girl gone bad. Abusive father started molesting me when I was five. Mom drunk all the time, so I really had no role model. Got into drugs early, twelve or thirteen... Started turning tricks downtown at fourteen, and left home at sixteen when my parents threw me out after getting busted for the tenth time. Floated out to Reno and the rest is history."

Jake shook his head. "Sorry. I'm not buying it. That's a bimbo's story. Or something made for TV. Yours is a bit more complex, I'm gathering."

Amber laughed and slapped his chest playfully. "Are you calling me a liar?"

"Yep. Now let's have it. The truth."

"Okay. Here's God's own truth." She moved to the side and started working on his right arm. "My family is apple-pie American. Even more than yours. Dad is a scientist who works in the agriculture industry with soil conditioners and fertilizers. Mom stayed home and raised us all. Breakfast was on the table in the morning, dinner at night, and our lunches were packed for school. Dad was always there to bounce us on his knee or help with homework. I have two brothers and a sister. All younger. I went through school, graduated with high honors, and my boyfriend and I decided to go to college someplace where we could ski. I wanted Colorado but Nevada was cheaper, so we ended up in Reno.

"He was my one and only sexual experience when we left Nebraska. I'd been a skinny kid who had blossomed late. Braces and glasses. By midway through our first semester he was cheating on me regularly with any and every sorority bitch who'd have him, so we split. I was devastated. Thought he was the one I'd spend the rest of my life with, have kids, and eventually move back home with. Well, I wallowed in self-pity for a month or two, then got off my crying ass and took action. Took off the glasses, heavy coat and baggy sweat pants and started to live a bit.

"Well, I made some friends, and we cavorted through the bar scene. There were a few hot legs and wet T-shirt contests that I won. My self-esteem shot way up. I made some money—peanuts really—then one of the girls at a contest told me of some escort work she did. The money was good, and I gave it a try. No sex, at least at first. I could see there was big money in the entertainment and companionship business.

"I ended up joining a service. The money was good. It gave me management and a choice. Nothing said I had to take on anyone I didn't like. Being selective, I didn't make as much as the other ladies at first, but eventually, I built my own clientele. It was a great way to work through college. Sure, some of my clients were jerks, but any businessperson has that. They can be weeded out slowly and replaced with nice gentlemen. Most of the women in my line of work are tramps. But the few of us who've learned to work the business are comfortable.

"When I graduated with a degree in business admin, I found that a few companies were willing to take a risk hiring me for one-third of what I was making, so I stuck with my current occupation and proceeded to get my masters.

"With the masters in hand, I had the opportunity to make one-half of my then current salary working five times as many hours. The choice was obvious."

After completing the work on Jake's right arm, including a massage of each finger, Amber moved around and started work on the left shoulder. He could feel the tension being released from his body, muscle by muscle.

"Women are relegated to subservient positions in the business world. It would have taken me ten years of corporate climbing to duplicate my salary. I have sex less than an average housewife, and make $250,000 to $300,000 per year, declaring only a pittance for taxes. In a few more years I'll have enough to open a company of my own. I already have an idea and a new business plan diagrammed on the computer."

"Hmmm. Tell me about it," Jake said through lips that barely moved, his body melting into the chair in the warm tropical air as her skilled hands worked.

"Nope. It's a secret. You might copy the idea, then I'd be pissed at you and have to hunt you down and kill you," she laughed.

"We wouldn't want that. Okay, then tell me what makes you so different from the other girls at the service."

"You just hit the nail on the head. Some guys just want to buy a *girl* to knock off a quickie. Or to just plain get nasty and dirty with. The *girls* in my business offer that. The *ladies* offer something different. Companionship. A memorable evening, weekend, or whatever. We carry on intelligent conversation, don't get sloppy drunk or whacked on drugs, and take care of the *needs* of our clients. Men think they call the service to get laid, but in reality, the need is there for something they're not getting back home if they're married, or out of life in general if they're single. If you take them out and bone them in the first hour or two, you're done, have a few hundred bucks in your wallet, and they don't come back. Some of the *girls* end up taking on two hundred or more different guys per year.

"I have five clients now. I like to keep it about there, six at the most. Depends on how demanding they are on my time. You have to remember there are always one or two on the way out, so you keep options open. That's why I went on the initial interview with you. You, with your concocted tale, fit my profile. Someone from out of town who'll likely be in the area a few times per year looking to fill a void. Business professionals who can afford my services and want more than a hooker. About two-thirds are married, one-third single.

"The wedded ones are mostly searching for the way it used to be with their wives. Before kids and dogs and cats and the pile of bills and soccer games and Little League. They want an evening of *exchange* with a woman, without the baggage. Hire the babysitter, rush out to a movie or show, quick dinner, and then home. It isn't satisfying enough. It's too thick to get through, or over, with a time clock ticking. That's what keeps me in business."

"Doesn't bother you that you might wreck a marriage or two in the process?"

"Oh, I'm not the one wrecking the marriage. Speaking in terms you might understand; the boat has already hit the rocks when the guy calls the service. I've actually saved a few marriages by teaching hubby how to woo and romance again. I re-teach them in the art of candlelight, wine, and roses. Then I remind them of almost never seeing their kids again and having to split their assets right down the middle then make payments to the ex for the rest of their lives. For some, it's just an itch, and they go back to their wives with a better understanding of how *good* their life really is. I believe I help in those situations. If hubby had ended up with a bimbo into drugs and booze, he might actually ruin his life and marriage."

"So, is your next career marriage and family therapy?"

"Nope. Still a secret. Anyway, I'd prefer my clientele not be married. My perfect client is the businessman too busy for a relationship looking for a regular but brief period of romance without complications. There aren't enough of those though, so I have to put up with the cheating scum, too.

"In many ways, I'm like that cruise ship out there. Prefabricated romance, ready for those who want to board and can pay the passage. I yearn for something real, though. Lately more often."

Jake opened his eyes, looking directly at her face. She still worked on his arm yet stared out at the now distant lights of the ship. The candlelight reflected off her moist hair and her now red-brown skin. Almost unconsciously, he slid the arm she worked on out of her grasp and around behind to the middle of her back, then reached across his body and placed his right hand under her shapely bottom. With an ease that surprised her, she was lifted into his lap. He leaned down and kissed her gently but at the same time firmly.

When they released from one another's lips, she whispered, "Well, it's about time you took me up on my offerings. I was beginning to think you were gay."

"You broke me down. I'm like a fish following a chum line to your boat."

"I prefer to think of it more in terms of a lioness stalking her prey," she laughed teasingly. "But after today's experience, the fish allusion works fine."

"I still have that commitment thing back home, but I'll worry about that tomorrow," Jake suggested with a furrowed brow. "You're not going to think I'm cheating scum, are you?"

She made circles on his chest gently with her forefinger as she looked into his deep brown eyes. "Nope. You're open market. Having come to know you a bit over the last few days, I believe that if you ever *do* take that walk down the aisle, you'll be one of the few who will honor your commitment.

"But you're scared shitless of that cruise ship out there. And even more afraid of the tract home and the nine-to-five life that waits for you after the thing docks and you disembark. So you may never take that walk down the aisle." She pulled him back for another long kiss.

When their lips parted, he said, "You're wrong about that. I've had enough of a ski bum's life. I'm ready for a change."

Leaning away, she looked at him for a moment with thoughtful eyes. "Maybe. But it won't be the change you think you're looking for."

Returning her analytical gaze, he said, "I'll worry about that tomorrow, too."

He leaned down and kissed her again, but this time his fingers pressed deeply into the striations of the muscles in her back and shoulder, sending a robust signal the time for talk had ended.

CHAPTER 35

A vermilion glow over the smoky jungle greeted Amber as she awoke alone in the compact cabin of the *Gayle-Force*. The last time she'd seen the sunrise two days in a row was many years back. Propping the pillows up, she sat back for a few minutes.

She took in the view and sorted through the scents of the ocean, the jungle foliage, and food cooking somewhere nearby. All the aromas combined to form one inviting fragrance.

Amber Nelson couldn't remember the last time she'd felt so alive.

Wrapping the towel from the night before around her naked body she walked out onto the deck. She smiled as she found a bouquet of bright jungle flowers in a Pacifico bottle sitting next to two plates of freshly cut papaya and mango on the bait tank. The mess from their later-than-anticipated dinner was cleaned and stowed away. She remembered how satisfying the rare tuna had been. In fact, the entire evening had been gratifying, going as she'd planned.

Jake's wet toothbrush rested above the steering wheel of the boat. The kayak was gone, so she scanned the surface of the bay. Not far off shore toward the point, she saw him sitting and casting with a fishing rod. She yelled to him. On her third bellow, his hand shot up in a wave and the fishing rod went into a holder. He paddled back to the boat. As he pulled alongside, she said, "You've been busy this morning. Any luck?"

"Some. I had a pretty big one on the rod earlier." He gave her a sly smile.

Amber looked down at her bare feet. She blushed as she said, "No, you naughty boy! I meant the fishing."

"Yeah, that's what I meant too. Your mind is in the gutter, lady," laughed Jake. "Coincidentally, it was an amberjack. I was trying for roosterfish, but no luck on those rascals." His eyes scanned the surface of the bay as he said thoughtfully, "They should be here, but they're not."

"Ah, you seek the elusive roosterfish. I'm beginning to believe they don't exist."

"They do indeed, but they are not always where you think they are," Jake said as he hoisted himself out of the kayak and onto the swim step. "Let's go ashore with the photos. We'll take our fruit and augment it with some chorizo and eggs and coffee."

"Those sound like marching orders. So, the hunt is back on?"

"Yes, but it's nearing its end. I had an epiphany last night."

"Yes, you did. Four times. I think it was seven for me, but it may have been six. The last two maybe were one big one that ran together," she teased. "All right captain. Let me get some clothes on and fix my face a bit, then we'll go. And remember the mosquito repellent. You can tell me about your newfound enlightenment on the way."

"No, not yet. Right now, it's just a theory, but I'll do an experiment later to test my hypothesis. How long before you're ready?"

"Ten minutes."

"Okay. Call me over." Jake jumped back in the kayak, and after paddling away, resumed his casting with the fishing rod.

As Amber watched him, she smiled. The boyishness in him brought out the high school girl in her who'd disappeared years ago. She liked the feeling.

Glancing out at the kayak to see that he was not close, she opened his valise and took out the picture of Janelle. It was the one from the sun visor of his car.

Studying the photo of the lady in the swimsuit Amber spoke. "I only planned on borrowing him, but I may not want to give him back. Game on, honey. And all's fair."

CHAPTER 36

They ate a quick breakfast produced from what Amber proclaimed was the dirtiest outdoor kitchen she'd ever seen, yet the chorizo with eggs was surprisingly good and the view out over the bay made up for the lack of cleanliness. Jake said he'd eaten in much worse looking places. She again told him she was not surprised.

After downing two cups of coffee each (to Amber's dismay there was no tea available), they'd walked the beach for over a mile showing the photographs to the restaurant workers and shopkeepers. No one they met in the charming little fishing village recognized the figures in print, and Jake noted to Amber that this was the first place they'd stopped where people *hadn't* seen one of the trio. By nine o'clock, they weighed anchor and got underway. In the daylight, they were able to take a direct route, and the passage took less than an hour in the speedy little boat.

As they traveled, Jake put the boat on autopilot, and they scrubbed the *Gayle-Force* from stem to stern. He rinsed the fishing reels from the fresh water tank and wiped them down with a light coating of salt-resistant lubricant. Upon arrival, the boat was spotless. Bill and Gayle insisted they stay for lunch, but Jake told them he had something important to do back in Barra Navidad so after unloading and saying their goodbyes they bounced in the convertible through the jungle back to town. Even though he refused money for fuel, when he used the boat again, Bill would find three twenty-dollar bills under the cover of the GPS unit. Before leaving Jake caught Amber and Gayle exchanging winks, verifying his suspicion that Gayle had been a co-conspirator on the prior evening's events.

Arriving back in Barra Navidad just before noon, they went to their hotel and made good with the clerk on another two nights. Upon entering their room, Amber sneak-tackled him onto the bed, and with their first long kiss of the day suggested a shower and a nap with lovemaking mixed in. Jake declined, stating he had something important to do. They'd have time to take care of her wanton desires later. Suggesting she shower and join him afterward, he headed for the restaurant on the beach where they'd eaten a few nights before.

Amber arrived in the restaurant about an hour later in a new swimsuit and a tight-woven net sarong wrapped around her waist. The moderate afternoon crowd gathered to escape the merciless heat had just enough visibility through the mesh to know the bright yellow suit was a G-string style. As she moved gracefully through the tables under the palapa roof, the men there with ladies pretended not to look while the males alone stared openly. The women gazed too, with envy at the smoothness of her bottom and roundness of her cleavage.

Lowering her sunglasses on her nose and peering over the rims she surveyed the shaded tables. Jake was nowhere to be seen, and she nearly left to look elsewhere. Before exiting, a waitress tapped her on the shoulder and said, "There, señorita." The woman pointed to the beach.

Jake sat alone in the open sun. An empty wine bottle sat in the center of the table, and on the chair next to him sat a galvanized bucket, full of ice and beer. He wore his floppy canvas hat. As she approached, she saw his shirtless body was covered in droplets of sweat. The sand making its way over her sandals was searing hot, and her graceful walk turned into a sprint for survival over the stretch of beach between the restaurant stairs and his solitary table. Spotting her, he threw a towel down for her to stand on.

Composing herself as her feet cooled, she observed. He simply stared over the table at the sea, and she became certain the blazing sun had cooked his mind.

"You've been shopping," Jake said.

"Yep. Went to the *nice* hotel after I caught a shower." She unclasped the net sarong and did a runway style 360, being careful not to step off the towel. The small 'V' of fabric in the front of the suit fit perfectly on the lowest section of her flat tummy, and the rear was indeed a G-string at the base fringed by a series of tassels that made a semi-circle ending midway across her bottom. "You like?"

He smiled and nodded. "I like. Very much in fact." He pulled a beer out of the bucket, this time in a clear bottle rather than the brown they'd had since their arrival. He popped the top and handed it to her. She looked at him questioningly. "Thought I'd change brands. This is brewed locally," he offered. "Sit."

Feeling the white plastic chair with her hand, she determined it would not burn and took a seat. After a sip of the beer, she asked, "I thought you had something important to do?"

"I'm doing it."

They sat for a few more minutes. She sipped her beer again, then looked at him looking out over the table to the ocean. Eventually, she asked, "Doing what?"

"My experiment."

"Oh."

They sat. And sweated in the sun. A few more minutes passed. Her beer started to get warm, and she stuffed it back into the rapidly melting ice. Reaching into her bag, she withdrew sunscreen and rubbed some onto her face, then her shoulders.

Jake just sat. Staring.

"This is the stupidest experiment I've ever seen," Amber finally said. "I'm going to sit in the shade. It's roasting out here. We're the only idiots on this beach for miles except for the people in the water."

"Take a swim then."

Lowering her sunglasses, she said, "Do you think this suit was *ever* meant to *be* in water?"

"No, I suppose not," said Jake. He handed her one of the photos he'd carried for days now. "Help me with this research. Tell me what you see."

Withdrawing her beer from the ice, she studied the photograph. "It's Cindi, having lunch at an outdoor restaurant."

"How do you know it's lunch?"

"The clock on the wall behind her shows 1:15. So I'm guessing it's lunch."

"Okay. What time is it now?"

She put her arms out to the sides, palms up. "Do you think a watch goes with what I have on?"

His eyes moved from her feet to her head, scanning everything in between. "Good point."

"But, being the prepared lady I am, it's right here." She reached into her bag and withdrew her Rolex. "Says 10:52, but I haven't reset it. How many hours different are we here?"

"Two later."

"So that makes it 12:52 p.m."

"Yep. About the same time that picture was taken." He took a sip of beer. "Are you hot?"

"I already told you. Roasting."

"Cindi's sitting in the open sun. She look hot?"

Amber picked up the photo and studied it again. Her eyebrows rose as she said, "Nope. Very comfortable, in fact."

"Okay. Look at the wine on the table. What color?"

"Red."

"You see *anyone* drinking red wine midday since we got here?"

"No. It doesn't even sound good in this heat," said Amber as she sat straighter in her chair and looked carefully at the photo. "And the wine isn't really red; it's more of a ruby color, with a hint of orange-yellow-brown."

"What else?" he asked.

"There's more?

"Yep. Look carefully at the bottle and the table."

Her eyes shifted from the photo to the table, then back and forth a few times. "Sorry. I'm missing it. What's the difference?"

Jake pointed to a spot on the photo and answered, "The shadow from the wine bottle."

Amber looked at the bottle on their table. "Not so much here. In fact, almost none. So, what does this mean?"

Placing his thumbs and forefingers in a church steeple position, he said, "It means we've been duped."

"Enlighten me."

"Okay. Let's assume the time is correct on the clock in the photo. Her wine bottle is casting a much longer shadow than my test bottle. The sun is more directly overhead here than where she is, or was, when this photo was taken. That means this photo was likely taken at a different latitude than our present spot on the planet. We're at about nineteen degrees latitude here. That's about eleven hundred miles from zero latitude—the equator. I'd bet this photo was taken nearly twice that distance from the equator."

"Farther north?"

"Yep. Or maybe south. Wherever it is, the weather's cooler, too. That picture wasn't taken here."

They sat without speaking, each contemplating their breakthrough. The heat was forgotten for a moment.

"What about all the other photos, and local people seeing them from here up to Cabo?" questioned Amber.

"This lunch photo of Cindi is the most recent. Let's look at the other photos." Jake spread them out on the table. "Look at this one on Alvarez's beach. The jungle plants are bright green, with flowers. And there are white and gray puffy clouds. *Rain clouds.* Everyone's been talking about this being the dry season. The jungle is more of a brownish color now. The reason they got onto that beach is that the house was *closed* when the photo was taken. They didn't have to get by security."

He moved the photo of Tom and Cindi having a sunset cocktail in the same restaurant where they now sat. Pointing to the picture, he said, "Look at the horizon. The clouds are different here too. The ones we see at sunset are wispy. Cirrus. Not rain clouds, like these in the photo."

"Hmmm," mumbled Amber. "But they've been seen here in the last few days. Many people have verified that."

"No. The big guy, Monk, has been seen here. The last place Tom and Cindi were seen was Cabo.

"Last night, you told me I was doing a fine job of sleuthing. I disagreed. Why send photos and leave such an obvious trail? *They wanted anyone following to look here.* We could have spent weeks searching the coastline, and I'll bet if we go into Manzanillo, we'll find people who've seen that big guy. He's made *certain* he's been seen. His trail might lead from here to Xtapa, then Acapulco. We're not going to find them, because they're not here."

"When did you come to this conclusion?" asked Amber.

"It's been coming to light since we landed. Something didn't feel right. Then yesterday while we were fishing, I looked at a beer bottle on the boat and saw no shadow. It was a little cooler on the water than here but still wicked hot, and I realized the photo of your friend having lunch in the sun didn't make sense."

"You're convinced they're not here?"

"Yep. Like the roosterfish. All signs tell us they should be here, but they're long gone." He let the last syllable trail off as he spoke.

Amber looked at the photos, one by one. She shook her head and laughed, "God, we took the bait they put out hook, line, and sinker."

They sat for a few minutes. Jake closed his eyes and rubbed his forehead. Amber sipped at her beer a few times, but the level of the golden liquid in the bottle hardly dropped. They both sweated, but neither noticed.

"So," she asked eventually, "what now?"

Stretching his arms high above his head, he said, "One thing we know is Monk Phillips was here a week or so ago. You got that last e-mail about the same time he was here, so maybe he sent it. But maybe not." He put his hands flat on the table then said, "But that's the trail they've *wanted* us to follow. It was all way too easy.

"So, what now? I'm going home, that's what. I've still got two weeks to get in shape and ski in the world championships. It will take a few days to purge all this beer in my system, but I'll have time to work it through and polish skills a bit. There's a plane back to Los Angeles at six. Nothing straight to San Diego. It's not usually tough to get a seat down here, and I think we can make it." He rose and began collecting the photos off the table.

Amber still sat and stared out to sea. "Tell me about e-mail. Doesn't it leave a trail? Law enforcement people have traced it. So there must be a way to trace these to the source. I'm with you, Jake. That photo of Cindi lunching is likely the most recent. It had to be sent here, then forwarded. They must know the e-mail could be traced to a server."

He laughed. "All we have to do is find the one computer in Mexico from which the forwarded e-mail was sent to you? That will be next to impossible."

"I'd bet not," Amber smiled as she rose and reinstalled her wrap. "Let's go talk to the neighborhood professional."

CHAPTER 37

The real estate office was closed when they arrived, but Amber rounded up a few pesos and called from a pay phone. She left a message for Estela—she was a buyer interested in seeing at least one and maybe two of the most expensive properties featured on the flyers in the window. The story she concocted was she was staying on a boat in the marina at the Grand Bay, and wanted to see the property at 2:00 p.m. There was no way for the agent to return the call as their yacht had no phone and her cell battery was dead, but she'd be in Barra shopping, and would just 'swing by' the office at the given hour to see if anyone was there. She left no name.

Amber and Jake sat in a secluded corner of the restaurant across the street. Sipping bottled water and eating a light lunch of fresh ceviche and tortilla chips, they waited and watched. At 1:55, Estela appeared and unlocked the office, going inside and flipping the sign to the *Abierto*, or Open side.

Amber gave Jake a nod silently relaying, *Count on a real estate agent to never pass up a chance at a fat commission.* Without speaking, they stood and hurried across the street, having prepaid the bill.

Seated at her desk and working the computer keyboard, a look of both surprise and disappointment appeared on Estela's face as she recognized Jake and Amber. Recovering swiftly, she offered, "Well, *buenos tardes*, Mr. and Mrs. Cohen. I'm sorry, but I have an appointment. I have no time for you this afternoon."

"Oh God, I forgot we got married!" Amber gave Jake a look of mock perplexity. "Don't let me forget to stop at the palapa bar before we leave," she said to him as they approached the desk.

"What?" he asked, confused.

"You know, the Mexican divorce; we'll get our marriage annulled by the bartender," she answered.

"Oh," he nodded.

She said to Estela, "Don't worry. You have plenty of time. There's no one coming to meet you at two."

"Oh, I see. You are the woman from the mystery yacht." She pushed her keyboard away and stood. "Well, I have no time then this afternoon. As a matter of fact, you two should look for a new agent. I don't believe you are serious buyers. Please leave."

Rising, Amber walked to the window and turned the blinds, obscuring the view of the office from the outside. Jake stood in silence.

She walked around the desk and looked down at Estela. With a sudden sweep of her forearm, she pushed the items resting there off onto the floor. Taking a seat on the top in the cleared space she said to Estela, "Lady, you have no idea how serious I am."

"Get out."

Amber ignored her. "You're right. We're not buyers. I'm looking for Tom Wojicki and Cindi Light. Jake, get the pictures out."

As he reached into his valise, he said, "Amber, you can't—"

Her voice cut him off. "Just get the photos! I've bounced through the jungle or over the ocean or through airports for nearly a week now. While there have been enjoyable moments, my patience is at its end. The time has come for this bitch to come clean." She pointed her finger directly into Estela's face. "You snapped a photo of us the other day at the restaurant across the street, then spent an inordinate amount of time on the computer here while we ate. I think you sent that photo to someone through cyberspace, and I think you know where that someone is."

"How dare you come into my office and dump my desk on the floor! As I told you, I don't think you are real buyers of property, and I choose not to work with you. I'll give you one more chance to get out, then I call the *policia*."

She stood and smoothed her light cotton dress. As at their first encounter, her hair was impeccable, pulled back into a tight bun. Jake noticed her build was neither fat nor thin, but rather full yet with a hint of tone to the muscles as she looked down at Amber.

As the two women began to square off, he found himself silently sizing them up, noting Estela probably had twenty-five pounds on Amber.

"Don't stand there like a statue. Hand me the photos," commanded Amber.

He did as he was told. Amber held the first image of Tom and Cindi by the edge in front of Estela. "You know these people, don't you?"

Estela pushed Amber's hand holding the photo away and ordered, "One more chance for you. Get out!"

"I'll bet you know this one too," said Amber as she stood and thrust out the picture of Monk Phillips. Again, Estela pushed the photo away. However Jake noted a slight hint of recognition in her eye. He took a step forward and spoke.

"Estela, these people stole a great sum of money from my family. They nearly killed my father. We're willing to settle this without any action from authorities. Maybe you could pass along that message if you do know where they are."

"Bullshit, Jake! There is no 'if'. This bitch *does* know where they are. Or at a minimum, how they can be reached. And if you're right with your bottle-shadow theory, they're far enough away that they'll pack up and be gone before we or anyone can get there." Amber turned to Estela. "Nope. You're not going to contact them. You're going to tell us where they are, and we're going to arrive unannounced."

"Affairs in America have nothing to do with us here," Estela said with finality. "I know nothing of these people. Leave my office!" She pointed toward the door and stepped closer to Amber.

Amber looked at Jake, then rolled her eyes. "I'm sorry you have to see this, Jake," she apologized, then balled her right hand and brought it up under Estela's left breast in a quick and compact sweep.

Jake watched in amazement as she drove her fist deep into Estela's solar plexus with a punch that came up through the shoulder, ending with a rise of Amber's right heel, much like a major league baseball player's heel coming off the ground at the end of a home-run swing. The air left Estela's lungs with a hiss and grunt at the same time, then she doubled over and fell to the floor.

After a period of immobility, Estela slowly pushed herself up into a sitting position. Her breaths came in short gasps as she gulped at the air. "Take your time, honey," Amber advised as she squatted down to help her victim up. "In a minute or two you'll have enough wind back to tell us where our mutual friends are."

She helped the real estate agent into the desk chair, then placed Estela's hands on her head. "Hold there and try to push out on your lungs from the

270

inside as you breathe," Amber instructed.

Eventually, the natural color began to come back to Estela's face, and her breathing leveled off. She took her hands off her head and set them on the table. Amber resumed sitting on the desk and crossed her shapely legs next to the agent.

"Now, honey, why don't you tell us where we can find Mr. Wojicki and Ms. Light?"

Looking at Amber with malice, Estela's right hand shot out for the phone. It was caught at the halfway point by Amber's left hand, pinning it to the desk. With remarkable speed, Amber spun the hand upward and caught Estela's right elbow with her own right hand as it rose off the table. Her left thumb dug deep into the pocket between Estela's thumb and forefinger as Amber twisted and put pressure on the elbow with her right hand. Estela howled in agony as the pressure on her arm and hand forced her flat on the desktop with Amber rising to her feet behind.

"Estela, I'm pressing on the radial nerve between your thumb and fore-finger. If I press harder, it will hurt. Like this." Amber gave a push with her thumb and Estela squealed in pain. Upon releasing the pressure, the yelping stopped. "I can turn your pain on and off, like a light switch. I've also got your elbow which I can snap backward if you give me trouble." This time she pushed on the elbow, and again Estela howled. "Now, tell Jake where they are."

Between short gasps, Estela coughed out, "I don't know! I swear to you! Let me go! Please!"

Amber once more applied pressure to the nerve and elbow. Her helpless victim writhed and wailed with the pain as Amber said casually, "Sorry. Not buying it. I *will* break your arm if I have to. Wouldn't be the first time."

Once more Amber increased the pressure on both points. The howling reached a level that moved Jake a step forward to intervene, but between shrieks, Estela managed a couple of guttural "*sí's*" and "okay's," and Amber lessened the force.

"Please! Don't push again! I will tell you all I can. Let me up off this desk."

"No, you'll stay right there while we chat," answered Amber, "and if I don't believe what I'm hearing, I'm turning on the pain switch."

Jake suddenly remembered Sheriff Fred's warning. *A different set of rules applied once you're over the line.* Estela had crossed the line, and she was now subject to the conventions on this side of it. Yet he was too, feeling shame as he allowed the anguish on the desk to go on.

"Please! Listen before you cause the pain again! I know very little, but I will tell you all I know."

"We're listening," Amber replied.

"First, I must tell you, *I do not know* where they are. They, Tom and the pretty lady, come here many months ago. They look at casas and vacant land with me for many days. I know they were planning to run from the United States from something. Señor Tom wanted no other Americans around, so I guess that he was doing something bad.

"Finally he decide too many Americans here, so they leave and buy nothing."

"But that's not the end, is it?" Amber asked.

"Estela, I'm going to ask Amber to release you if you promise to tell the rest of the story. Deal?" said Jake.

"Sí! I will tell you everything."

Amber winked at Jake, then let the woman go. Estela remained flat on the desk for a moment, then slowly pushed herself up. Then she tested her right arm in different ranges of motion. Upon satisfaction that nothing was broken, she rose to her feet. Mustering all the dignity she could, she smoothed her dress, felt her hair to see that it was in place, and ran her hands over her face. A paperclip had embedded itself on her left cheek in the stickiness of the thick tropical air, and she removed it, massaging the indentation left by the metal. Finally sitting at the desk she shook her head, saying, "They didn't pay me enough for this shit."

Then she told them everything she knew.

———

Tom Wojicki and Cindi Light had come here in the rainy season. She showed them property for a few days but the presence of so many American expatriates had unnerved Tom, and he decided to look elsewhere.

She thought their relationship was done, but the pair requested a meeting with her at the office before leaving. She hoped they'd changed their minds and might want to make an offer on a home, but instead they outlined a rather simple plan to her and offered five thousand in American dollars for her help, plus future payments for further assistance if necessary. While the five grand wasn't necessarily a commission, it was quick cash without too much effort, accompanied by the promise of possible future payments.

Estela agreed that she would forward a series of future e-mails from them. Tom had explained that if traced those communications would lead to an internet service provider in Manzanillo, but he'd assured her they would not be traced beyond that point back to her machine. Estela would tell anyone inquiring they looked at property with her, but she thought they bought from another agent in an area farther to the south. Had Jake and Amber asked about Tom and Cindi specifically she would have immediately directed them on a southerly route.

She was to receive five hundred dollars U.S. currency for each contact. That was the reason she snapped the digital photo of them as a couple a few days prior, to forward it to Mr. Tom wherever he might be. The recognition of Amber's name from previous forwarded e-mails made her suspicious of the couple at the onset. She'd shown them property only until she received a response from Tom and his lady friend verifying Jake and Amber were a fraud and received assurance via the return e-mail that the cash was coming by Venmo.

With the computer still turned on, Jake stepped around Estela to use the keyboard. She started to protest but stopped as Amber shot her a stern look and said, "Go on with your story while Jake plays there."

Her account of the contact continued as she watched Jake tap away at the keyboard.

She never saw Tom and Cindi after their visit, and truly did not know where they were. They sent her e-mails, and per her deal, she did not forward, but rather retyped and reloaded the attached photograph files to be resent from an e-mail address that had been set up by Cindi Light before she and Tom left town.

Jake questioned her regarding their cyberspace whereabouts as he methodically searched through her e-mail cache. He pulled up a chair to sit in as he worked.

Being as helpful as possible now, Estela leaned forward and pointed to the communications that had been sent and forwarded. She explained that the big man had been here less than a week ago, but she thought he only passed through the area. With his phone battery dead, he'd stopped by the office but only stayed a few minutes to use the computer.

After forwarding the communications to himself, Jake continued to examine the in-depth properties of each e-mail as Estela bemoaned ever meeting Tom Wojicki and Cindi Light. After a few minutes of silently reading what appeared to Amber and Estela as gibberish on the screen, he looked at the dial of his watch, which he had reset to local time. The dial read 2:45 p.m. He pulled his phone from his pocket. Estela watched as he punched the country code for the United States and followed it with a series of memorized numbers.

"Caples Lake Resort." The phone was answered on the second ring.

"D.J.! Just the man I wanted," Jake laughed.

"Ah! The prodigal son. How's life in Cabo? It's spring-like here, but probably forty or fifty degrees below what you're basking in."

"I'm certain it's very nice in Cabo, but I'm in Manzanillo now. I'd guess about eighty-eight. You holding the fort okay?"

"Sure. Friday, Saturday, and Sunday nights were busy, but we're getting by. Janelle helped a lot last week, but she's back down at school, so you'll have to call there if you're looking for her," D.J. informed him. He added, "How's your dad?"

He answered, "Okay, I think. Hey, I'm really short on time, and I need a favor. You said it was spring-like. Is it sunny there?"

"Blinding. Snow yesterday but spring today. It's that time of year."

"Okay. Do me a favor. Grab a bottle of wine and take it out on the deck. Put it on a table and take some photos of it. Then text them to me. Get a few different angles. I'm especially interested in how the shadow of the bottle looks. At the latitude there. At this exact time of day."

"Would you like red or white?" D.J. asked mockingly.

"A cabernet, actually. I need the shape of that kind of bottle."

"Your wish shall be granted. I'm walking to the patio as we speak. Hey, how'd you end up there?"

"We just followed some clues," Jake said.

"We?" asked D.J.

"Yeah. Someone else is involved." Jake looked at Amber who sat cross-legged on the desk, staring at Estela as if ready to pounce.

274

"Lady?"

"Yes."

"Based upon Janelle's icy demeanor I think she's figured it out too. Okay. I'm hanging up to snap your shots. You'll have them in two minutes. Adios, my friend."

Jake terminated the call but did not put the device away. Next, he dialed Don Austin's number. It was answered on the first ring. Don, with a portion of his fine wine collection kept at the office, also promised similar photos within minutes.

Before hanging up, he said to Jake, "My diver who cleans my boat hull picked up a handgun off the bottom yesterday. The weapon had a silencer on it. You know anything about that?"

Jake hesitated then said, "Maybe. Save it, okay?"

Don answered with a drawn-out, "Yeah..." laced with skepticism.

As they said a quick goodbye, the text with photo attachments beeped in from the snowy peaks in the Sierra Nevada mountains.

"How much longer will you take?" griped Estela as she fidgeted in a chair.

Amber pointed a finger at the real estate agent. "As long as he needs." She turned to Jake and asked, "So, how much longer?"

"A bit... I suggest you both get comfortable," he answered as he forwarded the photos to Estela's e-mail to open on the 42" monitor she used to show buyers images of homes. Removing the photo of Cindi Light at the dockside café from his valise he began to study it carefully, comparing it to the ones on screen.

An hour and twenty minutes later after feverishly punching keys and clicking the mouse, Jake pushed the keyboard away. He announced, "I have no clue. The photos were useless." He wistfully shook his head and to Amber said, "Let's go. We're finished here."

"That's it?" Amber asked.

"Yes. We're done." He stood and turned to Estela. "I have a nagging intuition you'll go straight to the police as soon as we leave here and have us hauled in."

Estela said nothing but rubbed her arm.

"Three hundred dollars to keep us out of trouble?"

Turning her palm over at the end of her outstretched arm and flexing her fingers she said, "My arm is very sore. As is my hand. I think five hundred would be better."

They settled on $400, with Estela's word that the police would not be contacted, and they left the office. Amber thought it too high a price to pay but Jake assured her avoidance of a night or two in a Mexican jail cell was worth at least the amount forked over.

***

The shadows were lengthening with the breeze warm and sultry as they walked back down the cobblestone street toward their hotel. Amber was mildly melancholy as they strolled, yet Jake had a certain bounce to his step. She stopped and confronted him, "You're certainly chipper for someone who just got shut down."

"I'm trying to control my giddiness. The act was for Estela. I didn't want her to contact Tom and Cindi and tell them we're coming," he stopped and turned toward her. With eyes wide, he announced, "They're in Madeira."

"Where, pray-tell, is that?" Amber asked.

"It's an island chain. Off Portugal, of Portuguese domain. We're booked on a flight there day after tomorrow out of LAX. We could have gone from Mexico City, but the cost was double. Plus the fact that we have no clothes for the climate there. It's going to be a tad cooler than here. Of course, that's assuming you're still in on this."

With a mock look of severity, she asked, "Did you book first class? Coach all the way to Europe can be a brutal ride."

He shrugged as he said, "I am but a humble man."

Amber looked at his rubber sandals, tattered shorts, and his tee shirt as he stood grinning. The wardrobe could use improvement, but the smile was infectious. In her business, she'd developed a thick skin as a method of insulation from love and emotion. Yet the boyishness about him was so absolutely non-threatening she found herself being sucked in.

Only a moment ago she was depressed, thinking their time together was at its end. Now she was energized in the thought of their adventure continuing. Amber took his arm and started walking toward the hotel. She said, "I'm in. And coach will do. I'm certain you've been on worse rides."

276

CHAPTER 38

They caught the late flight out of Manzanillo to Los Angeles. Even after paying for her guarantee of silence, Jake was concerned that Estela would call the local *policía*. She was obviously a proud woman. Additionally, she might smell a bigger payoff if the couple was behind bars. It might cost a few thousand dollars for her to drop the charges, plus they'd have the local police to pay off.

Over Amber's protests, they threw their belongings into their bags and checked out of their hotel quickly. At the desk, Jake told the clerk that they were moving to the beautiful Grand Bay Hotel on the other end of town after they ate along the waterfront. All inquiries or messages should be directed there.

Another lie, but the necessity manifested itself as two black-and-white patrol cars arrived at the hotel just as they rattled away in their rental. The police cars sped off in the direction of the waterfront restaurants, while the convertible traveled toward the airport.

In the air and having successfully dodged incarceration, Amber questioned Jake as to why he was so certain the trio was in Madeira.

Jake explained, "I checked the properties tab on each message sent by Wojicki. Each communication was created hours later than the time it was received by the server in Manzanillo. So I pulled up a global time zone map and ran up and down possible locations in the grid of the time zone. I stopped on the west end of Spain. Cindi's incessant work on the language made me think this was their landing spot.

"But I didn't want to get duped again, so I checked other communications—sent items and deleted items—and found one sent by Monk Phillips to Wojicki four days ago. With his phone battery dead, the moron used Estela's e-mail. Through the grammatical butchery, he referenced he'd made certain he'd been seen in bars and hotels from Cabo to Manzanillo and told Tom to charter a boat called the *Tail Chaser* in three days so he could catch a 'Big Blue'.

"Any serious fisherman would name Madeira as one of the top three spots in the world for catching trophy blue marlin."

Amber responded, "That's probably why I've never heard of the place."

Ignoring her snub of one of his passions, he continued, "So I ran a search on 'Tail Chaser Fishing Charters'. There were three possibilities; it's a common name with big game fishermen."

"It's obvious big game fishermen are pigs."

Jake pushed his nose flat and uttered, "Oink, oink.

"Of the three potentials, I found one based in Madeira. But I still wasn't positive, so I reviewed the photos sent by my friends to the north. The photos from up at Caples Lake clearly showed a longer shadow cast by the wine bottle than the one you got from Cindi. The digital photos sent by my San Diego buddy Don, however, showed a nearly identical silhouette of the bottle on the table. His offices are in La Jolla, California."

"I know where La Jolla is. Geez, Jake, give me some credit."

"Yep, I know you *generally* know where La Jolla is. But you didn't know it sits at 32.8 degrees north latitude. Guess where Madeira sits?"

"32.8 degrees north?"

"Close. The biggest city there, Funchal, sits at 32.4 degrees north latitude. The 0.4 deviation between the two cities means there's only twenty-four miles difference in their distance from the equator. With the longitude of the time zone where Wojicki's e-mails originated and a reasonably accurate latitude from the shadow of the wine bottle, all I had to do was cross the points on the globe. Madeira is the only land there.

"Sitting there I yelled a resounding but silent 'bingo!' inside my head, then booked us through to Funchal, Madeira."

Reclining his seat and closing his eyes, Jake finished with, "Cindi wasn't learning Spanish; it was Portuguese."

They arrived in Los Angeles from Manzanillo in the early evening. Picking up Amber's Mercedes, they headed to his parents' home for a brief overnight stop (in separate beds, of course—Cohen house rules for non-marrieds).

Surprisingly, Anne Cohen was entirely supportive of the venture. While

Jake had been packing and the two women were alone, she'd confided in Amber that of the Cohen brood, he was the child best suited for this task. When Amber asked why, Mrs. Cohen's face tightened in reflection for a moment before answering.

"When Jake was little, he'd tell me he was going to hunt rattlesnakes behind our house. Those hills were full of bobcats, coyotes, cliffs, and all kinds of dangerous things. With the other kids, I was worried sick when they'd play up there. For some reason with Jake, I was never concerned. He always came home with rattles and skins."

Jake's mother ended the conversation by adding, "Frankly, when he left the house, I used to feel sorry for the rattlesnakes."

Before heading to the airport the next morning, they stopped to see Victor Cohen. Although he still couldn't talk, he looked less beaten up than when Jake had left the hospital five days ago. Jake explained their travels to date, leaving out the part about the run-in with Bennie Temple at the family beach house in Mexico. The idea of offering to split the plunder appealed to Dr. Cohen. He gave a nod of approval in Amber's direction when Jake told him the suggestion had originated as a result of their mutual input.

After a stop at a nearby mall for Amber's wardrobe augmentation, they were now headed to the island chain of Madeira, Portugal.

The first leg of their flight was from Los Angeles to Chicago's O'Hare where they changed planes. During the ground time, Jake called Chip Collins expecting to leave a message, yet was amazed to hear the deputy's voice. Collins relayed that Bennie had taken a walk on the beach the second morning after Jake's departure. When Chip had gone to look for him, he must have doubled back. Upon Chip's return to the house, he found the Toyota gone and the sparkplug wires on his rental truck yanked out and cut. Jake chided him on his fine detective work.

He and Amber flew through the night to reach Lisbon, Portugal. After clearing customs, they caught their scheduled flight into Madeira's capital city of Funchal.

The pilot's descent was anything but gradual as he nose-dived the passenger plane out of the sky. From her window seat, Amber caught a glimpse of the runway as their plane approached. It jutted from the island out over the ocean on pillars, giving the definite feeling that if the pilot made the slightest miscue, their wheels would be caught on the edge and the jet would do a fiery catapult down the runway. Or worse, they might not make the concrete path, and their plane would end up shattered where the rock met the sea below.

The plane cleared the fringe of the landing strip and abruptly came to a halt at the terminal. Jake pried Amber's clawed fingers off his forearm, and they grabbed their carry-on luggage. Upon viewing the indentations left by her nails, she giggled, "Sorry." Jake gave her his now familiar eye roll, and they disembarked the plane on a rolling staircase.

The weather was surprisingly cool as they walked across the tarmac. The azure blue of the ocean below had led them to believe the climate was tropical and both expected more warmth, yet the temperature was nearly identical to what they'd left in Southern California. Neither too hot nor too cold.

They rented another little Toyota. Jake, of course, wanted to start their search immediately but Amber insisted they find lodging and take a nap, as it was still the middle of the night on her internal clock. From a brochure she'd found at the airport, she decided to check out the Villa Echium.

The little B&B was clean and neat, with two villas for hire. One was being used by a group of four tourists on holiday from France, but the other was available at what seemed a very reasonable price. Through a conversation with the proprietor comprised of broken English, Spanish, and Portuguese they were able to rent the smaller of the two villas immediately. The bungalow offered a functional kitchen, sitting room, and bedroom. Everything was polished and maintained. French doors led outside to a grassy backyard and sitting area on a sunny patio.

"Not bad," said Amber as she flung her bag onto a small drawer chest. "For once a brochure didn't lie."

Jake stood at the open door to the patio and looked out over the yard. She came from behind and put her arms around his waist, running her hands up across his chest under yet another Tommy Bahama floral-print shirt purloined from his father's closet.

"Let's take a shower, make love, then take a nap," she whispered into his ear as she stood on her tiptoes. "It's been too long since we rocked that boat."

Jake turned and put his hands on her shoulders, straightening his arms as he took a step back. He looked directly into her eyes. "The boat was a one-timer. My mind wasn't in the right place. I'm committed to my relationship with Janelle. We'll be married someday, and I don't want to foul that up."

The smile on Amber's face slowly turned to a tight frown. Jake noticed the sparkle had left her eyes.

She walked over to the couch, sat down and put her shoeless feet on the coffee table. Rubbing her chin she offered, "You'll get married all right, then a few years down the road after a few kids and the pile of bills and whatever grind you end up in, you'll be back at my door, or someone like me. I'll be off the market by then. Retired. But there will always be someone else, as long as there are assholes like you to create the demand."

"So you've changed your opinion regarding my future fidelity?"

"Yep. You've shown your colors. Or I should say, the colors of your gender. 'Has a dick, is a dick,' we say at the service."

"Scintillating as this dialogue is, I'm sorry to say I have things to do. You're welcome to join me, but you need to adjust your attitude if you want to come along." He opened his bag and withdrew his shaving utensils.

"You should at the very least call her. She has a right to know where you are," Amber said in a louder voice to be heard over the running water in the bathroom.

"I will," he retorted with an edge as he started shaving. "When I'm ready. Right now I need to finish up with this, then I can deal with Janelle. She's going to ask about you, and I'm not going to lie. If I call her now, she'll have a few days to stew before I get home. It would be better for the two of us if I wait until I'm there."

"What a crock of shit! Who appointed you head of the household? I can see what your marriage will be like. A dictatorship. That'll be a hell of a relationship."

The door to the bathroom closed with a click.

Amber sat on the couch with her legs crossed thumbing through a magazine written in Portuguese. She pretended not to look up as he picked up the map provided with the rental car and studied it. She continued flipping pages in the publication she had no hope of reading. He moved toward the door, stopping before going out.

"Wanna go?" he asked.

Amber said nothing. Her eyes never left the pages.

"I'm going to call her. Your lambasting hit its mark."

"Great. I'll see to it that you receive a medal. Now get the hell out of here. The quicker we get this done, the better. I can get back to work, and you can go... Oh, never mind. Just get out."

He did.

As she heard the little Toyota rattle to a start and rumble away, she cried for the first time in many years.

CHAPTER 39

The island chain of Madeira was discovered in the early fifteenth century by lost Portuguese mariners running from a storm. The harbor allowed the sailors a haven from the howling winds that threatened to send them to a watery grave. After the discovery, the islands became an important port in the early exploration and exploitation of the African continent, as well as a stop-off point for the ships plundering the newfound bounty of the Americas. Christopher Columbus lived here after falling from the graces of the Spanish monarchy for failing to deliver the promised riches of his voyages.

Jake's knowledge of the local history was limited to that, and the fact they caught big fish here. His first stop was the waterfront retail and office complex that housed Tail Chaser Fishing Charters. The shop was easily located with the customary arbor and hooks out in front to hang the fish for photos after the catch.

The small space inside doubled as an extremely well-equipped tackle shop and headquarters for the charter business. Colorful lures and other fishing paraphernalia covered the walls and counters nearly completely, with the only open spaces filled with photos of the gigantic fish that lurked just outside the harbor.

The message to potential anglers was clear—to capture the monsters in the photos one needed a full array of the goodies offered for sale here.

Behind the counter was a big-boned yet attractive woman, who offered a, "May I help you?" The greeting was in English, yet carried an accent of the southern hemisphere.

"Aussie, Kiwi, or South African?" Jake asked. "Usually I can tell the difference, but there's a hint of something else."

"I'm an Aussie," she laughed, "but it's hard to tell anymore after rolling my tongue with Portuguese for so many years.

"With a tan like yours, you're either a fisherman or a surfer. Maybe both?"

He nodded. "I've just flown in from Mexico. Cabo and Manzanillo. Ran a little Bertram for a few days and put a little tuna blood on the deck. Released a few billfish too."

"Any blues or blacks?" she enquired as a fisherperson's bond formed. "How big were the tuna?"

Jake's head shook horizontally. "Only sailfish. The tuna were respectable; somewhere between ninety and one hundred. Pounds, not kilos."

"Sounds good, then" she replied. "You put some fillets on the barbie.

"My better half and me almost set up our charter business in Cabo years ago but came here instead. Both places have world-class fishing, diving, and surf. Less competition here, and not as bloody hot.

"We only planned on staying on for a bit—try to set a few world records and such—but the climate is so perfect we've just stayed. Been over ten years now. Set a few line-class records. The distance to the fishing is short, and not so rough as the big reef back home."

Her eyes got a faraway look as she added, "Someday we'll go home. But it's so damn perfect here, we just don't know when."

Refocusing on Jake, she said, "My husband's out on a bluefin tuna charter, but he'd be happy to take you on a tour of the *Tail Chaser* when back in port tomorrow." With an appraising once-over, she mentioned, "We're looking for a good leaderman as a deckhand or even a backup captain."

He told her, "Maybe. You never know. For now, I'm looking for these people." He placed the now well-traveled photos on the counter.

She raised her eyebrows and nodded. "The skinny man was in to book a fishing trip a few days ago. The big bloke came by and canceled when we told him the blue marlin won't be in for another two months when the water warms. Told us to keep the deposit to apply to a future trip.

"The skinny one—Tom, I think—stunk of stale booze and cigarettes and the big guy was so jumpy it made me nervous. Postponing the trip didn't bother me or my husband a bit. Spending a day with a drunk and hopped-up monster wouldn't be one of our preferred charters.

"Funny though; they didn't give us an address or phone number. Said they lived in the area and would check the fish reports to reschedule when the marlin were in. There was no woman with them."

Jake thanked her for her time and gave her his phone number, asking her to call if either of the pair was spotted again in the vicinity.

Exiting the little tackle store, Jake strolled along the waterfront. The sun had burned through the haze yet the temperature remained mild, warm but not too hot. People in the sidewalk cafés drank beer and wine as they ate late lunches. The urge to sit and have a cold beer himself gnawed lightly, but the world championships were still on his radar. He passed. He'd wrap things up here and still make it to Colorado in time to get a few days of practice in.

Wojicki was a known gambler, so the casino was on his list, yet he chose to meander through the restaurants and shops of the waterfront for now.

Only a few moments into his stroll he spotted the café where the picture of Cindi Light had been taken. From any angle, it looked like it could have been in Mexico. He sat down and ordered a coffee from a cute Portuguese girl who wore flat sandals and a light skirt and blouse. In her genuine smile, he saw the purity that Amber had noted in the town of Barra Navidad. She was another one isolated from the pressures of the 'civilized' sector of the earth.

When the photo of Cindi lunching was presented to the waitress at a refill stop, a look of immediate recognition came to her. "*Sim, estava aqui ontem,*" she said with a smile. "*Com um cavalheiro mais velho.*"

Communicating as best he could in Spanish, Jake gleaned that she was here yesterday with an older man. When he asked if they stopped in often, she replied, "*Uma vez uma semana.*"

"*Obrigado,*" he replied, having learned the word for 'thank you' at the airport.

They came into this café about once a week.

Close. He could feel it. Soon their paths would cross. It was a certainty.

Or was it a certainty? Doubt began to creep in.

He'd cleared Estela's computer of all the sites he'd visited and even deleted all her old e-mails. Could she have tipped them off somehow?

And what about Amber Nelson? He still didn't really know much about her. Was she right now out cutting a better deal with Wojicki and his trio?

Distrust. One of the symptoms of having crossed over the sheriff's line. Jake paid for his coffee and left the restaurant.

Looking up from sea level toward the thousands of homes chiseled into the bowl-shaped hillside cradling the city, Jake wondered under which of the red roofs Wojicki currently sat. Usually confident, he now felt uncertain.

Brushing aside the doubt, he pulled the map of Funchal up on his phone and located the casino. The distance was under a mile, so he chose to walk. After less than ten minutes on a brisk stroll, he found the building.

Climbing the marble stairs and going through the doors he left the quaint island outside. The interior environment could have been Vegas, Tahoe, or Reno, or any locale in the world that catered to the players of chance. Slots chimed, and bells rang when someone hit on a payout. Dealers stood stoically as players considered their cards before making tenuous decisions. Music played from an unseen lounge at the back of the hall.

At the casino bar, he ordered a glass of locally produced wine known as boal. When the wine arrived, he took a few sips and found it was excellent, tasting of the richness of the eroded volcanic soils of the island. Not exactly a red or a white, the ruby-tan color immediately reminded him of the lush hillsides that surrounded the city, yet the wine was light to the palate.

Leaving a few euros on the bar and sipping, he waited until he was certain the bartender had noticed the money, then he motioned him over. When the man arrived, Jake produced the photos of Wojicki and the others. Holding the images up at an angle, he pointed to each individual.

"¿Usted reconoce a cualquiera de esta gente?" Jake asked in Spanish.

The bartender answered with a headshake, "No. Eu não os reconheço."

No. Yet despite the denial, Jake was certain he saw recognition in the man's eye before the bartender walked away to wash cocktail glasses. Loading the photos back into the case, he left the wine behind and headed for the slot machines.

He played for a few minutes, actually winning some extra euros on a few pulls. Soon a cocktail waitress came by, and he ordered another glass of boal. When she returned, he had the photos out again, and again he received a denial. But the woman's eyes lingered a few extra seconds on the picture of Tom Wojicki. Jake tipped her, then she was gone. He retrieved his coins from the slot tray and placed them in the plastic cup to be converted to paper money at the cashier's station. He left the wine behind, after consuming only a few sips.

He presented the photographs once more, this time to the cashier handling the money conversion. With a brief crossover dialogue of Spanish and Portuguese, again a headshake told him 'no' to recollection of the faces. Jake folded the euros into his wallet and decided to stroll around the periphery of the gaming areas. He stopped at the lone sportsbook and surveyed the monitors, not surprised to find soccer games at the top of the odds board.

As he looked up at the panels, he heard from behind, "*Senhor, você parece procurar alguém. Talvez eu posso ajudar.*" The voice was firm.

Turning to see a man of darker complexion about his own height, Jake pulled at the words spoken in Portuguese. As his mind worked, he noted the man wore an impeccably tailored taupe suit and a tie of deep purple with taupe palm trees printed on it. His shoes were ornately woven leather loafers. He was of medium build with thinning dark hair, perfectly styled, pushed back and gelled.

"*Estoy apesadumbrado. No hablo portugués. Un poco español, pero el inglés es natives,*" Jake answered in Spanish, telling the man he spoke a bit of Spanish, but English was his first tongue.

With a nod, the man said, "English it shall be then. You seem to be looking for someone. Perhaps I can help?" The Portuguese accent was strong, yet the English words were clear and crisp.

"And you are?"

Smiling and extending his hand, he answered, "I am the casino manager, Juan Silva."

Silva's grasp was firm but not hard. The handshake was released, and Juan Silva continued. "You have asked three of my employees about people in some photographs you carry. May I take a look?" His eyes left Jake's as he pointed to the valise.

Handing the images over to Juan Silva he watched the casino manager shuffle from picture to picture. After what was too short a time of evaluation, Juan Silva handed the photos back. Touching his fingertips together at chest level he said again in an authoritative tone, "We live on a very small island, Senhor…?" Silva let the sentence hang as a question.

"Cohen. Jacob Cohen."

"Then, Senhor Cohen, as I said, we do live on a small island. So the staff is under explicit instructions not to divulge who comes and goes. It can cause problems locally. I'm certain you understand. So, the answer to your question of recollection of these faces from me, or any of the casino staff, is and will always be no.

"People do show up here from time to time, though. You might run into them on the premises. However, we want no trouble in the club. You must understand this. *Explicitly.*" Silva's eyes tightened as he let the notification of the sovereign state of his casino hang. Finally, he asked, "You have business with those in the photos?"

"Yes. They are from America, where they have stolen a large sum of money. They have run to your island here, but they have been tracked down. Tell them that *if* you should see any of them."

"And you are here to get the money back?"

"Yes. But only some of it. I believe we can reach a compromise that will allow Mr. Wojicki and his friends to stay here and have enough left over to help keep your lights on. If not, one of our agencies will come to drag the lot back home and lock him and his friends up for many years."

Silva smiled. "One man's winning or losing here will not 'keep our lights on', Senhor Cohen. This casino has been here for many years, and barring a natural disaster, it will be here for many more. I know no one by the name of Wojicki, but if I see any of those in your photos, I will let them know you look for them."

"Thank you. Do that for me, and I'll keep the sap coming to augment your income. Despite your denial, habitual losers are the lifeblood of clubs like this. Wojicki is good for at least a few pairs of Bragano loafers or silk suits and ties of Como, or whatever other vices you may have," Jake stated with a smile of his own.

"Ahhh! You have an eye for quality attire. It is a pity you do not put your knowledge to better use. You are in Europe now, and looking like a refugee from a Beach Boys song is not—how do you say it in the States? Cool, I believe." He let the jab settle a moment before asking, "Where might I say you can be reached if any of these people should materialize?"

"I'll drop in every now and then. Any certain time better for you?"

"Afternoons are best. It is slow now, but it gets very busy in the evenings. I remind you again of our policy of not having trouble in the club. The scar and purple around your eye tell me tribulation finds you. Problems will not be tolerated."

Jake nodded.

Silva looked Jake up and down then added, "Jackets and long pants are required in the club after sundown. Knowledge of this should save you some embarrassment," Silva said extending his hand, signaling their conversation had ended. Jake shook it, and Silva turned to leave. After a few steps, he stopped and looked back.

"Are you a gambler, Senhor Cohen?"

"I play a bit. Mostly poker, when I do."

The casino manager smiled, "Ahh! You prefer '*homem contra o homem*' rather than a game of chance."

Jake shook his head. Silva laughed, saying, "Translated to English—man versus man. You have the gaze of a gambler, Senhor. I would very much like to share a table with you sometime."

"Juan Silva, I couldn't afford your shoes, let alone sit at a table with you."

Looking briefly at his feet, then back at Jake, Silva answered, "Perhaps. I trust I will see you again?"

"Unless chance favors me elsewhere."

"*Adeus então para agora*," said Silva. He turned and walked away into the gaming area.

After leaving the casino, Jake spent the rest of the afternoon wandering the streets, checking the bars and cafés with no luck. His initial success in finding the fishing charter office and the café had buoyed his hopes, yet as he meandered through Funchal, his energy began to drain. Finally, out of options with the air cooling as the sun faded and the haze rolled in off the ocean, he walked back to the Toyota and headed up into the hills toward the rented villa.

He was tired, and the last thing he wanted to do was butt heads with an angry female. Maybe Amber would be asleep? He hoped… Or maybe her mood would be improved after a nap. He thought of Silva's statement that he preferred '*man versus man*' to a game of chance and laughed silently. Relationships with women were nothing but chance, and this one was even more of a gamble than most.

Never let the little head think for the big head, he reminded himself. Too late now. His problems were self-inflicted.

After a few close calls with oncoming traffic on the tight cobblestone roads, he arrived at the villa and parked. Entering, he heard the television tuned to a Portuguese station. Setting his valise on the breakfast bar next to an open bottle of local wine he walked into the small living area and plopped down in the armchair next to the couch where Amber sat. Jake purposefully did not make eye contact with her, looking only at the TV as he descended into the chair. He hoped to avoid a continuing battle.

She had her feet and legs up on the coffee table. His seat in the room was slightly forward of the couch, so he had to look sideways to see her. He avoided glancing that direction. Not interested at all in what was on the screen, he suddenly wondered why she was watching a program in a language she didn't speak. Maybe she was asleep, and this show had come on after she'd dozed off?

Eventually, he took a peek in her direction. With the slight tilt of his head, he saw only her legs on the table.

Funny, he thought; *I hadn't noticed a rose tattoo on her ankle…* He was certain he'd inspected that area on numerous occasions. Certainly, she didn't *get* a tattoo while he was gone today…

Spinning quickly he stood and found himself staring down at a woman who was *not* Amber Nelson. Speechless, he stared first into her blue eyes then scanned the rest of her.

He saw svelte legs that glowed with softness, a flat tummy showing above khaki shorts under a midriff blouse that housed round grapefruit-sized breasts. The female offered full lips, cheekbones just high enough, and hair of silk that could not be called either blonde or brown. The mane carried a natural shade of gold somewhere in between, showing time in the sun.

Amber had been right. She was indeed a beauty, yet as Jake looked at her, he recalled the trouble she'd caused. Her attractiveness had no effect on him.

"Hello Cindi," Jake said flatly, not extending his hand.

"You must be Jake." Her voice was hollow. He said nothing. She continued, "Amber's asleep in the bedroom. Just a catnap. Let me first tell you how sorry I am about all of this."

His eyes tightened and bore down upon her. She started to sniffle. Soon that broke down into a full-scale cry with her face buried in her hands.

Jake pinched the bridge between his nose and eyes and shook his head. He couldn't muster a speck of pity as the woman sobbed away.

CHAPTER 40

Amber appeared from the doorway, shooting Jake a 'what-have-you-done' look. She walked over and sat next to the woman sobbing on the couch, cuddling her against her shoulder. "Cindi, everything will be okay. We're going to fix this," consoled Amber in a motherly tone.

"No, we're *not*, Cindi," said Jake caustically. "We're going to send you to jail, where the next woman holding you won't be as gentle as Amber. Unless you want to give back the money you and that dickhead stole."

Amber looked up at Jake and hissed, "Can't you see she's been through hell? She's near a point of snapping. She knows she's screwed up big time and is truly sorry."

"Whaaa! Whaaa!" Jake mocked. "I'm not *playing* anything. Where the hell did you dig her up?"

"We were roommates for years, Jake," said Amber as she wiped the tears off Cindi's cheeks. "I know her schedule, so I guessed she'd be in a gym somewhere between two and four. I found a taxi driver and started looking at health clubs. Found her at my third stop. We've talked now for a couple of hours. She's on board with our plan. She just wants to get this over with."

He was quiet for a moment, looking down at the two women. All the days of pursuit had come down to a blathering woman throwing up the white flag of surrender. Jake wondered if Wojicki and Monk Phillips would so readily relinquish the plunder. Oddly, he found himself hoping they would not. He wanted vengeance. Letting them go would not settle the score.

The thought of revenge must be expunged, he decided quickly. A fast settlement was best. Get construction going and encumbrances paid back home.

Cindi began to regain composure and leaned away from Amber's embrace. Sniffling mildly, she looked up at Jake and offered, "I'm so sorry. No one ever meant for your father to be hurt. He just showed up that night and Monk went crazy on him."

"So you only meant to steal my parents blind?" Jake said.

"Jake, she *is* sorry. For everything. Can't you see she's alone here? She's stuck on a rock surrounded by water thousands of miles from home. It's worse than being alone. Tom's drunk all the time and won't give her access to any of their money for fear she'll bolt. The other one's whacked out on crystal meth and spends all his time staring at her like she's a piece of meat. It's no picnic," snarled Amber.

"Ahhh. Poor little Cindi," he mocked. "You didn't get what you wanted out of this, and now you want out. Sorry, my ass! You're garbage."

"Who do think called nine-one-one that night? I made Monk stop the car. I couldn't just leave him there. I'm not as bad as you think!"

"I'll see to it you get the Mother Teresa humanitarian award. Or at least a Girl Scout merit badge."

"Jake, you're done beating her up!" Amber yelled at him. "This isn't helping!"

Through clenched teeth, Jake exhaled a vociferous growl. He paced the length of the small room a few times. On his third lap, he stopped and looked at them on the couch. "All right. Let's hear your story. Then we go and see Mr. Wojicki and Mr. Phillips."

Cindi stood and looked defiantly at him. The wounded-deer demeanor was gone. In an even tone, she said, "He'll be drunk by now. And Monk will be sky high. Better to wait until tomorrow when they're both reasonably lucid. After eleven would be best. We'll meet at the house. It's really quite beautiful."

"Living it up on my parents' dough, while Dad lays in a hospital bed with his jaw wired shut eating through a tube."

Amber shot Jake another look. He put his hands up in a position of surrender. She nodded silently to him, then walked to the breakfast bar and poured three glasses of wine. She handed one each to Cindi and Jake. "Go ahead, Cindi. Tell Jake everything. Jake, you be a gentleman," she instructed as she gestured toward the small dining table.

Exchanging looks of mutual disdain, Jake and Cindi sat. Amber opened the refrigerator and withdrew cheese and bread and some pate she'd purchased that afternoon. She put out plates and set the meager spread out on the table on a cutting board, joining them.

Jake filled his plate and took a sip of his wine. Amber rested her hand on his forearm so she could squeeze a warning if he became agitated. They both listened as Cindi recounted the story.

"I met Tom when he came to the Carson Valley a few years ago. He quickly became a regular client. He used me more as a prop in the projection of his image than for sex. Tom worked out a retainer fee arrangement with me be his companion a few nights per week. Actually, we used each other; he gave me credibility among businesspeople, and I was his arm-candy, playing the part of the hottie girlfriend to the successful developer.

"He leveled with me early on he had IRS troubles. He'd made mistakes in handling his returns, and the back taxes, penalties, and interest were piling up so fast he couldn't stay ahead. I didn't much care as long as I received my monthly stipend.

"His pay, while damn good, wouldn't allow him to both get out from under his debt to the government and maintain his lifestyle. He started gambling in an attempt to augment his income. Gambling became a sickness. When he'd win, he was on top of the world. When he'd lose, he was so pissed he felt compelled to not just win, but needed to openly beat the clubs in retaliation."

Cindi took a sip of wine and ate a piece of cheese, then continued. "He rarely beat them, and between losses at the casinos and IRS garnishments of wages, he went broke. That's when he got hooked up with Nicki. His life had been heading downhill, but after meeting Nicki, it was a tailspin of debt and booze."

She added thoughtfully, "He really wasn't a bad guy. He just wanted to be recognized as a success. That image cost money, Tom financed it through Nicki, tried to win it back at the tables, and ended up deeper in debt than he ever imagined. Then there was the drinking.

"The 'good old boy' construction network is one of heavy drinking. Meetings, especially those after hours, were accompanied by cocktails. Tom did fine there, but afterward, he'd stop at the casinos. The free drinks at the tables did him in."

She took a deep breath, then continued. "He became nearly suicidal, owing over $700,000 to the government and another $150,000 to Nicki Stinnetti. I thought he was a goner. Then he got the miracle call from your dad."

Cindi looked at Jake, who sat tight-lipped.

"Your parents had money, and Tom didn't. So we came up with a plan.

"Despite his problems, Tom *knew* construction. I'd learned the escrow and title insurance business. It didn't pay what I made with the service, but it was legit work for a change. And I was good at it. It felt good. *It was real.*"

Jake saw a sense of accomplishment rise within her. Just for a second, but it was there. She sipped wine, then her mien dipped as she continued. "Tom said there was massive equity in their project, and the opportunity would arise to get to it somehow. We'd build trust, put me in control of the finances over time, and everything would fall into place."

Looking again at Jake, Cindi said, "Tom felt he had a score to settle with your parents. If they'd only allowed that one property to go to foreclosure years ago instead of taking the loss… He'd made it big, and believed your parents destroyed his world. So he decided the tables would be turned.

"We met with Nicki to outline the rudiments of his plan, then packed up and headed south. Monk was originally sent along as Nicki's employee to make certain Tom didn't slip away into oblivion. But the oaf demanded he be cut in, or he'd blow the whistle. We notified Nicki of Monk's newfound entrepreneurial spirit."

Cindi pushed at the cheese on the plate with the knife. "That's when the whole thing almost blew up. Monk and Tom were recalled to Carson City for a come-to-Jesus meeting with Nicki. I went too. Nicki's new leg-breaker took a poke at Tom to remind him who was still in charge. Monk leveled him with two swats. It sounded like a baseball bat hitting a watermelon.

"Right there, the power balance shifted. Nicki was left to trust us in a plan he knew nothing about. But Tom assured him it'd be okay.

"Tom sent an anonymous letter to his case worker at the IRS alerting them to the fact that he was indeed a partner in San Jacinto Development and therefore on the title to the land at Vineyard Meadows.

"Within a week the hammer fell. The property was slapped with a federal tax lien for nearly $750,000. The banker, even as a friend of your parents, wouldn't release a nickel on a new construction loan. The project was stalled. Tom played innocent, saying he never thought about the possibility of a lien.

"Your dad was undaunted. It wouldn't be a problem to complete the development with personal funds and pay the lien off at the closing of the homes from Tom's proceeds. While that strategy would gobble up Tom's profit from the first phase of the project, he'd at least be rid of the IRS lien. Tom would get out of the red and into the black on Phase II of the development. Heck, they were already grading the pads for the homes there. Completion was estimated at less than eight months. And your dad figured, why pay the interest on the construction loan to the bank? The money could be borrowed by the development company from their retirement accounts and a credit line against the home on the lake. The company would pay the interest to Victor and Anne instead of the bank.

"Well, Tom saw that as another slap in the face; your parents would get richer as his profit dropped. He held his tongue but was even more pissed at them.

"Within a few weeks, they got construction rolling again, funded by your parents' personal assets. Tom handled purveyance of materials and labor, but he fudged the budget, making gross underestimates in construction costs. Then he acted more surprised than any of them when they needed over $1,000,000 more to finish the project. He blamed the oversight on increased labor and materials costs, and his own optimism in trying to set too tight a budget. In all their years of working together, he'd never missed on an estimate.

"Your parents' finances were tapped-out, and Tom knew it. The credit line on the house was over the limit, and the personal loans taken against retirement funds depleted those assets to nearly nothing. There was no place left to draw cash.

"Your dad never worried, as over $7,000,000 sat in equity. The first phase of the project was nearly completed with only the $750,000 IRS lien owed against it. He just needed to find another $1,000,000 to finish up the homes."

Jake chimed in, "The prudent course of action would have been to simply pay off the IRS lien from the inception. With the cloud on title removed, the floodgates of institutional lending would open wide. But my dad would never do that. He'd feel the debt should be paid by Tom."

Cindi nodded. "Yep. That's what Tom thought too. Then a rumor, spread by Monk at the job site, of the shortage of funds and a huge IRS lien mysteriously reached the subcontractors and materials suppliers. They immediately pulled their workers and stopped delivering supplies. They raced one another to file mechanics' liens against the property. Fast cash was needed to get the contractors back on the job and open the flow of materials.

"Your brother and sisters all do pretty well. We were worried your parents might borrow the money from them. But Tom was right again; your dad's pride stopped him from telling the kids about the financial abyss he'd created.

"On the first day after the contractor's walkout, he called in sick to the hospital, drove to the bank early, opened their safety deposit box, and withdrew the collection of jewels. Tom directed him to a shop in San Diego and rode along as he hawked the items. As he left the high-end jewelry/pawn shop, your dad confided in Tom that it was vital the collection be redeemed. I guess it's treasured by your mom, with some pieces dating back through her lineage nearly a thousand years.

"The Cohen family jewels were hawked for a paltry $225,000. The cost to redeem the collection would be $250,000 due in six months."

"They're DeCorto family jewels," corrected Jake.

"Whatever. Didn't matter to the pawnbroker.

"Those funds were enough to get the building going again. Temporarily. Partial payments were made to the subcontractors and supply houses, with the promise of more in only a few weeks. But more money was needed. Just a little, only $1,000,000 or so.

"Your dad made one last run at the banker, Roger Scott. He wrote a detailed letter to be presented to the loan board outlining the financial position of the development. Yes, they had IRS and mechanics' liens that clouded the title to the property. But those were minor annoyances. The numbers added up to a huge position of equity. If the bank granted his request for $2,000,000, or even $1,000,000 at a minimum, there would still be well over $6,000,000 in equity with the homes and land as security.

"Roger Scott was a personal friend. They played golf and tennis together at the club and attended the same church. Your dad thought, surely Roger could see the safety in lending such a small sum on a short-term note. He assured your dad he'd present his case to the loan committee and they would seriously consider his request.

"What nobody knew was I'd been boffing Roger for some time. I pulled that little fart's strings like a puppet-master making a marionette dance." She laughed triumphantly. "I got video of him in all kinds of compromising positions; one with me ramming a dildo up his ass while he wore a Batman suit, for crying out loud. Not the kind of movie he'd want his wife to watch over popcorn and a cocktail, especially with a multimillion-dollar payout looming with the purchase of his bank by a national financial power.

"We *owned* the banker. Your parents' loan would be funded when Tom said so. Not a minute before.

"Stonewalled, your dad was ready to turn to his children in desperation. 'Wait,' Tom told him, 'I know a guy in Carson City...'"

"That's when the introduction was made to Nicki Stinnetti," Jake nodded.

"Yep. They flew up to Reno, made a short drive to Carson City, and met Nicki at his office. The walls were covered with photos of developments the lender had allegedly financed, and he presented himself as a legitimate businessman. A deal was worked out that day, and the funds would be wired immediately after Nicki had an opportunity to view the development. Two days later he and another guy we'd never seen before drove south and walked the project with Tom. Nicki was satisfied, and the funds would be wired within a week."

"Mom knew nothing of the loan, and still doesn't know about the pawning of the jewels," said Jake.

"The looks she gave Tom in those final weeks were of pure malice. That added fuel to Tom's contempt. He was certain your mom had no intention of continuing with him as a partner in the subsequent phases of the development. Their relationship was finished.

"So before leaving, Nicki asked Tom, Monk, and me to meet at a park near the project. He knew Tom planned on taking the $1,500,000 and running. That was okay; he just wanted to know *where* he was running. Tom wasn't off the hook until Nicki was paid off. Only at foreclosure when Nicki grabbed millions in equity would that debt would be canceled. Stinnetti had *never* put out that kind of money before for one person. The promise of a massive profit was worth the risk, but if this thing blew up, he wanted his money, and he assured us we'd be found.

"At the meeting, Nicki introduced us to his new associate, Bennie Temple. The little guy pistol-whipped Monk to the back of his head with his gun. Monk went down, but mad as hell, he quickly rolled to his feet, ready to charge and snap him like a twig. As he popped onto his toes, he found himself staring into the barrel of a gun. He backed down and took a seat on a bench, putting pressure on the wound to the back of his skull to stop the blood flowing.

"The balance of power had shifted back, Nicki explained. If he ended up screwed in this deal, his new hire, Bennie Temple, would be back to settle all debts.

"But instead of being scared, Tom's resolve strengthened. He was done being browbeaten, becoming more steadfast than ever.

"Your dad thought the 1.5 million-dollar loan would be his ticket out of the bind; he'd clear the IRS lien, clear the other liens, and have enough cash to finish the project.

"Tom knew otherwise. Once the money disappeared, there was no way for your parents to buy their way out. Adding the $2,000,000 and setting up your dad on criminal charges was brilliant. The increased debt ensured Nicki's payout. Your brother and sisters would never come up with over three and a half million, and we'd pocket two mil more. Whatever resources your dad could muster would be spent fighting legal battles.

"At the end, we'd hoped to end up with over $4,500,000. We stopped in St. Thomas to sell the jewels, but it didn't go as planned. Tom figured he'd get $1,250,000 but got only a half mil. All said and done, our total take was about $3,900,000."

"How are you splitting it up?" asked Jake.

"Tom gets fifty percent, I get thirty, and Monk twenty. The bozo doesn't deserve shit, but Tom says a deal was a deal."

"Such an honorable fellow," Jake mocked. Amber squeezed his arm. He asked, "So what about Stinnetti?"

Cindi answered, "Tom guessed after receiving an approximate $5,000,000 profit, Nicki will forget about the other $2,000,000. If not, he'll never find us anyway."

"I think that's up to me," Jake announced. "Finish telling us how you set my parents up, and how dad ended up beaten up."

"Zero hour arrived. Tom, allegedly feeling guilty over the IRS troubles and budgetary guffaws, arranged for your parents to have a Palm Springs weekend on him. Dr. Cohen would swing by the offices to sign and have notarized the loan documents for Nicki on his way out of town at 11:00 a.m. on that Thursday. Tom had set a tee time of 3:30 p.m. at PGA West, where your pop would play a quick nine holes before dark on one of the world's finest courses. He'd sign quickly, make the hour and a half drive to Palm Springs, and easily make his tee time after dropping your mom at the hotel.

"When he arrived at the offices, I buried him with not only the new note to Stinnetti but also a mountain of other documents to sign. The grant deeds to all nine homes, post-dated checks to contractors, authorizations for work, approvals for transfer of funds between Wine Country Escrow, San Jacinto Development, and Vineyard Meadows Limited Liability Corporation. In all, he signed his name over sixty times between eleven and twelve thirty. He didn't take time to verify account numbers on the transfer forms. I even got him to sign three blank pages by simply folding the papers one-quarter up the page and saying, 'Here too, Vic.'

"He made the tee time that Thursday afternoon, and on Friday afternoon, the note was recorded and Nicki funded $1,500,000 into the San Jacinto Development account. Tom relayed news of the deposit via text as your parents were eating a poolside lunch.

"But just hours earlier, unbeknownst to Nicki or your parents, Roger approved the request made for the original $2,000,000 on the construction loan and authorized the transfer of those funds into the development company's account. As far as your folks knew, in three weeks the homes would be completed and sold, and they'd be debt free.

"On Monday, your dad went to his medical office as usual. As he performed his surgeries, he had no idea we were cleaning out the accounts; the funds wired offshore, then finally to a bank here on Madeira.

"Tom left on Tuesday morning for Mexico, stopping in San Diego quickly to pick up the jewels. With a notarized authorization for the release in hand, he'd paid off the pawn with cash, then flew out of Lindberg Field. We flew separately to create different travel routes to follow, all of which led to Cabo San Lucas, then Mazatlán, and eventually Manzanillo. The trail was supposed to have ended there."

"Then Monk and I came up with a harebrained scheme to hawk all the office equipment to a reseller for a few thousand dollars before we left. That's where your dad stumbled across us clearing out the office."

"Where Monk pummeled him."

"Wasn't supposed to happen, Jake. I'm truly sorry."

Before he could reply, Amber's nails bit into his arm. He remained silent.

"We rendezvoused on the East Cape where we made a point of being seen, then flew to Mazatlán together from Cabo on a charter flight. From there Tom and I flew through Mexico City into the Caribbean, while Monk continued on to Manzanillo. We *wanted* him to be seen there.

"Tom had false passports made, and we re-entered U.S. soil in San Juan, Puerto Rico and caught a plane to St. Thomas. We traveled by boat to St. John and spent two nights at a luxury hotel while Tom fenced the jewels to a St. Thomas gem dealer. I wish we'd stayed there."

Her eyes took on a dreamy gaze. "The evening before the sale I wore the entire jewelry collection to dinner in the posh dining room. The looks from the snobbish crowd were of pure envy. It was beyond gaudy, but how often does a girl get to wear over $2,500,000 worth of trinkets to dine and dance under the stars?"

Coming back to reality, she continued, "Tom met the jeweler the following day. After getting fleeced on the jewels, we left the next morning for Europe, then flew to the island here. I've been here less than two weeks and already hate it.

"Monk arrived a day after us. The place might not be so bad if he wasn't here. Along with a slobbering Rottweiler Tom insisted on for protection. I don't know which scares me more—Monk or the dog. Both are dangerous, I assure you.

"Now Tom's drinking heavily again and makes a nightly jaunt to the casino. He's hit me a few times too. Monk's wired on speed; he found a dealer within twenty-four hours of getting here.

"I don't give a shit about the money. This is miserable, and I want out," she told Amber and Jake as she finished the tale.

Jake spun the wine in his glass. As the tan-ruby liquid settled, he shifted his eyes to stare directly at Cindi. "Then why don't you offer to give it all back?"

"I need money to live. I don't think I can go back to the States, at least not for a few years. Crimes have been committed; it'll take time for all this to go away. Tom would never go for returning all of it anyway."

Cindi bit her lip, pausing to contemplate. "There's also the fact that Nicki Stinnetti is hopping mad about the extra $2,000,000 we threw into the deal and the $150,000 Tom was supposed to have wired. If the project doesn't go to him in foreclosure, we're double screwed. We've got the law on one side, and Nicki with his new gun creep on the other. Honestly, he scares me more than the possibility of jail."

"He should."

"You've met him?" she asked.

"Jake shot him in the head," Amber informed her.

"So he's dead?"

"No. They tussled, and Jake got the better of him. Shots were fired, but one only grazed his scalp. He'll be back in business in no time," replied Amber.

Cindi sat back and gave Jake a look of appraisal. Gears were turning in her head.

"Does Wojicki know how much you got from the banker?" he asked her bluntly.

Her look changed to one of surprise. "I have no idea what you're talking about."

"I met with Roger. He didn't say how much, just that you hit him up again before leaving."

She bit her lip before answering. "No. Tom doesn't know. My services, my money there. Tom didn't have to fuck that little worm over and over. If I set up a meeting, we leave that out."

Jake's eyes shifted to Amber without turning his head. He caught a nearly imperceptible raise of her eyebrows as they exchanged glances.

"How much?" he asked.

"Fifty thousand," she said, shaking her head.

Jake smiled at her for the first time. He stood and said, "I'm not buying it. I'm willing to forget I ever met you, or found Tom Wojicki, or flew to this rock, but you need to be forthcoming. If I find out you're lying, or discover *later* you've lied to me, the deal is off. Even *after* we transfer the funds. Instead of a lengthy extradition, I may just tell Nicki where to find you. That would be easier than the onerous process of having you dragged back to California through the international legal system.

"We *will* finish Vineyard Meadows, Cindi. My brother and sisters will kick in the necessary funds. There will be no foreclosure. Then Nicki will come looking, and I'll give him the map with a big 'X' marked on your doorstep."

Cindi rubbed her forehead with deep massaging strokes.

"How much from the banker?" Jake asked again.

Without looking up, she answered, "One hundred fifty thousand. I wanted more, but that's all he could muster on short notice."

"But you kept a copy of your recording. When the well runs a little dry you'll just call up your old friend Roger Scott, won't you? For now, $150,000 is all, but you'll be back for more later. If we make a deal, you'll need to cough up a chunk of that too. Half."

"Bullshit! I made that money. Fair and square. You have no right to ask me to kick that in!" Turning to Amber, she moaned, "Where the fuck did you find this guy?"

Amber, reaching out and putting her hand on Cindi's, said, "I didn't find him; he found me. He's right. You're in trouble. He knows it. And you know it too. It's time to settle."

"Half or Wojicki and Monk are informed of it. Then they'll want their piece of the pie," Jake stated.

Jake could see the gears turning again as she sat staring at her wineglass.

"I'll help you with the math," offered Jake. "If you gave one-half back, at the percentages you've given in round numbers you'll get $585,000 out of Tom plus $75,000 in your work as an amateur cinematographer for a grand total of $660,000 in cash and prizes. That'll last a while. Plus, you have the video. You can dip into that for years to come; it'll be your annuity."

"What about Nicki Stinnetti?" Cindi asked.

"Your problem," Jake answered.

She looked at Jake and calmly said, "No deal, then. I've seen firsthand what happens when you cross a crook. In Miami. A client was shot in the face and the chest on his yacht. I have no idea why. Blood and gore everywhere, then the shooter pointed that big fucking gun at me and said, 'Bang.' He laughed and left the boat. So did I, after peeing my pants. I never want to look up the barrel of a gun again." Jake noted she shuddered slightly. "We've got to reach an agreement with Nicki, or the whole deal is off."

"I'll work it out," he said as took a few steps to the bedroom and returned with the satellite phone and tablet computer. He activated the screen and pushed the button to start the phone.

"What are you gonna do, call him? You have his number?"

"No. I'm going to get it. Then I'll call him."

"How? I'm certain it's unlisted," Cindi stated. "Tom has it, though."

Jake held up a finger as he punched numbers into the phone. Cindi looked at Amber who returned a 'palms-up' gesture of ignorance.

"Fred. Jake here… The eye is fine; better every day. And yes, I've found them… It's better you don't know. All I can say is we're far, far away. We're working out a deal. I need Nicki's phone number. You have it?"

Jake waited a moment as he listened then said, "Okay. Five minutes. No, I'll call you. Thanks, Fred. I owe you." He pushed the button to terminate the call.

"Fred Asaro?" asked Cindi.

"The same."

"How do you know him?"

"I dated his daughter years ago. Lauren."

"We graduated together. She was gorgeous. Had that country-queen thing going for her. She'd have made a fortune at the service with that act. So you're the mystery man she ran off with after high school. Everyone wondered about that."

Jake smiled tightly. "We were both kids. She was eighteen, me barely twenty-one. She went off to college after it ended badly. My fault."

"Imagine that," Amber added sarcastically.

Jake passed over Amber's dig, responding, "Anyway, her father and I were friends. I helped with the teams. We skied together too."

"Yeah, I remember. He coached wrestling and football. So I end up heisting the family of a friend of my hometown sheriff. And here you are with my best friend. Lucky me…"

Jake ignored her as he again dialed the phone. "Hi, Fred. Got it yet?" He used the digital keyboard to record the numbers. "Cell?… Home?… Office?… Thanks. I owe you again. Beer when I get back?"

Jake listened for a few seconds as his eyes shifted from Cindi to Amber.

"I won't. See you then." He pushed the button to terminate the call.

Amber looked at him with a puzzled expression. "What did the 'I won't' mean?"

"The sheriff told me not to trust anybody.

"Let's call Nicki."

CHAPTER 41

"Where the fuck are you?" The voice was loud enough to be heard through the receiver on the satellite phone ten feet away.

"Far away Nicki. And I'm with them. Cindi Light is sitting within arm's reach. In a place you'd never find them. How's the plumbing?"

"Fuck off. Grab that cunt by the hair and slap the shit out of her for me. I'll give you fifty grand to do it."

"Cash?"

"Any way you'd like it. Fucking gold bullion if you want. Just kick her ass for me. So what the fuck do you want? I'm sure this is no fucking social call."

"Nicki, please, the language! Must you throw an F-bomb in every sentence?"

"Fuck off."

"That's redundant."

"God damn it, just tell me what you want."

"That's better. Popping off on the third commandment now," laughed Jake.

"Get to the point, will ya?"

"Okay. Bottom line here. I've found them. We arrange for charges to be pressed and order extradition. That means they're in a foreign country, by the way."

"I ain't stupid, asshole! Bennie won't miss you next time. All I have to do is say the word, and you're toast."

"You really need to be careful about what you say on an unsecure line. You never know who's listening."

Nicki was quiet for a few seconds before he said, "Go on."

"They may choose to turn themselves in instead of being caught. Either way, after testimony, a conspiracy to defraud between you and Wojicki will come up, and the note on my parents' property will be declared invalid. 1.5 million dollars… Poof! Gone!"

The line was silent for a moment. Finally, Nicki ground out, "I'm listening. Tell me what the fuck you want."

"If they come back on charges, it will take months, maybe years, to unravel. There's a high likelihood your note becomes invalid and void, not to mention you'll have charges pressed against you.

"Wojicki will go to jail, and your personal debt from him will go uncollected too. You'll end up with nothing, and you might even go to the pokey yourself. We'll get Fred to arrest you; he'd love that."

"My attorney said this was a safe investment."

"Your attorney either was unaware of the plot or he assumed that Wojicki and friends wouldn't be found," Jake stated.

"I gotta check with some people on this. I still don't know what you want." His tone was less defiant. The seed of doubt had been planted.

"I'm working out a deal. You'll get your 1.5 million back, plus interest. The prospect of millions for you in this is history."

Nicki's silence told Jake the loan shark was digesting the revelation. He'd thought he was on his way to the biggest payoff of his life; now he'd be lucky to get his initial investment back.

Jake continued, "I'll get you the hundred fifty grand Wojicki owes you too. That's 1.65 million, plus a little interest. If we can't work it out, you'll get nothing."

"What do I gotta do for all your generosity?" harped Nicki.

"Accept that it's over and put a leash on your hired gun. Then agree to accept the payoff and forget you ever met Wojicki or Cindi Light."

"I gotta talk to some people. Gim'me the number where you are."

"I'll call you. Maybe a conference call with your attorney would help you understand. It's still early there. What do you say we'll talk in a half hour?"

"I don't need no fucking conference call! I just need to talk to a few people, that's all. I can't believe this shit! Some fucking punk-ass ski-bum Jew-fart giving me ultimatums."

"I'll call you in thirty minutes. Be one hundred percent straight with your attorney. Use the term 'conspiracy to defraud'. He, or she, will tell you to take my deal and run. I can get the hundred fifty grand in a few days. Your choice Nicki, 1.65 mil, or zilch."

"Thirty minutes, fuck-head!"

The line went silent.

CHAPTER 42

Worried Tom would be concerned about her absence, Cindi went home. She agreed to call in the morning after she'd set up a meeting.

Amber, who'd been strangely quiet, cleaned up the dishes. As she worked, Jake noticed she bit her lip and fidgeted in the small kitchen.

"What's up?" he asked.

"Nothing," she answered without looking up.

"You still miffed about this afternoon?"

She rolled her eyes. "Jesus, don't flatter yourself. It has nothing to do with you."

He took a seat at the table, pretending to look at the computer screen.

"Blackmail," she blurted out.

He shrugged his shoulders and said, "You're surprised?"

"Why didn't you tell me before?"

"Didn't know."

"You said the banker told you."

"I lied. I guessed it, so I threw it out, and she jumped on it. Got another $75,000 back for my folks, less your percentage, of course."

"Hmmm," Amber rubbed her chin lightly.

"What's that supposed to mean?"

"So you can't be trusted either."

"These people are crooks. They've created a different set of rules. I'm just playing along."

"Yeah, right. So what now? If we can get the money out of them, will you alert the authorities after we're paid?"

Jake said nothing but crossed his arms at the table.

"I'm not on board if you plan to turn them in. You agreed you wouldn't."

"My folks have been wronged, so maybe I should leave it up to them."

"I told Cindi the deal was that if they gave the money back, she'd go free. No law. No pursuit. I'm not going to let you make me a liar!" snapped Amber as she threw the kitchen towel down.

"You want her to live happily ever after, huh?"

Amber came and sat at the table, saying nothing. For the first time since they'd met, he noticed she looked worn out. Or maybe wounded at finding her friend to be more crooked than anticipated.

Pouring salt on the wound wouldn't help. "Okay. I'll stick to my agreement. We won't turn her in."

She looked at him, fatigue in her eyes. "Thanks. I'm pooped. Tuck me in?" she asked as she stood and turned toward the bedroom.

"Sure. But I can't stay."

"You weren't invited to," she said as the door closed behind her.

Jake set wine and water glasses on windowsills and behind the door, each with a knife, fork, or spoon dropped into it. While it wasn't a sophisticated burglar alarm system, he was satisfied it would create a clatter if an intruder attempted entry. He carried three more makeshift noisemakers into the bedroom and set those on the lone windowsill there.

If Cindi's acceptance of the pact was an act and they came back for them tonight or early tomorrow morning, Jake wanted to be ready. He'd sleep with a butcher knife on the coffee table.

Amber was in bed with the sheet up over her waist, wearing one of his tee shirts. He sat next to her and gently rubbed her shoulders without saying anything. After five minutes he softly said good night with no response as she breathed evenly.

Checking his watch, he saw that an hour had passed since his call to Stinnetti. He went to the living room and called on the satellite phone.

"Yeah." The answer was gruff.

"Hello, Nicki."

"You're late, asshole."

"Fire me. So, what's the verdict?"

"After consultation with my associates, the consensus is the quicker I get your fucking Jew family and the goddamn Polack and his whore out of my life the better off I am."

"So you'll take the $150,000 Wojicki owes you now and the 1.5 mil on the note when the homes are sold?"

"Yeah, as long as I never have to see neither one of you fuckers again. If I do, deal's off. If I end up fucked in this, I'll hunt every one of you down."

"Right, just like you found us here in…" Jake let it trail off. "You thought I was going to tell you, didn't you?" He laughed into the receiver.

"Fuck you."

"Okay, I've had my fun for the day. Let's have the wiring instructions. I'm meeting with them tomorrow. It might be very early your time; maybe 2:00 to 4:00 a.m. But they'll need to hear it from you that they're off the hook."

"Fuck that. Call me after ten."

"Nope. I want to hear you in a bad mood. I can only imagine your demeanor at that hour. You're so pleasant now, in the middle of the day."

"I'll sleep with my cell phone next to the bed. How the fuck did you get this number anyway? Good ole' Sheriff Fred, I'll bet."

"Okay, here's where you wire the money…"

CHAPTER 43

The dawn was gray with haze, cool but not cold. The drafty bungalow allowed air to creep in, equalizing the inside temperature with the outside. Amber smiled as she thought of it being called a 'villa'. Not exactly. Yet it was quaint. Very much what one should expect in Europe, she decided.

After brushing her teeth, she went to check on Jake on the couch.

Gone. Did the man ever sleep? She shook her head and went to boil some water for the tea she'd purchased the day before.

She looked about for a note of some sort but found none. The kitchen clock showed 7:20 a.m. Back home at this time, it would be bright daylight, if it wasn't snowing of course. Probably never snowed here.

Would all this be wrapped up today, or in the next few days? The injection of approximately $200,000 into her personal account was appealing, yet sadness had taken hold. Yesterday had been an emotional abyss, with Jake's rejection and the revelation that Cindi was a more ambitious and industrious crook than expected.

She was certain the relationship with him would have been short-lived anyway; she just wasn't prepared for it to be cut off so abruptly. *Real.* It felt good, for a change. Not just the sex, but rather having a man as a partner and friend. What they were doing was fun and exciting, too. Now it was winding down.

And Cindi. Blackmail, along with the other crimes. Maybe Jake was right, and Amber had overestimated her friend's moral fiber. Part of her embarking upon this quest had been to save Cindi's ass. Maybe it wasn't worth saving.

The rattle of an engine and a car door closing outside signaled Jake's return, breaking her out of her musing. She would not be weak again. It was business now; get it done, get the money, and go home. A year closer to retirement.

He bounced in and announced he was taking her to breakfast. The day before neither had eaten much, so the prospect of a full meal was appealing.

They had to kill a few hours, and they could see a little more of the island. In his early morning travels, he'd found the perfect spot.

Breakfast was at Reid's Palace Hotel, perched on a spectacular bluff overlooking the harbor at Funchal. The garden room where they ate offered a panoramic view of the ocean to the south and the city to the west. During their meal, the sun burned through the thin marine layer to create a perfect temperature on the open-air patio. It had to be one of the most beautiful dining settings in the world, they agreed as the maître d sat them at their table.

Jake had smoked salmon benedict, eggs lightly poached, and declared the hollandaise the most exquisite he'd ever sampled. Better even than his own. Amber tried crepes made tableside rolled around a cream cheese blend with fresh berries, nuts, and topped with shaved powdered sugar. She declared that she never needed to eat anything else; if death found her at that moment, she would go happily.

Most of the patrons in the restaurant seemed to be from various parts of Europe, but one stout-looking older couple overheard their English and introduced themselves.

John and Grace had sailed their boat from Florida to the Mediterranean immediately after hurricane season seventeen months earlier to tour the Greek and Italian isles. Now on the last leg of their journey home, they'd stopped here for a respite before the rigorous Atlantic crossing. The boat would be put up for sale the minute they got home, as Grace had had enough of the ocean. It had been the journey of a lifetime; however, she dreaded the monotony of those final twenty or so days they'd spend without seeing land between here and Miami. They'd be on their way in a week or two after recharging their internal batteries at the hotel here, John told them.

Jake worried about paying the fare for breakfast, let alone wondering what a few weeks at this joint would cost.

Their new friends admitted to accosting every American they ran into for news from home whenever possible and grilled Amber and Jake about the goings-on in the USA. Accurate news was difficult to get here as views of America were shrouded by local sentiments, differing from country to country but rarely favorable. John remarked with a wink and nod that the attitude from the Europeans should be a little different, in that they'd all be speaking German or Russian if not for the intervention of America.

Amber surprised Jake with her ability to provide up to the minute accounts of homeland affairs from political maneuverings to Hollywood trysts and even threw out some sports teams' standings, statistics, and recent player trades. Jake and John exchanged stories of the sea and the Pacific crossing to Polynesia, which John had done himself a few times.

Before parting, Jake asked if they had run into any other Americans on Madeira. They told him no; he and Amber were the first, but they'd only sailed in a few days ago. Now the daunting 3,300 sea miles before their next landfall on American soil had them contemplating selling the boat and flying home. They would take a huge loss as there was simply no market here, but the boat had served its purpose, and they were tired. It was just a thought anyway; John was determined to complete the voyage.

Grace invited them to dinner that evening, but Jake and Amber declined, thanking them for the offer. Perhaps another time, if their stay on the island would permit.

Upon returning to their flat, they found Cindi sitting in a little convertible, obviously annoyed at having to wait. She'd talked to Tom, and he was ready to meet. Exchanging glances with Amber, Jake said, "Let's do it."

Cindi suggested they ride together, but Jake opted to follow in their vehicle. When he told her the loan shark was in on the plan, she bit her lip and nodded.

They wound high above the city on the narrow roads. Cindi showed blatant disregard for the pedestrians and cyclists they passed, nearly annihilating those who didn't move to clear the road and using the horn liberally to tell the world to 'get the hell out of my way.' Amber told Jake Cindi's careless driving was a result of the stress. Jake retorted they were watching a self-absorbed bitch behind the wheel. Amber found it hard to argue as Cindi demonstrated utter indifference to anyone unlucky enough to be on the pavement.

Within minutes they reached the home. They saw Cindi reach to the sun visor and activate a remote control to open the tall gate. Surveying the property, Jake noted a ten-foot high block and plaster wall that appeared to completely encompass the grounds. At what he guessed to be twelve-foot intervals the wall rose in two-foot columns to support wrought iron, each piece twisted ornately to come to a point on top and form an upward arch between the plastered protrusions. Even on the tops of the raised block sections iron spikes protruded skyward six inches. While the grape-leaf designs welded to the arches offered a pleasing façade, the spiked wall was indeed a formidable barrier to the outside world.

Cindi waved at them to follow her in, but Jake pulled the little Toyota parallel to the wall outside. They got out and walked through the gate. Cindi had parked her car in a carport next to one other, and space existed for a third vehicle.

The driveway was covered in paver tiles, and the home was a textbook Mediterranean villa. Red clay tile roof, palms, and flowering climbing vines over white plaster arches that supported the roof where it overhung the patio in front. The interior courtyard past the driveway offered a fountain and garden sitting area. As the electric gate rolled shut, Jake pointed to a monstrous fresh turd in the grass off the drive and said to Amber, "Big dog. Be careful here."

Shaking her head, she replied, "Only you would notice that."

Cindi walked over and also looking at the pile said, "Damien. Our Rottweiler. Came with the house, by order of Tom. Bonded instantly with Monk; I think they share the same IQ. He's chained most of the time, but if he gets loose, watch out.

"This way." She turned in the direction of the home.

As they followed, Jake noticed a small sailboat on a trailer in the massive carport, with an old windsurfer hanging from the beams. Next to the sailboat sat two wave runners on their trailer. All the toys were pre-stocked with the dog before their arrival.

They had known for quite some time they'd be coming.

Walking through the massive wooden doors suspended on iron hinges, they entered a room with shining hardwood floors, an open-beamed ceiling, and a stunning view of Funchal and the ocean beyond floor-to-ceiling windows. It appeared that the world fell away beneath their feet.

The smell of coffee wafted in from the kitchen. Jake still had not seen the dog.

"Have a seat," offered Cindi, "Tom'll be out in a minute." She disappeared through the door from where the coffee bouquet emanated.

Amber sat on the end of a couch in front of a glass coffee table and patted the seat next to her as she looked at Jake. He shook his head and put his back against a column, crossing his arms and raising his right foot against the support to knee level. From this spot, he could see every door or entry into the room.

Cindi returned shortly with a tray containing matching oversized coffee cups and set it on the table. From one cup a teabag hung, which she handed to Amber. She picked up another and set it in front of the largest chair in the room on a coaster, then disappeared through an arched entry down the hall toward the back of the house.

Jake walked over and picked up the bowl-sized cup she'd set on the table. Taking a whiff, he set it back down. "Spiked," he said to Amber. She nodded, bobbing her teabag in her cup. He returned to his column.

Cindi appeared shortly from the archway, followed by Tom Wojicki. Jake felt a wave of rage as he looked upon him.

He was tall, yet rail thin. The index and middle finger of his right hand showed mild tobacco staining. The Dockers-style pants hung loosely off his butt and his polo shirt bunched where it was tucked in at the waist. The arms didn't come close to filling the band at the end of the short sleeves. He carried a folded light jacket and set it on the arm of the chair. Jake guessed his height at about six two or six three, and he couldn't have topped one hundred and sixty-five pounds. His thinning hair was slicked back in a combover on his scalp, and his cheeks and nose showed red spider veins creeping across his face.

Jake knew Tom was in his mid-to-late forties, yet he looked every bit of sixty-five.

He looked at Jake for a moment then sat, not offering a handshake. As he picked up his coffee, Jake noticed a slight wobble to the cup as he lifted it to his lips. After sipping deeply, he set it down and wiped his mouth with a linen napkin. Crossing his long claw-like fingers, he looked from Amber to Jake.

Cindi stood behind his chair, her eyes keen and lips tight, not offering either a smile or a frown.

"I must congratulate you. How did you find us?" Wojicki's voice was monotone.

"Doesn't matter. Did Cindi outline our deal?" Jake questioned.

He looked at Jake and with a sideways nod answered, "Yes, yes. It all sounds fair. Even more than fair, I suppose. But I must hear it from you. You'll take a split of half the money and let us go?"

"That's the deal. You need to pay off Stinnetti too. He's agreed to forget about you for one hundred and fifty thousand. Says that's what you owe him."

"Nicki's okay with it, Tom. I talked to him this morning before they arrived," Cindi interjected as she put her hand on his shoulder.

Jake raised his eyebrows slightly. She knew the deal was done before he'd told her this morning. He wondered what else she might have cooked up.

Wojicki nodded slowly, staring at his coffee cup. "I'll wire the funds today." His gaze turned to Jake. "I didn't steal the money; I'm not a thief."

"When you see them, tell your mom and dad I'm sorry about the beating. That was never part of the plan. But they owed me. Without me, the development company never would have gotten off the ground. I started it, ran it, and made them a ton of money. They never treated me like a partner. Should have rat-holed our company funds and declared bankruptcy when the housing market went to shit years ago. Then Stinnetti never would have gotten his hooks in me.

"They put me in this position. I really had no choice."

With a headshake, Jake said, "Wojicki, people, like water, find their own level. You'd have found a way to screw up your life no matter what. Let's get this done so you can go back to smoking and drinking yourself to death, and my family can finish the project."

"I'm quitting both the booze and cigarettes. Soon," he said as he put his hand on Cindi's where it rested on his shoulder. Jake almost felt sorry for him. He had no idea his beautiful young lover was about to bolt, leaving him alone.

But he wouldn't be alone, Jake thought suddenly. "So, where is the loser who beat the hell out of my dad?"

Cindi spoke. "He's out, with the dog. Probably with some new friends he's made on the island. Meth heads. We're not going to tell him about any of this until the money's gone."

Jake nodded. "Doesn't matter to me. Just so the funds go back."

"It'll be done today. Then you fly out of here and leave us alone, right?

That's the deal?" Wojicki asked.

"Right." Jake unfolded a letter-sized paper from the side pocket of his cargo shorts. With a few steps, he dropped it on the table in front of Wojicki. "Here are wiring instructions for my parents' account and the escrow trust account. The distribution amounts for each account are noted. The buyer's deposits have to go back into the trust account. It's possible that might avoid a commingling charge. Wiring instructions for Stinnetti's account are there, too."

Wojicki picked up the paper and studied the figures. Putting it down after a moment, he looked at Jake, who had returned to his spot against the support post. "You gotta split Nicki's payoff with us. He's all of our problem, not just mine."

Without hesitation, Jake answered, "Nope. Your problem. You pay him off."

Tom reached over the table and opened a brass case. Pulling out a cigarette, he lit up and sat back in his chair. He inhaled deeply then blew the smoke out toward the center of the room. "You're just like your father. The debt to Nicki is a result of his poor judgment. So it's half his. It seems we're actually $75,000 apart in negotiations."

"What are you talking about? You said we had a deal," Jake said as he closed his eyes and shook his head.

"I'm willing to split everything. That means *everything*."

Jake turned his head and looked at Amber, who had been quiet throughout the exchange. With a quick wink of his right eye, he said, "Let's go. We're done."

She rose to her feet and said, "Yep. Sorry, Cindi."

"I wonder who'll get to you first," Jake said thoughtfully. "The FBI and IRS investigators, or Nicki's guy? The authorities will be armed with an extradition order. On the other hand, you *won't* see Nicki's guy. He'll just plink you from the shadows."

Jake pointed his forefinger at Wojicki and brought his thumb down like the hammer of a gun. "Plink. You're dead." Then he turned the finger to Cindi and made the same motion. "Plink. You too."

She looked down at Tom and patted his shoulder. In the sincerest of tones, she said, "It's over, honey. Pay them off and be done with it."

Resting the half-burned cigarette on the ashtray, he looked up at her and answered, "No, it's not over," as his hand slid inside the folded jacket and came out with a small handgun. He pointed it at Jake first, moved it slowly in Amber's direction, then brought it back to bear on Jake.

"Looks like a Glock 17, right?" Jake asked casually, while silently cursing himself for not recognizing the possibility of a concealed weapon. With the right eye again he gave Amber another assuring wink. She'd gone slightly pale.

"What are you going to do? Kill us both?" He asked as he put his hands up, palms out. "Don't be silly. With a murder charge, they'll find you for sure."

"Tom. You're going too far. It is over. Put the gun down!" Cindi implored.

"No! It's not over. We worked too hard on this. If they won't split the payoff, we kill them and pack up again. We'll dump their bodies in the ocean on the north side of the island. We'll pay off Nicki ourselves, then take off. Maybe South America. Chile or Peru. Even Brazil. Nobody will find us. I didn't steal the money; I simply took what was mine!" He sounded like a child having a toy taken away.

"People know we're here, Tom," said Amber. Her voice quaked slightly, but she went on. "With a murder charge, the authorities *will* find you. You'll go to prison. You're not a murderer."

Turning toward Amber, he left the gun pointed at Jake, but the barrel moved a few inches off center. He said wildly, "You have no idea what I'm capable of! I'm running out of options!"

As Wojicki addressed Amber, Jake used the foot he had against the support as a launching mechanism. He sprang off the column and covered the ten feet that separated them in an instant. Wojicki's arm swung in an arc following him, but he couldn't keep up. Jake caught the extended gun hand as he went by, yanking Tom out of the chair and spinning him to the floor. Wojicki squeezed the trigger in desperation, and a shot blasted out, but Jake, now on his knees, had Tom's arm and hand pointed out away from the interior of the room. The tinting film on the window kept the glass from shattering as the bullet passed through, leaving a tiny hole. With vise-like force, Jake's left hand pinned Tom's wrist to the floor, and as the right hand twisted the gun away, another shot went off, leaving another hole in the window just above floor level.

Wojicki clawed like an animal with his free hand first at the weapon, then realizing it was out of reach, the hand moved to Jake's face and scratched wildly. The gun, now firmly in Jake's right hand, swung back into Wojicki's face. Jake grasped the weapon by its side and twice more hammered the steel across his assailant's nose and lips. On the third impact of metal against tissue, Wojicki drove forward and buried his face into Jake's chest to shelter his mug from more blows of the gun. The animalistic clawing stopped.

Jake shucked him hard to the floor, and standing, looked at the bloody spot where Tom had hidden his face. He wiped the blood off the gun onto the tail of the already ruined shirt. After his marginal cleaning of the weapon, he popped the clip out, sliding out the bullets and allowing each to rattle to the floor. In a final act, he actuated the slide to clear the chamber. Certain now that the gun was unloaded, he threw it into Wojicki's lap.

Crossing his arms with the clip still in hand, he looked down and said, "Okay Tom, you should know at 4:00 p.m., local time, an autosend e-mail will go out to four different people, one of whom is Nicki Stinnetti. The communication contains information revealing your whereabouts. Two others are law enforcement entities, and the last is my parents' attorney. The e-mail tells them the reason they're receiving this communication is that I'm likely dead, killed by you or one of your party. It outlines everything. Stinnetti's note goes into litigation. He'll be extremely pissed, and you won't have enough money to buy your way out then.

"It'll be a race between the authorities and Nicki to see who gets you first. By the time you get organized to make a run for it, the immigration or customs inspectors at the airport will have your pictures plastered all over the walls of their offices. They might not take you in, but you aren't going anywhere. Nicki will come. Hell, if I'm alive, I might just stay here and watch the fun.

"This caper is over."

All were quiet for a moment, and the look on Tom's battered face faded to one of stunned acceptance. Then it was Amber, not Cindi, who rose off the couch and picked up the napkin off the table. She walked over and knelt where he sat on the floor and gently began cleaning up the blood where it flowed from his nose and cuts on his cheeks. He reached out and took the cloth, giving her a nod signaling 'Thanks,' and continued the cleanup himself.

As he worked, he muttered with a headshake, "How the fuck did you find us?"

Amber said, "In Manzanillo, Jake figured out the trail you left was a sham. He deciphered the digital encryptions on Estela's computer and the flaws in the photos we had, leading us here."

"She said you found nothing," Tom noted. Picking up his spiked coffee and cautiously taking a long pull, he added, "You were always a disappointment to your father. 'Surf and ski bum,' he said. You're the last of your family I'd have thought would come."

"Surprise!" Jake chortled. He continued in a more level pitch. "The money? They'd have figured something out. It was the pummeling you idiots gave him."

"Monk," Wojicki muttered with a headshake.

Jake said thoughtfully, "And the jewels too, I suppose. They're my mother's. The collection has been in her family for hundreds of years. The DeCorto side. Dad had no right to hawk them. The fact that a scuzball like you possessed them even for a minute, or that tramp adorned herself with them, sickens me. Where are they?"

Cindi gave Jake a stare of cold loathing. Wojicki smiled wickedly over his coffee cup before draining it. He said through puffy lips, "I hawked them to a jeweler in St. Thomas. He's Arabic. He actually believes they may be part of a set taken from his ancestors. They won't be for sale."

"What jeweler?" Jake asked flatly.

"The store is called Global Passions on St. Thomas. I can't tell you exactly where because I didn't meet with him there. Found him on the internet. We met at his estate on the north side of the island. His name is Amir Mojabi.

"He's surrounded by a small army. They carry automatic weapons. You won't get the collection back; he's infatuated with the jewels." Tom's lips formed a tight smile. It was a small victory for him.

"We shall see," Jake answered. "So, what's the bottom line here? We have a deal, fifty percent back and you square the debt to Stinnetti? Or do I release the hounds?"

Tom picked himself off the floor and sat in the chair again, mustering as much dignity as he could. Cindi replaced her hand on his shoulder, the gesture wrought with insincerity. He tossed the empty pistol on the table and said, "It seems we have no choice. We'll wire the funds today. Then you go away, and we'll never hear from you again? Right?"

"Once the funds are wired, I will not disclose your location. Everyone lives happily ever after," answered Jake.

"Done then," stated Tom. "Get out and good riddance to you."

Turning to leave Jake asked, "Global Passions? Amir Mojabi? In St. Thomas?"

Tom dabbed the napkin at the gouges on his face and squinted up at Jake, "Yep. Remember, getting the jewels back isn't part of our deal."

"Ready?" Jake asked Amber. She nodded and stepped toward the door. Before following, he said, "We'll check the accounts every few hours. When the funds are returned, we'll go. You don't need to get up. Hopefully, we'll never see one another again."

"One can only hope," muttered Tom, but Jake and Amber were already out the door, too far away to hear.

CHAPTER 44

"Jesus!" hissed Amber as they backtracked down the narrow mountain road. "Why didn't you tell me you were going to pounce on him!"

Without looking at her, Jake smiled. "I winked."

"Yeah, I caught it. I thought you were reassuring me. I was scared shitless, but I doubted he was going to shoot. We could have talked our way through."

"Wasn't going to take a chance."

"You know what I think? I think you wanted to rough him up. A bit of vindication for what they did to your father. You didn't need to clobber him as many times as you did."

"Well, next time you have a gun pointed at you, I'll be sure to use greater restraint in saving your ass."

"Fortunately, there won't be a next time. As soon as the funds are wired, I'm going home. You can continue chasing the jewels wherever you care to go."

At the gate Cindi had assured them she'd wire the amount she'd committed to the night before. Although she didn't know from the numbers scratched on the paper, her contribution went directly to Amber's account.

"You'll find another $125,000 in your account after my parents receive the money."

She corrected him. "It should be $127,500."

Always the businesswoman, Jake reminded himself.

After a quick shower and a change of his bloodstained shirt and shorts, Jake and Amber decided to go sightseeing as they waited for the verification of the incoming funds. The rugged coastline of the north side of the island was breathtaking. Jake spotted breaking waves at numerous points along the base of the cliffs. Surfers could be seen carving smooth turns on the faces of the large swells before they cascaded over into frothing whitewater.

"I'm coming back here," Jake stated with a boyish smile and a faraway look at the blue water as he drove. "Surf, big fish, low cost of living; it's my kind of place."

"Yeah. It's your kind of place all right," muttered Amber. Under her breath, she added, "Never-never land for you, Peter."

They enjoyed a late lunch at an outdoor cafe where they split an angel hair pasta dish made with fresh tomato and basil, and a cucumber and green leaf salad. A melancholy air came over them as each knew this might be their last meeting.

She wanted to reach out and hold his hand with no promise of anything beyond. The fear of rejection stopped her.

Jake, too, felt a loss at the ending of the chase. The prospect of going back to his normal life nagged at him, but he wasn't certain why.

He and Janelle would enjoy a summer in the sun and live happily ever after if she forgave him for his slip in commitment. He guessed she would. Grudgingly.

They knew where the jewels were and could begin the official process of retrieval through legal channels. Getting the rocks back was his father's problem now. He'd done his part.

So why did he feel such a pit in his stomach? Assuming Wojicki and company came through with the transfers, the major problems of his family were solved.

He looked over the tawny wine he held and stared at Amber. She was stunning.

Bewitching... Once again, he remembered the description from the night of their meeting.

They'd made love through a night and a morning. The act had been gratifying, but it wasn't a sexual void he was now feeling. It was the looming loss of her companionship.

Suddenly he realized that Amber Nelson challenged him.

In his world of reclusion, he was seldom challenged. Now a woman entered his life who tested him, forcing decisions and bringing the aspect of nourishing argument into his existence.

Looking contemplatively at Amber across the table he wondered what life with her might be like. Goal-oriented, obstinately stubborn, strikingly beautiful, extremely intelligent, passionate love-maker, and scintillating conversationalist. Mean as a gunnysack full of snakes when crossed, with the tenderness of a mother putting a Band-Aid on a child's skinned knee when necessary. Independent yet mildly needful. The complete package.

Like the aged wine he sipped, time and knowledge gave Amber Nelson great depth. Jake felt himself wanting to explore those depths as they sat together, from a philosophical standpoint as well as a sexual desire.

But she was a prostitute, he reiterated mentally. *Ultra-high end, but still a prostitute*. She lived on the other side of Sheriff Fred's line. Loan sharks, drunken gamblers, hired killers, con artists, blackmailers, and whores had crawled through the fissure and invaded the respectable world of his family. He repeated to himself, *she's here to collect her ten percent*.

The breach needed closing. They would all move on with life, each on the side of the line where they belonged.

"Figure it out, Dr. Cohen?" Amber's voice snapped him out of his deliberations. She was smiling at him, slyly. *Knowingly*.

"Yep," he answered as he set his empty wineglass on the table.

She reached out and took his hand, giving it a reassuring squeeze. "It's been fun, hasn't it?" she said.

"Barrels," Jake answered as he lifted their joined hands high in the air in a triumphant gesture.

The hands fell and parted after a moment, and they received a few odd stares from other patrons of the establishment as they both burst out laughing.

CHAPTER 45
SATURDAY A.M.

Yesterday's *London's Times* sat in a heap on the seat next to him, read from cover to cartoons. Sipping coffee, Jake web-surfed on his tablet as he waited for the plane that would take him back to Lisbon. From there he'd get a flight home. He was standby, but the attendant had assured him there was always room on the Saturday flights. It was a day people flew *in* to the island, not out. The first plane had come and gone with no space available; the one he waited for now seemed to be his ticket home. The attendant told him there were four openings as of forty minutes before departure.

At 10:00 p.m. local time the previous evening, he'd spoken to his mother. She joyously verified the incoming deposit of a combined $1,950,000 to the company accounts. His father's condition was rapidly improving, and the news of the arrival of the funds would help in lifting his spirits. Victor would be home in a few days. Jake gave her wiring instructions for $127,500 to be sent out with no questions asked. The balance due Amber came directly from Cindi's transfer.

She and Jake were too tired for celebration; he actually had to wake her to tell her the news. He then fell asleep and was out for ten hours straight.

When he woke, he showered quickly and said a brief goodbye. Her plan had changed; she was staying on here for a few days with Cindi. Jake was annoyed but said nothing. They embraced, she kissed him on the cheek, then he left. He offered to leave the rental car, but she said they'd use Cindi's convertible for transportation. She'd square the bill with the proprietor on the villa and move into the big house for the remainder of her stay.

The outlaws were flocking together. Although of higher moral fiber, Amber was indeed one of them. *She lived on their side of the line.*

A mid-sized jet touched down and taxied toward the terminal. The stairs were rolled across the tarmac to meet the fuselage, and soon the cabin door popped open. One by one the visitors came down. Jake watched with mild interest, noting the diversity between the dress of the Europeans coming to this island and the Americans heading to Cabo San Lucas and Hawaii. There was a formality about travel here that had been abandoned at home. Americans went on *vacations*. Europeans went on *holiday*. *Holiday* was obviously more formal.

One man even sported a classy brown fedora at an angle on his head as he disembarked. In the mountains and in Southern California such caps were not seen, especially worn crooked, Jake laughed silently.

Before his fingers reached the keyboard to initiate the shutdown mode, his eyes opened wide. He sprang to his feet to bring his face to within inches of the glass. Craning his neck to get a better look, his eyes found the modish passenger sporting the fedora.

The hat was indeed worn at an odd angle. As he disappeared through the door to the terminal, Jake noted he was shorter than most of the other men.

Quickly Jake shut his computer down and gathered his bag. Even without a good look at the face, Jake knew the angled hat was not a fashion statement. It was worn to cover the crease in the man's scalp. A crease that Jake had bandaged himself only a week prior.

Bennie Temple had arrived in Madeira.

CHAPTER 46

Working backward through the terminal Jake reached the car rental counters. Bennie arrived from the direction of the deplaning passengers. Jake quickly took a seat with the *London Times* high up in front of him. The baggy cargo shorts and Racor's Edge sweatshirt might give him away, but at least he had on a pair of cross-trainers instead of his rubber sandals Bennie had seen at their last meeting. He concealed himself as best he could.

Paperwork was waiting at the counter. Temple signed quickly and headed to the rental parking lot. Jake found the clerk at the counter where he'd turned in his car three hours ago. It took a painstaking eight minutes to line up another car. While he waited, he watched Bennie drive off toward Funchal.

Once behind the wheel, Jake drove like a madman to catch the fellow well ahead in the Peugeot sedan. Bennie had to stop a few times to decipher signs and maps on his phone. Catching him just outside the city, Jake stayed a good distance back.

The plane that was to have taken him home rumbled overhead. He cursed himself for not getting on. He could still forget about it all and go home.

Yet he drove on, telling himself he'd only observe and see what played out. He could fly out tomorrow. Or the next day.

Bennie drove along the waterfront eventually reaching the Hotel Santa Maria where he pulled in, got out of the car, and went inside with his bag. The valet took the vehicle away as Jake parked in the lot. He went inside, *London Times* in hand, and watched as Bennie received his key quickly.

The simplicity with which he checked in told Jake he was expected. The rental car had been waiting too. Someone had prearranged Bennie's itinerary. Someone who knew the island.

After check-in Bennie went to the elevators, declining a bellman's help. He disappeared as the door slid shut. The old-style arm above the elevator doors stopped on level III out of a possible IV.

Jake walked over and punched the 'up' button but gave up after thirty seconds of waiting and sprinted up the stairs. Slowly peeking out of the door on the third floor, he found an empty hallway. He strolled the entire level and found closed doors except where the maid service worked to ready the rooms for the next guests.

There was a sitting room with a veranda overlooking the pool at the end of the hall. Jake took a chair and opened the *London Times*, ready to snap it up as cover when any door opened. Then he waited.

It had been just after noon when Jake took the seat. During his waiting and watching he'd moved to the veranda as the day had warmed, leaving the French doors open. The sunset had been exquisite, and now the air cooled with the onset of evening. He'd gotten up a few times to use the head and buy a bottle of water downstairs.

A few room service carts came and went during the afternoon, becoming more frequent as the dinner hour approached. Jake saw people come and go and one by one he eliminated the possible doors behind which Bennie Temple probably slept off the jet lag. The staff had come to recognize him, and a few stopped to ask if they could bring anything. Surprisingly a manager had not come to send him away.

A few more hours passed. Finally, Bennie emerged from a door down the hall. He wore a stylish brown tweed sports coat over a cream-colored polo shirt with tan pants. His shoes were polished brown cap-toe walkers. The fedora was in place to cover the crease in his head. Jake almost rose to compliment him on his outfit but decided approaching would be imprudent. Better just to follow and see where he might be headed in his smart attire.

Words he'd heard spoken two days ago came back to him. 'Jackets and long pants are required in the club after sundown,' Juan Silva had told him.

Bennie was headed to the casino.

Panic struck him as he looked at his shorts, cross-trainer shoes and baggy sweatshirt. His thoughts turned to his bag in the car. Two wrinkled Bamboo Cay shirts, one stained with blood from his scuffle with Wojicki. Another pair of shorts and a pair of jeans, two tee shirts, another sweatshirt, and the rubber sandals.

He needed a clothier. Quickly.

CHAPTER 47
SATURDAY NIGHT

Nothing off the rack ever fit. The size forty-four jacket and thirty-two-inch waist were a mismatch. Most men who carried that broad width at the shoulders were taller by three or four inches. Without having time to have the cheap coat taken in or adjust the sleeves, it draped like a gunnysack over Jake as he walked through the casino doors. The faded jeans with a cheap white dress shirt and sports coat, while always in style in the western United States, were a fashion abomination here. Yet few noticed as the heavy crowd pulled at machine handles and uttered prayers over flung dice and dealt cards as they guzzled drinks.

Still in his cross-trainers, Jake melded into the periphery of the mob, hoping to stay out of sight until he could pick out Bennie or one of the hitman's possible targets. The sound from the disco was muted by heavily insulated doors, yet the deep bass thumping could be felt through the floor as Jake walked by the entrance. He knew the type of action Wojicki craved would not be found in the dance hall, so he continued until he reached the lowered pit with the high rollers' tables.

Scanning the tables, he didn't see Tom or any of the group. His eyes moved to the bar and slot areas hoping to pick out a familiar face.

Recognition came quickly. Standing tall, a bowl-shaped wineglass in hand, was Amber Nelson. She looked stunning in a deep burgundy silken dress. The low back revealed her thin waist that rolled downward into a perfectly rounded hip. Traveling upward from the waist, the shoulders showed enough time was spent at the gym to sculpt an alluring 'V' in her shape. Her hair cascaded in shiny curls and the makeup was perfect.

She too seemed to be scanning the crowd.

Staying to the sides of the building he walked around the gaming area until he was behind her. As he pulled alongside, he said, "Hello Amber."

Turning, she set her wineglass on the table. Without saying anything her head tilted to one side, and she gave him an odd squint. Then Amber Nelson unleashed a full roundhouse right, catching Jake between the left cheekbone and the jaw.

Not expecting the punch, he didn't move with it to absorb the impact. Flying backward he was surprised a lady could hit so hard. Then the second one came in from the left hand. Instinctively his hand shot up and caught hers. With vise-like force, he pulled her by and wrapped her up with both arms in a bear hug from behind. Still, she kicked viciously backward at his shins and drove spiked heels at his feet.

Jake promptly realized he had two choices—take her down and immobilize the surprisingly dangerous legs or push her away to put a safe distance between them. Surmising quickly she might make another run at him if loosed he spun her to the floor, slowing her fall to avoid a hard impact on the carpet. Once down, he secured the legs between his own knees.

Now she bit at him, getting only mouthfuls of his ill-fitting coat sleeves as he had a grip too low to be reached with her pearly whites. With nothing else left, she threw her neck backward to try to headbutt him. He kept his chin tucked into her back and absorbed three shots from the back of her head on his forehead, knowing that each time she made an impact it hurt her as much as it did him.

Finally, the writhing stopped. Jake looked around. Their action had gathered a crowd. Close by he noticed a pair of very expensive looking loafers. Italian. Then strong hands grasped at him from both sides and began to pull him upward.

"Let go of the lady, Senhor Cohen." It was the voice of Juan Silva, the casino manager.

Two casino bouncers held his arms and lifted him off Amber. She rolled onto her bottom and smoothed her dress before rising. Juan Silva reached out to help her up.

"Many people were betting on the lady," he said to both combatants as Amber reached her feet. "Are you injured?"

She again adjusted the dress and pushed her hair back. Then she flexed her bare arms and moved her fingers. "No. I'll be fine. Thank you for your intervention. I might have killed him otherwise."

Juan Silva nodded and laughed. Then he looked at Jake.

"We saw you come in on the monitors and I followed you. Within ten minutes you are involved in a fight. With a woman, no less!"

"I just wanted to say hello," Jake offered with a shoulder shrug, "and she clobbered me."

"Yes, I saw. I can only imagine what you must have done to her to initiate such an act."

She pointed a polished fingernail at Jake. "We made a deal. You lied, you bastard."

"The lady and I will be fine now," Jake said with a nod to Juan Silva. "Thank you for your intervention."

The suave casino manager looked at Amber. Fire still burned in her eyes and her face was tight with fury. As a seasoned gambler, he was an expert at nonverbal communication. Under his gaze, Amber submitted. "Yes, we'll be fine. Thank you, Juan Silva."

"You are welcome, Ms. Nelson."

Jake raised an eyebrow at the fact Amber and the manager knew one another.

Juan Silva looked Jake up and down, then said, "If you wish to be a patron in my establishment, do not cause any more problems. I know you didn't start this—how do you say in America? Ruckus?—but trouble follows you. The clothes you wear look like hand-me-downs. Truthfully, I should have you removed from the club permanently." He shook his head and exhaled.

"I thought I was making a cutting-edge fashion statement," Jake joked.

"Yes, you are. But it is a *bad* one." To the men who held Jake's arms, he said, "*Deixe o ir livre.*" They let him go.

"No more trouble, or you'll be removed." Juan Silva straightened his tie and left them.

CHAPTER 48

"You saw Stinnetti's hit man tonight," Jake stated as he motioned toward a seat in the lounge.

The crowd gathered to watch their fracas had dissipated, with only a few lingering to see if the melee might re-erupt. Juan Silva's two heavies stood at a distance, yet close enough to intervene quickly if Amber decided to once again loose her rage.

Looking directly in his eyes, she said, "Jake, you're a lying piece of shit."

He pursed his lips. "Ahhh, you think I called Stinnetti in."

"If not you, who?"

"Who saw his man first this evening?"

"Cindi. She spotted him in this bar," Amber muttered slowly.

"Whose idea was it to come to this casino tonight?"

"All of us. We decided we wanted to wind down. The last few days were rather stressful for everyone."

"But who *suggested* the outing?"

Amber's head moved from side to side in denial. "Cindi."

"It wasn't a coincidence that you ended up here at the same time as Bennie Temple. It was orchestrated, Amber.

"I picked Bennie out at the airport and followed him to his hotel. He didn't check-in; he just picked up a key. It was waiting. Somebody checked him in earlier."

She pondered. "How do I know you're not lying?"

"Compare track records."

Biting her lip, she focused on her wine for a moment.

"Why?" she asked.

"Money, probably. And maybe freedom. Probably both."

"What are you saying?"

Jake took the wineglass from her hand and took a sip. He postulated, "Cindi wants to get away from Tom, but Tom holds the purse strings. If she leaves the money stays. Monk Phillips is in for a cut of it all too. Cindi is scared of him, I think."

Amber nodded. "I met him today. He's bonkers. They still haven't told him about the money. God knows what will happen when they do."

"Bennie solves two problems for Cindi. Bang, bang." Jake made a gun shape with his forefinger and thumb, bringing the thumb down twice.

"But Cindi wouldn't do—"

"Yes, she would," Jake interrupted. "Think about all she's done. Blackmail. Embezzlement. Forgery."

Amber inhaled deeply, letting out the breath in a puff. "She brought Bennie in to kill them."

"Yep. But not right away. She wants to *scare* them first. If she simply wanted him dead, she would have given him the address of the villa. I don't think he has it, or he would have gone there. She needs to get the money before they're offed."

Amber nodded now. "Tonight was all an act. She spotted Bennie and pointed him out to Tom. They left, allegedly before he spotted them. I stayed to watch him. He's never seen me. He stayed a few minutes after they left, then went out.

"You're right. Tom's scared shitless now. Of course, he thinks you broke your promise and ratted him out."

Rubbing his chin, Jake said, "That's okay. Bennie's back at his hotel, I'd bet. He won't be back tonight. He's played his part for this evening. They just wanted him to be spotted. No one but you and Juan Silva know I'm still here."

"So, what do we do?"

"We wait."

"Jake, I'm not going to sit and wait for people to get killed."

"If my hunch is right Bennie's not going to kill anyone until Cindi has the money or a way to get it."

Amber gently bit her lip as her head shook. "I don't like it; something bad is going to happen."

"There is another shot at more of the money here," said Jake with raised eyebrows. "Remember your ten percent."

"You made a deal with them."

"They're crooks, Amber. The money they have is stolen, and now one is trying to sell the other two down the road and keep it all. I can smell it. Deals mean nothing in their world."

She continued biting her lip, but her head had stopped shaking.

"You may even end up saving a life or two," he added.

The lip biting stopped. "You have a plan?"

He nodded. "I'll stay with Bennie. You keep me posted on what happens at the villa. Text me with updates. He's staying at the Santa Maria Hotel. I'll be there."

She reached into her purse, pulled out a pen, and scribbled the hotel name on the back of a random receipt. "I'll keep you posted. I really don't like this."

"I'll stay with Bennie as much as possible, but I can't watch him one hundred percent of the time. Be very careful. Call if you can without being overheard. If not, text." He gave her his cell number.

"Looks like we're partners again," Amber laughed.

"Destiny." He winked and laughed too.

CHAPTER 49
MONDAY MORNING

A room with a view of the parking lot had been available on Saturday night. Jake communicated through a mixture of sign language and Spanish to the hotel clerk that he wanted to be able to see his vehicle, and they obliged him with a spot offering a panoramic view of the asphalt, happy to rent one of their worst rooms.

Bennie's car hadn't moved all day Sunday and Jake had followed him on foot along the waterfront, to restaurants, and into the city. Mostly, he spent the time in his room, with Jake camped out either in the sitting area at the end of the hall or behind a cracked door.

Amber and he had traded one text wherein she noted Tom and Cindi had a few closed-door discussions, and Amber was convinced they'd cooked up a plot.

Cindi played the situation beautifully. She cursed Jake for their current woes and vociferously vowed revenge. If he'd called in Stinnetti's man, the law wasn't far behind. They needed to hightail it and take the money with them.

Amber showed her dramatic talents with a believable performance of disgust for Jake and willingness to help. She hoped Juan Silva and Tom did not meet or converse, where their encounter in the casino might be mentioned.

Not surprisingly, Monk Phillips had been left out of discussions. He was either gone most of the day or in his own suite downstairs with the dog. Amber was convinced that wherever they were going or whatever they were doing, they were leaving the big man behind.

At 8:00 a.m. Monday morning, Jake's phone rang. He punched the icon and said hello as he silently closed the cracked door to the hall.

"Something's up. They packed and left together," reported Amber.

"They're gone?" he asked as he walked to the window to see that Bennie's car hadn't disappeared from the lot.

"Not for good. The bags are still here, with two empty ones. They're stuffed in the closet, I'd guess so Monk doesn't see them. Tom got on the phone early, then they left. Told me they'd be back in about two hours. Cindi suggested I should fly home today if possible. If I couldn't get a flight, I should check into a hotel somewhere."

"So, it's coming down today. Anything else?"

"Yes. Tom used the house phone to call. Before I called you I hit redial. The man who picked up spoke poor Portuguese but shifted to English when he realized I didn't understand him. He runs a yacht charter company."

"Australian accent?"

"Yeah. I suppose. It wasn't exactly British, but I couldn't place it. How'd you know?"

"Wild guess," muttered Jake. "It makes sense. They're converting the accounts to paper money. That's what the two empty bags are for. A boat would be the only way to get close to $2,000,000 out of the country; the airport would be too risky."

"Could they arrange one so quickly though?"

"For the right amount of money," he said cracking the door, an eye on the hall.

"Where would they go?"

Jake thought for a moment. "East to Europe. Once past the Rock of Gibraltar inside the Mediterranean, they could go anywhere. South of Spain or France, then on to Italy and the Greek Isles. Maybe North Africa, or the West Coast there. I'd bet on Europe though. That's assuming Tom is alive to make the trip. I'd bet Cindi is planning on making a solo voyage."

"What now?"

"Which car did they take?"

"Let me check."

Jake heard the clicking of heels on the tile, a door closing, then vicious growling and barking of a large dog in the background. In thirty seconds she was back on the line. "Cindi's convertible."

"*What* was that noise? It sounded like you were being eaten."

334

"The dog. It's chained up in the entry. He's huge and scary as hell."

"Be careful. Pack your stuff and get a cab to my hotel. I'll have a key waiting at the desk."

"Got it. I'll be there in less than an hour. Where are you going?"

"Fishing."

CHAPTER 50

The *Tail Chaser* was a 47-foot Riviera Flybridge yacht neatly backed into a slip. Sure enough, Tom Wojicki and Cindi Light were touring the boat as Jake looked down from the walk above. He pulled his floppy canvas hat down low and took a seat in the restaurant where he'd stopped a few days before. Ordering coffee, he watched as the couple walked around the boat.

At one point, Wojicki flicked a cigarette butt overboard into the bay. The sandy-haired captain gave a slight headshake in disgust as he followed behind.

Stacked on the dock next to the yacht were monstrous piles of provisions. Heavy flat fuel bladders laid on the transom waiting to be filled to increase the range of the yacht.

This boat was being prepared for a long trip.

The orientation to the yacht went on for twenty minutes as Jake ate a beignet and had a refill on his thick European brew. Tom and Cindi shook hands with the captain and stepped off the boat. With his bill already paid, he quickly rose and trailed behind them to the parking area. Waiting until they were seated with the engine running, he fired up the rental. He tailed them for five minutes until they landed at the casino where they handed the car to the valet and went inside.

Confident he knew the reason for their visit, Jake went back to the marina. After re-parking the car, he ambled to the dock through the open security gate and stood alongside the *Tail Chaser* next to the pile of supplies. Soon the captain emerged from the salon and saw him gazing admirably at the sportfisher.

"She's a beauty," Jake offered.

"Thanks, mate. We're damn proud of her. Ten line-class world records have hit her decks," answered the captain as he grabbed a case of bottled water off the pile and stepped back aboard.

"Any chance of getting work with you in the next week? Your wife said you might be looking."

"None," he answered looking up from under his baseball cap with a grin. "Some old codger and his hot little betty 'ave booked her for a month. Sixty thousand euros and he pays for fuel and provisions."

"Wow. That's probably half a year's worth of charters."

The grin got bigger on the skipper. "Yep, mate. And at the slow time of the year. I'll be back when the bigeye and blues are startin' to arrive. Had to reschedule a few trips, but they'll go on a quality boat."

The captain looked Jake up and down. "When we get back, we'll be needin' help. Leader'ed before?"

Jake nodded and offered, "Yep. Plenty in Cabo. I know diesels too. Need a hand with the provisions?"

The skipper looked over the stack and wiped his brow. The sun was winning the battle with the morning haze, and although not hot, the air was thick along the docks. "That I could, mate. Let me show you where to stack and stow. Assuming you'll be workin' on her soon, it'd be good to get to know your way around. Let's start by gettin' that pile there into the boat."

Jake grabbed a case of canned fruit and handed it down. The Aussie took it and stacked it in the open deck area next to the fighting chair. In less than ten minutes the pile was in the stern of the vessel. Then the captain showed him the staterooms and galley, along with the bulkhead storage areas.

Jake stacked and stowed after the brief orientation, and the skipper went to work on the fuel bladders, raising the deck hatches to access the engine room. He hopped down below to hook up the lines to the auxiliary fuel tanks, telling Jake he'd be a few minutes and to watch himself on the open hatch. A few times the skipper called to drop a tool down to the engine room, but for the most part, Jake was alone in the task of stowing the supplies.

As he stowed, he pulled a pair of diagonal cutters from the unattended toolbox. Every few moments, Jake emerged to grab another armful of supplies, and after checking to see the skipper was working below and asking if he needed anything, he disappeared into the salon and stateroom areas. Fifteen minutes later he called down into the engine room that the work was done.

The Aussie popped his head out of the hatch and nodded approvingly at the empty deck. "Well then, if you're here in a month, you're hired. A hundred euros a day and we split tips with the crew."

"We leave for the Med tomorrow at gray light. First stop is south of Spain for fuel, then they decide where from there. My wife's cooking and taking second watch. We've got someone to mind the store."

"Staying on board tonight?" Jake asked.

"No. My wife wants one more night in our own bed. It'll be our last night alone together for a month or so." He winked at Jake and continued, "The charter guests will. They'll be sleeping like babies in the master stateroom when we leave. Can I pay you for the half hour of work?"

Jake shook his head and said, "No thanks. See you in a month." He turned and hopped up onto the dock, walking away. Just another boat bum on the docks.

As the captain ducked back into the engine room, he realized they hadn't exchanged names. The fellow had been a nice enough bloke though, he decided as he tightened the clamp on the fuel line. Saved him a half hour at least.

CHAPTER 51

When Jake returned to the room, he found Amber fresh from the shower wrapped in a towel. She was fluffing her hair with a portable blow dryer, and the short terrycloth swatch barely covered her bottom as she worked with her arms up high. He blushed a bit as she caught him surveying her figure.

Raising her arms even higher she revealed about half of her near-perfect rump beneath the towel and smiled from the mirror. "You can look all you want, but don't even think of touching it. It's fifteen thousand bucks now."

He laughed and shook his head. "It's great to see you. Even in all your modesty."

Turning the blow dryer off, she loosed the towel and dropped it on his head as she walked by. At the bed, she reached into her bag and pulled out thong panties. He turned his head and pretended not to look as she shimmied into them. Then she withdrew a lacy black bra and turned her back to him as she fastened it into place.

"What should I dress for?" she asked as she looked down into her bag.

"What?" Jake asked.

"Your plan. Surely you've thought of something. I want to be in on it. What do I need to wear?"

Exhaling deeply, he sat at the small table. "I don't have one. And when I do, you're not going to be involved. The guy down the hall is a killer, and I'm not going to allow you to risk your life."

"Such chivalry," Amber mocked as she rolled her eyes upward and put her hands over her heart. Then pointing a finger at him, she said, "I'm in this for the money now, and I'm willing to take a risk or two."

"What happened to the motherly care of Cindi?"

She answered in a wintry tone, "Screw Cindi. I have no more patience with her! You're right; she's bad."

Amber's eyes became moist and her head sagged from the usual proud tilt. He stood and wrapped his arms around her. She buried her head in his shoulder and gave a few sniffles, but after a moment pushed away gently and said, "Thanks. I'll be over it soon enough."

"I'm sorry Amber."

"No apology necessary. Let's move on." She grabbed a tissue and wiped her eyes then her nose. Tossing the paper in the garbage, she confronted him. "We need a plan, so come up with something. I want my money."

"There's the businesswoman I know," he said with a smile. "Get dressed. I can't have a serious conversation with you wearing next to nothing."

She reached into her bag and removed a pair of tan shorts and an orange-and-white-striped pullover sleeveless blouse. From the tags, he realized she'd obviously been shopping. She worked her way into the clothes and reviewed the fit in the mirror as Jake gave a rundown of what they knew.

"They've chartered a boat to get away. They're planning on leaving Monk behind. Actually, Cindi is planning on leaving *both* of her men behind, I'd bet. This morning I followed them from the boat to the casino."

"The casino?" Amber interrupted with wide, questioning eyes.

"Where else would you convert nearly $2,000,000 to cash?"

"Ah. Our friend Juan Silva will take a small fee, no doubt."

"No doubt," Jake nodded. "They won't have the money until late today. It'll have to be wired to the casino account before Juan Silva converts it to cash euros for them. The boat leaves at first light tomorrow.

"So somewhere between the receipt of the cash and tomorrow morning Miss Cindi has to get Tom, Monk, and the hit man together. Probably when they go back to get their bags."

Amber's face took on a serious look. "We've got to stop it."

"Stop it?" asked Jake incredulously. "I thought we'd let it happen and retrieve the money afterward."

"You made a deal with him."

"And I kept my end of the bargain. Keeping that alcoholic bag of bones alive was never part of the pact. It's not my fault their little threesome is imploding. Better to have Monk Phillips and Tom Wojicki dead and gone. Then all we have to do is pay a visit to Cindi on the boat tonight. She's sleeping there. Alone, if her plans work out."

Amber hissed, "We're not going to stand by and let two people die!"

"Why not? We'd be doing the world a favor."

"Murder? A favor to the world?" she contested. "No, we are going to stop this. I do want the money, but not at the stake of two lives."

Shaking his head, he fired at her, "You asked for a plan, and I gave you one. Why are you so hell-bent on saving their sorry asses?"

"They're people, Jake. Just like you and me. They've made mistakes. However, their lives aren't worth the money. Allowing them to be killed to make getting the money easier is almost the same as killing them yourself. We put this in motion. We owe it to them."

"No Amber. *We* did not put this in motion. *They* concocted a plan to defraud their business partners and a loan shark. *They* set this in motion."

"I'm just not willing to let them die. You shouldn't be willing to either."

Realizing he'd slipped to a level where he was receiving a lesson in morals from a prostitute, Jake said, "Okay. Plan changed. We *try* to save their sorry asses, then get the money. But the retrieval of the funds is more important than the continued existence of a thug, an alcoholic piece of shit, and a black-mailing embezzler.

"Your life is more important, too. I don't want to put you at risk. If this gets dicey, you walk away. Or run."

With her eyes again bright, she said, "Jake, you're so cute when you're gallant."

"You may take this lightly, but I've met Stinnetti's shooter. He's as serious as a heart attack."

"My cholesterol is low. I've got nothing to worry about," she chuckled. Then she asked, "So, what's our new plan?"

Squinting, Jake answered, "The plan, dear lady, is to crossbreed a helicopter, an elephant, and a rhinoceros."

"What are you talking about?"

"You don't get it?"

"No."

"The plan. It's a 'hell-if-I-know.'"

"God," muttered Amber as she pinched her nose at the bridge. "Let's see if we can't think of something better."

Jake's eyes grew wide as he smiled. "I thought that was pretty good. A hell-if-I-know."

Still shaking her head, she answered, "I get it. It just wasn't funny. Now let's come up with something better. Shall we?"

341

CHAPTER 52
MONDAY AFTERNOON & EVENING

Guessing Cindi would not lead Tom into an ambush on the boat, or anywhere in public, it would need to be someplace secluded. It had to be their secluded villa. Jake surmised that was why their bags had been left behind, so a return trip would be necessary.

Jake would watch the house and Amber would watch Bennie Temple. They needed an additional car for the task, so another Toyota was ordered from the rental agency and delivered to the hotel. Jake took it and wound his way up the mountain road.

He found a spot neatly out of sight about one hundred yards up the road offering a view of the home and began his campout in the early afternoon. In less than thirty minutes, he got his first look at Monk Phillips as the big man walked out of the house and unhooked the Rottweiler from the post in the yard. The beast jumped off the ground and landed in the bed of the truck, easily clearing the raised tailgate.

Before driving off, Monk retrieved a paper tucked under the wiper. After pausing a moment to read the note and tossing it in the driveway, the engine rattled to life, and the electric gate slid open. Then he was gone, heading down the narrow mountainside road toward town.

Jake had seen guys as big as Monk before. Most of the time they'd been coming at him full tilt, pulling from the tackle or guard position and leading a running back around the hash marks on a football field. He hadn't seen too many bigger, he added in an afterthought. The fellow was at least six five, and more likely six six.

Any lingering ambition of avenging his father's beating disappeared after seeing the giant. His absence from the home was appreciated.

After the brief excitement of Monk's exit, the waiting continued.

Amber had taken Jake's place at the hotel, moving from the veranda to the room, watching Bennie's room and the parked car. She was fortified with water and snacks. Jake had left behind his copy of the *London Times*, and she filled her time reading stories of British royalty and economic dread in the isles.

At 3:00 p.m. sitting on the rattan couch in the hall, she saw Bennie's door open. He looked up and down the passage, and she caught him staring for a moment too long at Jake's door. Convinced it was closed his gaze moved to the veranda where she sat. Anticipating his appearance, she had on the outside of the *London Times* a copy of the *Jornal da Madeira*. Bennie looked for a moment at her, but the bold headlines in Portuguese convinced him she was a local.

It was clear, however, that he was perusing the area for a familiar face.

A sense of worry came over her, and she bit her lip as she realized Bennie knew Jake was in the vicinity.

The stout little man walked to the elevators and after a short wait stepped in with his luggage in hand. Before the doors closed, Amber was on her feet heading to the stairs for a downward race with the lift.

She spotted him going through the lobby, and after stopping at the desk and dropping the key, he strolled to the valet area. Reaching into her small purse, she withdrew the keys to the rental car and made for the parking lot. As she slipped in behind the wheel, she saw the car Jake had pointed out rolling up to the valet portico. Bennie handed the attendant a bill and pulled out. She turned the key to start the car and follow him. The engine cranked, yet it didn't fire. She stopped and pumped the gas a few times then tried the starter again with the same result. The engine turned over but didn't come to life.

Amber shook her head as she walked to the valet stand where she asked for a cab. The man there picked up a phone and rattled quickly in Portuguese. Hanging up, he offered a heavily accented, "Ten minutes."

She called Jake. No answer. She texted, 'Bennie on the move. Picked up car & checked out. Rental would not start. He knows you're here. Waiting for a cab.'

———————————————————————————————

At 3:10 p.m., Cindi Light's convertible stopped at the gate as it slid open. Backing in under the carport, she and Tom got out and went inside, carrying two canvas bags with them. The gate was left open.

Moments later, they emerged from the home, carrying luggage and packing it in the trunk. Then they went back inside.

Starting down the hill the instant they disappeared into the home, Jake heard the muted sound of his phone ringing inside the car. There was no time to answer as he trotted around the switchback in the road toward the villa. He knew Bennie could not be far behind and wanted to take a position to surprise him.

As he estimated his position at halfway between the villa and his vantage point, a sharp 'pop' filled the air. He stopped in his tracks and listened. Another 'pop' followed.

He started moving again, now faster, then realized the silliness of rushing toward an armed killer with no weapon of his own. Slowing, he rounded the last bend and pressed himself against the high wall of the villa. As he crept along the rough plastered surface, he cursed himself for leaving such a great distance between himself and Wojicki. While it was less than a hundred yards as the crow flies, the switchbacks in the road tripled the distance. Bennie must have arrived and plugged the drunk during his trot down the hill.

As his heart pounded, he rethought the position he'd taken. The hill was very steep, and the driver would have to apply a heavy foot on the accelerator to make the ascent. Jake hadn't heard a vehicle. He'd seen and heard Cindi's car winding up the hill on the switchbacks three to four minutes before their arrival. He guessed he'd covered the distance in less than two minutes on foot.

The realization became all too clear as he neared the open gate: Bennie Temple did not pull the trigger that fired the shots he'd heard.

The sound of a starting engine inside the wall roused him. He shot across the street and ducked into the bushes as Cindi's convertible screeched out of the driveway, spitting gravel at him from the tires as they spun. Instantly she

344

was around the bend, the hum of her car's engine rising and falling as she sped up and slowed between the curves on her way down the hill toward the city of Funchal.

Jake trotted across the street and surveyed the grounds as he passed through the open gate. All was quiet. The crumpled note was on the ground in the drive. He stopped to read it.

Monk,

Tom wants to meet at 3:45 p.m. sharp. Here. Come back from town then. We're getting the money and leaving. They know where we are.

Placing the note in his pocket, he continued across the yard to the entry.

Stepping through the door, he heard nothing. He continued through the room where they'd met two days ago and noted the bullet holes in the window as he passed on his way to the bedroom.

With an unconscious nod and a swallow, he continued down the hall.

In the bedroom, he found his father's business partner face down on the tile. Blood flowed from a neat little hole in his ribcage around the backside of his body and pooled on the floor. Upon closer examination, Jake saw a trickle of blood from his head, just above the temple.

Now with robotic motion, he bent down and touched the wrist, looking for a pulse.

Nothing.

Careful to not touch the blood running across Tom's lifeless face, he performed a carotid pulse check on the neck with the same result. The man was dead.

He looked down on the body. The man was a drunk, embezzler and a gambling addict, to name only a few of his vices. He'd cheated Jake's family, a loan shark, and was preparing to dupe one of his partners in crime.

His death, however, was not a foregone conclusion.

Jake didn't pull the trigger but was responsible nonetheless.

Life on the other side of the line was harsh.

Nudging the body gently with his toe he said, "Sorry Tom."

"Ain't too pretty, is it kid?"

Jake twisted toward the voice and saw Bennie Temple standing in the doorway. As he instinctually started toward the killer, a gun snapped up to chest level. The same gun Tom Wojicki had fired at Jake two days ago.

"I know how quick you is now. Thing is, I'm quick too. There ain't no sand or sun to blind me. So just relax."

Jake leaned back from his coiled stance and put his palms up. He hadn't heard the car pull up. He noticed surgical gloves on both of the killer's hands.

Bennie looked at him quizzically with his hat on sideways. "How'd you get here?"

"Rental car."

His face twisted in thought, Bennie said, "I paid a guy to fix it so it wouldn't start. Guess that fucker owes me some money. Anyway, it don't matter.

"Listen, kid, I got no beef with you. I'm here to do a job. My boss would prefer I popped you too, but we're square. You could'a let me die on that beach, but you didn't. Nicki just wants that guy and the big fucker. Looks like you did half my job already." He pointed at Wojicki's body with his left hand, but the gun never moved.

"He was dead when I walked in," said Jake looking down.

"Wooooo," Bennie said with a long exhale. "The whore popped the bastard! Well, he had it comin', one way or another."

He raised his wrist to see his watch without taking his eyes off Jake. Jake looked at his own wrist. 3:35 p.m. Monk Phillips would be arriving shortly. Cindi had undoubtedly alerted Bennie of the time of his planned return.

Still, with no wavering of the gun, the hit man sidestepped over to the dresser where he picked up a small backpack. Jake hadn't noticed it as his attention had been on the body.

The barrel of the weapon remained trained on Jake as Bennie unzipped the satchel with his free hand. He removed a stack of crisp euros, bound by a white band. Jake saw more bundles in the pack as Bennie zipped it back up.

"How much?" Jake asked.

"What the fuck do you care?" Bennie retorted. Jake remained silent but raised his eyebrows slightly. Nodding Bennie said, "Ten grand. Can't really fly with much more than that. It's a side deal I made with the whore.

"All right. What the fuck am I gonna do with you? I got a 6:25 flight off this rock." Bennie rubbed his chin with his left hand. "You keep quiet about this, and we won't have no troubles. Start talkin', and I'll find you. Turn around and put your hands behind your back. Face the bed," he ordered.

As Jake complied, Bennie swung the weapon in an arc and drubbed him just behind the left ear. His knees buckled at the impact, and his first thought was this blow was about two inches to the left of where the bat had caught him a few days ago. As he fell forward onto the bed, he remembered being thankful the crack had not hit the same spot, which was still tender. Then as he tried to get his hands underneath to push himself up he heard Bennie's voice mumble, "Most fuckers go out in one shot. Tough son of a bitch, aren't you?"

The second blow directly on the back of the head ended all thought, and Jake flopped onto the bed in an inert state induced by the sedative administered by Bennie—two doses of stainless-steel gun handle. Although it would be painful upon waking, the treatment was preferable to the prescription that came from the other end of the Glock.

Jake didn't hear as Bennie offered, "We're even now kid." Then the hit man closed the door and walked to the living room, taking in the panoramic view of Funchal and its harbor as he waited.

CHAPTER 53

Cold water splashed liberally on face roused him. Initially groggy, he sat from the waist. As he tried to throw his legs over the edge of the bed, he mumbled, "Where's Bennie? Where's Bennie?"

"It's okay, Jake! He's gone!" said Amber.

"No. No. He's waiting! Hiding somewhere. He has a gun!" He staggered to his feet, only to fall sideways and land on Tom's body on the floor. He pushed off the corpse and rolled onto his hip, pawing at the air.

Amber knelt down, catching a forearm across the face as he thrashed at the fuzziness. She pushed in after the blow and got hold around his chest, cradling him from behind.

"It's okay," she repeated. "We saw him drive away."

Jake shook his head, trying desperately to clear his vision. After attaining a hint of coherency, he looked at her and asked, "We?"

She nodded upward to the right. "Our rental wouldn't start so I grabbed a cab. My driver caught Monk coming up the hill. I waved him down, and we rode together in his truck. We went by and saw Bennie's car in the drive. We found yours up the hill, so we waited there watching from the turnout.

"Bennie walked around the grounds a few times, disappeared into the house, and then he'd come out and look again. At 4:35 he got in his car and left."

Jake's eyes followed her upward nod, and he saw the tall blond man towering above. His lips were pursed in disgust as he looked down at the two of them on the floor.

Amber went on. "We came down and found you on the bed, with the gun under your hand, Jake."

He squinted and nodded. "Bennie must have put it there after he clocked me. He paid someone to sabotage the rental car."

"So you're sayin' Nicki's guy did this?" grumbled Monk above them.

Jake's head moved from side to side. "Cindi. Before Bennie got here." He looked at Amber and added softly, "Sorry. I didn't expect it. I had time to stop *him*. I just didn't expect she'd be the one to…"

Amber's face showed disbelief. She looked at the body, then back at Jake.

"You don't believe me," he squinted. "Your friend did this, Amber. She killed him and took the money."

She stood, her head hung in sadness. "The only thing I know for certain is there is a man dead on the floor, and I'm a part of it somehow. We're responsible, even if neither of us pulled the trigger."

"Where's the money?" interrupted Monk in a growl.

A tear rolled down Amber's cheek. Hearing the malice in Monk's voice Jake stood quickly, hanging onto the dresser for balance. "No idea," Jake said.

Monk's finger rose and pointed at Amber as he stepped forward toward Jake. "She just said you're responsible. I don't give a flying fuck who pulled the trigger. All I know is I should have…," he looked down at Wojicki's body as he attempted mental calculation with numbers beyond his grasp, "…a lot. You're tellin' me Tom's whore has it? My money? All of it?"

"It never was your money. It was stolen from my family. Looks like neither of us ended up with it."

"You show up here, and everything goes to shit!" Monk said as he advanced. The huge man held his left index finger out at Jake's face, only inches from his nose.

"You weren't smart enough to take it on your own, weren't smart enough to keep it, and you're not smart enough to get it back," Jake said with a smile.

A thunderous right hand swung out from Monk's side. Jake saw it coming and ducked under the blow, stepping away from the dresser. Monk didn't lose his balance, and as he quickly turned to pursue, he found Amber standing between them.

"Stop it!" she yelled. "You two should be ashamed of yourselves! This man's dead and all you can talk about is the money. He was your partner!" she yelled, pointing at Monk. Then her finger moved to Jake. "And you told him everything would be fine if he made the deal. He's not fine. He's dead!"

"What deal?" muttered Monk.

Jake answered, "We agreed to take half and let you go. So we split the money. But Cindi had other plans. She called in Stinnetti's killer to keep all that was left after she got rid of you two."

"Asshole!" Monk shouted down at the dead man, then cocked his right foot and kicked Tom's body viciously in the ribs. The crack of the bones breaking was sickening as he caved in the man's side. Amber turned her head away in horror at the sight and the sound.

He turned back to face Jake. "Where is she?"

Jake looked him in the eye and said, "No idea."

Amber, shaken by the ordeal, shot Jake a look. It was not lost on Monk.

"You're lying. You know where she went!"

"Forget about the money!" Amber yelled. She pointed to the floor and said, "What do we do about him?"

Jake looked down. "Nothing. We leave him here, get on the first plane we can tomorrow, and fly home."

"We can't just leave him. We've got to do something!" Amber implored.

"His body won't be found for days," said Jake as he picked the gun up off the bed. Opening a dresser drawer, he found a tee shirt Wojicki had intended to leave behind. He flipped the safety to the 'on' position and wiped the weapon clean of fingerprints, then threw it on the floor next to the remains of his father's business partner.

Flies had begun their congregation on the coagulated blood and the areas around the entry holes the bullets had made. The three looked down on the corpse.

Monk said callously, "There's gonna' be dancin' rice on him tomorrow."

"Dancing rice?" questioned Amber as she looked at Jake.

"Maggots," he answered.

Turning pale, she charged into the bathroom and retched repeatedly over the toilet. Jake went in and helped Amber stand erect after she finished emptying her stomach. She ran some water from the sink and rinsed her mouth, then wiped it dry on a hand towel. When she caught her breath, he pulled her close, and she sobbed softly on his shoulder.

She implored Jake through the tears, "Do something. Please! We can't just leave his body to rot. We owe it to him. He trusted us."

Leading her out of the bathroom, he said, "Walk up the hill and get the car. The keys are on the floorboard. I'll wrap him in a blanket to keep the bugs off while you bring it down. There's really nothing more I can do."

"Jake, we should go to the police with this."

"We're not going to any fucking police," growled Monk who had followed.

Amber's eyes were wide as she looked into Jake's, pleading for an answer. Rubbing his chin, he responded to the nonverbal question. "He's right. We'll get a flight out tomorrow. As early as possible. By the time the body is found, we'll be home in the States. The authorities here may dig into this a bit, but they'll give up quickly. They probably don't care about the death of an expatriated American on the run. Tom Wojicki did not exist here. Tom Miller did. There aren't many ties to us.

"Bring in the police, and we could *all* be here a long time. We'll piss off a loan shark and a killer back home in the process. Better to leave all this behind."

She nodded slowly in acceptance. "You'll cover him up?"

"Yes. I promise. You go get the car."

She walked out the front door. Jake heard the dog barking wildly as she passed by through the courtyard. He looked at Monk then toward the bedroom. "Give me a hand?"

"Fuck it. Leave him there. She'll never know."

Jake shook his head and walked past him. He pulled the cover from the bed, then knelt down and put his arms under Wojicki, making certain the bedspread wrapped completely around the torso. His head throbbed as he lifted the body onto the bed, flipping it over onto the back with the spread centered underneath. He pulled the legs straight, thankful that rigor mortis had not taken hold. The hands were carefully laid on the stomach. Before covering the man for the final time, Jake again checked the pulse, both carotid and wrist. Nothing. And the body was noticeably cool. The man was dead.

Wrapping him up, Jake used the forefinger and middle digit of his right hand to close the unblinking, bloodshot eyes.

There was sadness in those orbs. Not just the sorrow of death, but an emptiness in the life they'd seen. Tom Wojicki's existence, at least in his latter years, had seen little joy, Jake reflected as he wrapped the spread tightly over the body that smelled of stale booze and cigarettes.

He wanted to say something, but nothing came to mind. He left the room.

Reaching inward to find solace that the wrong done his parents had been avenged, he discovered only emptiness.

Once out the door, Jake strode toward the gate. He estimated the crude internment of the body had taken four to six minutes. Amber should be waiting by now in front. Oddly, Monk was absent.

The Rottweiler yanked wildly at its chain as he passed within ten feet of the beast, slobbering as the massive white teeth were bared in growls between barks. He continued past the restrained dog and the house, where he turned the corner to the driveway.

Jake stopped in his tracks as he found the tall wrought-iron gate closed. Looking around at the high white plastered wall he remembered his survey of the compound a few days ago. The barrier went entirely around the home, constructed to follow the slope of the hillside.

It would serve equally well to keep someone *inside* as it would to keep unwanted visitors out.

The gate itself was made of ornately twisted iron bars, spaced about six inches apart, beginning on the ends where it met the wall from what Jake guessed was a height of about twelve feet and rising to the center in a smooth arch to over fourteen. From an architectural standpoint, it was not a balanced structure; the gate was an eyesore, with sharp iron spikes pointing toward the sky.

He strode over to the entrance and pulled at the bars. Even with his legs pushing off the column with all the force he could apply and his hands on the bars it would not budge. He tried yanking, hoping a sharp snap might loosen the gate from its hold and get it sliding along the track. Still nothing.

Amber drove up, stopping outside. Only a few feet away, she rolled the window down. "Let's go," she said.

"I'm ready," Jake answered from behind the iron structure, "but it seems Mr. Monk has other plans." He raised his hands and looked up at the gate. Then he looked around for the big man. He saw nothing but the dog barking and crazily yanking at the chain in the courtyard entry.

"It's okay. I'll climb it," he told her.

The iron crossbar holding the vertical rods together was at about nine and a half feet off the ground. Although he hadn't done it in a year, or maybe even two on second thought, he was able to grab a basketball rim at ten feet with a good leap. Taking a few steps back he got a running start and jumped.

Elevating easily to the necessary altitude his hands got a firm grip on the crossbar as his legs thumped into the vertical bars with a swing. With a quick pull-up, he got his chest level with the crossbar and raised his right foot to hook between the upright spikes. All that was left was to balance on the gate and step through the spikes, then drop down the other side.

In his last pull to straddle the spikes, Jake's hands instantly clenched on the metal as his body shook uncontrollably. The foot between the spikes lost its grip, and he hung in the air, quivering as waves of electricity coursed through him.

After an agonizing ten seconds, the voltage was cut off, and Jake fell to the ground. On the *inside* of the barrier. With muscles in tight spasm, he sat in a heap.

Emerging from the carport, Monk grinned a sardonic smile and towered above, taunting, "Pretty good dance you did there, buddy. The airborne electric slide!"

Jake's arms and legs still pulsed with the memory of the violent current. He cursed himself for not realizing the fence might be electrified.

Monk said loudly, "You two ain't leavin' me here with nothin'. *You* may be able to fly away and leave all this behind, but it looks like I got shit: a dead man here, probably a warrant back home, and no way off this fucking rock. Even if I found a ticket out, I got no money. We need to work out a deal, or you don't go. Far as I'm concerned, I'll put you back there with Tom. I got nothin' to lose." Then he kicked Jake, hard, in the back under the shoulder.

Seeing the blow coming, Jake rolled to lessen the impact. Had it not been for the combined tightness and weakness of his muscles he might have avoided it altogether. Yet even with the giving move, the power of the three-hundred-plus-pound man knocked the breath out of him as he went flat in the driveway.

Amber had gotten out of the car and stood at the gate. "Don't hurt him anymore!" she implored as Monk cocked his foot for another kick. "We don't have the money. But we know where Cindi is!"

Looking up, he didn't follow-through with the leg swing. "Where?"

As Jake pulled himself up to a sitting position, she answered, "On a boat. She's not leaving until morning. There still may be time to catch her."

"Take me to her," he demanded.

"No," said Jake as he slowly stood. "We're going to see Ms. Light this evening, but you won't be coming along."

Putting his hands up in a defensive position he began circling the big man. His legs felt sluggish and heavy. His hands would not make tight fists.

Over the years through mountain and beach bars, Jake had been in his share of scuffles. At about one hundred eighty-two pounds himself, he'd factor in the estimated level of training, physical condition, size, and assess the overall toughness in his would-be opponents. It was an imprecise equation to be sure, but Jake's computations put the biggest man he'd ever want to face at about two forty or two fifty in a stretch.

His rules for skirmish told him to hightail it and save his ass. Yet he had nowhere to go. The wall ran around the entire villa, and Monk likely had hit the switch sending the current back into the fence.

He could probably outrun the giant. Jake tested his legs with a few quick steps sideways. They were unresponsive, the muscles still in spasm. And then there was the dog... Monk could let the dog loose, and Jake knew he couldn't outrun the animal for long.

Could he reach the gun before Monk or his monster of a mutt caught him? His eyes looked toward the house for an instant.

"You won't make it," Monk said, as if reading Jake's thoughts. "I'd snap you like a twig, just like I did your daddy, but then she'd drive away." He nodded in Amber's direction. "And she knows where that bitch is with the money." Turning to look at Amber through the bars, he nodded, "Don't you?"

In the second his head was turned Jake moved in with all the speed he could muster, knowing that no matter how big a man was, his testicles were soft. As Jake raised his knee to snap his lower leg out and deliver the blow his muscles again protested, lethargic from the shock waves. He forced his body to complete the kick, but it felt as if his blow was delivered in slow motion.

At the end of the leg snap, Jake felt an unexpected hardness. Monk had raised his left knee high and turned it slightly inward to absorb and deflect the blow with the rigid shinbone.

Training. A novice would have reacted to natural instinct and reached down with his hands to ward off the blow, leaving his face open for attack.

Monk Phillips was no novice. His hands were both up high to protect his head, and he countered the attack with a meaty left jab followed by an overhand right. Jake took the jab on his right forearm and knowing the right would follow tried to duck underneath it. The motion came naturally, but the left jab of the monster was so powerful that even though blocked, it stood him up to take the full force of the crashing right.

It came, and Jake took most of it with his left forearm. Even checked, the blow had so much power it drove his arm back into his own head. He stumbled backward going down on the tile, rolling instantly as Monk kicked at him, barely missing in a roundhouse with his right leg. At the end of the roll, Jake found his feet and popped up, squaring off again.

As he danced on his toes, he kept a good distance from the hulking man. His head throbbed as the bashing reactivated the pain from the cracks of the gun butt. Monk made a few advances and threw a few punches that Jake was able to sidestep as he retreated. Jake countered with a couple of combinations, but Monk took those mostly on the arms and massive body. Each of Jake's counterpunches was delivered as he stepped to the side or backward, and without the forward press of his legs, he could generate little power. The inability to make tight fists lessened the impact of his blows.

"That's all you got?" Monk mocked, absorbing another combo on his thick forearms. He again jabbed at Jake, who moved sideways and slightly backward out of the way of the gorilla-sized fist. "Quick bastard, though," he laughed. "I can't catch you." Then, grinning another sardonic smile, he lowered his hands and turned, walking away.

"But it don't matter how fast you are. You ain't quicker than Damien."

Monk was off to loose the Rottweiler on him! The dog seemed to sense his opportunity to use Jake as a chew-toy as he thrashed against his chain, slobbering and barking wildly.

"We'll take you to Cindi!" yelled Amber from the other side of the gate. "Don't let the dog go."

Monk's stride never broke. Jake looked around once more for an escape route and saw none. He took off full tilt and caught the gargantuan hominoid before he reached the chain to release the animal. On the big man's back instantly, Jake wrapped his arms around the waist. Trying a heel trip by putting his toe against the back of Monk's left foot and leveraging backward, he was unsuccessful in taking him down. The move worked on normal-sized opponents, but Monk felt the throw coming and braced against it by leaning forward. To get extra leverage, Jake leaned out to the side, a critical mistake as he exposed his face only for a second. It was a second too long as the big man demonstrated quickness of his own in throwing an elbow backward and catching Jake in the side of the face in a tooth-rattling impact.

Most men would have released their grip and gone down with the elbow, but Jake fought through the pain. Knowing the dog would mangle him if he lost this battle, he held on even through the clenched weakness in his hands. A second and third elbow came but his face was pressed firmly into Monk's back, and the blows could not find the intended mark.

The big fellow tried to spin in the waist hold. Jake spun too, staying low and not enabling him to reach around with the massive mitts and get hold of his head. After two times around for both of them, Monk gave up and started back toward the dog, simply dragging Jake along. Now within ten feet of the beast, Jake again pressed on the heel and Monk put even more of his body into a forward lean to avoid the heel trip. At the peak of the push away, Jake instantly released the pressure and went with the bigger man, wrapping the large left leg with his own and tripping him forward.

Their combined weight hit the lawn as the takedown worked perfectly. Monk coughed out air as he landed, yet instantly reached back with his right arm to get a hand on his opponent as most inexperienced grapplers do. Jake seized the opportunity and got hold of the appendage under the elbow in a chicken-wing grip over Monk's back. Momentarily he had the upper hand over the larger man. Jake knew from experience that if he waited long enough his foe would reach back with the other hand and he could catch that elbow too. The double-chicken-wing was a devastating wrestling move, the very one that had cost him a high school state championship as a sophomore.

Pressing his chest into the single-wing hold on the elbow and sprawling his legs out and to the side like outriggers for stability Jake pawed at the left arm, trying desperately to get a hold on it. Three times he hooked the elbow, but the power of the giant pulled the arm forward to keep Jake from locking it back. Between pulls, Jake landed compact punches on the ear and back of the head with his left hand. The blows did little damage individually yet in succession must have started to hurt as Monk reached up and covered his ear with his left hand. Still, he kept the elbow out forward.

Jake reached for it again. Monk must have felt the weight distribution change just slightly. With the weight center shifting, he was able to get a leg underneath.

The powerful leg pushed forward as Monk rolled his shoulder downward, yanking his captive arm loose from the hold. Jake's body flew in an arc as the grip was broken, yet even as he went by, he caught a handful of the flowing blond hair in his left hand. Using the mane as a handle, he instantly pulled himself close in and took another handful of the hair with his right hand. He hid his face below his arms and again spread his legs in a sprawl position with the toes downward desperately trying to find a hold on the lawn.

Monk hammered relentlessly with his massive fists at his body. He was unable to get full swings, but the power he mustered in the compact punches was taking its toll.

Jake dared not look up as he would expose his face to the blows, yet he estimated his legs were now scant feet from the jaws of the ravenous dog. He wondered how long it would take for Monk to realize that rather than pounding him to a pulp all he had to do was use his mass and drive them both ahead a few feet, allowing the dog to have his way.

Either way, from the pounding he was absorbing or the fangs of the beast behind him, Jake was about to lose this battle. Advice from his wrestling coach in high school came to mind; *when all else fails, cheat.*

He loosed his thumbs from the mane of his opponent and drove them into the eyes, twisting the hair with his fingers for leverage. The hammering stopped as Monk clawed first at Jake's hands then at his eyes. With his head buried between his forearms, Jake's face remained protected, and he pressed slightly deeper into the sockets with his thumbs.

"You're blind if you move again!" yelled Jake

The image of a massive man staggering in darkness with a white cane must have come to Monk. All movement ceased as he held his hands out to the side in an open position of surrender.

Jake took a few deep breaths and assessed the situation as he maintained even pressure on the eyes with his thumbs. Looking backward, he saw his toes were within inches, not feet, of the dog's jaws. The beast had stopped barking and now simply growled as they exchanged looks.

Knowing the man he now held could see nothing with the thumbs in his eyes, Jake pulled to his knees and cocked the right one back, then swung it forward with all the force he could muster. Actually pulling Monk's head toward the oncoming knee, he held firm as the top of the knee caught Monk square in the nose. All movement stopped, and Jake removed the thumbs from the eye sockets, preserving his hold on the hair. Twice more he brought the knee forward, these blows landing on the forehead.

Jake let the hair go, and Monk fell to the ground, motionless. Standing, he looked at the dog. He couldn't be certain, but he thought the Rottweiler had a distinct look of disappointment on its face. "Not today, Damien," he said as he walked away toward the carport.

As he passed the gate, Amber said, "I thought he was going to kill you!"

"That makes two of us," he answered as he looked at the iron structure, oblivious to the blood running from his nose and the re-opened scratches on his face. "Probably a button or switch in the carport." He strode toward the enclosure to find the remote actuator.

As he rounded the corner of the wall, he heard Amber yell, "Jake! Run!"

Poking his head back around the partition he looked first at her and saw she stared toward the spot where his battle had just ended. Monk had crawled to where the dog was secured and worked with his hands at its collar.

The beast shot forward like a sprinter out of the blocks as the clip on the chain was released. Jake did a lightning-quick survey of the surroundings and realized there was no escape from the approaching fiend. He turned and took four steps to where the wave runners sat on their trailer. Upon reaching the machines, he bounded up onto the seat of one with the memory of the dog's leaping ability as it had cleared the truck's tailgate earlier. As he bent his own legs to jump, he heard the claws of the animal clicking on the paver tiles as it closed the distance between them at full speed.

Jake pushed upward as the mass of fur and slobbering jowls rounded the wall of the carport. He caught the bottom of the carport truss with his hands and swung his body around the wood member as Damien launched himself off the tile. His father's baggy shirt was shredded as the Rottweiler flew at him and caught the tail as he pulled himself to the top of the truss support.

The dog spit out the piece of shirt with a shake of its bear-sized head and turned back for another leap. Jumping first on the wave runners and straddling both seats, it pushed upward at Jake who now had his feet on the four-inch-wide truss base nine feet above the floor. At the apex of the animal's leap, Jake grasped the upright support between the roof peak and the truss and pulled his feet up. The dog missed his toes but managed to lock its teeth onto the beam.

Amazingly, the brute hung from its jaws, fangs sunken into the wood as it growled staring upward at him. Then with a shake of his head, he freed himself and dropped to the carport floor. Jake clamored through the trusses to a position above an open space where the dog would not have a launch platform on the wave runners.

Damien growled and barked as he spun in circles on the floor beneath.

"This just keeps getting better and better," Jake called out to Amber, who was obscured from view.

"Jesus! You're alive!" she called back. "I thought the dog got you when I saw the piece of fabric fly."

"You'd think I was wearing Milk-Bone underwear," he called out. "Where's Monk?"

"He staggered off into the house."

"Criminy. He's getting the gun." He again cursed himself, this time for not disposing of the weapon the first time he'd held it days ago. "I guess he needed another shot or two with my knee. Any ideas? I'm fresh out."

"Yeah. I'm going to do something before he kills you."

Jake stared down at the dog from his perch. The mutt growled and ran back and forth in front of the carport.

Suddenly the dog trotted off. Jake presumed, correctly, that his master had appeared. Although he couldn't see them, he heard Amber and Monk talking.

"Where's your boyfriend?"

"He's in the top of the carport. And he's not my boyfriend."

"Damien didn't get him?"

"Almost. Listen, Monk, beating each other to death isn't going to get either of you any closer to Cindi and the money."

"I'm done using my fists on that little fucker. He about clawed my eyes out. This'll take care of him."

Although he couldn't see him, Jake pictured Monk brandishing the gun.

"Shooting him won't do any good either. I'll go to the authorities if you do. Then you'll be broke and stuck here for a long time, in jail."

There was silence for a moment as Monk contemplated.

"So, what do you wanna do?"

"I'll take you to Cindi. And to the money. Then you let Jake go."

A quiet period came again as he thought about it.

"Deal."

"Okay. Chain the dog up again and let's go."

"Nope. Damien will watch our friend. If he gets by the dog, he's got the electric fence to deal with. I'll turn him loose *after* I have the money."

"Jake, you hear all this?"

"Yep."

"You okay with it?"

"Do I have a choice?"

"No. I just want you to know the plan. We'll be back in an hour, maybe two. Can you make it that long?"

He saw a portion of the carport had plywood installed between the trusses for storage. He started working his way toward the section through the bracing. "Yeah, I'll be all right."

Monk appeared below. "Don't get no ideas. The electric to the fence is coded on a box in the house, and you ain't got a remote." He held his keys up and shook the fob attached to the bundle. "Damien will get you if you try to wander around."

Monk disappeared from the carport.

"Where are you going?" Jake heard Amber ask.

"I'm packing a bag in case I have to leave in a hurry. I have to clean up a little, too. It'll take about five minutes." To the dog that tried to follow, Monk barked out, "Stay!"

Damien returned and sat obediently below the rafters of the carport, panting.

Amber yelled in to Jake, "We'll have you out in no time! Just be patient. Monk and Cindi can hash it out, then you and I will get the first flight home tomorrow."

Leaning his back against a support member, he found the most comfortable position he could. They were both quiet as they waited for Monk.

Soon he emerged into the carport, a medium-sized duffle in hand. He wore a fresh but wrinkled pair of camel-colored pants and a polo shirt. Looking up at Jake sitting on his perch, his face was washed but red and puffy.

360

"The nose is broke," he said low enough to keep Amber from hearing, "If I have time, we'll finish this."

"I'm counting the moments," Jake answered.

Monk walked to the gate and Jake heard the mechanism opening it. Damien followed.

"Stay," was Monk's last command as the gate rolled closed and the car sputtered off for the waterfront.

Jake settled in with his back against the support column of a truss. The beast obediently came back and sat below on the floor of the carport, a hopeful look on his face.

CHAPTER 54

Small waves generated from boats moving in the harbor rocked the *Tail Chaser* gently as Cindi Light attempted to enjoy a glass of boal in a chair on the aft deck. The sky over the harbor turned from red-orange to purple with the fading day. Music mixed with the sounds of traffic drifted along the waterfront.

The captain and his wife had given her a rundown on the basic systems for her stay aboard this evening. She'd explained Tom had business that had arisen and would join them when they reached the south of Spain. With the trip paid for in cash in advance, Cindi thought the boat owners looked relieved the man who obviously smoked and drank heavily would not be along for the 565-nautical-mile crossing to the port of Cadiz. The captain informed her heading into the trade winds the average speed would be about twelve knots per hour, and the crossing would take about two days. He and his wife had gone home for one more night on land.

Her self-inflicted indenture to Tom Wojicki had ended.

Bennie Temple had undoubtedly finished the job on Monk Phillips and was on a plane headed for America. She knew Jake Cohen was on the island somewhere; both Bennie by phone and Juan Silva earlier today at the casino had confirmed the fact. She pulled the baseball cap she wore down tighter on her head and hiked the blanket up around her neck to keep any passersby on the walkway above from recognizing her.

Jake couldn't possibly know she was here. She was safe.

Tomorrow morning, before dawn, the big engines would rattle to life, and this boat would be gone to Europe and the Mediterranean.

The captain had stated they'd be in radio contact for about 220 miles; beyond that point, the curvature of the earth's surface would block the transmissions to and from here. Cindi prayed silently the bodies of Tom and Monk would not be discovered until they were past the point of contact.

No matter how tightly she pulled the blanket around her, she couldn't ward off the chill. She watched the people at the restaurant above the marina. Some wore light sleeves; however most were in T-shirts and shorts. Weren't they freezing?

Suddenly Cindi realized the chill she felt wasn't in the air. It came from within. Taking a long pull from the wine glass, she shuddered and hoped the alcohol would warm her blood. As she mused, a familiar voice barked out from the walkway above.

"Which boat?" The man's growl was unmistakable.

A woman's voice answered him, too low to be identified.

"The goddamn fishing boat?" thundered Monk Phillips as he walked toward the water.

Cindi dove from her chair to the deck below the rail, spilling her wine.

"There it is! Right fucking there!"

The pounding of footfalls on the gangway alerted her; Monk, very much alive, was on the way down. The gate twenty yards away rattled loudly as he tried to open it.

"Goddamn thing is locked!"

"Be patient. If you make a scene, the police, or whatever they call them here, will be all over us!" It was a woman's voice. Familiar. *Amber Nelson had brought Monk to her.*

"The bitch has almost two million dollars. A lot of it's my money! I'm gonna rip her head off!"

Cindi peeked up over the rail of the boat. The two stood at the entrance gate, Amber with her arms crossed facing him. Her first thought at the site of her roommate with him was one of betrayal, yet now, only seconds later, she could think of no one else she'd rather have to smooth things over with the crazed giant.

He must be aware of the plot to kill him, she thought as she crouched.

People on crystal meth were unpredictable, she knew, yet the one advantage the drug offered was those under its influence loved to talk. They generally felt enlightened by the stimulation of the brain as it fried with the constriction of the blood vessels.

"Let's calm down," Amber said as she put a hand on his arm. "If you want any part of what is on that boat, you'll need a cool head."

The tone was perfect, Cindi noted as she cowered. *Way to go, Amber; save my ass!*

Monk hissed as he let out his breath. The gate shook again, but this time the banging was shorter and lacked the angry rattle. "Whad'da you suppose I should do?" His words carried no profanity and were almost level.

"First, let's just wait here. Calmly. Like a couple who was out and left their key behind. Someone will be along, and we'll get in.

"Then, you two need to work out a deal. You can't kill her, or even rough her up. You don't know she meant to have you… meet Bennie. If you make a ruckus, the police will come. They'll start asking questions. None of us will get out of here, and they'll take what's on that boat."

"Okay. I'm calm," he snarled.

"Good. Now let's wait."

Cindi realized eventually, they would get through the gate. She stood, and offered in a low shout, "I'll let you in."

Stepping onto the rail, she hopped on the dock and walked to the gate. Upon letting them in Monk gave an icy stare as he walked past the woman who'd plotted his demise. Amber gave a head shake of disgust.

"We need to talk. Climb aboard," Cindi offered as she walked to the boat.

Monk offered no hello, but rather blurted, "Where's the money?"

"In the stateroom," she replied, a beaten quality in her voice.

Amber hopped up on the rail and dropped to the deck. Monk followed, and the boat listed heavily under his mass as he stepped on the starboard side. The motion made him visibly uncomfortable, and he grabbed a rod holder for balance.

"I wanna see it," he demanded.

Cindi nodded and opened the cabin door. She went in, and he followed.

"Fuck!" he griped as his head hit the doorframe that offered only six feet three inches of clearance. "This thing was made for midgets."

The headroom in the interior cabin was slightly better at six foot eight, but he still had to duck to miss the fishing rods mounted to the ceiling. They walked through the cabin and descended three steps to the hall. Two staterooms opened on each side of the boat amidships. Cindi continued forward to a teak door and opened it, revealing the forward stateroom. The clearance had shrunk in this area below decks to six four, and Monk had to cock his neck slightly as he moved. He hit his head again as he failed to duck low enough at the forward stateroom doorframe.

"Fuck!"

"Just remember to duck a little lower," Cindi said.

"My head is sore. That's all," he snarled.

"I'm guessing you already knew, but in case you didn't—Jake never left the island," explained Amber. "He and Monk had a bit of a battle at the villa."

Cindi raised her eyebrows, "Is Jake dead?"

"No. He won," Amber said with a smile.

"Bullshit! I'll whip that punk-ass jew-motherfucker anytime. He just got lucky."

Cindi looked at Monk closely in the light of the stateroom. "Looks like he did a job on your face. Your nose looks crooked." She moved her head at different angles as she examined him. He pushed her face away. Roughly. She stepped back.

"Forget my nose. Where's the money."

Opening a closet, she withdrew two multicolored canvas bags. As she worked the zipper of one, she asked, "So, where is the elusive Mr. Cohen?"

"With Damien. Behind the electric fence," growled Monk.

Cindi nodded as she flipped the top open. "We won't be seeing him then." Her voice trailed off as the contents of the bag came into view.

Neatly wrapped euros, the equivalent of approximately $950,000, were stacked inside. The other bag was opened with the same amount revealed. Monk whistled. Amber remained silent. Cindi ran her fingers gently over the cash.

They were quiet for a moment, each lost in thought as they ruminated over the loot. Finally, Cindi said, "What now?"

"Good fucking question," replied Monk.

"You two need to do some talking. I'll moderate," offered Amber. "And we need to do it quickly before Jake does something stupid and the dog eats him."

"Where's Tom?" Cindi asked innocently.

Both Amber and Monk shot her looks. Monk's was of confusion, yet Amber's was of revulsion. It was not lost on Cindi.

"He's dead. And Cohen says you did it," Monk answered.

Saying nothing, Cindi bit her lip and shook her head horizontally.

Two empty plastic gas cans. A few sections of wrought iron probably left over from the construction of the fence. Four folding beach chairs. Various fertilizers and pesticides with the warning labels written in Portuguese. Paint to match the hues of the rooms in the home. An old windsurfer and mast. A cheap aluminum tennis racket and mesh bucket full of worn-out tennis balls. A skateboard. Beach toys for kids. A single person foam raft. An old set of double water skis…

Jake took inventory of the items stored in the rafters as he sat on the plywood. Damien had relaxed from his sitting position, and he rested on his side, yet remained alert. Twice Jake had dangled from the beams, and each time the beast had charged him, once nearly clamping onto his leg as he did a pull-up to escape.

He'd crawled through the rafters, covering the entire area, looking for an exit to the roof. The eave extended too far to reach around and get a hold on the tiles. The clay roofing material offered no hand hold anyway. The thought of bashing through the sheeting and tiles above his head had come to him. Checking the seams on the plywood where it met the rafters, he found heavy glue residue and the shanks of large screws where a few had missed the lumber. Driving his shoulder upward twice, he realized the roof sheeting would not give.

Maybe he could kill the dog? With what? The pesticides were his first thought, but it was quickly dismissed; it might take days for the mutt to succumb to the poison, and he'd have to figure out a way to get it into the animal.

Crawling over to the mesh bucket of tennis balls, Jake estimated the diameter of the opening. He looked at Damien's bear-sized head, and back at the bucket. The steel container would fit over the dog's face. Could he make a muzzle to cover the jaws and head? Absolutely. The line on the sailboard boom was long enough to reach around the head. But how would he get it on the dog? He guessed the brute weighed over a hundred and forty pounds. Could he out-wrestle the mass of muscle, jaws, and teeth long enough to mash the bucket over its head? No, he decided quickly. Growing up with German Shepherds, he knew that at play the dogs would allow the upper hand to a human occasionally, yet if the jostling got too rough, the power of the animal would be evident. Their biggest Shepherd was no match for a

Rottie, and the one he now engaged was an aberration to that breed, stronger and larger than any he'd ever seen.

The wrought-iron sections of the fence caught his eye. Could he build a spear and take the dog with it? Working his way to the stacked iron bars, he found them welded together in four-foot sections. Checking each weld joint, no weak points were found. Maybe he could just drop the sections, points first, on the dog? Jake shook his head. That likely wouldn't kill the beast, and would probably just infuriate him more.

At a loss for an answer, he crawled back through the rafters to his perch on the plywood. Damien moved slowly on the paver tiles underneath and sat, panting lightly as he looked up at his detainee.

Absentmindedly, Jake picked up a tennis ball from the wire bucket. Rolling it in his hands, he continued his deliberations. Without a thought of the motion, he bounced the ball off the carport floor and back up to himself.

Instantly, Damien was off the floor after the bouncing ball. The dog just missed the rising sphere as Jake caught it on the rebound. He looked at the ball, then at the beast below, who now looked up in rapt attention. Again he bounced the ball, and this time the dog smothered it before it could rise and return. A loud pop announced the end of the tennis ball as it was crushed by the powerful jaws.

His captor liked to play ball.

Surely, a dog wouldn't want to eviscerate a playmate? As a test, Jake pulled another tennis ball from the bucket. He hung one-handed like a monkey and threw the ball out of the carport. Damien instantly gave chase. Jake grabbed another ball and swung down onto the seat of the wave runner. The beast had retrieved the ball and now galloped on his return trip to the carport. Jake cocked his arm and threw again, the ball sailing past the dog's head.

Damien's stride never broke as the object passed by, and the first thrown ball was spit out in two pieces as the pulsating mass of muscle, fur, and fangs charged at Jake. He was back in the rafters with a pull-up. His captor jumped up with his paws on the seat of the wave runner, panting and looking up.

Jake looked at the remnants of the two mangled tennis balls. *So much for the prospect of making friends.* Damien's primary goal was to do to his hostage what he'd done to the balls. Perhaps the dog enjoyed the chase as foreplay to the final mangling of its prey.

He thought... The dog chased the balls and picked them up in his mouth, at least long enough to crush them. Jake still had a sizable inventory of tennis balls. Could he distract Damien and escape while the dog gave chase?

Even making it to the perimeter wall, he still had to get *over* it. The top section had enough voltage coursing through to cook a hot dog on contact. Getting *to* the wall was only part of the answer. Clearing the barrier was the key, quickly enough to beat the dog's return.

He had no ladder, and nothing long enough to scale the wall. Once committed to the jaunt, there would be no time for a return trip to this sanctuary. Out, up, and over. It had to be done in a few seconds. If he didn't make it, Jake knew he'd become a chew toy for Damien or be barbequed on the electric grid on top of the wall.

Perhaps the dog would enjoy the taste of his flesh after it was cooked a bit.

A newly found determination blossomed. The shaking weakness from the electric shock was gone. The blow to his head from the gun butt was forgotten. Clarity took hold.

For the third time, he did an inventory, this round focusing upon each item individually. The windsurfer mast passed over as useless on the first two accountings caught his attention.

He again worked through the rafters until he reached the carbon fiber reinforced shaft. Hoisting the approximate fifteen-foot mast up through the beams, he slid it across the support members to the front of the carport. Next, he crawled back to the plywood platform and pulled out the skateboard. Finally, he collected the bucket of tennis balls, and he crawled to the front beam over the entry and driveway.

He suspended the mast between the beams, then turned it perpendicular to the front of the carport. With all the force he could muster, Jake shoved the shaft out into the driveway. Clanging to the tiled surface, it slid to a stop midway between the carport and the wall.

Damien looked up at him curiously. The beast's gaze alternated from the mast to Jake. The panting stopped.

Next Jake dangled the skateboard down between the rafters. With a swinging motion, he loosed the device out into the drive. It came to rest alongside the windsurfer mast. Damien followed it out.

"Don't pick it up," Jake muttered.

As if in defiance, the Rottweiler opened his jaws and grabbed the board, beginning to carry it back into the carport. Instantly a tennis ball bounced by his head. The skateboard was dropped, and the dog gave chase, ending the life of another of the green spheres as he ran it down, chomping it to pieces.

Again Damien came to rest beneath Jake, proudly dropping the shredded remains of the ball in front of his paws. The beast looked at Jake, then to the driveway.

Jake surmised, if he could have talked, the monster mutt would be saying, *"You're not going to make it."*

Grabbing another ball, he hung down and threw to the farthest corner of the drive. As he watched Damien chase the ball down, he timed the retrieval. Seven seconds to the grab. While the dog sauntered back, Jake surmised that with the motivation of a mauling, the return trip could be made at least as quickly.

Fourteen seconds. He needed more time.

Five times more he threw and timed. On the fifth toss, the dog's trip to fetch had increased to ten seconds. *Times two, maybe enough,* he thought. *Yet possibly not.* He had only one chance. Success had to be a certainty. He did not wish to provide himself as the dog's repast.

The supply of balls wasn't a problem. He worried that Damien's motivation to chase them would wane. A longer chase area was needed, yet his tosses were already to the farthest corner of the drive.

The carport protruded from the main structure of the house at a ninety-degree angle. Looking at the wall, Jake quickly calculated the angle necessary for a bank shot off the barrier to send the ball behind the carport alongside the house. Hanging once again, he let a ball fly with all the force he could muster.

The felt and rubber ball hit the wall on the fly and began a rebound to perfectly clear the carport and obscure itself as it passed to the side of the house. Damien, however, had calculated the bounce and caught the ball before it passed by.

Jake scratched his head. He'd have to get the tennis ball around the carport. That would put the dog going away, and increase the distance between them as he tried for the wall. Hanging, he couldn't throw hard enough to give the ball the necessary speed to get by the dog. There had to be a way to hit the wall high enough and with enough force to get the ball by his playmate.

The tennis racket... Another crawl through the rafters and return to the front of the carport. Now, with the racket in his right hand, he locked around the rafter with his left elbow. In his left hand, he held a ball.

Damien sat up, watching. His panting stopped.

Jake dropped the ball in his left hand and swung hard with the racket in his right, catching the tennis ball in the sweet spot at the bottom of the arc. The twang told of a direct hit, and a telling rubberized thump notified him of contact with the wall. Instantly Damien shot out of the carport. Just as Jake was ready to drop to the floor, the dog came charging back in after the bouncing object. The ball bounced around for a few seconds before it was secured and instantly crushed by the jaws.

He'd hit the ball back to himself. Yet it was encouraging. The speed of the ball off the racket was too much even for this swift animal.

Once more Jake readied for the swat. Damien was onto the game now and was poised for the run. The ball was dropped and swatted with just a bit more angle, the thump of the rebound heard, and the dog was off.

The shot was beautiful as the ball visibly bounced past the carport. The scraping of toenails on the tile could be heard as the chasing mutt changed directions when the sphere passed. Abruptly, however, the dog stopped just before passing out of sight around the wall.

Damien stood, obviously torn by his desire to disembowel his prisoner and the lure of the ball. Jake instantly realized the mutt's dilemma. He sat back in a relaxed position. The comfortable body tilt relayed in his best dog language, *I'm not going anywhere.* He even forced a yawn.

The dog's brow furrowed in suspicion. He stared for a few seconds longer, then bought the ruse and disappeared around the carport.

Quickly swinging down to the tile Jake listened. Certain the dog was still moving away, he trotted silently to the skateboard. Hoisting it and arching backward, he heaved it over the wall.

He estimated his ground time at seven or eight seconds. Two backward steps and the mast was in his hands, the tip facing the wall. Keeping his right hand at his waist and his left at shoulder level, he drove off of his left foot and began a run at the barrier he estimated to rise twelve feet above the driveway.

In high school, he'd played at the pole vault station during track and field practice. Jake had picked up the flexible stick and cleared the bar at as high as thirteen feet. Far below the state meet record, but a respectable elevation for a beginner.

His last attempt was now many years behind him, but he remembered the technique from the coach.

Keep the pole level as the run accelerates, lower the tip evenly as you approach the box. Allow the forward momentum of the run to flex the shaft, raising it above your head.

DO NOT JUMP, Jake reminded himself as the tip of the mast hit the base of the wall. Allow the energy of the flexed pole to LIFT you into the air. Hang from the pole as you are lifted. At the exact millisecond, your body leaves the ground, you may pop from the knees and ankles, but do not jump.

Jake prayed the windsurfer mast would hold together as he rose into the air. The carbon fibers could be both heard and felt through the shaft as they cracked under the inordinate arc forced upon them. Still, the makeshift pole held as it lifted the body into the air.

As the pole goes perpendicular, two things must happen. You must rotate the pole and push over the bar. Do not push out on the pole. Push STRAIGHT DOWN. This will elevate you over the bar as you rotate in the air.

Too late, Jake realized he needed to rotate. And he pushed out, not down. The sequence that started out so beautifully ended in a botched attempt. At the top of the wall, the momentum stalled as he missed the downward push. Cursing himself as he failed, he got a foot out to push off the white plaster. His hands were inches from the wrought iron, yet knowing it coursed with electricity, he fought off the natural inclination to grab on.

Going down to the tile from twelve feet was going to sting, but the push off the wall diverted his trajectory just enough to roll with the impact. Still, he hit hard enough that the wind was knocked out of him as he took the ground on his left side. Almost blacking out, he heard the mast clank on the tile as it followed him down.

The sound was sharp and definite; if he heard it, the dog did, too.

Knowing he was down to scant seconds, he pushed past the pain and sucked deeply to fill his lungs. Scrambling on all fours, he had the mast back in his hands before he rose to his feet.

Damien's snarling could be heard as he dashed from the front yard toward the drive. Jake thought he detected anger in the growl. The animal was pissed about being duped.

Instinct told him to run away from the sound of a vicious animal coming at him, yet Jake rose and ran toward the oncoming beast, mast in hand.

More space was needed for a second approach at the wall.

In the fading light of the day, he could see the slobber flying off the dog's jowls as he turned with less than thirty feet between them.

Once more he raised the mast and ran at the barrier. As he made his approach, the noise of clicking of the toenails on the tile grew closer with each step. Jake did not look back. He planted the tip of the mast smoothly into the base of the wall. The pole flexed and again groaned with carbon fibers cracking as his body lifted.

Another sound filled the air during his ascent—the distinct snapping shut of the dog's jaws inches below him. The monster had missed.

This time at the apex of the rise he pushed down on the shaft and rotated. At the exact second necessary, he let go of the mast and allowed his momentum to carry him over the charged wrought-iron spikes.

Now up and over, the impact with the road on the other side loomed. Already short of breath, he landed on his feet, bending the knees and buckling into a roll. The abrasive pavement rashed his right forearm first, then his right cheek as he spun over. As he slid to a stop, his Bamboo Cay shirt rose up, the asphalt scraping his lower back.

Jake could both smell and taste blood as he lay still on the road. Finally, flexing his hands and straightening out his arms and legs, he pushed to a sitting position. As he performed a self-triage of his injuries, he heard a whimpering from behind. Turning as he rose, he saw Damien behind the iron bars of the gate.

The dog whined as he pawed at the air between the bars. Jake walked to the gate as he brushed loose pieces of asphalt off his arms. He put out his hand to meet the paw of the dog.

Damien's eyes seemed to be saying 'Good match' as his paw met Jake's palm. As he released the paw and turned away, he heard the sad whimpering of the dog as his playmate left him behind.

With no cars passing by and no prospects of a lift down the hill, Jake flipped the skateboard onto its rubberized wheels and stepped aboard. Years of practice in riding mountain roads back home on the sidewalk surfer were put to use as he descended toward the city of Funchal.

CHAPTER 55

The trio chose the café on the waterfront where they could see the boat. Neither Monk nor Cindi wanted to let the vessel holding the cash out of their sight. They took a corner table and Monk ordered a beer, telling the waitress to keep them coming. Cindi had another glass of boal and Amber sipped a coffee.

Talking quietly, Cindi denied everything. "I can't believe Tom's dead," she said. Sniffles came, but Amber noticed the whimpering was not followed by any tears.

"I have no idea who killed him," Cindi proclaimed. "He told me to wait here with the money, and his meeting with you was to say goodbye and leave your share. He felt it was better we split up at this point. That's what he told me."

"There was no money at the villa," Monk stated.

"Maybe Jake or Stinnetti's hit man took it," she suggested. "Or maybe Tom lied to me, and it's all down there." She pointed to the boat. "I haven't counted it."

She shuddered. "I was lucky Tom sent me down here, or I might be dead too."

During the conversation, Amber noticed Cindi scooted her chair closer to Monk's. *Her old friend was working him.*

Nobody had mentioned multiple bullet wounds, yet Cindi continually referred to the lethal *shots* that killed Tom. And how did the hitman end up at the villa at the exact time of Monk's return? The holes in her story made the yarn sound almost ridiculous. Yet Monk bought it all, blaming Jake and responding to her advances.

Suddenly Cindi bolted upright, stating, "The boat is moving!"

Amber calmed her. "All the boats are bouncing with the waves. The other boats and dinghies running in the harbor are leaving wakes."

"Yeah, it just seemed to be moving more than the others. Just nerves, I guess..." She sat back but kept a wary eye on the cabin door to the boat.

Monk announced, "We gotta get out of here. We'll leave together. I ain't lettin' the money out of my sight."

While not wanting to include the beast in her plans, she had to get him off the island. He'd be a loose end. She could tie that up later, but for now, having him nearby was best.

"We'll take the boat," Cindi announced. "It's provisioned for two passengers. When I checked out with the port captain's office earlier today, there was no passport stamp. So you don't need to check out. Do you have your passport, or is it up at the house?"

"Grabbed it before we came down the hill, along with a bag of my stuff," he answered. "What about the captain? Won't he wonder why I'm here instead of Tom."

"We'll tell him the truth. Some of it, at least. We're leaving Tom behind. We decided to ditch him. With a few thousand extra euros, I think they'll be okay with the change.

"By this time tomorrow, we'll be nearly halfway to Spain."

Another beer for Monk and another wine for Cindi, and the two were planning an itinerary for their landing in Europe. Amber watched the metamorphosis of the relationship in amazement as Cindi cuddled up to the behemoth. Her hand found its way to his shoulder and onto his forearm. She showed what appeared to be genuine concern for his injuries, even mopping his brow with an ice-wrapped napkin. They commiserated on what a lying bastard Jake Cohen was and how his involvement caused all their woes.

The body of Tom Wojicki was forgotten as the two huddled closer in their chairs along the waterfront.

Amber watched with repulsion. Finally, she stood and said, "It looks as though you two have worked this out. Shall we get Jake down?"

The smile on Monk's face turned to a frown and his brow furrowed. He looked at Cindi, then at the closed door on the boat fifty yards away. Her eyebrows raised slightly at the prospect of Monk leaving. Amber caught the slight motion; Monk did not.

He reached into his pocket and withdrew the keys with his remote control attached. "I'm not leaving the money," he growled as he tossed the keys to Amber. "I got everything I need from the house. What I don't got, I'll buy in

Spain. The button with a 'I' opens the gate. The 'II' shuts off the power to the fence. The dog knows you. You'll be fine. He likes chicks. Only hates men."

Cindi took one more shot at disengaging herself long enough to reposition some of the money. She could hide a chunk away that he wouldn't know about. Patting his arm, she said, "She can't handle Damien. Run up the hill and help her. I'll wait for you in the stateroom."

He looked at Amber and then at Cindi. "We'll all ride together," he announced.

Cindi now looked mildly panicked. Her gaze shifted to the boat. "Amber, you can handle the dog. Monk and I need to stay here. There's too much floating out there to leave behind."

"Shit," muttered Amber as she rose. Turning away, she walked to the car. Opening the door and reaching in she withdrew Monk's bag. She dropped it in the lot, got in, and drove off.

On board, Cindi reminded him to duck for the low doorways as she led him to the main cabin of the yacht. Playing along beautifully, she offered a massage as she stripped down to her lacy G-string panties.

Lust had built within as he'd watched Tom have her. The massage had barely begun before desire overcame him and he took her roughly.

When it was over only a few minutes later, he confessed that he'd dreamed of having her for himself for years. She concurred that during the time spent with Tom she too had fantasized what it might be like to feel his muscular body wrapped around hers and she'd longed for his touch. Finally, she proclaimed, they could, at last, be together.

Before dozing off, he checked the closet. The bags were still there, neatly zipped and stacked where they'd left them before going to the café.

Satisfied the money was safe and spent from the battle with Jake and his interlude with Cindi only moments before, Monk Phillips was quickly snoring peacefully in the oversized main stateroom berth.

Slumber, however, did not quickly find Cindi Light. She'd gotten rid of Tom, yet now faced an even more daunting task. How would she ditch the leviathan?

Money fixed things, and she had plenty. Once on the firm ground of

Spain with what equated to over 1.9 million American dollars in euros, she'd say a final goodbye to Monk Phillips, one way or another.

CHAPTER 56
TUESDAY MORNING

The twin 1,100 horsepower Detroit diesel engines spun the propellers on the big Riviera yacht. She pushed through the water at speeds varying from twelve to fifteen knots, depending on whether the boat was climbing the face of a wave or accelerating as it surfed down the backside. The rise and fall became rhythmic as the *Tail Chaser* pounded eastward into the trade winds.

When they'd left the dock at Funchal a few hours ago, the captain had knocked gently on the door and informed Cindi that they were leaving the slip. She said she'd sleep in and join him and his wife topside later. Her eyes never closed after the engines rumbled to life. Monk had stirred but was snoring softly again; she knew he'd slumber a while longer. Coming down from a crystal meth high, he always cashed in on a few hours of extra sleep.

Initially, the ride had been smooth and comfortable as they'd left the harbor. When the trip was booked and paid for, the skipper had explained that once out of what he called the "lee" of the island the ocean would be rough. The trade winds blew through the end of this month and well into April.

His prediction held true as Cindi felt her stomach rise as the boat fell and then sink as the boat climbed over the next mound of undulating water.

Throwing her legs over the side of the bed, her feet found the teak floor. In an upright position, the wave motion was accentuated. Swallowing hard, she knew she needed fresh air. She yanked on the designer warm-up suit she'd worn the night before, then stumbled out the door and down the hall. Once up the short staircase, she saw the salon door to the aft deck and sprinted through, throwing her body over the starboard gunnel and barfing into the water as she hung on to the rail for dear life. She wretched over the side three more times, emptying the contents of her gut into the ocean.

As she leaned over the water, she felt a hand on her back. "You'll be all right in a few hours." Cindi rose to find the captain holding her by the waist-band. He added with a smile, "We don't want you joinin' the fish now."

Wiping her mouth, she looked out at the frothing ocean. It was anything but blue, as the wind whipped the surface and the morning sun reflected off the churned water, she saw only white where the waves crested with dazzling silver in between. The vision only made her feel worse.

"Are we safe?" she muttered.

"Oh, God yes!" laughed the captain. "This would be a *nice* day on the Barrier Reef back home. Miss *Tail Chaser* has seen far worse than this. We're in the worst of it now; as we near the continent we'll see much-improved weather. By tonight even, seas will be 'alf this size."

"If you're down here, who's driving?" Cindi asked as she licked her lips.

"She's on autopilot, but me wife's watchin' from above." He pointed up to the flying bridge. The skipper's wife sat behind the wheel with sunglasses on and her blonde hair in a braid coming through the strap of a baseball cap. "Let's get you inside a moment."

Once in the salon, he seated her quickly on the couch, then opened the windows on the starboard side. "You'd do a bit better with all the windows open, but we're takin' too much water on the port. You're welcome to ride on the bridge if you'd like. Better breeze up there, but the boat rocks a bit more."

Breathing deeply, she answered, "I'm fine here for now. Thanks."

"I take it you won't be wantin' breakfast?"

Shaking her head, she answered, "God, no."

Nodding, he offered, "Might help if you lay down then. Less movement down under, if you get my drift." Pointing to his stomach, he moved all his fingers at once.

"Do you have pills or one of those patches?"

"Pills, we have." He walked to the galley as though there were no waves at all. He withdrew some white pills from a plastic container in the spice rack and brought them to her with a bottle of water. "These will help a bit, but they work better if you take the buggers before you leave the dock. Once you're sick, it's usually too late."

She tossed them in her mouth and swallowed the water behind them. "While I'm waiting for these to kick in, I need to discuss something with you."

"I'm all ears. Go ahead now," said the captain.

"Our plans changed last night. We have another passenger aboard."

The skipper lowered his sunglasses on his nose and asked, "Another passenger?"

"Yes. Our friend, Monk. You've met him at the office."

"The big bloke?"

She nodded.

"I thought the bow was riding a bit heavy this morning." Biting his lip, he said, "We gotta turn back, then. I have to change the crew list with the port captain. You should have told me before we left the dock."

"We don't really have to go back, do we? Can't we just change the list when we get to Spain? Or make a new one?"

He breathed in deeply and exhaled before answering, "No, Ms. Cindi, I 'ave to run by the rules or they'll take my charter permit away. They'd probably never match up the crew list in Spain, but I can't risk my business. They might even impound the *Tail Chaser*. We're turning back."

He stepped toward the salon door.

"I'll pay you 5,000 euros to keep going," she offered.

Stopping, he looked at her for a moment, then cleaned his glasses on his shirt. "You really don't want to go back to that island, do you missie?"

"I'm running away from Tom," she stated. "You've met him. He's a drunk, smokes incessantly, and he's abusive. We all made some money together back home. I took my share, and I'm leaving. You're right; I don't want to go back."

"The big bloke, he's in this with you?"

"Yes. We're leaving Tom behind."

Without looking at her, he examined his glasses. "Doctoring a crew list is serious business. I wouldn't risk it for 5,000."

Cindi knew men, and she was on the right track with this one. It was only a matter of how much now. "How about 10,000?" she asked, trying to sound firm.

Holding his glasses up for another inspection, he said, "Twenty."

"Twenty!" she exclaimed. "That's ridiculous. We've already paid a fortune for this trip."

Now he looked at her directly. "You're asking me to violate international and maritime law. I'm a risk-taker, lass, but the reward has to be worth the jeopardy I'm putting myself and my operation in.

"I'll leave it up to you, but you've gotta make your choice in a hurry. We're not moving forward without the money. I know I'm asking a lot, but it ain't me who's smuggled a passenger aboard and sneaked off the island."

Cindi didn't answer immediately as she evaluated matters. Tom's body likely wouldn't be found for a few days. Twenty thousand euros was unadulterated extortion. The boat was already paid for.

Her lips pursed to give the order to turn back, but she stopped herself. What if the body *was* somehow found? There was still plenty of money to last a long time down below, even if she paid the exorbitant fee for passage.

"Keep going, skipper. We'll pay it," she said with a sigh and a headshake.

"All right, then. Let's have it now," he nodded. "I assume it's in cash."

"Yes, it's cash. That means I have to go back down below, huh?" she muttered with dread at the prospect of going where the airflow was poor and the rise and fall of the boat greater in the bow.

"Yeah. It's best we get this business done. No sense lettin' it linger."

Cindi rose and shot off like a sprinter, planning to grab one of the bags of money and be back topside in only seconds. At the cabin door, she gently pushed it open, trying to not disturb Monk.

"What the fuck's going on?" he muttered from flat on the bed.

"You're awake?"

"Yeah. I'm trying not to move. I stood up once and about puked."

"The skipper says it will start to calm down this evening. I'm sick too, but we need to just live with it."

"If I don't die first. Hell, that might be welcome. Is it any better up top?"

"Maybe. I felt a little less queasy on the deck," Cindi answered. She changed to the subject at hand as she opened the closet. "The captain wants another 20,000 euros to take you on as a passenger."

Sitting up abruptly, Monk hit his head on the ceiling. Cradling his face, he went back down on the bed. "Twenty grand!" he exclaimed. "That son of a bitch is out of his fucking mind. I'm gonna talk to him," He threw his legs over the side of the bed.

Cindi put her hand on his shoulder in mock resistance as he rose with no chance of holding him down. He reached for his pants as he brushed her aside then wiggled in. As he worked in the cramped cabin, she said, "He's adamant, Monk. You're not going to change his mind."

"We'll see about that," he said, shaking his fist in the air. Attempting to pull the polo shirt over his head, he paused and turned a shade of green. Coughing and gagging a few times, he threw the shirt aside and ducked into the connected bathroom, emptying his stomach into the stainless-steel sink. He ran a little water to clear the bowl and splashed some around his mouth to clean off the remnants of vomit.

"It's his boat. We have no choice, honey," she said, purposefully adding the 'honey' to remind him they were now a couple. "We can afford this. We'll have plenty left over."

Licking his lips and taking a swallow of water, he stumbled out of the head and flopped back onto the bed. "Fuck it. Give him the money. I couldn't fight anybody if I had to right now."

Cindi withdrew one of the bags from the closet, setting it next to Monk. As she unzipped it, she froze in horror as she found the interior empty. Quickly she pounced on the other bag and ripped open the zipper to find the interior void of the coveted euros she'd stacked there less than twenty-four hours ago.

"Did you move the money?" she shrieked as she tapped Monk on the shoulder.

He sat up halfway. "No," he answered looking at the bags. Reaching in, he moved his hands around. His face went blank, and his mouth formed a soundless 'O'.

Cindi glared at him as she spat, "What did you do with the money?"

"I didn't touch it. It was there last night."

She began tearing through the closet with both hands, ripping out everything that had been sitting under the canvas bags. The hunt went through the entire master stateroom and the adjoining head.

The euros were nowhere to be found.

Grabbing at his bare shoulders and using her fingernails as claws she yelled into his face again, "What did you do with the money!" She shook him, the nails biting deeper into the flesh of his shoulders.

His right hand flew up, and his ogre-sized fist caught her left cheek. Flying backward into the bulkhead her body thumped against the closed cabin door before crumpling to the floor. She rested there in a fetal position and sobbed softly, more at the shock of the disappearance of the stacks of euros than the blow received.

Again he rose off the bed, this time bending to avoid the low ceiling. "Calm down, you stupid bitch! The money was there last night. I didn't take it. In case you didn't notice, I ain't left the cabin since we got on board," Monk said.

Pulling herself up the bed with her hands, she stood and worked into the head where she again threw up in the sink. She rinsed her mouth. Looking into the mirror at the redness of her cheek, she pushed gently with her fingertips. Convinced the bone was not shattered, she returned and stood by the bed. Breathing deeply she asked, "You're certain it was there last night?"

With his head in his hands, he growled, "Yeah. It was there when we came down from the café." Removing his hands from his face, he thought for a few seconds. "But I only looked to see the bags was there. I never looked inside."

Closing her eyes and shaking her head, she exhaled loudly as she said, "It was that bastard, Jake Cohen."

Shaking his head, he said, "Impossible. We watched the door the whole time we was up there."

Looking up, Cindi saw the round plexiglass hatch above. She reached up and checked the three handles to be certain they were latched. The clasps were secure, and the small gray tab on the bottom was turned to the 'locked' position. Checking each one, she found it turned easily when a minimal amount of force was applied.

The locks on the hatch did not work.

"Whoever it was must have come through this hatch," she stated. "The lock is broken."

He looked at her. Even with his purple-shrouded eyes, the suspicion was evident. "There was nobody on that dock. We'da seen anyone there. You took the money while I was sleeping!" His index finger was extended as he advanced upon her in the small cabin.

The memory of his punch in the face still fresh, she stepped backward with her hands up in front of her.

He quickly reached under her elbows and brought his left hand to grasp her designer sweatshirt where it was zipped to the 'V' above her breasts. Yanking her face close to his he hissed, "The doc's kid was right. You set me up with that hitman, didn't you? It was you who killed Tom, too. You was leavin' me behind. That is, if that little fuck Bennie didn't get me. God, I've been stupid."

With an overhand whack, Monk brought his open hand down across her face. Ducking behind her forearms, she was able to shield herself from the direct impact, yet the power of his three-hundred-plus pounds knocked her to the floor.

He went down with her to one knee, his left hand remaining secure on the polar-fleece fabric of her top. His right hand was raised to deliver another blow.

"That's quite enough, mate!" The voice came from above them. Monk's huge paw hung in the air as he looked up. Hiding behind the arms covering her face, Cindi looked up too.

In the open doorway of the cabin stood the Aussie captain, wielding a Ruger Single Six, a small caliber revolver. It was pointed directly at Monk's chest.

"Don't be a fool, mate. With long loads, this little gem has the power to stop even a big bloke like you."

Monk lowered his hand and stood, releasing the hold on Cindi's sweatshirt.

"What in Christ's name is going on here? When I heard the bang against the door, I grabbed 'Little Betty' and came runnin'. Now I find you poundin' this lass? A big fellow like you, you ought'a be ashamed, mate."

Sitting on the floor, Cindi said, "Someone got in here and stole our money. Must have happened while we were at the café last night."

The skipper rubbed his chin and asked, "What was the fight about, then?"

"He thinks I took it."

Looking at Monk then at her, the captain shook his head, saying, "Does this mean you ain't got the money to pay his passage?"

"I told you, it was stolen last night," Cindi said, looking at the floor dejectedly.

Looking at the empty bags on the bed and the clothing and other items on the floor, he asked, "How much?"

"A lot."

"There was no one on that dock," Monk said shaking his head. "We watched the boat the whole time from the café. She took it. It's here somewhere on this martini shaker you call a boat."

With the gun still leveled the skipper laughed, "Bit of sea has you under, 'ay mate? Big bloke like you, reduced to near nothin.'" He looked at them both and continued without a smile. "Well I don't give a bit of a damn where it is, but if I don't get the fare, we're turning 'round."

Sitting still on the teak flooring with their belongings scattered about, she said, "There's no money. The lock doesn't work on that hatch. He must have come through there." She pointed upward without looking.

The captain looked at the hatch, then at them. "Move into the head a moment," he said to Monk as he motioned with the gun. With the opportunity to be near the sink, Monk made no argument about relocating.

The skipper examined the locking mechanisms for the hatch with his left hand as he kept the gun in his right. Closing the hatch and securing the swing arms he said flatly, "Lock pins 'ave been cut. Had to have been done from inside."

As he slid off the bed, he continued, "There was footprints on the bow this morning when we left. I didn't think nothin' of it, as I was more pissed about the spilled wine in the stern."

Cindi's forehead rested on her hands. "Shit," she muttered.

The captain nodded thoughtfully and said, "Footprints I saw went straight to the anchor. Whoever it was must've come over the bow from the water. Behind the tower and the salon structure you wouldn't have seen 'em from the waterfront."

Cindi shook her head and said dejectedly, "It was Jake. Had to have been."

The skipper asked, "Jake? Curly-haired bloke? Kinda wiry-muscled, and with one eyebrow 'alf grown in? And his face was scratched, I recall."

Looking up, she said, "You've met him?"

"Helped me stow supplies yesterday. Must've jimmied the latches while he worked. Knew just where to cut to make it look like the arms was locked."

Climbing to her feet, Cindi looked directly at the captain and yelled, "You're responsible for this! We chartered this boat, and you're responsible for the safety of our belongings!"

"Well now, let's see... You didn't tell me you was bringin' bags full of money aboard, now did you? Or about a stowaway? This Jake bloke told me he knew boats, and anyone who knows boats can get into one. She's a boat, not a safe.

"And this one is turnin' 'round right now. You can file a complaint with the port captain or the local coppers about your theft if you'd like. This whole thing smells worse than the lowest of tides." He turned and left the cabin.

CHAPTER 57

Isabella had been cleaning the villa for over ten years. Being a long-time employee, she knew the guard dog that patrolled the grounds well. She also had a remote for the gate, which she used, then she drove her car inside.

She parked, patted the dog on the head a few times, and went inside to begin her normal duties. As always, she started with the laundry, so she stripped the bed in the guestroom as she had done close to two hundred times. She piled the sheets in the hall to be picked up on the way to the washing machine and moved, as she'd always done, to the master suite.

Twenty minutes later the *polícias* were there. The *polícias principais*, the chief, held her hand and comforted her as she sipped a brandy poured from the bar. The color had come back to her, and she had valiantly mustered the strength to restrain the Rottweiler for the officers after the shock of finding the body. Between sips of the thick liquor, she told the inspector everything she knew of the residents here.

Americans. Just arrived. Plenty of money. The one living below used drugs; she'd seen his paraphernalia. The dead man, a heavy drinker. Younger girlfriend. Pretty. Sexy, too. Not much else was known. She was paid in cash.

The *polícias principais* had his Public Security Police, or PSP team, thoroughly scour the premises. The island had not seen a homicide in years; crime here was generally limited to pick-pocketing and purse-snatching along the waterfront and near hotels, with the occasional mugging of a tourist. On the rarest of occasions, a star-crossed lover would pull a knife to avenge his or his woman's honor, and someone might get cut or stabbed, requiring an emergency room visit or short stay in the hospital.

Inspector Jorge Calista had enjoyed many years of moderate tranquility as the *polícias principais* on Madeira. The job was not like Jorge's past position in Lisbon. There he dealt with international criminals at all levels. He'd seen his share of hardcore police and investigative work and had had enough of it. The job here offered a state of semi-retirement, and he enjoyed it.

Except for today. Brutal murders took away the serenity he'd attained. Or created. Either way, he now had to do some real police work, and he wasn't happy about it.

Photographs were taken, then the body was bagged and put on ice. With no lab on the island, the corpse and all evidence would be flown to Lisbon for evaluation. The room and house were sealed with yellow caution tape. A forensics specialist would be flown in from the continent to search for more clues. Jorge knew he'd be scolded for his sloppiness at the crime scene, yet he didn't much care. The murder of an American new to the locale was of little importance. Probably on the run from someone and something back home, and that 'someone' had found him.

Before any work on the crime scene, Polícias Principais Calista had called the airport terminal and ordered all departing Americans be searched, and any suspicious characters be detained. Even the slightest thing out of order should be investigated, he'd instructed.

The killing of a foreigner was generally at the hands of another of the deceased's countrymen, and his first act was to cut off the escape route.

On the way down the hill his phone rang. It was a customs official. They already had a suspect in custody. Inspector Calista immediately left to interrogate him.

CHAPTER 58
TUESDAY MIDMORNING AT THE AIRPORT

Amber walked toward the ticketing windows pulling her rolling bag. She didn't have a flight, so she'd likely be on standby. First class would be requested, yet any seat would do.

Upon returning to the villa last night after her less-than-rewarding meeting with Monk and Cindi, she found Damien as the only occupant. Jake had somehow escaped.

At the hotel, his belongings were missing, with a wet towel hanging on the rack. No note, no goodbye.

Amber had slept fitfully, with recurring dreams of being chased and attacked by a Rottweiler. Now she was tired and simply longed to go home.

She prayed silently for a first-class seat. She would have a few glasses of bubbly and comfortably snooze as she found her way back to America.

As the agent worked on the computer, Amber noticed flashing lights and numerous police vehicles about the drop-off areas. "What's going on?" she asked as she pointed toward the commotion.

"Ah, Senhorita Nelson," the man said, "There has been a murder! An American, like yourself, and they have another American in custody." The ticket agent leaned across the desk, and half-whispered, "They caught the killer trying to get a flight out this morning."

Frowning and at the same time nodding, she looked in the direction of the lights and vehicles. The lead car drove away toward town, and the entourage followed.

The agent looked up from the computer screen. "It would appear that we

389

are booked, but you would be first standby. I can nearly guarantee something will open up if you are willing to wait."

Still looking in the direction of the vehicles, Amber stood silently. Her professional side told her to be a good businesswoman and take the first available flight. With the recent infusion of funds, a year had been cut off her scheduled retirement date.

Jake Cohen and his family could fend for themselves. He seemed to be a cat who knew how to land on his feet.

"Senhorita? Would you like for me to book you onto the standby list?" The agent's voice roused her from the deliberations.

Her gaze switched from the departing police vehicles to the airline employee, yet she did not immediately speak. The attendant raised his eyebrows and gestured with an open palm at the computer screen.

"I'll wait for a guaranteed seat. Thank you for your trouble." She pulled her bag away and went to find a taxi, cursing herself as she moved along.

The agent shook his head and muttered in Portuguese about the craziness of women, and Americans.

CHAPTER 59
TUESDAY EARLY AFTERNOON

The skipper backed the *Tail Chaser* into her slip, where *policías* waited on the dock. He'd had the good sense to call in the officials.

It was time to go back to fishing. Put the passengers on the boat, put some fish on the deck, then say goodbye the same day. Two days was the maximum exposure. The lure of the large payment for a charter to the Mediterranean had caused the skipper and his wife to compromise their standards.

All in all, though, this would work out okay. He'd keep their money and send them away. Not bad for a day or two of provisioning and a few hours at sea. Sixty thousand euros made the morning's excitement worthwhile.

From inside the salon, Monk and Cindi looked out at the three officers as they talked to the captain on the dock. There would be nowhere to hide. They would have to face the questions and give answers. The officers stepped aboard, and the captain opened the door.

"Let's go now, you two. Time to hop off," he said with a wave of his hand.

The *policías* stood silently outside on the deck. Cindi looked at Monk, who returned a blank gaze. She nodded toward their bags, and Monk picked them up. She asked the captain, "Why are the police here?"

Lifting his baseball cap, he ran his fingers through his coarse hair then nodded in Monk's direction. "Don't want no trouble with King Kong here. Told them the truth. We had a charter that went bad, and my wife and I thought there might be a row. These men are just here to make certain you leave peacefully."

With a nod, Cindi squinted and said, "I want a refund of the charter fee."

Replacing his baseball cap, the skipper said thoughtfully, "Well now, let's see… These officers tell me there's been a murder. Up in the hills. An American. Tom Miller was his name. Imagine that! My original passenger…

391

They've got the bloke responsible. They think anyway. I think maybe they've got the wrong bloke. If you want to raise a fuss about a cockamamie charter fee, I think we'll enlighten those men on deck as to the original charter plans and passenger change."

He let the threat sink in before he continued. "Or we can all keep our mouths shut. The description of the suspect they have matches the man who I'd guess jimmied the locks on the hatch. It'd do my heart a bit of good to see him locked up for a time. Messin' with a man's boat is the same as messin' with a man's wife.

"I'd suggest you hop off now and never come 'round again." The captain gave a thumb signal toward the door.

Monk started to say something, but Cindi cut him off. "Let's go." She left and marched past the officers on the deck outside the cabin. Monk followed her, uttering a final "Fuck!" as he hit his head on the cabin door while leaving.

Cindi Light's plans for a quick exit off the island had changed. The knowledge that Jake Cohen was still here would keep her around for a day or two at least. Certainly, it was about the money, yet now it had become personal.

While cleaning out the cash, he'd grabbed her thumb drive too, on which she had the video she planned to use as an annuity.

He'd made a fool of her, and the seed of vengeance had taken root.

CHAPTER 60

Polícias Principais Calista had, during his storied career, solved numerous international crimes while on the European mainland. Terrorist cells had been dissolved as a result of his investigations. With bold intervention into planned acts of mayhem, he'd saved hundreds, even thousands of lives throughout Western Europe. Once, while following a trail of clues leading to the capture of the leader of a terrorist cell, he happened upon the island of Madeira.

With the terrorist neutralized, Calista brought his bride of thirty years back to the island. He covered the trip with the façade of a vacation, his true intention being to allow her to become captivated with the simplicity and warmth the island offered. The ruse worked; she was enthralled as they'd lunched in the heart of old Funchal and explored the vineyards above the city.

The best police officers do not wait for things to happen; rather they set in motion events to bring about their desired result. Calista had befriended the local *polícias principais* upon his initial visit and found the young man a reflection of himself thirty years ago. The man felt stifled and wasted as an officer on this rock, far from the action of international intrigue in Europe.

Within a few months the young lion officer from Madeira had a position with Interpol and the old cat Calista was the new leader of the island *polícias*.

The transition had been years ago, and it had worked out well. Jorge was comfortably quelling the criminal activity of the city and the island. He'd been enjoying the semi-retirement the job offered, and the island enjoyed him. From a law enforcement standpoint, the islands of Madeira were running agreeably well.

Until today...

The evidence had been flown to the mainland for analysis. There was nothing to do but wait, and most officers would have done just that. However, Jorge Calista was not made of the mettle of most officers. With his suspect safely behind bars, he brought Jacob Cohen's belongings into his office. Pouring himself a cup of thick coffee, he removed the tablet computer from its case and turned it on. While the machine booted up, he opened the wallet of the prisoner.

The usual pictures of mom and dad. Brother and sisters. A strikingly beautiful young woman. Driver's license and one corporate credit card. Nothing startling. Opening the billfold, he found a few hundred euros and a few hundred in American currency. Between the bills, however, he found the cards of two American police officers. He tossed those on his desk and put the wallet aside. Then he ran a search on the now-ready computer and sorted the documents by history of creation or modification. Printed pictures were taken from the case and reviewed, and a thumb drive was inserted into the tablet's USB port.

Calista read and spoke English fluently, and as he opened the most recently modified documents, he picked up his cup and began deciphering the text. It was early afternoon, and he hoped the coffee would keep him from napping as he sat alone in his office. It was always mildly embarrassing when one of his officers found him asleep in his chair.

Five hours later, Calista appeared outside Jacob Cohen's cell. The day was fading, and the light streaked from the barred windows at the western end of the building. The *polícias principais* inserted a key in the lock and swung the door open. He brought a stool in from outside and sat upon it, facing the prisoner who was flat on the bunk.

"What's up?" questioned Jake without rising.

"I wish to talk with you. Sit up, please."

"Do I have to? You have no idea how much pain I'm in."

Calista laughed, "Yes, you have to. I wish to see your eyes as we speak. A man's eyes sometimes tell more than his words."

"Won't do you much good. Mine are swollen shut. Nearly anyway," offered Jake as he rolled into a sitting position.

Nodding the chief said, "You look bad, but I've seen much worse. You'll live."

"You should see the other guy," groaned Jake as he stood and walked to the sink, washing his face with cold water and rubbing gently around the eyes to break up the crud formed from the fluids discharged by the swelling. After drying his mug, he turned and looked at the chief through the puffiness. "Aren't you taking a big chance, being alone in a cell with an alleged killer? With the door open, too?"

Laughing again the officer said, "I have been told this afternoon by three people that you are not dangerous. Two of them were police officers. Are you a killer?"

"No. With whom did you speak?"

"A sheriff from what he says is a little town in Nevada in America. Then a detective from Southern California. Both said you were not likely a killer."

"You said you spoke to three people."

Calista smiled. "Oh yes. The third was a woman. Extraordinarily beautiful. She stopped by, and we chatted for nearly an hour. Her lips formed words, but it was her eyes that convinced me she was telling the truth. Those eyes also carried wounding."

"Is she okay?" Jake asked with concern in his voice.

"Yes. She will be fine. Sometimes it is the wounding of the heart that is most devastating. Yet Ms. Nelson seems in control. Quite a lady, in my estimation.

"I read the notes in your computer. Those match up to her story, for the most part. Also, I read the online articles of your father's beating and the disappearance of the funds from his building company. The detective I talked with has verified the account. The small-town sheriff described a man who matches the description of the victim here, a drunken gambler with ties to a—how do say it? Loan shark? He believes this man was killed by the employee of that loan shark, and not likely by you.

"The woman who stopped by concurs. The shooter employed by the loan shark was here on the island. I checked her description of the man with the sheriff, and it matches. Everything checks out, with a few minor holes to fill.

"In your bag, there is a thumb drive containing a movie of a young woman having sex with a man. Older. The man does not seem to know he was on camera. I'm guessing the movie was used for blackmail. Is this your father?"

"No. It's my father's banker."

"Ahhh," Calista said with a nod. "The man from your notes."

"So?"

"It means there is enough doubt of your guilt for me to release you. Temporarily, until the evidence results come back from Lisbon in a few days. I have also spoken with our forensics expert there, unofficially. The gun was covered with fingerprints, from a much larger hand than yours. He did, however, find prints matching yours on the ammunition clip inserted in the weapon." Calista's eyes locked on Jake as he made the revelations.

"Additionally, our laboratory found burned powder residue, along with dried blood and saliva of the victim on a shirt taken from your bag. The technician scraped some skin particles from under the victim's fingernails. Early results on that analysis match the DNA on the sample we scraped from inside your cheek this morning. The scratches on your face are from the hands of the deceased?"

Jake said nothing, silently cursing himself for not wiping down the clip of the weapon.

Calista nodded with satisfaction that his question had been answered and went on. "At the villa, we found a piece of fabric in the driveway that matches a shirt found in the rubbish can of your hotel room. That shirt has been sent to Lisbon too for analysis."

Jake rubbed his chin as he thought of Damien and the bite that nearly got him as he'd scrambled into the rafters. Calista laughed again.

"I'm glad you find humor in my predicament."

Still smiling, the *polícias principais* said, "In my business, you must learn to believe your comrades. I trust the opinions of the two American officers who say you are likely not guilty. And I trust the eyes of the woman who spoke to me on your behalf.

"Yet, in my business, we must also trust the evidence. You may spend a good deal of the rest of your life behind bars in Portugal if found guilty."

"So, which do you believe? My confidantes, or the clues?" asked Jake.

Calista put his elbows on his knees and his fingertips together, resting his chin on the point where the index fingers met and offered, "I don't—as you say in America—give a shit. Americans killing Americans over problems in America is a complete waste of our time. My life would be easier without you."

Now it was Jake who sat trying to read the face of the man sitting in front of him.

The chief went on, "The evidence is not yet official, nor has it been returned. If that evidence comes back, I will have to hold a trial. A motive exists, and the facts will support a conviction. Presently though, *officially* we have no evidence. With three vouching for you, I can release you on your own recognizance.

"But if you are still here when the forensic tests are returned, you will be tried and convicted."

Realization took hold. *The officer wanted him off the island.* He felt dense for not picking up on the hints. He stood. "So, I'm free to go?"

"Yes. The packaged lab results will be sent from Lisbon midday, the day after tomorrow. I have circulated to the airport security office your photograph and your name. You cannot leave by plane, and I have alerted the ferry and cruise ship terminals to hold you.

"Officially, I'm telling you *not* to leave Madeira. Also, officially, for the record, I must close the obvious escape routes," said Calista as he rose. "Again, the officers I spoke with told me you were industrious, and both concurred that if I released you, you'd likely slip away. Quietly.

"I trust the words of these men." He held an open palm to the cell door.

"Your belongings are on the table in the entry. Remember, if you are still here you will be officially arrested and charged in less than forty-eight hours."

As Jake walked past the officer, he extended his hand, saying, "I'll need less than twenty-four."

Jorge took it and smiled. "Please, no more trouble on my island home."

Jake nodded, released the grip, and started down the cell block toward freedom. Calista's voice stopped him.

"Mr. Cohen, one last thing. When I spoke to the sheriff, I grew to like him very much. His demeanor was much like a character of a Western movie from your country. He offered to take me hunting for elk. Tell him I will take him up on that offer, and that he is welcome to come here and fish with me. He will catch the biggest fish of his life. I guarantee it. But he may not keep a trophy, as I practice catch and release whenever possible."

Jake nodded and smiled as he said, "I'll let Sheriff Fred know you'll be joining him. I appreciate your sportsmanship, Principais Calista." He tapped his forehead in a salute then disappeared from the cell block through the doorway.

CHAPTER 61

Moments after Jake left the jail, Calista was in his office tidying up before going home. Just as he turned off his desk lamp and pulled on his light coat, an officer tapped on the open door. He informed the chief two Americans wished to see the prisoner. Jorge told the officer to send them in.

Less than a minute later, the officer showed the couple through the door. Now sitting behind his desk, Calista waved to the chairs on the other side with his open palm.

"You must be the other guy," the chief stated as he looked at the black eyes and puffy nose of Monk Phillips.

"What?" grumbled the big man.

"Never mind," laughed Calista before turning to Cindi. "I have spent a long day here. Much of it looking at video and pictures of you, Ms. Light."

"My name is...," Cindi realized quickly that pronouncing herself to be Cindi Miller would immediately associate her with the victim. "Cindi. Please, call me Cindi."

"Yes, Cindi. Tell me, what can I do for you?"

"We wish to see the man you have in custody."

"Why?" The *policías principais'* eyes narrowed and bore upon her.

"We wish to talk to him," she said.

"This young man seems to have a way with women; so many want to talk with, or about, him," laughed Calista.

"What?" Cindi Light asked.

The chief's eyebrows rose as he stated, "You are the second beautiful American woman who has visited here today."

"Amber..." Cindi bit her lip. *She was still here.* Was she in on the theft of the money? She had been the one to suggest the café last night.

"Why yes, that *was* her name," Calista said in mock surprise. "Amber. She said the man I had in custody was not guilty, that another American on the island killed Mr. Miller. What do you know of this killing?"

"We know nothing of the incident. We just wish to see the man you have in custody."

"Why?" The chief's eyes were still locked on hers.

"We only met him a few days ago. He seemed like a nice guy. We just want to find out what happened, and if there is anything we can do to help."

"Did you kill Thomas Wojicki?" Calista's question was sudden. Cindi was blindsided but recovered quickly.

"No. I don't even know a Thomas Wojackstone, or whatever his name is."

Watching her reaction, the seasoned officer stated, "A man was killed here yesterday. The man taken into custody in connection with that killing possesses photographs of you with the victim. The deceased's name was Thomas Miller; however, we believe his name in America was Wojicki. The photos, Cindi, are a tie between you and the dead man."

"Am I being questioned as a suspect? If so, I'd like to have an attorney present."

"You came to see me, Ms. Light. You are free to leave at any time."

Cindi squinted at Calista. "May I see the prisoner?"

"He has been released. Only a few moments ago, actually."

"What! You let a murderer go free?"

"I thought you said he seemed a 'nice guy.' Now you're calling him a killer?" Cindi answered, "Men are often not what they seem, Inspector."

"Nor are women," Calista answered. "Mr. Cohen has been ordered to not leave the island. In a few days, evidence will be returned, and he will either be charged or set free. Part of that evidence is a gun. There were fingerprints on it from a very large hand. Could those be yours?" He looked at Monk.

Monk fidgeted in his chair, saying nothing. Cindi rubbed her chin as the chief sat back with his hands folded across his slightly round belly.

"We're done here," she said as she stood. Monk didn't stand right away, but a rap of her knuckles against his shoulder roused him. "Thank you, Inspector. We'll be going."

"Please do. The makeup does not hide the bruise on your cheek any more than the expensive clothing you wear hides who and what you are, Ms. Light. There is a tie to you and the victim of a murder; I should lock you up now. You and your friends have caused havoc in our quiet city. I would ask that you take your problems and go back to America. Any more trouble, with any one of you, and I will lock all of you up. For a long time."

Saying nothing, she stepped out. Monk followed.

The police chief rose and walked out after they cleared the lobby. Any lingering doubts of Jacob Cohen's guilt had evaporated when Calista had looked into the eyes of Cindi Light. In those eyes, he saw treachery and the burning of unfinished business. He also saw the coldness of a killer.

Closing his door behind him, he hoped they would all go away, and he could continue to fade away into retirement, peacefully.

CHAPTER 62

Amber Nelson and Jake Cohen were hiding somewhere on this island. Cindi had checked the outgoing flights, and no planes had departed which would have given them an exit last night. They spent much of this morning and afternoon at the airport, watching the gates and drop-off zones.

Last night after leaving the *polícias* station, they'd roamed the haunts of Funchal. Cindi found a computer store and paid a few euros to print photos of Amber she had on her phone and of Jake she found on the internet. They presented the images wherever they went. Bartenders, waiters, cab drivers, and counter help at nearly every bar and café in town had images of both. None they met had seen them. Cindi wrote her number down on each page and offered a reward.

The hunted had turned into the hunters, and they were having no luck. Until just after three p.m.

Outside the arriving flights gate, Cindi stuck her head inside a cab in the line for trips to the city and had her first break. The driver had transported the woman in the photo yesterday. He couldn't remember where initially, but when offered twenty euros, his recollection skills improved slightly. When the twenty turned into fifty, he became downright clairvoyant.

The woman was staying at Reid's Palace. He'd taken her there yesterday and waited while she'd booked a room and checked in. After the stop, he'd driven her to the police station and waited there for an hour before taking her back to the hotel.

After rounding up Monk, they were off to Funchal's finest hotel in the same cab that had transported her friend yesterday. Cindi prayed they would not pass one another fifty feet apart on the road as they traveled, with her prey arriving at the airport at the same time they arrived at the majestic Reid's Palace.

The workout felt good. Amber had stretched slowly but deliberately, then hit the machines for an hour of working her upper and lower body. Fifty laps in the pool topped off the routine.

Now it was off for a quick rinse in the shower followed by a massage before dinner. Reid's Palace would be a great place to unwind from the stresses of this escapade. The pace Jake set had been blistering. Changes between time zones were ignored, and they'd relaxed only on a few occasions. Even in those brief downtimes, they'd been planning, compiling data, analyzing, and considering their next move. It would be good to take two days here for personal rebuilding.

With the substantial injection of dollars into her accounts, she'd pamper herself before heading home. Perhaps tonight she would even order something deliciously sinful at dinner.

Anger had stopped her from seeing Jake while at the jail yesterday, her pride damaged at his rejection. It was extremely rude on his part to not give the courtesy of closure.

She thought about it as she wrapped the plush robe around her and headed from the showers to the spa. *Men.* They could be counted on for one thing. *Nothing.* On second thought, they actually could be counted on to do the exact *wrong* thing, especially in a woman's time of need. Jake had lived up to the expectations of his gender.

Yet despite *his* lack of caring, he was in trouble, and she would not abandon him.

She'd gone back to the station this morning, surprised to find Jake released. They'd also let her know that he'd been informed of her visit. Another sign that he wanted finality; he hadn't asked of her whereabouts.

Her instinct told her that he'd be okay, and she'd convinced herself that her staying on here was a personal choice to enjoy the island. In actuality, the choice was based on her desire to see that no harm came to him, but she would never admit it.

Until Amber knew Jake was safe, she wasn't going anywhere.

As she walked from the workout facility to the spa and adjusted the turban she'd fashioned, she stopped abruptly upon seeing a familiar face. The look she received was one of pure malice.

Cindi Light rose out of a chair and blocked her path. "Where is my goddamn money?"

"Well hello to you, too," replied Amber evenly. "Shouldn't you be somewhere near Spain about now?"

"You and that asshole took my money, and I want it back!" Cindi growled.

"Shouldn't that be 'our' money? Or have you already cut Monk from your team?"

"He's outside looking for you, too. And how I deal with him is none of your business. I want that fucking money back. Where's Jake?"

Amber smiled slightly. She didn't know exactly how he'd done it, but somehow Jake had commandeered the cash.

If Jake had acquired the money, she was due her percentage. The prospect of tracking him down to claim her share suddenly gave her a renewed vitality. *This was not over.* She now had a reason to keep looking for him.

"Get that smirk of satisfaction off your face!" Cindi snarled.

Amber stepped to pass her in the hall and said, "If you'll excuse me, I have a massage appointment." Cindi grabbed her arm and spun her abruptly to a stop. Amber's jiu jitsu training kicked instantly into gear, and she caught her assailant's wrist, twisting the arm up behind her back and stepping forward to jam the unsuspecting woman into the wall outside the spa door. Cindi kicked viciously backward once, catching Amber on the shin with the heel of her sandal. Amber countered with a twist upward on the wrist from the elbow she held. The kicking stopped as pain shot up Cindi's left arm into her shoulder.

Amber whispered into her ear, "I'm the one who's supposed to be getting a massage, but if you'd like I can *give* you one. Hard or soft. Your choice."

"Let me go, you fucking bitch!"

"Cindi dear, I feel like the love is gone from our relationship." She let Cindi go free. Peeling herself off the wall, she rubbed her upper arm and elbow as she glared at Amber.

"Now, that's better behavior," declared Amber. "To tell you the truth, I don't know what has happened to the money, but I daresay it's not yours. I don't have it, I didn't know you'd lost it, and I've not seen Jake in nearly two days. The most important thing on my mind right now is my massage, so if you'll excuse me, I'll be off."

She walked past Cindi. Turning back, she said, "If you wish to discuss this topic, please join me for dinner tonight. I expect you to be civil. The Dining

Room at Reid's is beyond the behavior you've exhibited here. We'll meet in the lobby at, say, seven thirty?"

Flexing her fingers, Cindi answered sarcastically, "See you there, old pal."

"Please dress appropriately." Amber winked at her and walked into the spa.

She didn't relish the prospect of dining with Cindi, but she needed to know how much money had been taken. An accurate billing would be necessary to present to Jake when she finally caught up with him.

CHAPTER 63

The Dining Room at Reid's Palace was everything that would be expected in a castle. The patrons were beautifully attired if not wholly beautiful. While no membership card existed, it was a club reserved for the matured wealthy.

As her chair was scooted under her shapely bottom by the attendant, Amber decided she, and the two others at the table, would never be part of the club. Their dinner this evening and her stay at the hotel was on a visitation pass. It could be purchased short-term, but membership was off limits. That was okay; her clientele included members of the 'old-money' group, and she knew first hand of the conjured demons that tormented the mega-rich.

Social grace filled the air from the epaulets on the shoulders of the maître d's tuxedo to the guests and the European flair they carried. Except at her table.

Monk sat awkwardly in a velvet chair far too small for his massive frame. The restaurant had attempted to provide him with a jacket; however none would fit his bulky shoulders. They made an exception to allow him in without proper attire, yet he was the only male in the room in shirtsleeves without a jacket and tie. His battered face did not lend to the environs either. He looked like a Brahma bull grazing with the gazelles. Nobody dared stare. However, the entire room felt his presence.

Cindi looked the part. One of her recent wardrobe acquisitions was a satin black strapless gown. She'd had the wrinkles pressed out and wore it low. Gray pearls circled her flawless neck and matching spheres dangled from sterling silver wire beneath her ears. She removed her black mesh shawl and placed it on the back of her chair revealing tanned and toned shoulders. After her scuffle with Amber, she'd freshened up, wishing she could have had her hair done but doing an adequate job on her own, allowing it to flow down the back of her neck with the bangs waved back lightly and held by spray.

Amber, too, was clad in a black gown, although hers was not cut quite so low in the front but with a diving back, exposing the sway of her spine and the curvature inward to her flat tummy then out again over the rump. Black and gold sequins covered the portion above the waist in the front. She wore no jewelry save her earrings and a thin gold watch. The fabric of the dress was gathered to expose her figure, and although not as revealing of her bosom as her dinner partner's, the gown carried a style that made a one-word statement. *Wow.* Her raven hair was styled up off her shoulders, gathered loosely underneath and falling over the collection point to frame her face.

Even without the giant at the table Cindi and Amber would have silently made their presence known in the room. With him, the low chatter of the guests at many of the tables was conjecture as to who these women were.

'They must be actresses, and the big man is their bodyguard.' 'No, they are sisters of one of Europe's most prestigious families.' 'I distinctly heard them speaking English, and not of the continental accent. They are Americans, and they must be models.'

The only thing anyone agreed upon was the fellow with them was their protector. Neither of the gorgeous females showed any interest in him romantically. From a distance, nobody could see the makeup covering the bruised cheek of the blonde.

After ordering a double appetizer of escargot, a bottle of Pouilly Fuisse and salads of endive leaves filled with bleu cheese, foie gras, and port-soaked walnuts, they selected entrées. Monk was more concerned with portion size than culinary wizardry and bought the largest cut of beef available. Cindi selected Icelandic cod en croute. Amber chose stacked diver-harvested scallops piled with wild baby mushrooms and a sherry cream sauce. As the waiter finished taking their order, Amber suggested that she and Cindi each try a cup of lobster bisque between the salad and the entrée.

After the wine was poured and pleasantries exchanged, they lowered their voices, leaned a bit closer together, and began talking business.

Amber planned to find out how much money Jake had gotten away with.

Cindi believed Amber was connected to the theft. The blonde held her anger in check, yet her vehemence percolated through curbed vocalizations.

Monk sat listening, comprehending the spoken words but missing any underlying meaning or innuendos.

Cindi recounted their discovery of the missing funds while at sea. Upon completing the account of what transpired, including a derisive narrative on *Polícias Principais* Calista (whom Amber found to be delightful), Cindi dabbed at the remaining garlic sauce on the escargot platter with French bread (Monk had devoured the entire appetizer instantly) and nibbled.

The one piece of information that did not arise during the chronicle was the amount of money Jake had reclaimed. Amber knew Cindi was being careful to not divulge the sum.

The ladies had daintily worked on their salads. Monk devoured his, wiping down the china with the bread. They exchanged looks of disgust as he slurped and smacked his lips during the process. Each silently implored a higher power to help him abstain from picking the plate up and licking it clean. Thankfully, the attendant snatched the platter away before an embarrassing incident arose.

The lobster bisque was next, with each fine china cup placed in front of the dinner guest. However, before they could sample the potage, a young second attendant stumbled ever so slightly as he poured wine, knocking the cup of red-orange cream infused with tasty crustacean into Cindi's lap with the base of the bottle. Her napkin and the dress protected her thighs from being badly scalded. However, she jumped up from her chair instantly, a look of disbelief on her face.

The patrons in the dining room all looked in her direction, some even being so bold as to turn their heads but most simply using the shift in their eyes to take in the incident. *Really! We'd think you common folk could behave with civility when visitation is allowed.*

"Madame, *eu sou assim pesaroso para meu* clumsiness," said the attendant as he stepped back.

As the head waiter arrived, Cindi's eyes bore viciously into the offending young man. He shrank into the plush carpet. The lead server calmly snatched the bottle from the hand of the horrified underling, and with a nod, dismissed him. Turning, he placed the wine back on the table and said to Cindi, "Madame, if you will come with me, we will remedy this mishap. In a few moments, it will be as though nothing happened." Reaching out, he took her hand gently and stepped toward the foyer.

Cindi looked back at the table in disbelief as the floor captain led her away. She wanted to resist, but social correctness moved her forward and away from Monk and Amber.

The seemingly clumsy second attendant folded a hundred-euro note into his wallet. In the center of the bill was a kiss of burgundy lipstick in the exact shape of Amber Nelson's lips.

"Well, Jake sure put the screws to all of us, didn't he?" Amber said with a head shake as she focused on Monk. He'd lifted the cup of bisque off the table and was scouring the bottom with the bread. Stuffing the red-orange-coated crust over his lips, he didn't hesitate to speak, crumbs flying like meteorites from his mouth in Amber's direction.

"Son of a bitch is in for an ass-whipping when I catch him," he managed to spit around the lump on his tongue. A meaty hand came up, and a massive index finger bobbed at Amber as he continued, "I know you think he won when we fought. He just got lucky; it won't happen again. Fucker's toast." Shaking his head, he tore off another piece of bread and wiped again at the cup.

"Man, is this shit good or what?" he said while licking his fingers loudly. "Best damn food I've ever had."

"Yeah, it is. Too bad you're going to have to give up this lifestyle, now that Jake took your money," she commiserated. "How much did he get?"

Monk's lips pursed. He became edgy in his seat.

"Would you like a beer?" Amber asked. "You don't look like a white wine fellow to me."

Crossing his arms, he leaned back and visibly relaxed. "Yeah, I *would* like a beer. *She* told me not to have any, but this crap tastes like grape syrup poured over a barn door."

Amber gave a quick wink to their server. He moved over, and she placed the order. "Beer is on the way." She reached out and patted his hand. He looked satisfied and more content.

"You're a hell of a lot nicer than she is," Monk said in a contemplative growl. "Just as pretty too, although she might have a better rack."

"Well, thank you," answered Amber, ignoring the fact that her bosom had just been relegated to a lesser status. She changed the subject. "Too bad about the money. I guess a million each would have gone a long way."

"I wish it was a million," he said before draining half of the delivered beer in one pull. Amber again caught the eye of the server and pointed at his glass with a nod. "You didn't get a million each?"

"Naah. Wasn't that much. It was a lot though. Would'a lasted a long time," he said as he emptied the glass. The backup beer arrived in the nick of time.

"You know, Jake cheated me too. Owes me a bundle. Maybe more than he got from you." Casting them both as victims, she hoped to gain an edge.

"I doubt that. How much does he owe you?"

Her lips now pursed in a flirtatious smile. The eyes twinkled magically, and she patted his arm. "No. You go first. Then I'll tell."

She'd turned it into a playful game. Men were so easy to trick.

"Nine hundred, fifty thousand, give or take," he said proudly. "And I plan on getting it back or beating that amount of shit out of him when I catch the fucker."

"Wow. That's more than he owes me. So, your share was $475,000?"

He took a long pull on beer number two, then answered, "Nope. Nine fifty was my share, though I never really counted it. Cindi just said there was 1.9 mil in the bags."

He looked at Amber and felt a need to defend himself. "I was gonna count it. Bastard just got it before I could. How much does he owe you?"

"One hundred ninety thousand."

"Still a lot, but not as much as me," he said with slight pride that his amount was higher. "So, how we gonna get it back?"

Uh oh, thought Amber. He used the word 'we' far too easily. This was a connection that needed to be broken quickly.

"He's gone, I think. I'm going to forget about it, and go home," Amber announced

"This was supposed to be my home. Now I got no place to go and no money," he said forlornly. It was the first bit of feeling she'd seen in him. Although it was self-pity, it made her slightly sad. "I reckon there's a warrant out on me in the States for roughin' up the doc. Maybe for the money thing, too. That asshole Tom got me into this, and then that fucking Jew doctor had to stop by the office that night. It all went to shit right there."

Amber's compassion instantly evaporated. Dr. Cohen probably was still lying in a hospital bed eating through a tube, and Tom Wojicki was flat too, wrapped in plastic and cold as ice in a coroner's cubby. This crass idiot had no regret.

Cindi arrived back at the table looking no worse for the incident. The eye-catching dress she wore showed no signs of the bisque that splattered on it and her hair and makeup were as if she'd just arrived. Her eyes instantly locked on the empty beer glass on the table then bore into Monk. All six feet five inches of him shrunk as she stared down with utter disdain.

Amber interjected, "They do a good job here. You look stunning. Let's have them get another cup of bisque and start over."

"No, fuck the soup," Cindi said as she sat. The attendant who placed the linen napkin in her lap raised an eyebrow slightly. "Let's cut the crap and get down to business. That's what it's about with you, isn't it, Amber? All business. How much are Jake and his family paying you for helping?"

Amber let the server leave before answering. "No, Cindi, it is not just about business. It was at first, but I've seen now what the lust for money can do to people. And I've felt the real world outside our business. I baked cookies, with an apron on, and went to Bible study with Jake's mom. I liked it, and I like them. I visited his father in the hospital, too. It was unimaginable that you could be involved in something like that." She shook her head.

"What I'm doing is a good thing; I'm helping right a wrong. You used to be…," she paused searching for a word, ". . . nice. You're not nice anymore."

With her eyes, half-closed Cindi retorted in an even voice, "The world's not nice, Amber dear. Live with it. That cozy kitchen where you plopped dough onto the Teflon sheets isn't as warm as you think; it is full of judgment and hypocrisy. I didn't come here tonight to talk about philosophy or my shortcomings; I came to find Jake Cohen and my money."

"It's *our* money, Cindi," Monk corrected her.

Looking at him, she nearly spat, "Whatever." Then she looked back at Amber. "We made a deal. He broke it. Now I think he's screwed you, too, hasn't he?"

Picking up her wineglass Amber twirled the golden French liquid, then finally answered, "Yes, he's screwed me, too. I was to get ten percent of whatever we got back. But he's gone and didn't pay up." Purposefully, she didn't mention that she'd already received her initial stipend.

Cindi's arms crossed, and her head shook as she said, "You bitch. How dare you sit in judgment of me? You sold me out. For money."

Amber's looked directly into Cindi's eyes. "No. The money was secondary. I was trying to save you. From prison, from Tom, or the troubles you now have. But now I can see you're beyond saving." She took a long pull of wine.

"Well, thanks for the favor," Cindi spat.

A team of servers arrived with their entrées on a silver cart. The scallops were presented with the sherry cream sauce, flambéed tableside, and poured over the stacked mushrooms. Monk's filet mignon was sliced and covered with a flaming brandy sauce as well. He looked forlornly at the portion size on his plate.

Simultaneously, as the conflagrations on Amber and Monk's plates dwindled, Cindi's cod was placed before her, and the silver cover lifted off to reveal a gorgeous fillet of North Atlantic deep-water fish covered by a broiled potato glaze.

"What? No fire for me?" Cindi asked the waiter jokingly.

"If there's a God, he'll take care of that when you meet him," Amber chided. She lifted her wineglass and tipped it toward Cindi and Monk. "Let's enjoy our entrées. Quickly, that our paths might part."

"I'll drink to that," said Cindi with a nod.

Rather than joining in the toast, Monk started in on his filet mignon, devouring half of the cut in one bite. With his mouth full he worked out, "Man, is this shit good!"

Closing her eyes, Cindi pinched the top of her nose and shook her head slowly in repulsion. Amber smiled and again tilted the wineglass toward them, this time offering, "May your union be eternal. You deserve each other."

With her eyes still closed, Cindi said, "Shut up and eat."

Amber did just that, deciding the scallops stacked high with the baby mushrooms and sherry sauce might just be the finest thing ever to pass her palate.

Monk waited in longing while the plates were cleared. He'd finished in two bites and sat hungrily by as Cindi and Amber had lingered longer than he'd preferred over their seafood entrées. He took a pull at what was now his fourth beer, trying to quell his appetite with the golden-amber liquid.

Just as their head server was about to offer a choice of sauternes, ports, brandies, and desserts, someone called out from behind.

"Why hello, Amber! What a pleasure to see you again!"

Not recognizing the voice, Amber turned. An older man in a navy blue one-button dinner jacket, white cotton pants with three-inch blue whales embroidered randomly, and a red ascot tucked in over a white silk V-neck T-shirt stood before her. His mostly salt-colored hair was thinning but lightly gelled, looking as though it had been recently windblown and forced involuntarily into an unnatural position. Amber pictured the fellow with a firm grip on a steering wheel in the cockpit of a sailboat, the gusting breeze blowing salt spray past his leathery tanned face and a tight smile.

The woman at his side had the tanned skin too, but her features were softer. Even at what Amber guessed was an age well over sixty, her green eyes sparkled, and she carried an elegance that fit the locale. Her hair streaked of blonde-red and gray was longish and not styled, but rather pulled up and back into a ponytail with a tie of a wide silk band of red and navy alternating stripes. She wore a navy dress, and a light six-button jacket of what Amber guessed was white silk over a cotton sailcloth smock of red and white vertical stripes open at the neck.

Their nautical regalia was light and carefree yet somehow fit the elegance of the Dining Room with a quirky statement made boldly yet silently. 'We belong, but we will not conform.' Both were thin and fit; not muscled from workouts in the weight room, but instead toned from the rigors of labor on a boat and likely many hours on tennis courts and golf courses.

Cindi and Monk sat in bewilderment at the couple's appearance and their recognition of Amber. Catching on to the lapse of etiquette, Amber stood and made introductions.

"Cindi and Monk, this lovely couple is John and Grace. Jake and I met them at breakfast here a few days ago."

"Ah, such a lovely young lady," John said as he took Cindi's hand and kissed it lightly. "And you, sir, look like you should be playing for my Dolphins back home." He shook Monk's hand with vigor. The big man said nothing.

"A pleasure to meet you both," offered Grace as she alternately shook each of their hands.

"John and Grace are in the process of sailing from Miami through the Mediterranean. They've been at it nearly a year and a half. They're on their way home now. The last leg of their sail," recounted Amber.

"If only what you said were true," said John sadly with a headshake.

Amber's eyes widened. Her questioning look shifted to Grace. "Why, I thought you knew," she said. "We've sold the boat. We'll be flying home in a few days."

"But how would I have known you sold…," Amber's voice trailed off. She suddenly knew who the purchaser of the yacht was, and she asked, "When?"

"Why, just this afternoon. He came to us this morning with the suggestion. The deal was made over coffee on the veranda here. He worked today to get funds, and we cleared out our belongings," offered Grace. "He only gave us the money two hours ago. The American Consulate here notarized the transaction."

Amber stood silently, digesting the recitation. Cindi sat in rapt attention at the table too, not missing a word. Monk licked his lips as he watched a flaming Bananas Foster being prepared at a nearby table.

"We assumed you were going with him, but as we gave him a ride back to the boat, he explained that you two had separated. He said you were just friends, and really nothing more."

"Has he left Madeira yet?" blurted out Cindi, who had risen to her feet.

John looked at his no-frills stainless-steel Rolex and answered with a nod, "We helped him load provisions, and he and I topped off the fuel and put fresh oil in the diesels before sunset. Then he rode back here with us in the cab. Said he wanted to say farewell to you, lovely Amber.

"That was over an hour ago. I gathered you two missed one another?"

Amber bit her lip and nodded.

"Only an hour?" exclaimed Cindi, now wide-eyed. "Where was the boat parked?"

"One does not 'park' a boat, young lady. Boats are *moored*," John corrected her playfully.

Her eyes rolled as she asked again, "Okay, where was the boat *moored?*"

"That's better!" he laughed with a wink. "We'll turn you into a vixen of the sea yet. The *Concubine* was moored at the main marina in town."

"The one by the fishing store? Next to the little café?" Cindi asked as she gathered her purse and wrap.

"Why, yes. You've spent some time at the marina?" he asked.

"Some of my finest moments," Cindi answered. "Monk, stop eye-balling that dessert and let's go! We might still catch him."

"Oh, I doubt you'll make it. Jake said he'd be underway by 8:00 p.m. He was ready to cast off momentarily," John stated.

"It's worth a shot. Dinner's on you, old pal. Gotta run." Cindi grabbed Monk by the hand and started off. Quickly she stopped and turned back. "The *Concubine*?"

"Yes. She was truly the only other woman for me." He put his arm around Grace. "Now he's stolen her from me."

"Join the crowd." Cindi started to turn away again but looked back and asked, "He say where he was going?"

"Why yes, he did. Miami. I told him he could keep the boat there at our dock until shipping arrangements could be made to California."

Amber had wanted to stop him from the disclosure, but it happened too fast.

"How long will that take him?" Cindi asked.

John's brow furrowed as the navigator in him calculated the distance in consideration of the speed of the yacht. "Three weeks if he pushes her. More likely three and a half. Depends on whether or not he stops in the Bahamas."

"Well, if you'll excuse us, we'd like to bid him farewell if he hasn't gone yet." Cindi led Monk away.

Grace raised her eyebrows and said to Amber, "It seems they've left you with the bill."

"No. I offered. Will they find him at the marina?"

John shook his head. "Not a chance. If you didn't see him here, he's gone. He seemed on a mission to get off the island."

"Better him than me. John, you are the love of my life, but I just couldn't take another three weeks at sea," offered Grace. "Thank you for your sacrifice." She kissed him on the cheek. She asked Amber, "Care to join us for dinner? You'll get to watch a couple of old people get roaring drunk."

Amber smiled genuinely for the first time today. Knowing Jake was safely off the island made her feel better. Yet with the satisfaction came an odd emptiness.

"I've eaten, but with your permission, I'll sit and join you in getting smashed."

Grace noticed her eyes were slightly misty. "We've all suffered a bit of a loss today, haven't we?" She put her arm around Amber's shoulders.

"We're just friends. Hell, maybe not even that really. More like business associates."

Grace nodded and said, "Uh huh. Sure you were…

"Well if you'd like to be there waiting for him when he pulls into our dock, you're more than welcome. Coral Gables is wonderful this time of year."

"No, thank you. I'm going back to Reno. I'll catch him later, and we'll settle up."

John's face had a wry smile upon it. Grace noticed and asked, "Why the smirk?"

With a headshake and the smile still in place, John answered, "It wouldn't do you a bit of good to be on our dock in Miami. He's not going there."

"What?" said Grace. "That's where he told us he was heading. And that's what you told those two."

"Those two have mayhem in their hearts and most certainly mean him harm. Besides, I told them the truth. He did *say* he was going to Miami."

"But you think differently," his wife announced.

"I *know* differently," John stated. "While he was putting fuel in the boat, I checked the GPS. He'd already programmed in the waypoints for his destination."

The women waited. Finally, Grace growled at him, "Quit the theatrics and tell us, or I'll cut off what little sex we still have."

"Please, not that!" he mocked. "With my *Concubine* gone, I need you more than ever!"

He looked at Amber then at Grace and finally revealed, "Our friend is heading directly to St. Thomas in the U.S. Virgin Islands."

Amber's lips pursed and she nodded. John continued, "Let's get a table and drink to a pleasant voyage for him, shall we?"

And they did.

CHAPTER 64

The sails did not vibrate as the Mylar took the set in the light puffs of moving air. Tomorrow, away from the wind shadow of the island and out in the trade breezes, the sheet lines would be hauled in, and the boat would be tested. The mild groan of the hull as a vessel plows forward under the force of the wind into a wave coupled with the sweet humming she emits as she surfs down the face creates a rhythm unlike any other of this world.

After a day or two, Jake decided, he would fly the spinnaker and make this boat sing her own distinct melody.

For the first hour of the journey, the *Concubine* had to be pushed by her little Yanmar diesel engines. Now, free of the hole in the wind created by the island of Madeira the boat heeled gently as she took the light breeze over her port beam. The offshore buoys were well-marked on the GPS chart plotter, and Jake steered the fifty-foot Fountaine-Pajot catamaran under sail toward open water. The engines coughed one last time giving way to near quiet as they were shut down. Behind him the lights of Funchal were still bright along the waterline, dispersing into an umbrella of muted luminosity as they faded into the descending cloud cover. Looking back at the beautiful city glowing against the night, he vowed to return someday. Ahead of him was the near total blackness of the ocean with the break between the horizon and the water indiscernible.

The charts had been studied, and the waypoints had been programmed to offer clear passage around any obstacles, submerged or exposed above the surface. Still, Jake set a depth alarm for three hundred feet. His final act for the evening was to set the alarm on the radar for four miles. If any vessel or obstacle above the surface came within that radius, another squeal would erupt and rouse him from the sleep he desperately needed.

With the warnings set and one last look around at the surrounding blackness, Jake rolled the sleeping bag out in the cockpit and crawled in. To his disappointment sleep did not come immediately. The exhaustion had increased

416

exponentially over the past days, and his battered body needed rest.

His mind, however, raced with thought as he closed his eyes.

On the skateboard ride down the hill into the city to find a taxi he'd taken two spills in the gray of evening, picking up a few more cuts and scrapes. It had been simple to commandeer the inflatable dinghy from the courtesy dock so he could motor through the harbor. The silent paddling over the final few hundred feet to reach the boat was easy enough. He'd felt some joy as he'd pulled himself over the bow anchor of the *Tail Chaser* and slithered through the jimmied hatch to find the bags full of euros two nights ago. He'd expected to have to give Cindi a whack or two to subdue her (actually he might have been looking forward to it), but he was giddy to spot her and the entourage at the café above the dock. As he'd exited the sportfisher with the money, his only regret was that he would not be there to see the expression on the face of Ms. Light as she discovered that her coveted loot was gone.

John had reluctantly sold the boat at one-half of her market value. Grace had been Jake's ally in the coup. Dreading the upcoming crossing, she reminded her husband they could *give* the boat away and feel no ill effect financially. The *Concubine* should go to someone they liked, and John had professed, "*Jake reminds me of myself twenty years ago.*" Grace corrected him, "*More like thirty, dear.*" So the deal was done, with the promise that if the boat were ever to be sold, the old owners would have first rights to her.

An afternoon of provisioning had been spent, with a quick trip to the U.S. consulate for a notary stamp on the contract. Then a checkout with the Harbor Master, who signed him through without a blink of an eye. Jake wondered whether *Polícias Principais* Calista had left that door open on purpose.

Juan Silva had made out well, taking a fee on the transfer of funds each time a wire was sent or received. The last transfer had been the final deposit to his parents' account. The debonair casino manager would probably be sorry to see them go.

A pang of guilt had arisen in not saying goodbye to Amber. He'd intended to bid his farewell, but when he'd arrived at the Palace, her dinner guests were a deterrent to the closure. Better to say a silent *adieu* than tangle with either Monk or Cindi. She'd get her additional ten percent when he sold the boat he now piloted.

He wriggled to get comfortable on the padded bench seat in the cockpit of the yacht. The queen-size berth in the master cabin was inviting, however he felt more secure out in the open air with a view of everything around him. The autopilot was set to steer his new toy to a waypoint on a Caribbean island 2,700 nautical miles downwind.

Getting acquainted with a new boat took time. Most newly acquired yachts were taken on short excursions and day sails until the owners were ready for more adventurous outings. He would sleep above deck tonight and for a few nights to come until he and the *Concubine* formed a symbiotic relationship wherein they trusted each other completely.

With enough twisting and contorting he found a position where his aches and pains were at a minimum and fought to clear his head. He needed sleep. One by one, the jumbled ruminations of the past weeks were put aside until only one image remained.

Jake's mind could not erase the vision of the unblinking eyes of Tom Wojicki as he'd wrapped his body in the sheet. It was too easy to say he'd gotten what he'd deserved. Jake had made a deal with him, and although he hadn't pulled the trigger, his arrival here had kicked off a chain of events that led to the killing.

The eyes had begged for something... Explanation? Perhaps... Or was it forgiveness? He couldn't be certain, but the eyes haunted him this night and would for many more. His lack of action allowed a life to end.

In the end, he realized what he'd seen in those eyes before he'd covered them. Blame... Tom's death had been preventable.

So, Jake accepted the blame for the death of Tom Wojicki.

Over the next twenty-one days at sea, his guilt in the matter wore down, but never went completely away.

It might have cheered him to know that at the exact time of reaching the midpoint of his Atlantic crossing, his good friend and protégé, The Flyin' Hawaiian, Brian Chang, won his first World Mogul Skiing championship. But instead, the shadow of death hovered over his wake, chasing as the trade winds pushed him forward.

What Jake could not foresee was more death lay directly ahead, with the twin bows of the catamaran pointing toward it like directional arrows as the boat rose and fell with the waves.

THE END

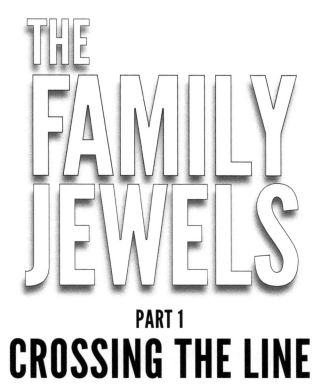

PART 1

CROSSING THE LINE

Look for the ongoing saga of *The Family Jewels* as Jake Cohen and his cronies will be back soon in *Pain Kil'lah*. Here's a snippet of what to expect as the quest for the sacred jewels continues in a battle of wits between Cohen and crazed terrorists trying to create a new world order!

Outside the Global Passions office the limousine came to a stop. The driver opened the door. As Jake moved into the portal, he felt a foot on his rump. Before he could react, the massive Nasir kicked forward, sending him flying out of the car. He landed in the street, the pack he held breaking his fall. His steeping anger reaching a boil, he flew off the pavement at the guard, elbows in tight and cocked to unleash. A left jab landed cleanly on Nasir's cheek as he exited the vehicle, followed by a well-placed overhand right that caught the guard square in the nose.

The big man didn't flinch at the blows as he stepped forward driving a knee upward into Jake's solar plexus, knocking the wind out of him.

Jake sagged to the ground with the air pounded from his lungs, rolling to avoid the guard's next shot. Nothing came, and he found his feet. As he gasped for breath, he saw Nasir walking toward the door, stemming the blood flowing from his nose with his hand. The lock mechanism buzzed and he disappeared into the building. The limo pulled away and Jake stood in the middle of the street half-doubled over, both elbows scraped from his slide across the cobblestones.

He inhaled slowly and as deeply as possible to regain his breath. His hands moved along the ribs, one-by-one feeling for any that might be broken. He guessed he might have a few cracked bones, but there were no complete breaks.

Picking up his pack, he stood, ignoring the pain in his midsection. Unzipping it, Jake reached inside and removed the package of diamonds. With a quick sidearm toss, the velvet box landed on the top step of the Global Passions place of business. Upon impact it exploded, with exquisite diamonds flying like shrapnel over the steps and sidewalk.

Jake turned and walked up the street to his car, where he sat for a few moments writing on a piece of paper retrieved from the glove box. After starting the engine, he U-turned and drove past the jewelry brokerage.

As the car passed the stoned Rastafarian apparently asleep in the door-way across the street, a piece of trash thrown from the window hit the ganga-peddler in the head. The wadded-up paper was reeled into his tunic and unfolded out of sight of the gem dealer's many eyes on the street.

The words scribbled made the Rasta's mouth form a yellow-toothed smile as he read. *Meet me at Hurricane Hole, St. John. Tonight. Your new partner, Jake.*

Nasir kept his eye on the telescope until the sail of the catamaran disappeared to the west under the fiery sunset. In Farsi, he said to Amir Mojabi, "He is gone."

Standing on the roof of the Global Passions building, Amir replied, "Do not believe it. He threw $100,000 in diamonds back at me. This man is a DeCorto. They have always come. He will return."

"I will have all the harbors watched. The GPS transmitter will continue to send us his position for over four months. By that time we will be gone. The unit is outside the range now, but if he comes within fifteen miles, we will know it.

"If he returns before our departure, do we have your blessing to kill him?"

Amir gazed at the crimson on the horizon. "You not only have my blessing; you have my direct order to remove him."

"It will be at the pleasure of me and my men Amir," said Nasir as he placed the ice pack over his swollen nose.

Lightning Source UK Ltd.
Milton Keynes UK
UKHW021528301219
356115UK00014B/3589/P